Happy Sun Farm

Behind the Facade

Deven Greene

PANTHERA
PUBLISHING

Cover design by Vila Design.

For the small farmers who work when it's too hot, too cold, too early, or too late, in order to feed our nation.

Happy Sun Farm

Behind the Facade

Prologue

FOG ROLLED IN AS the sun set on the verdant hills, silent but for the small animals carrying out their daily tasks of finding food and safety while caring for their young. Below in the valley, the mist-shrouded a smattering of primitive structures—the permanent home of twenty thousand guests of Hwasong, the largest political prisoner camp in North Korea.

All the inmates—men, women, and children—were serving a life sentence for anti-revolutionary activities or being within three generations of a person convicted of that same high crime, so-called guilt by association. Those imprisoned solely because they were related to a convicted enemy of the state lived separately on the grounds, never allowed to see their denounced relative again. Their living conditions were horrible, but not as horrible as those who had committed a serious offense.

A group of a hundred men, women, and teens wearing orange jumpsuits, tired after a long day of hard labor, shuffled into the large auditorium, hurried along by shoves and baton whacks from the guards. Already seated was an equal number of prisoners wearing blue jumpsuits, men, women, and teens who had arrived by bus a half-hour earlier from a nearby housing block. The inmates dressed in blue were emaciated, their skin loosely covering the bones underneath, while those in orange were thin but without signs of starvation. The people in orange were silent as they glanced around and sat in the vacant seats between those in blue.

If the two groups of prisoners had questions about why those in orange and blue were intermingled in this way, none dared to speak up. Ten guards armed with guns and batons stood around the room's perimeter. After all the inmates were seated, one of the officers stepped to the front of the room and commenced the evening ritual of indoctrination. The session of self-criticism would be next.

Prisoners who occasionally slumped forward from exhaustion were struck with a baton. He or she would either straighten up or fall to the floor before being pulled by their arms out of the room, never to be seen again.

As the officer droned on about the greatness of the country and their Supreme Leader, Kim Jong Un, the guards around the perimeter continued to look straight ahead. None of the convicts seemed to notice the fine aerosol being emitted from nozzles that had poked through small holes in the ceiling high above. The mist silently spread to all corners of the room for several minutes before the apertures closed, and the spouts crawled back into the ceiling.

A short session followed in which several prisoners were required to admit to recent shortcomings, such as not working as hard as they could have or eating more than needed to survive. The other prisoners responded by agreeing that the behavior described was shameful.

When the meeting appeared to be over, the inmates in orange looked around, ready for the usual order to file into the cafeteria for a small meal. However, the doors remained shut, and all were told to stay seated. The lights dimmed, and a movie began, showing scenes of happy North Koreans at parades and concerts, playing sports, and attending school. For eleven hours, during which time the guards were replaced by a fresh batch, one film after the other played as the prisoners were forced to watch.

One of the prisoners in an orange jumpsuit began to moan. In the dim light, the officers exchanged knowing looks. The sounds of distress became louder and deeper as several more inmates, all wearing orange, began to groan. The guards started to place buckets at the feet of the prisoners in orange. Within three hours, almost all those wearing orange were groaning, doubled over in pain, as they vomited into buckets. The vomit became increasingly tinged with blood as the night turned to day. Blood and stomach contents spewed onto the floor as the prisoners became unable to control their forceful retching.

Soon, the sounds of explosive diarrhea filled the air. Unable to exert any control over their bodies, the sick fell to the floor as bloody bodily fluids from both ends of their gastrointestinal systems streamed out of them, into their clothes, down their pant legs, and onto the floor. Blood oozed from their mouths, noses, and eyes.

At first, the convicts wearing blue sat still in their seats, fear drawn on their faces, but without suffering physically. At some point, one, then another, abandoned their seats and stood near the back of the room. Seeing that there were no repercussions, others followed.

Within eight hours of the start of vomiting, two prisoners in orange had died. The deaths began to mount as those in blue looked on in horror, wondering if they would be next. Two buckets were placed near them for their own hygiene needs while they waited.

Seventy-two hours later, the doors opened. The prisoners in blue, still emaciated but as healthy as they were when they had entered the building, were escorted outside into waiting buses to return them to their housing block. All of the prisoners in orange lay on the floor—dead.

Chapter 1

I HANDED MY DRIVER'S license to the airport security agent at the Indianapolis airport and scanned the boarding pass on my phone. As I had come to expect, the gray-haired man looked up at me and smiled. "I ain't never seen that name before. Kinda takes me back."

"I know," I said. "I get that a lot." My dad was only two when John Lennon was killed, but his parents indoctrinated their son on everything Beatles. He, in turn, spent countless hours listening to Beatles music with my mom. I think they got stoned a lot when they were doing it, but they never admitted it to me.

Given that their favorite Beatles song was "Strawberry Fields Forever," I strongly favored that hypothesis. When I was born, they couldn't resist naming me Strawberry. Oh, and my last name is Fields. Now you know why people often have something to say about my name. I'm a run-of-the-mill blond, not a strawberry blond. I think that would have made my life unbearable.

I pulled on the cuff of my long-sleeved shirt, grabbed my driver's license, and was about to walk off when the man said, "You must be a student at Purdue. Going home to visit the folks?"

"Something like that." I was in no mood to talk. I know the man was trying to be pleasant and make his day pass more quickly with small talk. The large P on the front of my baseball cap was known by all in the area to signify Purdue University, where I was, in fact, a student. I forced a weak smile and adjusted the shoulder straps on my backpack before walking off.

After passing through the luggage check without incident, I headed toward my gate. First class was already embarking, but I still had to wait a while before my boarding group was called. I had bought my ticket the previous night and was in the last group, my seat near the back of the plane. Fortunately, the flight to Bakersfield, with one stop in Phoenix, wasn't in high demand, and almost a quarter of the seats in the rear were empty. With ample space in the overhead bin, I lobbed my backpack in and took my aisle seat. The man sitting next to the window glanced my way and nodded. I nodded back, glad he didn't want to chat.

I remember taking off, but not much after that until I heard a male voice asking me if I was okay. I must have dosed off and wasn't sure how much time had passed. I opened my eyes to see the concerned look on the flight attendant's face, a pudgy middle-aged man who was bent over, his face close to mine. We were cruising at altitude, and tears were running down my face. Embarrassed, I tried to wipe them away. "Sorry," I said. "I was dreaming about my dad. I'm on my way to his funeral."

"So sorry, dear. If you need anything, just let me know. I'll comp you a drink if that will help."

I declined but thanked him for his offer and reflected on my mother's hysterical call the day before. She had come home after spending all afternoon with a friend shopping and going to lunch when she found my dad dead on the kitchen floor. She had often confided in me that she felt terrible going places without him, but since he refused to leave the farm, she'd been doing things independent of him for quite some time. He'd been in good health—physically, that is—so his death was a big shock.

I reflected on the situation, different from what I had planned for before my dad died as the plane sat on the tarmac in Phoenix. I was all too aware that it was too late. I was heading home, ready or not. Hardly the family reunion I had anticipated.

I started to study a book on the economics of short-run decisions. After reading the first paragraph three times and still having no clue what it was about, I shut my eyes as the plane took off for the last leg of my trip. I'd be landing in Bakersfield in a little over an hour.

My rest was short-lived. The flight attendant came by with a cart and asked me if I would like vanilla, raspberry, or peach yogurt. I looked at the available items—individual servings of Happy Sun Farm yogurt. I'd had their yogurt before, and it was delicious.

"You're lucky," the attendant said. "Happy Sun Farm has donated a ton of yogurt to be served on our flights all week."

I decided it was probably no use trying to sleep and chose the peach flavor even though I wasn't hungry. As I started to eat, my mind wandered to Happy Sun Farm. I had never heard of them until about a year earlier when their dairy and agricultural products began popping up all over. The company heavily advertised on TV. They boasted about all their products being non-genetically modified, or non-GMO. I didn't have a problem with genetically modified food myself but knew that a lot of Americans did. All the produce my dad grew was non-GMO because he suspected all genetically modified food to be part of a government conspiracy. A conspiracy to do what, I didn't know.

Although I didn't have time to watch much television, when I did, it was hard to avoid the Happy Sun Farm commercials featuring wholesome families frolicking and picnicking in a green meadow. The smiling sun logo served to reinforce that warm and fuzzy feeling emanating from their commercials. I wondered if they had a model I could follow to pursue success for my family's farm. I'd noticed their rock-bottom prices, which was surprising since they must have spent a ton on ads. What I wouldn't give to find out the secret to their success.

I finished the yogurt, then scraped the container for the last traces of peach delight and put the empty carton in my beverage holder before I dozed off again.

I dreamt of Perry. We were having coffee on campus, talking about something important. I didn't remember much more than it wasn't a happy dream. I awoke with a jerk when the plane hit turbulence, and passengers were instructed to fasten their seatbelts. I pushed thoughts of Perry away as my mind drifted to the last conversation I'd had with Mom. She had told me she was so upset, she couldn't promise to meet me at the airport. Never a strong woman, I knew it was beyond difficult for her to cope. She couldn't run the farm by herself, but I'd promised to move back there permanently after I graduated at the end of the summer. I'd speak to Mr. Aguilar, who owned the farm next door, and ask him to assist until I returned. He was always ready to help out neighbors in need.

Planning the funeral invaded my thoughts next. It would be a small affair. Dad didn't have many friends. I wondered if he had life insurance, although I doubted it. A brother or sister would have been nice. Someone else to share the burden with, but the reality was it was just me and Mom. My aunt said she would fly out in a few days if my mother wanted her to, but for the time being, I was all Mom had for support, and she was all I had.

I'd driven by the Grigsby funeral home with my mother numerous times when I was young. I'd never been inside, but always imagined it would be a strange place, like a haunted house, with black crepe hanging from the ceilings and matching drapes covering the windows. Soon, I'd be stepping inside for the first time.

While the circumstances weren't joyful, I looked forward to seeing Mom, the house I grew up in, and the farm. Ever since I was a toddler, the strawberry fields, which shared my name, seemed magical. I always felt particularly at peace in that area of the farm. Just being there soothed me when I did poorly on a test, was hurt by my classmates, had a disagreement with my parents, or was ashamed, which was almost daily before I left home.

Surely, the strawberry harvest would be over when I arrived, the plants already thinned before filling in with new plants. But seeing the compact, low-lying plants with their scalloped shamrock green leaves would cheer me up, as always. I'd be sure to find a few strawberries that had escaped harvest. I envisioned myself being warmed by the sun as I lay between the rows of plants while I dined on the juicy red delicacy, like I'd done in some of my happiest memories as a child.

The plane landed abruptly, with a slight bounce that roused me from my thoughts. I knew it would take a while to exit the aircraft since I was in the back, so I texted my mom, hoping she would let me know she was waiting for me in the cell phone lot. After the plane had taxied to the gate and I was in the terminal, I hadn't heard back from her yet. Once outside the building, I rechecked my phone. Still no reply. Looking around, the familiar silver fifteen-year-old Toyota Corolla my mom drove was nowhere to be found. Neither was my dad's twenty-five-year-old white Chevy truck, which never looked white.

Frustrated, I phoned my mom again. No answer. Was she so despondent she was unable to answer her phone, much less get out of bed? I stepped out of the terminal, into the hot June sun and bought a ticket for a transport bus serving rural Kern County, which had a stop ten miles from my home. A lengthy ride was ahead of me. I hoped I could rouse my mother or summon an Uber once I reached my stop. If not, it would be a long, sweltering walk to the farm.

I found a seat on the bus near a window and closed my eyes, the unpleasant odor reminding me of one of the smells on the farm. Diesel. I'd been romanticizing about how nice it would be to be back amongst the crops of one of the richest agricultural valleys in the country. Birds flying, butterflies and bees floating in the air, small animals scampering. I'd forgotten about the noxious diesel odor from farm equipment, which often drifted through the air. Despite that, and all the bugs, worry about weather, and price instability, farming was in my blood. The bus started up. Fortunately, no one sat in my row. Soon, the gentle swaying back and forth lulled me to sleep.

I was startled awake by a male voice asking, "Hey, is that you?"

Chapter 2

LOOKING UP, I SAW a man about my age standing in the aisle to my left. I wiped the side of my face, embarrassed as I became aware of the small amount of drool on the right side of my mouth. As I collected my bearings and straightened up, I responded in the cleverest way I could think of. "I'm me, if that's what you mean." I quickly regretted my words. I probably sounded like a bitch when he likely thought I really looked like someone he knew.

"Sorry, I didn't mean to startle you. It's just that you remind me of someone I haven't seen in years."

I looked more closely at the man, who was now sitting in the outside seat across the aisle. "Are you CJ?" I asked. He was so much bigger and more muscular than I remembered.

"Hell, yeah! I knew it was you." A broad smile spread across his face. "Strawberry Fields. Man, it's been a long time. Whatever happened to you? Here one day, gone the next. You've no idea the rumors that spread around. Some were not so nice. Most of the kids thought your old man murdered you and buried you under the broccoli. None of us were brave enough to knock on your door and ask questions. Me, I always thought you'd run away from home."

I pulled down on the sleeves of my shirt before answering. "That's not exactly what happened. I wasn't a runaway. I went to live with my aunt in Indianapolis. Haven't been home since. Not 'til today."

"What brings you back now?"

"My dad died."

CJ's smile melted. "Damn. I had no idea. We all thought he was such a mean cuss, but I never wished him any harm."

"I'm afraid he was a tortured soul. Ever since he got back from Afghanistan. I always hoped I could return home and get him the help he needed, but that won't be possible now. He died suddenly yesterday."

"Heart attack?"

"He wasn't even forty-five years old, so I doubt it. My mom was pretty broken up when she called me, so she couldn't tell me much. I'm sure I'll learn more once I'm home."

CJ was one of the kids I hung out with when my dad let me out of the house. I had a crush on him back then, but he never noticed me in the same way. He was popular and had many groups of friends, so I didn't see him as much as I would have liked to. A terrible student, CJ was very sociable. I could tell he was smart and kind, and I thought he was sexy as hell. I pictured him auctioning off cattle when he grew up. That was a long time ago. He was most likely married now with three kids. Overruling my usual cautious nature, I asked, "Say, do you have a ride home from the bus stop?"

"Yup. My truck's parked right there. Someone needed it to haul some stuff while I was gone, but he promised to leave it in the lot near the bus stop for me today. You need a ride?"

I smiled with relief. "Sure do. I hate to ask, but I don't think my mom can pick me up, and I'm not sure if I can catch an Uber out there."

"Uber is pretty iffy in the rural areas, but I'd be happy to take you home. I think I still remember where you live. People still call you Berry?"

"Just friends and family." I don't usually consider myself lucky, but I felt incredibly fortunate to have landed a ride to my house.

"I hope that includes me, even though it's been a while."

"Of course. But you'll have to tell me what you've been doing for the past ten years or so."

"Nothing exciting. I managed to graduate from high school and got some community college under my belt. Unfortunately, my parents both passed away a few years ago. I inherited the pasta sauce business, so I suppose that makes me a businessman."

"I remember. Mama Baroni's Delizioso Pasta Sauce. My mom used it often. We all liked it."

"I've kept it going, but the business is in a bit of a slump right now."

"Sorry to hear that. I suppose people are cutting out pasta since carbs have gotten a bad name."

"That's not it," CJ answered. "We can't keep up with the demand because we're having a hard time getting tomatoes."

Skeptical, I cocked my head. "That doesn't make sense. They grow tons of tomatoes around here."

"That used to be true, but believe it or not, a large agribusiness has bought up a lot of the farms in these parts, and they're ripping out all the tomatoes to grow other stuff."

"Sorry to hear that, but it sounds crazy. This is one of the best places in the world to grow tomatoes."

"I know. I'm not worried though. I'm working out deals from farms farther away. I'll have to pay a little more for shipping, but it'll be okay. Once I have a good supply of tomatoes, I'll be in the black again. I've got other interests, anyway."

"Like what?"

"I started a private boarding school for troubled kids."

His answer surprised me. "You're a teacher?"

"Naw, but I hired a bunch. There's a lot of troubled teens around here. Lots of drugs. I can't even tell you how many of 'em have died from fentanyl overdoses."

"Where's the school?"

"Not far from my factory. I have a younger cousin who got into drugs real bad when he was fourteen. He's the reason I started the school in the first place. I was afraid he was gonna die. So I bought that old supermarket down by the Hanson place, turned it into a school, hired teachers, and appointed myself as The Coach for All Sports."

"Gosh, sounds like you're a real doer."

CJ smiled. "It's been a lot of work, but I'd do it again. My cousin turns eighteen and is set to graduate high school next week. He's clean and will be starting at the community college in the fall."

"I'm impressed. You're having a real impact on the community."

"I like to think so."

"It's none of my business, but how do you keep the school going, financially, that is? You must charge a ton for tuition." I envisioned a lot of rich kids from Bakersfield or the large agribusinesses in surrounding areas being dropped off for school in black limousines.

"It's free for those whose parents can't pay. The school gets small donations from the more well-to-do families, I get grants and kick in a bit myself—things like that. I really like those kids. They can be difficult when they first arrive, but I get through to most of 'em. Some of them surprise me with how smart and talented they are." CJ paused. "Say, you haven't been here in ages. Bet you haven't kept up with too many of the folks who are still around."

"None, to be exact."

"We'll have to fix that. Give me your cell number, and I'll get you back in touch with some people. After you get through the funeral and all that."

"Sure. I'd like that." I started to feel some of that attraction I'd felt towards CJ when I was in middle school. A sense of guilt began invading my thoughts. I'd been dating Perry exclusively for the past eight months. Handsome and brilliant, I had pictured settling down with him after we finished school. A fellow agricultural finance major, he could earn big bucks working for one of the large conglomerate farms in Kern County, where my family farm was. We were perfect for each other. On paper, anyway. That initial spark I'd felt when we were first together had worn off. I often told myself I was expecting too much. Life isn't like a fairytale.

When Perry had dropped me off at the Indianapolis Airport that morning, we'd briefly kissed, but there was no feeling. I knew I wouldn't miss him and ascribed that to the hurt I was feeling from losing my dad. Now I wasn't so sure about that.

I gave CJ my number, then asked for his. Thoughts swirled in my head about having a quick fling with this past obsession of mine before heading back to school, if he was interested. I checked his hand. No wedding ring, not that it meant he was unattached. I didn't have much time to find out.

"So, what's that P on your hat for?" CJ asked.

"Purdue. Purdue University. I'm a student there."

"I'll be damned. I always knew you were smart. Here I am, talking about myself, and I didn't ask what you've been up to."

I wished I didn't blush so easily. With my fair complexion, I knew there was no hiding my embarrassment when that familiar warm feeling crept over my face. "Nothing terribly interesting. I graduated high school, then enrolled in Purdue. It's only about a ninety-minute drive from where my aunt and uncle live. They're paying for my tuition. Purdue has a great agricultural program, and I'm majoring in Aggie finance. Plan to finally graduate at the end of the summer quarter after a little more than four years there."

CJ whistled. "That's gotta be a tough major, but a lot of the farmers around here —the ones that are left, anyways—could use some help in that area. Are you planning to come back here, or make big bucks by going off to one of those giant corporate farms that are taking over?"

"I was planning to come back and help my parents with the farm. Now it'll just be my mom. I've got a lot of ideas about how she can improve productivity with new equipment, take advantage of farm subsidies, then leverage her capital and expand. With a larger operation, she'll be able to take advantage of economies of scale."

CJ smiled. "I'm glad you want to come back, but, you'll see, it won't be easy. Many folks have already left the area."

"Bought out?"

"You know it. Agribusiness is taking over. Maybe you can do something to put a stop to it. Lots of these farms have been in families for generations. Call me old fashioned, but seeing all these places bought up rubs me the wrong way."

I must have lost track of time because I was surprised when the bus stopped and announced we had arrived at our destination. Several people got off with CJ and me, and the bus pulled away, kicking up dirt in the process. We were standing in front of a gas station next to a dirt parking lot. It was then that I noticed just how much CJ had grown in the past ten years. When I had left, I was a bit taller than him. Now, he towered over me.

I figured the muddy white Ford with the rusted chassis was his. I started walking towards it when CJ grabbed my shoulder and pointed in another direction, saying, "Mine's this way."

Chapter 3

I WAS MOMENTARILY EMBARRASSED and speechless, taken aback as he led me to the lone Chevy Silverado, a blue pick-up truck so clean it seemed to sparkle in the sun. "Beautiful truck," I said. I was wondering how he could afford such an expensive ride.

CJ opened the passenger side door. "It's a little hard to get into, so you might want to use the running board," he said as he pointed to the small platform below the door.

"Thanks," I said as I stepped onto the platform and slid into the seat. The new car smell was hard to miss.

CJ closed the door and walked around to the driver's side. He removed the windbreaker he was wearing, tossed it into the back, and took his place behind the wheel. Being six foot two, about a half foot taller than me, made it easy for him to reach the seat. I was still looking around, marveling at all the screens on the dash and the controls on the steering wheel, when he shut his door. He was wearing a grey T-shirt, exposing his muscular arms for the first time.

"What's that tattoo mean?" I asked, noticing the Asian characters displayed on his right forearm.

"It's a Chinese character that means live long and prosper. Or so I was told. I was, and still am, a big Star Trek fan."

"Me, too. But I don't have a tattoo like that."

"Do you have any tattoos?" CJ asked, smiling mischievously. "Any tattoos anywhere?"

I wondered if he was flirting with me. At a loss for words, the best I could come up with was, "Wouldn't you like to know?"

"Now you've got me curious." As we pulled onto the road, CJ waved at a passing car. "That's the father of one of the boys in my school."

"I suppose a lot of people around here know you."

CJ laughed. "Yeah, but that's not always a good thing. Some folks in these parts got it in their minds that I should run for the state assembly."

"That's impressive. Are you going to do it?"

"I'm thinking about it. I flew into Sacramento early this morning for some meetings, which is why I just arrived back at the Bakersfield airport. I hadn't been to Sacto since our school trip there when I was in high school. I didn't have time to see much this time, but I met with some folks in the know about what would be involved if I decided to throw my hat in the ring."

"Sounds like a big decision."

"I want to give it more thought. Hell, I don't have a fancy diploma like most of 'em. Just an AA degree."

"That's more than Jessie Ventura had when he was elected governor."

"People keep reminding me of that."

Looking around as we drove by the farmland I was familiar with, I was struck by the changes. "What happened to the Dodson house?" I asked.

"Gone. Gone like lots of 'em. You'll see, there's been a lot of changes around here."

"I suppose I expected to find some differences in the area, but the more I see, the less I recognize." We turned down the road leading to my parents' farm, and everything felt so unfamiliar to me. "This isn't anything like I remember," I said.

"This area has probably changed more'n any other place in the county. Most of the farms have been bought up by a large Chinese agricultural conglomerate. I've got nothing against foreigners, but it just doesn't seem like a good idea to me for so much of our farmland and housing to be owned by people who answer to another government. That's why some folks around here want me to run. I tend to speak my mind, and they think I could get our state to regulate such things."

"I, for one, will do what I can to keep our farm in my family's hands. I want to hang on to that land, expand the farm, and have something to pass on to my kids."

"You have kids?"

I have a knack for saying things that will embarrass me. "I don't have kids now, but I hope to someday."

"You got a boyfriend?"

I thought for a moment, then made a split-second decision. I lied. "No."

"Well, here we are at your house. One of the few still standing."

"I see what you mean. None of the neighboring houses are still here. Even the Aguilar's house is gone. I don't recognize the place, with all the super high fencing around everything. Who does that?"

"The new owners. Good luck holding onto your farm."

"Thanks for the ride," I said, starting to open the door.

"Here, let me help you."

Before I could stop him, CJ dashed to my side of the truck, swung the door open, and grabbed my hand to support me as I exited the vehicle. Even with the running board, it was a doozy of a step to the ground. He held my hand a bit longer than necessary, then let go. "Tell your mom hi for me."

"Sure," I said before turning and heading up the long driveway to my front door.

I heard the Chevy pull away as I walked under the apple trees providing shade over the walkway. CJ intrigued me. No longer the adorably cute, somewhat rascally pubescent I remembered, he was now a strong, handsome, fully developed man with a good moral compass and the ability to get things done. A genuine boot-strappy kind of guy. I started thinking about how I should react if he were to call me, but I needed to think about my dad, my mom, and everything she was dealing with.

The front door was locked. Just like it had always been when my dad was alive. Back then, with crime almost non-existent in our communi-ty, there was no need to lock the door other than paranoia. But things had changed with the passage of time. People were worried about crime even in rural Kern County. I no longer had a key, so I knocked loudly. The sound of footsteps was soon followed by the face of my mother, still beautiful but looking older than the last time I'd seen her, greeting me. Her graying shoulder-length hair was disheveled, and she was in her bathrobe. When I hugged her, I noticed she smelled of booze. I didn't remember her drinking much, but figured she needed the relief alcohol provided during this trying time.

"I'm so glad to see you," she said after a long hug. "Come to the kitchen with me. I want to introduce you to someone."

I followed her the short distance through the living room into the kitchen, thankful a friend had come by to comfort her. I was surprised to see a trim Asian man, around fifty years of age, dressed in a suit. He was seated at the kitchen table, an array of papers before him.

A glass half-filled with brown liquid sat next to a bottle of Maker's Mark in front of the pulled-out seat where I assumed my mother had been seated. "Berry, I'd like you to meet Mr. Chang."

The man shot up to a standing position, and his deadpan expression quickly transformed into a smile, a smile that appeared forced. "So glad to meet you," he said, extending his hand. As we shook briefly, he added, "It's Chen, not Chang."

Feeling blindsided and not particularly sociable, I asked, "What's going on, Mom?"

"Sit down, and I'll explain later, Dear."

"I'm not sitting down until I get an explanation."

"Have it your way. Stand if you want to—you were always so stubborn. You'll find out soon, anyway." She paused. "I just sold the farm."

Chapter 4

I STOOD IN SHOCK, unable to speak. Shaken by my dad's sudden death yesterday, I was utterly dumbfounded by my mother's words telling me she'd just sold the farm. This was the land she and my father had worked so hard on for so many years, the reason I had devoted the last four years of my life to studying agricultural economics. The land I was planning to transform into a viable concern to support my parents comfortably and pass on to my children. I staggered to the closest chair and sat while my mother returned to her seat in front of the whiskey bottle.

"I knew you wouldn't approve," she said.

"Don't do it, Mom," I shouted.

"Too late. I already signed the papers."

"What did this man talk you into?" I yelled, not giving Mr. Chen the satisfaction of looking in his direction.

"Where are your manners? Mr. Chang has been so caring and understanding. He brought me this expensive bottle of Makers Mark, the sign of a truly classy gentleman."

"Classy? Is that what you call it? He was just trying to get you drunk so you'd agree to sell the farm!" I started crying. "Please, Mom. You can still cancel the sale. California law allows you to back out of a real estate deal."

"My apologies, Miss Fields," Mr. Chen said, "but you should know that once the papers have been signed, the money has been transferred, and the notary has recorded the sale, the transaction is final. Your farm, house, and all surrounding land is now owned by Happy Sun Farm."

I was in disbelief as I realized the company, whose name seemed to be popping up all over the place, promoted by a glossy ad campaign, was actually a predatory Chinese company that had nothing to do with a happy or smiling sun. I turned to my mom. "See? You can still back out. All you did was sign the papers. None of those other things have happened yet."

"Again, my apologies," Mr. Chen said, "but I already transferred the money to your mother's account, and the notary public was recently here to record the sale. She left just fifteen minutes before you arrived."

This guy was slick. "You purposefully got her drunk so she'd sign the papers. I'm sure I'll be able to have that contract thrown out."

"This is what your mom wanted. Isn't that right, Wanda?"

"That's right. I've grown to hate this place. All it does is lose money."

"Don't you see, Mom? I'm going to turn that all around. I sure wish you'd answered your phone when I called you earlier today."

"You called?"

"Yes, and I left several messages."

My mother pulled her phone from her bathrobe pocket. "Looks like it got turned off. Sorry, Berry, I don't know how that happened. I would have answered it."

I looked at Mr. Chen, a forbidding expression on his face. I interpreted that as an attempt to convey he was in charge, had turned off my mother's phone, and there was no point in contesting the contract. He and his company knew how to win.

Unsure how to respond, I asked my mother, "How much are you being paid?"

"One and a half million dollars. Can you believe it?"

"No, I can't. This farm must be worth at least two million."

"Pardon me for interrupting," Mr. Chen said, "but you should know that my company, which owns most of the land around here now, can produce crops much more efficiently than a small farm such as this, and we are able to sell our produce at much lower prices. I'm sorry to say that this farm has been losing money for years. It's completely useless as a source of income for your mother. We tried to purchase it when your father was alive, but he refused to sell. I'm very sorry for your loss, but your mother is looking at this a bit more pragmatically and realizes that our offer is quite generous."

Feeling defeated, I turned back to my mom. "I suppose if this is what you want, you could invest one and a half million dollars and manage to live on the interest."

"Half the money went to pay off the mortgage," she said. "Your father was using this place like a piggy bank."

That shouldn't have surprised me, but it did. I shook my head. "You can't get by comfortably forever on just seven hundred and fifty thousand."

"I can get a job. I'll get by."

I asked Mr. Chen if my mother could stay in the house, perhaps rent it for a modest amount.

"We have generously offered to allow her to stay here two weeks, rent-free. After that, the house will be demolished."

I shrieked. "Demolished? Why would you destroy a perfectly good house like this? My mom and I could rent it from you." This was the house I grew up in. Although I hadn't visited in ten years, I always pictured myself coming back to live on the property with my parents and future husband, probably Perry. There was plenty of room to build a separate cottage for me and my future family. Once my parents were gone, I wanted to live here, in the house I grew up in. Despite the difficulties with my dad, I still had fond memories of running around outside in the sun, eating fresh strawberries, grapes, and peaches that were in plentiful supply. I'd heard the expression, you can never go home, but didn't think it applied to me. It would take me some time to adjust to the new reality.

"We have no need for an old house. We will plant here," Mr. Chen said.

"Where will my mom go?"

"I'm afraid that is not our concern. Again, so sorry for your loss, but I must leave now for another engagement."

Chapter 5

MOMENTS LATER MR. CHEN had let himself out, and I was left with my mother, whose head was now on the table. Whatever pain she had been in had been wiped away by the whisky.

Our roles had clearly switched. Before I arrived, I had expected to help my mother make arrangements for my father's funeral, but it seemed clear she was so unable to cope, I might have to do everything myself. Then, there was the matter of finding her a new place to live and moving all her possessions.

I jiggled my mother's shoulder and asked her what she wanted to do next. Look for a place to live? Make arrangements for my dad's funeral? I didn't even know if they owned a burial plot. Each of my questions was answered with what could best be described as a grunt.

I went to my old bedroom. Gone were my posters of Justin Bieber and the Jonas Brothers. In their place were floor-to-ceiling bookcases stocked with bottled water, canned food, guns, ammunition, batteries, camouflage clothes, and other goods a survivalist might collect.

My old bed had been pushed to the middle of the room and was covered with manuals on how to survive after an apocalypse. Until that moment, I hadn't realized how far off the rails my dad had veered. After clearing everything off, I found clean sheets in the hall closet and made the bed. This was going to be more difficult than I had thought.

The sun was setting, and I helped Mom brush her teeth and change into pajamas. I put her to bed, hoping I could have a more productive talk with her in the morning. I found leftover chicken in the refrigerator. Not very tasty, but I was starving and wasn't picky. I read a bit of the same eBook I had tried to read on the plane, then went to sleep.

I awakened to the sound of crows making a ruckus outside the window. Disoriented at first by the disarray surrounding me, I quickly remembered the events of the preceding day and the reason I found myself ensconced in chaos.

I made my way to my mom's bedroom, where she lay on her back, snoring loudly. I found the makings for coffee in the kitchen and brewed a fresh pot. Soon, the comforting aroma of freshly made coffee filled the air. I poured two cups and carried them into the master bedroom. I shook Mother awake, fluffed the pillows behind her, and helped her sit up in bed. Although her eyes were still closed, I shoved one of the cups of Joe into her hand. After a few sips, she opened her eyes and looked at me. "I have a terrible headache," she said.

"No kidding. You drank a lot of whisky yesterday."

"Now I remember. That nice Mr. Chang came by and bought this dump. Little does he know how much he overpaid."

"I'm not so sure Mr. Chen is so nice or that he overpaid," I said as I sat at the foot of the bed," but it seems there may be no going back. Now you're going to have to move out."

"I won't miss this place."

"Where will you live?"

"I'll worry about that later."

Her words did little to comfort me. "We're going to be busy deciding what to do with all your possessions. We also need to arrange Dad's funeral. Did you find out why he died?"

"The coroner's office said it was a heart attack."

"But he was so young. Are they sure?"

"I'm not about to question them. They're the experts. It runs in families, and your dad's father, Grandpa Ted, died of a heart attack."

"But Grandpa was eighty-two."

"I think your father had high cholesterol."

I cocked my head. "Think? Did he have it measured?"

"He didn't trust doctors, so he hadn't been to one in years. He ate a lot of eggs. I told him not to, but he didn't listen to me. Didn't listen to me about much, but I suppose the eggs did him in."

"Maybe someone killed him. Did you ever think of that?"

My mom gasped. "Of course not. No one would have a reason to kill your dad. You must be watching too many TV shows. Besides, there was no sign of a struggle or anyone breaking and entering. As a matter of routine, they took a blood sample and said they'd do some toxicology but didn't expect to find anything."

The suddenness of my dad's death didn't seem right. Sure, some people die unexpectedly from a massive heart attack, but the way he died so abruptly, followed by Mr. Chen sweeping in, struck me as strange. I believe coincidences do happen, but this one bore investigating. I didn't want to go there, but wondered if my mother could have had something to do with Dad's death. The farm hadn't been doing well financially, and I suppose she'd wanted to sell, but he didn't. I'd watched enough episodes of Dateline and Snapped to know the wife is often the culprit. I couldn't believe my mom could do such a thing—I hoped she didn't—but I had to know. I wouldn't tell the cops if she did, but I needed to find out for myself.

I had no desire to grill my own mother about her possible involvement in my father's demise. Instead, I asked some uncomfortable questions about their finances and learned that they received a small pension from the VA, a pension she would continue to get as long as she didn't remarry. My dad had won two plots in a nearby cemetery at a county fair eight years earlier. Mom thought he was the only one who entered the drawing, but at least there would be no grave to pay for. Expenses for my father's burial would be covered by the VA.

"Don't worry about the cost for everything," she said. "It will be minimal, since I'm not planning on having a funeral.

"Don't you want a service so people can pay their respects?"

"You and I would be the only ones there. Actually, you'll be the only one. I plan to leave town this afternoon."

I became aware that my mouth had fallen open. "All your stuff has to be out of the house in two weeks. What about all the arrangements? Aren't you going to be around for Dad's burial?" The words came out quickly.

"I can't deal with any of this. You're the one with the brains. Your dad's at Grigsby's. I'll get you the name of the cemetery and the plot number. Put anything that looks worth keeping in storage. If I ever see this place again, it will be too soon."

I followed her as she carried her coffee into the kitchen and sat at the table. "What am I going to use to pay for all this?" I asked.

"Mr. Chang made me a new bank account. I'll give you the checkbook. There's plenty to pay for whatever you need. I have to pack now. Someone will be by to pick me up in a few hours."

"Where the hell are you going?"

"I'm taking a vacation. Please don't be mad at me, but I need this. You don't know what it's been like since you left home."

My mother looked frazzled, about to break. I hadn't appreciated the strain she'd been under looking after my dad and was sympathetic, but didn't think I could ever forgive her if she killed him. "Who's going to pick you up?"

"A friend of mine. Someone you don't know." She paused before continuing. "His name is Harrison." She glanced in my direction as soon as she'd spoken, as if wanting to gauge my reaction.

"Harrison? A man?"

"Yes."

"What the hell, Mom," I yelled. "What sort of friend is this? Is he gay, or is he a secret lover?" I wasn't concerned that my words might upset her.

She let out a long sigh and plopped into a chair. After sitting for an uncomfortable amount of time, she spoke. "I suppose I'll have to tell you all this eventually."

"Tell me what?"

"I loved your dad until the day he died, but he was very difficult to live with. He became more and more paranoid and believed in all sorts of conspiracy theories."

"I saw my bedroom has been turned into some sort of survivalist haven."

"So you know what I'm talking about. I needed to find someone to help me through all of this, and that someone is Harrison. He was divorced a few years ago, and a mutual friend saw my need as well as his. She introduced us and, yes, we became lovers. He's smart, kind, and supportive. I love him, and he loves me."

I couldn't control the anger that boiled up inside me. "You say you loved Dad, but now you tell me you love this Harrison guy."

"I know it may not make sense to you, but I became more of a caretaker to your dad. I loved him more like he was my brother, or even my child. Harrison—well, I love him differently. Like I used to love your dad."

As much as I tried, I couldn't stop the tears running down my cheeks. "Is that who you were with when Dad died?"

"Yes, I was with Harrison. I just didn't want to tell you."

"Did Dad know about him?"

"I never told him, but I was gone a lot, and he may have suspected something. He never said anything, though, and I don't think he would have cared if he knew. His obsession with conspiracies and survivalism occupied all his time. So there you have it. The whole truth, and nothing but the truth."

"Damn it, Mom. I'm having a hard time hearing this," I said as I felt my eyes water.

"I know, Dear. I'm sorry about the suddenness of all of this, but try to understand. Harrison and I haven't spent any significant span of time with each other. I came home to your father every night. Now, Harrison and I will be traveling together, starting in Hawaii. I've always wanted to go there. We'll find out if we're really compatible. I believe we are, and if we both think so, we're going to get married. After his divorce, he bought a lovely home in a nice area of Bakersfield. I picture myself being very happy there."

I sat in dazed silence as my mother left the room to pack. Reflecting on the past few years, I acknowledged that I'd been so busy I hadn't spoken to her nearly as often as when I first moved away—probably only ten times in the past year. If I'd made an effort to speak to her more, she might have divulged how difficult her life was, maybe even her extracurricular activities.

This was not what I had expected when I left Indianapolis yesterday. That seemed so long ago. I couldn't help but wonder if my mom wanted to get away so quickly because she felt guilty being in the place where Dad died—guilty because she had killed him. Maybe even with Harrison's help. The whole truth and nothing but the truth? I would look into that as soon as she was gone.

Chapter 6

TWO HOURS LATER, MY mom received a message on her cell. "Harrison's here," she said. "He doesn't think this would be a good time to meet you, so I'll just leave. Plenty of time to meet him later. I think you'll like him."

"Don't count on it." I was determined never to accept that man.

Mom looked at me and grimaced. "Don't be mad at me," she said. "I know I'm leaving you with the burden of taking care of your father's remains and the house, but I can't bear to be here anymore. I hope you never feel as helpless and depressed as I feel right now because that would mean you've reached an unbearable level of suffering."

Were those the words of a murderer? I hoped to know soon.

Shortly after my mother's abrupt abandonment of me and the home she'd lived in for over twenty years but was unlikely to see ever again, I drove her car to Grigsby's Funeral Home. Only two other vehicles were in the parking lot when I pulled in. I sat looking at the steering wheel for a few moments before walking to the pristine white, two-story colonial building with blue shutters matching the front door. The surrounding well-maintained lawn was green, no doubt sustained by squandering the precious water needed by the farmers. Red rose bushes in bloom flourished around the perimeter.

I wasn't sure if I should knock or open the door. I knocked. Seconds later, I heard the sound of shoes hitting a hard surface. It reminded me of the sound made by tap shoes I'd had as a child. A man in a black suit opened the door, invited me in, and introduced himself as Mr. Grigsby. His demeanor was subdued yet friendly, an affect he had likely perfected over the years. I explained who I was, and he responded with the familiar "sorry for your loss" said so frequently in movies and TV shows. I told him of my desire for the most economical burial for my dad but was unable to escape his polished presentation of costly funeral and casket options. Although I was determined from the outset to opt for the plainest pine box, I felt guilty choosing the rock-bottom option after being escorted around the room filled with pricey, comfortable-looking final resting places for loved ones who surely deserved the best that could possibly be afforded by their bereaved family members with credit being so readily available.

It was easy to understand how someone less determined, less wise to the manipulations of an unscrupulous funeral director, would fall victim to a man like Mr. Grigsby, but even at the age of twenty-two, I was worldly enough not to succumb to the feelings of guilt he was throwing my way. Plain pine box, no embalming, no service, burial at the Shady Hill Cemetery, plot number 178. Once he understood I would hold my ground, he began to usher me to the door.

"One more thing," I said. "I want to see my dad's body."

"At your request, there won't be a showing, so that will not be possible."

"His body is here, isn't it?" I asked. Mr. Grigsby reluctantly nodded in the affirmative. "Then please take me to see him."

"He hasn't been prepared."

"I don't know what you would do to prepare him, but he's my dad, and I want to see him now."

"That would be highly unusual. At any rate, it would be unsafe for me to take you into the room where we store bodies."

"Then bring him out here."

The man's eyes narrowed. "Suit yourself. I'll take you to our morgue."

I followed behind, walking more quickly than usual to keep up with him. He led me down a pristine white hallway with a shiny wood floor towards the back of the building, then made a sharp right through a pair of double doors into a dingy corridor. Looking down, I noted the dirty linoleum. We came to a partially opened door with a large red sign reading "Authorized Personnel Only." Below that was a placard with "DANGER" written in white, surrounded by a red ellipse. A third sign read, "Formaldehyde, Irritant and Potential Cancer Hazard." I figured if it were safe for him to enter, it would be safe for me.

Mr. Grigsby pushed on the door until it was fully opened, revealing a square room twice the size of my bedroom-turned-survivalist supply room. On the counters and shelves around the perimeter were jars of chemicals, bottles filled with solutions, and trays of metal instruments. Several large blue drums, labeled as hazardous material, were inside, under the counter on the floor. A sizeable porcelain sink occupied one corner. In the middle of the room was the usual center of attention: a stainless steel table about six feet long, like ones I'd seen on TV where murder victims are autopsied.

Remaining silent, the funeral director opened a large metal door opposite where I was standing, exposing a sizeable walk-in refrigerator holding two gurneys, each with a body loosely covered by a white cloth. He checked the toe tag on the closest refrigerator resident, then moved on to the next. Taking care to prevent his jacket sleeves and hem from coming in contact with the gurney, he wheeled the body to the space adjacent to the fixed metal table and announced, "This is your father."

I stood still momentarily as fear, trepidation, and curiosity competed for top tier in my mind.

"Well? I haven't got all day," Grigsby said.

His words snapped me into action, and I walked toward the amorphous form under the cloth. I took a deep breath before I slowly pulled the covering down halfway, revealing my father's body from his head to his mid-torso. His arms were flexed awkwardly, and his face was mottled. Both of his pale blue eyes were open, his pupils appearing unusually small. His mouth was hideously agape, with an unsightly dried brownish-red crust. He was wearing the jeans and T-shirt he'd been found in. I saw no marks or injuries on the exposed areas. No blood stained his clothes. I wondered if this is how people appeared when they died of natural causes. He didn't look at peace. He looked troubled.

"Did he look like this when he passed?" I asked.

"He seems more relaxed now than when they brought him in. His arms and jaw were rigid, but now it looks like the rigor mortis has passed."

"Is this what people look like after they've died from a heart attack?"

Mr. Grigsby tapped his foot impatiently as he answered curtly, "Sometimes."

The constant click, click, click of the shoe hitting the floor made me nervous. I was about to cover my dad's body again, when something struck me as odd.

"I don't see where they cut his chest open," I said.

Mr. Grigsby rolled his eyes. "He didn't have surgery. He was already dead when they found him."

"But he had an autopsy. They always make a Y-shaped incision. I've seen it on TV."

"They didn't do an autopsy. Lots of times, the medical examiner doesn't need to do that. They use other information."

"Did the police investigate?"

"I was told they went to the scene, but they found no evidence of foul play. Look, if you think he died of something else, talk to the medical examiner. I've never known him to be wrong. He already did his investigation and cleared the body for burial. His department delivered the body here."

This may have seemed like an open-and-shut case of a heart attack to the police and the medical examiner, but this was my dad, and his death, all alone after years of mental torment, was hard for me to accept. Maybe the medical examiner was never wrong before, but was wrong now. Perhaps I was being irrational, and it was guilt that made me want to blame someone. I might have felt differently if I'd had the chance to see him again and re-established a relationship with him. If only he'd lived another few months.

I scheduled the burial for two days from then and left for the home where I'd grown up. The house was small but jammed full of things, mainly what most people would classify as junk. I wouldn't have time to go through every item carefully and decide what to keep and what to throw away. The sun was still up, so I went outside to look over the fields. Walking between the rows of almond trees, grapes, tomatoes, and peaches brought back memories of my childhood, when I would play hide and seek with my mom and some of the kids in the neighborhood. When I reached my favorite place, the strawberry fields, my eyes teared up as some of my fondest memories surfaced.

The strawberries had been harvested weeks before, but I foraged through the leaves and found a handful of luscious red fruit that had been missed by the pickers. I closed my eyes and ate everything in my hand, imagining I was seven years old, eating strawberries without a care in the world.

My world changed gradually as I grew up. When I was in the fourth grade, my mom told me my father suffered from something called PTSD. He had caught it in the war in a faraway place called Afghanistan. At the time, I was confused. I didn't understand PTSD. I didn't know where Afghanistan was, or why my dad was upset by being in a war there, where he was one of the good guys.

Mom said he'd been a happy, industrious, kind-hearted man with a lot of smarts when she married him. They were still in their teens, and their first years together were happy ones. My father built their home on the plot of land he'd managed to purchase by doing odd jobs and scraping funds together. When they were barely twenty-one, he enlisted in the army after seeing footage of the Twin Towers engulfed in flames. Mother was pregnant with me at the time, and I was born while he was overseas. In anticipation of my birth, they had decided on my name before he left.

I remembered my dad being kind, gentle, and a lot of fun when I was very young, but even then, he had periods when he was melancholy, paranoid, and prone to violent outbursts. The kind, gentle, and fun dad was almost completely replaced by the sad, paranoid, and sporadically violent dad by the time I was twelve. Nighttime was often the worst, when he would wake screaming and kicking from a dream. Therapy through the VA didn't help. It was a long drive from our farm to the VA hospital, and he stopped going.

He'd probably suffered from PTSD all throughout my childhood. Like many kids with a disturbed parent, I interpreted his behavior as a reflection of my own shortcomings. I became insecure and withdrawn. Although my mother did her best to comfort and encourage me, I felt unworthy of love.

When I was in middle school, Mom sent me to live with her sister in Indianapolis. I attended high school there and became close to my aunt and uncle. They had an accounting business, where I often worked on weekends until I enrolled at Purdue. I was helped immensely by the therapist they found, who helped me learn more about myself and my dad's PTSD.

I had planned to visit my parents ever since I moved to Indiana, but something constantly got in the way. My classes, a party, a sports event, a concert. I really could have gone, but truthfully, I didn't want to. I never felt ready, and my mom didn't encourage me. Until I got the call from her telling me Dad had died, I had been looking forward to returning home in August with my degree in hand.

With my knowledge of Aggie finance, I was sure I could turn the family business around from where, according to my mom, they barely eked out an existence, to an enterprise where they could grow and prosper. I'd tried to explain it a number of times when I talked to Mom on the phone. It's all about borrowing money and leveraging what you have so you can modernize and eventually expand. I'd arrange for Dad to get the best psychiatric care possible. My parents would enjoy their later years in financial comfort, with me by their side.

The sting of a mosquito roused me from my mind's meanderings. The sun was setting, and the insects were out in full force. Many things had changed, and I needed to rethink the trajectory of my life. The only thing that hadn't changed was the bugs.

Chapter 7

ONCE INSIDE, MY PHONE rang. Perry. I hadn't thought about him all day. I filled him in on the events since my arrival, how my mother sold the farm and left me to take care of everything. I told him what had happened, but not how I felt.

"Doesn't sound like a big deal to me," he said. "From what you've told me, the farm wasn't worth much. Now you won't be stuck with it."

"Don't you remember me telling you how I want to move back here and turn it around?"

"I remember, but never thought you'd really do it. I always figured it was a lame idea, and you'd come to your senses eventually. Now you don't even have to think about it. You should be relieved to be rid of it."

His words reminded me that he had a way of belittling many of the things that were important to me. While Perry was full of good ideas, he always seemed to find a way to make my ideas seem silly.

"I have a lot to do," I said, not wanting to argue and cause myself more distress. "No time to talk." After I ended the call, I realized he never even asked if I wanted him to attend my dad's burial. Turns out, I didn't want him there. While Perry had a lot of good qualities, I couldn't count on him for emotional support. The passion in our relationship was waning. I was beginning to think he wasn't the man of my dreams, but maybe someone else was.

Shortly after we disconnected, he called back. Or so I thought. Instead of hearing Perry's voice, I was greeted by CJ. I had to admit to myself, I was glad he called. Maybe it was because I'd been friends with him years ago or because I appreciated his genuine, down-to-earth nature. Whatever the reason, I felt more comfortable talking to him than Perry.

I told him how shocked and upset I was that my dad had died suddenly before we had a chance to reconnect, and that my mom had sold the farm, the farm I had grown up on and loved and planned to breathe new life into. I'd taken an almost instant dislike to the cold businessman, Mr. Chen, who plied her with booze so she'd sign the papers. Now she had only two weeks to move out and empty the house. To make things worse, I learned she'd been having an affair with a man she'd met through a friend, and she'd taken off with him, leaving me to take care of everything.

I was heartbroken that there would be no funeral and my mom, his wife of over twenty years, wouldn't even attend his burial. Not a fitting farewell for this man who had sacrificed for his country, only to be haunted by PTSD and spend the last decades of his life spiraling into depression and paranoia.

"Seeing my dad lying on that gurney at the funeral home," I said as tears silently trickled down my face, "he looked so pained. Knowing I would be the only one to attend his burial was almost more than I could bear."

"Let me come with you to bury your dad," CJ said. "I didn't know him much, but I have great respect for all veterans. After that, we I'll go by the VA and get a flag for his coffin."

Why hadn't I thought of that? "That would be nice," I said.

Despite CJ's kindness, I felt more alone than I could remember after we disconnected. My mind was going crazy places. I was almost convinced Mom had murdered him, perhaps with the help of her new lover.

Darkness had fallen outside, and I was isolated in the house, a long way from anyone I knew. My father was dead, and my mother was on a plane to Hawaii. She had proven herself useless or worse. I had no siblings, no friends nearby I had kept in touch with to console me. My aunt and uncle were far away, as was Perry who was unhelpful anyway. I found myself strangely wanting CJ to keep me company. He had a comforting way about him. His voice, his looks, his words—it was hard to pinpoint, but everything rolled up into him was what I wanted at the moment.

Needing to keep busy, I began searching through my mother's things. I didn't know what I was looking for exactly, but If I got lucky and found an incriminating note from Harrison or a bottle of poison, I'd know she was involved in my father's death. The small desk in the entryway near the front door contained pens, mostly out of ink, pencils with broken tips and hard, useless erasers if any eraser was left, a jumble of recipes, receipts, coupons, paperclips, and a screwdriver.

Satisfied there was nothing pointing to my mother's guilt there, I stood facing the front door, wondering what I should rummage through next. My eye focused on a wire traveling from a small hole above the door, down the side molding, to a plug near the baseboard. I turned on the outside light and opened the front door. Looking up, I saw a small camera mounted above the molding. Duh. My father, with all his paranoia, had mounted a camera to view the outside, should the house come under attack. The small green light above the lens indicated the camera was still running.

I slammed the door and ran back to my old bedroom. There had to be a recording device mixed in with the jumble of guns, flack jackets, and food rations. After searching through several piles of miscellaneous items, I was no closer to finding it. With my face covered in sweat, I pushed my hair back from my forehead and looked around.

Could my old closet hold the key? I swung the door open and was surprised to see what looked like a Star Wars control center. Unbeknownst to me until then, the closet had been enlarged, the footprint extending beyond the house's original exterior. A bulky wooden desk with a desktop computer was in the center, the computer screen facing me. Flashing green LED lights pierced the darkness on either side. A comfortable-looking chair on rollers faced the computer. I couldn't make out much more. Details of the room were hard to discern, as it was lit only by the overhead light from the bedroom.

I retrieved a powerful flashlight I'd seen on one of the bedroom shelves holding canned food. Shining light on the inner wall of the closet, I found a switch. I flipped it, and the secret room was immediately illuminated, revealing what could be best described as a man cave for the paranoid.

Unlike the bedroom outside the closet, the area within it was pristine. The only clutter was a cup, half filled with water, on the desk. A combination fax and printer occupied a nearby small stand. Paper and printer ink were on a shelf below. Behind the desk was a window looking out onto the fields. Shelves lined the walls, filled with survivalist manuals, copies of American Survival Guide magazine, grenades, tasers, pith helmets, flak jackets, tools, electronic equipment, and at least twenty neatly stacked and labeled hard drives. My dad's old ham radio, which I remembered from my youth, was on a top shelf.

I slid into the chair facing the desk. I'm not an information technology expert, but am still a member of Gen Z, so I am pretty comfortable navigating computers. I located the start button on the tower beneath the desk. While hearing the familiar whirring and humming sounds as the computer booted up, I pressed the monitor power switch. Moments later, the Windows logo appeared. I shook the mouse to locate the arrow key and was immediately confronted with a login screen. Shit. At a loss to guess the username and password, my chest tightened, and I placed my chin in my hands. Think! Think! I told myself over and over. Maybe my mother knew, but I didn't want to call her about it even if she wasn't on a plane yet. She might worry about something incriminating on his computer and interfere with my investigation. I tried using my dad's name and birthday as username and password. The usual "username or password is incorrect" message appeared.

I opened the pencil drawer and spotted a notebook. Thumbing through, I saw addresses and phone numbers. All the names seemed to be in code—there was no recognizable login information. A scrap of paper, loose next to the notebook, was folded over. I opened it to reveal the word "Strawberry" overlying "O215O2712!"

My eyes teared up instantly, seeing my name, then my birthdate and birthweight followed by an exclamation point, the zero's substituted with capital Os. This had to be the holy grail.

Chapter 8

I QUICKLY TYPED MY newly acquired information into the login spaces, held my breath, and pressed enter. The screen instantly changed to an image of a post-apocalyptic world, complete with dead bodies strewn over tanks and rubble, collapsing concrete structures, and, almost comically, giraffes, gorillas, and lions roaming around. The sky was dark but light enough to see the mushroom cloud in the distance. The picture was disturbing, but I rejoiced. I was in.

My hands were shaking as I searched through the icons on the desktop for the mail symbol. There was none. Then I looked for an internet browser logo. There was none. The only icons before me were for folders and security equipment. It didn't take me long to realize this computer was air-gapped—there was no connection between it and the internet serving the house, which linked up the TV and a laptop computer my mom had taken with her. I should have expected as much. Attached to a hub, this computer was hooked up to other devices, probably monitoring equipment, via ethernet connections. Everything was hardwired.

I clicked on the folder labeled "Land" and discovered a myriad of images of our family farm. Pictures of neighboring farms were in subfolders with dates, addresses, and often descriptions of the goings on. Another subfolder labeled "Entry" showed an image of a security booth and a yellow arm across the adjacent road, stopping traffic. Other pictures in that folder revealed a large sign reading "Happy Sun Farm." Behind it stood a partially obscured large sculpture of a smiling sun, identical to the familiar company logo, atop a sturdy-appearing wooden A-frame stand. I quickly scrolled through the dozen or so pictures of the sculpture taken from different angles. Other images in the folder showed Happy Sun Farm trucks exiting behind the security booth. I wondered how Dad took those pictures, as Mom said he never left the farm.

More images showed my father had kept close tabs on what was happening at all the surrounding properties. He had documented the dismantling of a solar farm at the Shelton's place, as well as the removal of the tomato plants heavy with fruit, ready to harvest. The new owner's activities were strange, indeed. A large agricultural concern would be expected to make smart, financially sound decisions, but this appeared to be reckless. Perhaps, being a foreign company, they were unfamiliar with optimizing the use of this highly productive farmland.

When I came upon a folder labeled "Surveillance," my pulse quickened. This could hold key information about my dad's death. Or it could show nothing of note. I clicked on the "Front door" folder. Numerous subfolders were inside, indicating the week of the recording. The dates went back at least three months. I clicked on the folder for the current week. I was surprised to see a subfolder for each day, beginning with Sunday.

My dad had died on Friday. It was now Sunday night. My muscles tensed as I clicked on the Friday folder. Empty. This wasn't going to be easy.

The Thursday folder held multiple subfolders, each labeled with a different location. I clicked on the one identified as "Entry" and was soon looking at a video of the area outside the front door.

It started at midnight, according to the time stamp. The camera was sophisticated, using infrared technology when it was dark outside, allowing me to see a raccoon roaming in the patch of weeds that used to be a flowerbed near the walkway. I sped through the tape at high speed and witnessed the sunrise, my mom leaving and returning with groceries and Amazon packages, then a man I didn't recognize coming to the door. He was dressed casually, in overalls, a T-shirt and work boots, and was carrying a large empty glass jug. Before knocking on the door, he ran his fingers over the top of his head through his thinning hair, which appeared light-colored in the black-and-white video. I slowed the playback to twice normal speed and saw him speaking to someone who opened the door and invited him in. The man wiped his feet and entered. Ten minutes later, he exited carrying the same jug, now filled with clear fluid.

Seeing that brought back memories from my childhood when neighbors came around with bottles and jugs to buy whiskey from my parents' still. They'd given up the business years ago, or so I thought. Perhaps they'd stopped making whiskey but started production again to make ends meet. That might explain how my dad could afford all his expensive electronic equipment.

I started skipping through the video to speed up the process. Aside from another customer arriving with an empty jug and leaving with a full one, nothing else of note took place. Whatever happened to my dad occurred after the last video in the file. I needed to locate the most recent recording and the live video feed, which I assumed was still coming in.

I opened "Devices and Drives" and discovered a drive labeled "Active." I held my breath as I clicked on the icon. I was greeted with numerous camera icons. I clicked on the one labeled "Entry." Voila! There it was. Live feed of the front door. It was currently dark outside, but the camera's infrared capability captured a few leaves blowing around in the walkway in front of the door.

My heart was thumping quickly as I reversed the video. I saw myself arrive at the house after visiting the funeral home. I backed the recording to the beginning, time-stamped noon, the day of my dad's death. I sped through minutes of inaction, then my mom leaving the house at 12:07. I slowed the speed to "normal" and watched. For an hour, the image on the screen was less interesting than the chess match Perry had dragged me to. Nothing was happening.

At 1:22 p.m., two young girls I estimated to be around seven years of age, were holding hands as they walked towards the front door. When they were close, I saw they were both adorable, laughing and talking. One had long dark hair in a ponytail, and the other had curly mid-length light hair. The dark-haired one held a small box, about two inches square. The box was closed, and the surface appeared shiny. They stood in front of the door for a while, looking around nervously and taking turns whispering in each other's ear. The curly-haired one reached out to ring the bell, then withdrew her arm. This action was repeated several times by each of the girls. I envisioned them daring the other to ring the bell of the crazy man's house. Finally, the girl holding the box pressed the button decisively.

The duo stood silently, occasionally giggling while covering their mouths. Seconds later, the door opened. The girls looked momentarily nervous, but as the braver one, the one with the dark hair, began speaking, they both appeared to ease up. I saw an arm reach out and take the box. I recognized the eagle tattoo above the elbow as being my father's. Once the box had been taken, they spoke a few seconds more, and the door closed. The girls looked at each other, shrugged, laughed, then skipped away.

Hours later, my mother returned looking happy, as one might expect from someone who just got laid. I could only imagine what she saw when she entered the house, and I wondered if she had been surprised or had found exactly what she expected. Fifteen minutes later, a team of emergency responders arrived with equipment and a gurney, followed ten minutes after that by two police officers. I watched as a body, presumably that of my father, was wheeled out on the gurney, covered in a sheet. The body appeared to be lying sideways, in a fetal position. Mother followed, comforted by a female police officer as she walked with her hands covering her face, her shoulders shaking. Although there was no sound in the video, I imagined her cries of despair. Her grief looked genuine. After seeing what was on the recording, I couldn't imagine she had anything to do with my dad's death.

I still wasn't convinced my dad died of a heart attack. Perhaps someone entered the house another way. I spent the next five hours reviewing videos taken from cameras positioned around the house perimeter. Nothing but small animals and leaves swirling in the air.

My mind traveled back to the girls. Who are they? What had they given my dad? They appeared too young and innocent to be involved in something nefarious, but I had no other leads. I needed to find them and that box.

I searched the room I was in, my old bedroom, my parents' bedroom, the living room, and the kitchen. No box. The sun was rising. I was out of breath and exhausted from my search. I hit my forehead with the palm of my hand. Of course! I needed to look in the trash. The bathroom waste can was nearly empty, as were the ones in both bedrooms. I dreaded going through the kitchen garbage, but there was no getting around it. I found a pair of disposable vinyl gloves to wear, placed paper towels on the floor next to the waste basket and began sifting through the contents, transferring each item to the paper towels after I had examined it.

Carrot peels, coffee grounds, junk mail, and a copy of People magazine were on top. Hadn't my parents heard of recycling? I didn't have to dig too deep before finding it. There was no question in my mind that this was the box I'd seen on the video. I wiped away the coffee grounds and studied it. A two-inch cube made of metallic silver-colored cardboard. The box was open, with the flap lid partially torn. A gray circular seal, which I hadn't appreciated on the recording, had been broken. Wondering what I would find, I opened the box and looked in. Empty. I was left wondering what had been inside.

Chapter 9

I PLACED THE BOX on my dad's desk next to the computer screen. In my mind, it was evidence of something. I just didn't know what. It was 5:30 a.m., and I was exhausted. I lay down on the bed and quickly fell asleep.

Three hours later, I was awakened by the sound of a large engine behind the house. Still in my clothes, I splashed water on my face and ran out the back door. What sounded close by was actually about three hundred yards away. I ran towards the source of the noise, a large, motorized piece of equipment slowly moving through the almond orchard. I had assumed that since I had two weeks to move out of the house, the farm would be idle during that time. I was wrong.

As I approached the equipment, the smell of diesel became strong. The vehicle was one of the largest, if not the largest, piece of farm equipment I'd ever seen. A behemoth bulldozer-like contraption was making its way down a row of almond trees, felling them, grinding them, and working the crumbs into the ground, all in one pass. Several rows of trees were already destroyed. I got close enough to look at the operator of the equipment, who appeared to be concentrating on the work ahead of him. He was wearing a dark suit. It was an Asian man, but not Mr. Chen.

Sure, almond trees required a tremendous amount of water, but they'd been on the farm since I was little, and I felt a sense of loss seeing them disappear so unceremoniously. I told myself I'd better get used to it. The farm was now in new hands, and they had their own vision of how the land would be used.

In the distance, I saw a tractor pulling planting equipment, which was dropping seeds into the ground where radishes used to grow. This would have been an ideal time to harvest the crop planted in May. If they were re-planting radishes, they were making a big mistake. This was not the optimal time to be sowing them.

I looked to my right and saw a dozen farm workers picking plums. The familiarity of the scene took me back to a pleasant time in my childhood and made me smile. I walked towards the men and women, some standing on the ground, others on folding ladders reaching into the trees. Not much had changed in this corner of the farm during the ten years I'd been gone. The workers were Hispanic—dark-skinned, with black hair visible under their bucket hats or baseball caps. All wore long pants, colored shirts, boots, and gloves. Over-the-shoulder straps kept their four-gallon bean-shaped white plastic baskets at chest height for easy collection of fruit. After they were full, the baskets were emptied into large bins on the ground. When I was younger, I often followed behind as workers loaded the large fruit bins onto flatbed trucks at the end of the day, helping myself to whatever fell on the ground.

I didn't recognize any of the workers until I laid my eyes on Diego. Noticeably older than the last time I'd seen him, he was one of the few workers on our farm who spoke English, and I remembered playing tag with his daughter, Martina, who was about my age.

"Diego!" I yelled.

He turned and looked in my direction, his furrowed brow indicating he didn't recognize me.

"Remember me?" I shouted. "I'm Strawberry Fields. You worked for my dad."

Before I finished speaking, a smile spread across Diego's face. "Berry," he said as he started walking towards me. "So glad to see you, and so sorry—"

His words were interrupted by a bespectacled Asian man wearing a suit who seemed to appear out of nowhere. In a heavy accent, he yelled at me. "Miss Fields, you must leave. No trespassing." Then he turned to Diego and shouted, "Return to work."

The smile melted from Diego's face as he changed course and sheepishly walked back towards the tree he'd been picking fruit from.

I don't know if he turned around to look at me again because I immediately headed back to the house without looking back. I didn't want to do anything to jeopardize Diego's job. I would have enjoyed talking to him, an incredibly kind man who I knew would have spoken to me about my father, which was something I would have found comforting. I felt like crying, which is exactly what I did once back inside the confines of the house.

I made coffee and sat at the kitchen table to think. I didn't know where to start. Call storage companies and arrange to move everything into a large rental space? Consult with an attorney? Call the police with my suspicions?

My phone played the Strawberry Fields Forever ringtone I had downloaded, announcing a call. I didn't want to speak to Perry or my mom at the moment. I smiled seeing the name CJ on my caller ID.

He asked how I was doing, and I immediately lied, answering that I was fine.

"I don't believe you. I felt bad leaving you all alone last night, but I had to get home. I'm going to come by. You shouldn't be alone at a time like this."

"But—"

"It's settled. See you in twenty."

The call disconnected before I could object.

Chapter 10

I TOOK A QUICK shower and combed my hair. I didn't have time to look through my mom's clothes for something attractive—perhaps fetching—to wear, so I wore my jeans and a long-sleeved blue shirt I had brought with me. I was still tying one of my shoes when I heard a knock on the door. I checked the live feed on the front door camera and saw CJ standing straight, looking forward, holding a package of store-bought donuts.

I finished tightening the bow on my Asics and opened the door.

"I figured you could use something to eat," CJ said. "Sorry, this is all I had. Not too fancy, but I hope you like them as much as I do."

"Come in the kitchen. I'll pour you some coffee. How do you take it?"

"I'm easy. I like it black." I warmed my coffee in the microwave and poured CJ a fresh cup. He sat at the table, and I brought both cups over before taking a seat.

"It's awfully nice of you to come over," I said. I enjoyed his company, but there was an awkwardness I needed to clear up. "I'm not sure you should be here. Certainly not if, for instance, you have an emergency at home."

CJ looked stunned for a moment, then laughed. "I'll bet you think I'm married."

"Well, you did mention something was going on at home last night. I just figured—"

"I had a meeting at my house with some people in the town about the election. I'm single. No girlfriend. There, I've said it. Now I can put all my cards on the table. I don't like keeping secrets, anyway. I like you. Always did. Maybe I didn't know the best way to show it when I was a kid, but I'm not a kid anymore."

"Yes, I can see that."

"I'd really like to help you through this tough time. I'd want to do that for anyone I met in your situation, but I'm thinking—I'm hoping—we'll have something that lasts after you settle everything."

I knew my fair skin was betraying me again as I felt my face heat up. CJ grabbed my hand, which was resting on the table, before I could get up and walk away to hide my face. "I know you're hurting and don't know many people around here. Just know you can count on me."

I looked into CJ's eyes. He seemed so genuinely concerned. He was right. I hadn't connected with anyone else in town besides Mr. Chen, who wasn't exactly someone I could confide in, and Diego, who couldn't talk to me. I didn't even know who still lived in the area. I followed my best instincts and decided to trust CJ. My memories of him were of a good, honest, dependable pre-teen. He could have changed in the ten years that had passed, but a lot of people trusted him enough to want him to enter politics. Maybe that would corrupt him, but he didn't seem corrupted yet.

"It's more than that. So much has happened." I started to tell CJ more details about everything that had transpired in the short time since I'd arrived, but I was at a loss as to where to start and broke down in tears. He scooted his chair closer to mine and put his arm around me.

"I don't blame you for crying. I cried when each of my parents died. It's only natural, but know that you'll get over it."

His warmth was comforting as I continued to sob, bent over with my hands covering my face until I felt all cried out. I sat up and sniffled. He handed me a napkin from the napkin holder in the middle of the table so I could blow my nose and wipe my face.

"Feel better?" he asked. I nodded in the affirmative. "Okay, then. Tell me everything that's happened. Take your time."

I inhaled deeply a few times, then began. I may have sounded disorganized and frazzled, but that didn't hold me back. I'd already told him about my mother selling the farm, leaving with her lover, and my visit to the funeral home.

I started by describing what I'd found in my old bedroom and the shock of discovering how much my dad had gone off the deep end with survivalist gear and surveillance equipment. I admitted to suspecting my mother of murdering my father, but after finding a recording of her coming home after he'd died, I was convinced she was traumatized by his death. She just showed it differently than me.

The girls with the box were an enigma. I'd found the box, which was empty, supporting my suspicion that my dad had been poisoned. On the video, I'd also seen men collect what I assume was whisky, so I believed my parents operated a still as they'd done years ago. There were pictures of crops and a solar farm being ripped out on surrounding farmland that Happy Sun Farm had taken over. I had walked around the property and saw the Happy Sun people destroying perfectly good almond trees. Then I came upon a farm worker I knew, but when we started talking, I was told to leave.

CJ listened to everything I said without interruption while eating a donut and drinking coffee. Once finished, I sat back and relaxed. A large weight had been lifted, and I breathed more easily. The knot that had been tightening in my stomach had dissipated, and I helped myself to a donut.

"As you probably know by now," CJ said, "Happy Sun has bought up just about all the farms around yours. Your dad was one of the last holdouts."

"Do you think they might have murdered him to get the farm?"

"I didn't say that. They've aggressively bought land by making generous offers, but there's been nothing illegal. Most of the farmers have taken the money and left the area."

"What about the others? There must be others who haven't sold."

"From what I know, almost all caved eventually. Right now, I'm curious about those girls who brought the box. Would you mind showing me what they look like?" He'd clearly been paying attention to all the information I'd dumped on him.

"I'd be happy to," I said. "I hope you can identify them."

CJ followed me into my dad's lair. "Whoa," he said," you didn't exaggerate. Your dad really was preparing for the apocalypse." He whistled when he looked over the monitoring equipment. "This must have cost a fortune."

When I brought up the front door video, he looked attentively. I found the segment where the girls approached the front door, spoke to my dad, and turned away.

"Damn," he said. "I know most of the folks around here, including the kids, but I don't recognize those girls." He sat on my bed to think. "There's a group of Gypsies camped out about ten miles away. They keep to themselves but have been known to pull off petty crimes, like stealing things. Once took a sheep from Steadman's place and slaughtered it. They have lots of kids running around. Most look pretty grubby, not clean and dressed up like these girls, but it could be one of 'em, I suppose."

"I'd sure like to look into that," I said. "Can you take me there?"

"Sure. They don't talk to strangers unless they have to, but it's worth a try. I'm going to be tied up for the rest of the day. I need to go to a meeting at my company soon, then I have a long baseball practice scheduled. At six, I have another meeting with my state assembly backers. My day tomorrow is pretty clear, though. After your dad's burial, if you're up to it, I'll take you to the Gypsy compound." He paused a moment before continuing. "You should know that everyone around here is aware that your parents have a whisky still. Best barley and corn whiskey around and pretty inexpensive. I think the income from that helped a lot."

"Where is it?"

"Your dad built a really nice shed out back, near the old one. I've been there several times myself."

"It belongs to Happy Sun now."

"I suppose they'll dismantle it and plant something in its place." He paused before continuing. "Most folks around here know about your dad passing, but don't be surprised if some of 'em come around with empty jugs looking for moonshine. Right now, I think you should start going through all the stuff in the house, deciding what to keep and what to leave here for the Happy Sun people to dispose of. You can label everything with Post-it notes—what to leave here, what to give away, and what to store. There are companies that will hold a yard sale for you, but they have to be reserved way in advance."

"Too late for that now."

"The population has fallen since Happy Sun moved in, so there wouldn't be a lot of buyers anyway. My pick-up's got a big bed, so I could take whatever you want to keep to a storage unit. You'll save big bucks by not hiring a moving company."

I agreed to start labeling things, and CJ left for his meeting. Just before exiting the house, he paused awkwardly for a moment, then bent down and kissed me on the lips. I made no effort to stop him. I didn't know what this would lead to, but was willing to take the ride.

I retrieved Post-its and a pen from my mother's desk, then started in my parents' bedroom. I'd box up my mom and dad's clothes and shoes separately and donate my dad's things to charities later. Most incidentals like toiletries could be left behind. Furniture, other than the broken lamp, could go to storage, although I didn't have a clue if my mom would want any of it. I assumed Harrison's house was already furnished.

The living room was easy. I marked everything for storage. The kitchen was another story. Lots of cookbooks, bric-a-brac, even a cupboard filled with broken plates waiting to be fixed. While I was deciding how to organize the kitchen contents, the doorbell rang. I ran to my dad's computer and checked out the feed from the front door camera. I saw a young Hispanic woman wearing sunglasses and a yellow baseball cap with the letters CAT across the front. CAT is an abbreviation for Caterpillar, a large manufacturer of farm equipment. The woman looked familiar, but for a moment, I couldn't place her. Then it hit me. Could it be?

Chapter 11

I RAN TO THE door and swung it open. "Martina!" I yelled. There was no doubt in my mind this was my childhood friend, Diego's daughter.

We hugged and I led Martina to the living room where we sat, me on the couch, she on one of the stuffed chairs. We both started talking at once, then laughed. For a moment I felt like I was six years old, fully comfortable with my friend and my surroundings.

"I'm so glad to see you," I said. "I wondered if you were still in the area. I saw your dad, but didn't get a chance to ask him."

"I know. I came the first chance I got after he told me you were here. He wanted to talk to you more yesterday but didn't want to lose his job."

"No need to explain. He's working for Happy Sun Farm now, and they seem to be pretty strict."

"Yes. I don't know how much you know, but things have changed around here a lot."

"So I've been told. I haven't had a chance to drive around and see for myself, though."

"First, I need to tell you how sorry we both are about your father."

"Thanks. It really hit me hard. We hadn't spoken in years, and I was planning to come back in a few months to reconnect with him and help out with the farm, but now I'll never get the chance." I didn't want to dwell on my problems, so I asked, "What's going on with you and your parents?"

"As you can see, Dad is still working in the fields. Mom died of COVID a few years ago after she started working as a maid for the Samson's."

"So sorry to hear that."

"Thanks, Berry. It's just the two of us now. Ever since Mom died, my dad has lived in the housing he used on your farm when he rotated through here. He hasn't worked anywhere else since then. The place is fixed up pretty nice now, with electricity and his own bathroom, but I moved out to be on my own. A year ago, your father helped me get a job at the JiffMart. I live in an apartment I share with two others about five miles from here. Until those assholes at Happy Sun took over, I would visit my dad a few times a week."

"I've never heard you use such strong language before," I said.

"I know, but the company is run by terrible people. Things have changed fast around here. As you know, the farms get their seasonal laborers using brokers, and the few left in the area all work with Happy Sun exclusively. They pay more than the others, which is nice for my dad and his fellow pickers, but it's clear to me they're trying to drive all the other farmers around here out of business, and they are succeeding. Your father was one of the last holdouts. Had he lived, he never would have sold. My dad was always loyal to your family so he didn't go to Happy Sun even though they offered him more than your dad could afford. Now he has no choice. He really loved your father, although he thought he was a bit odd with all his survivalist ideas."

"I understand. Seems he was preparing for Armageddon."

"A few years ago, your father became too paranoid to use his cell phone, so he gave his to my dad. Still paid for the service, though, so Dad could call me. He would call me regularly, but a Happy Sun supervisor crushed the phone under a tractor. Now, Dad has no way to reach me."

"How did you learn I was here?"

"Dad and I often met at the northeast corner of your property so I wouldn't have to look around for him in the fields. Then your father died, and things changed fast. I hadn't heard from my dad, so I went to our meeting place yesterday evening, hoping he would go there. Luckily, he showed up after I'd been waiting a half hour. He said he'd been checking at least once an hour. That's when I learned about the phone and what happened yesterday when he saw you."

"What do you know about Happy Sun Farm, other than that it's run by a bunch of assholes?"

Martina chuckled. "My dad and I didn't buy into all your father's conspiracy theories about them, but there is something funny about the way they do things. When they started buying up land, your father asked my dad to use the phone to take lots of pictures of the surrounding land they'd taken over. He wanted to keep track of everything Happy Sun was doing. They have a lot of security, with high fences and guards keeping outsiders off the land, but it was easy for my dad to walk around unnoticed. He blended in with all the other workers, so he got lots of pictures. It is strange, I must admit, that they rip out perfectly good crops, like corn, nuts, citrus, and vegetables, including tomatoes. Even took down all those solar panels the Sheltons put in. I heard they were quite profitable now that the equipment was paid off."

"What are they growing instead?"

"Fruits and vegetables. They built a large packing house right on the grounds, where they package their produce. They finished building it eight months ago. When Dad told me about it, I applied for a job there, or I wanted to, anyway. I thought I'd make more there than at the JiffMart and could save a lot of money by living in my dad's place here."

"What happened?"

"I didn't get far. I drove to the entrance and stopped behind the yellow arm they have there blocking traffic. I thought it was strange that I couldn't just drive through, and for a moment wondered if I'd taken a wrong turn, but there was a Happy Sun Farm sign and a giant smiling sun sculpture behind it on the side of the road, so I knew I was in the right place. A guard came out of the kiosk they had there and came up to my window. He seemed very suspicious. I know my car is old and all that, but what do they expect in a farming area? Anyway, I sure was surprised. I've never seen a farm with a guard."

"That does seem odd," I said. "What did the guard say?"

"He asked me what I wanted. He was Chinese and had such a heavy accent I could hardly understand him. I told him the truth, that I wanted to apply for a job in their food processing plant, but he said there were no openings, and I had to leave. That's when I noticed that all the people around there—other guards, a few people walking nearby in suits, and even the truck drivers—they were all Chinese."

"What did you do?"

"What could I do? I drove up a bit where I could turn around and left. On my way out, I saw an area where local trucks were dropping off supplies and leaving. There was a large sign with a picture of a cell phone inside a red circle with a red line through it, meaning no cell phones allowed. Everything about that place is strange."

"I'd love to talk to your dad."

"He can't talk to you. He'd like to, but he's afraid."

"The worst thing they could do is fire him. I'm sure he could find work elsewhere. All the farms are harvesting now."

"There aren't many other farms left around here. Happy Sun owns most of the land, and the few that remain are all going under. The only reason your father had any laborers was because he gave them all housing and work all year round, so they were very loyal."

"How did he manage that?"

"Lots of people around here took out loans against their property, so I suppose he did, too." Martina chuckled before continuing. "Also, remember that still he had?" I nodded. "Well, he greatly expanded that business. His whiskey is awfully popular around here, and I believe your father made a lot of money from it."

"If everyone around here knew about it, how did he get away with it for so long?"

"The local sheriff here loves the whiskey, and rumor is your father gave it to him for free. I believe it was only a question of time before the people at Happy Sun pressured the sheriff to shut down the operation so your father would run out of money and have to sell." Martina paused, seeming to consider whether she should continue. She took in a deep breath and exhaled. "For the workers, when it comes to Happy Sun, there's an issue of safety."

"They use unsafe chemicals or harvesting equipment?"

"Nothing like that, but a number of the workers are afraid. A local laborer named Carlos used to work for Mr. Jeffers. Happy Sun offered him a lot more money and got him to work for them a week ago."

"Mr. Jeffers—yes, I remember him. He used to visit my dad and was always nice to me."

"Apparently, he was barely making a go of it for the past six months. When Carlos left, Mr. Jeffers was on the verge of losing his farm. He told my dad, who told Carlos. Carlos felt so bad he left Happy Sun and went back to work for Mr. Jeffers so he could save his farm. Two days later, one of the Happy Sun workers found Carlos's body in the dirt outside the living quarters."

"He was dead?"

"Afraid so. One of the Happy Sun bosses came by and announced that Carlos had come back the night before and begged for his job back. They told him to sleep in his old cabin and start work in the morning."

"How did he die?"

"Good question. Happy Sun has their own doctor from China. He examined Carlos's body and said he died of a heart attack on the way to his cabin. They carried him away in a wheelbarrow and said they would notify the coroner. There was never an investigation."

"That seems very strange."

"The rumor is people from Happy Sun killed Carlos and left his body where everyone would see it. A warning to the others not to leave. No one believes Carlos came back to Happy Sun and begged for his job. They think the Happy Sun people kidnapped him from the Jeffers farm, killed him, and left him where the other workers would see him."

I sat back as the information sunk in. Was Happy Sun Farm so determined to buy up all the land in the area they'd be willing to kill to accomplish their goal? It wasn't a stretch to think they could have been behind my dad's death. Secretive and threatening, while trying to portray a friendly image with their logo, I wanted to find out more about the company.

Martina and I continued to visit, the conversation turning to what we'd each been up to the past ten years. As we spoke, in the back of my mind I wondered how I could learn more about Happy Sun. We exchanged phone numbers, and Martina left an hour later.

I continued the task of labeling the items in my parents' house. Looking in the kitchen bookcase, I began to reminisce when I started going through the photo albums. I looked like such a happy baby, toddler, and young child. As I got older, there were fewer pictures of me smiling. My dad was smiling in a few of the photos taken when I was a baby, but the smiles looked forced. By the time I was about five, he always looked somber. Over time, my mom had changed from a happy, playful young mother to a less cheerful older mother who rarely smiled. There were few pictures taken after I left the house, mostly of my dad working on the farm or sitting expressionless in front of a birthday cake.

Looking back on those times with the advantage of age, it is evident that whatever demons my dad had suffered as a consequence of his time in Afghanistan, he never recovered. My mother did her best, but with time, his anguish, bitterness, depression, guilt, or whatever he felt took a toll on both my mother and me. I was thankful I had the opportunity to spend my teen years away from the toxic environment. Perhaps if my dad had lived, if I had moved back here when he was alive and gotten him the help he needed, he and my mom could have lived out their lives in happiness. If not happiness, then in a state happier than it was.

My distrust of Happy Sun was strong. They desperately wanted the family farm and it wasn't a stretch to think they were responsible for my father's death in some way. Troubled as he was, my dad didn't deserve to be murdered.

The sun was starting to set when I poured myself some coffee and sat at the kitchen table, trying to think of a way to explore Happy Sun and find evidence. CJ called and told me his meeting was almost over. He could come by in an hour. I told him it was too late. I was tired, but I'd see him the next day at my father's burial. He said he'd already picked up the flag for the coffin and would pick me up at ten in the morning. After ending the call, I changed my clothes. I'd lied to CJ. I wasn't tired. I was going to do some investigating.

Chapter 12

IT WAS A WARM, humid day in Pyongyang. The Taejong, or general, stood in front of a large picture of Kim Jong Un hanging on the wall behind him. He displayed a rare smile as a tall, thin, middle-aged man with thick glasses and sparse gray hair entered the room. "Please, have a seat, Dr. Gang."

"Thank you, General Bai." The distinguished scientist sat, after which the officer resumed his seated position.

"I called you here, Doctor, to let you know how pleased we all are with your accomplishments. You have proven yourself to be a true visionary. As you had predicted, I just received word that the last type of produce bearing the genes you inserted passed the final hurdle of inspection. They will now bear the non-GMO label, which is so important to the Americans. Sales of our product have been brisk, and this should make it even better."

"It has been my honor to be of service to our government."

"The operation under your direction has been progressing flawlessly. Do you anticipate we will be able to complete it within the year?"

"Sooner than that. It all depends on the market penetration of our products. The way things are going now, I predict we will be ready in six months, at the most."

A sinister smile grew on his face. "Excellent."

Chapter 13

I SAT ON THE couch wearing the black clothes I'd changed into, waiting for the sun to go down. When it was pitch black outside, I was ready to go. I almost panicked when I couldn't locate my cell phone but found it between two cushions on the sofa after a frenzied search. I took several deep breaths to calm myself and ventured out behind the house. Using the light on my phone to make my way, I walked in the direction where I remembered my dad's still had been, about 200 yards from the house. When I reached the location, all I found left of it was an old shack with a few shoulder bags used for harvesting produce. I shone the light around outside randomly until a shed twenty-five yards away came into view.

I walked to the wood building, about the size of a three-car garage. The double doors were unlocked, and I stepped inside, closing the doors behind me. The sweet smell of alcohol brought back memories of my childhood, when I helped my father tend the still. Feeling around, I located a light switch and flipped it. Two stills, each comprised of a large copper pot with a long neck reaching the ceiling, bore no resemblance to the amateur glass still my father once operated. A heating element was at the base of each vessel. Mash was heated at each bulbous base which was continuous with a much narrower neck above, where the alcohol vapors traveled upward. This structure tapered to a pipe leading to a cylindrical condenser, where the vapors were cooled to a liquid state.

My first thought was that since no one was tending the operation, each pot could have become overheated and started a fire. On closer inspection, I noted the heating elements were operated by timers and had shut off. This equipment was much more sophisticated than what my dad had when I was younger. Another run of whisky production could be started any time. A large container filled with mash was nearby, ready for use. Happy Sun Farm was now in the moonshine business, although they didn't know it yet.

Looking around, I saw six sizeable jugs full of clear liquid, which I assumed were alcohol. Twelve large plastic drums with white lids, twenty gallons each, were lined up against one wall. I opened the two closest to me and recognized barley. The next two were filled with corn, the fifth contained sugar—all the ingredients for the mash my father was famous for.

The sixth container was empty. I kicked the seventh one lightly, expecting it to be empty, too, but it held its position as my foot made a thud deeper than expected. Curious, I started to remove the lid. Almost immediately, my nose burned and my eyes watered. I had no memory of any caustic material involved in the manufacture of alcohol.

I closed the lid and backed away to an area where the air was fresher, smelling only of alcohol. I breathed deeply several times. On the final inhalation, I held my breath and returned to the drum. I lifted the lid, peeked in, then shut it and backed away. I turned off the light and sat in the back corner, opposite the containers. With both hands pressed tightly against my mouth, I resisted the urge to puke. I'd just seen a black-haired man in a blue shirt folded into a drum filled with what I suspected was sodium hydroxide or another strong alkali. In the short moment I'd looked at him, his outline appeared blurry, as if he were dissolving.

In my mind, Happy Sun Farm had just changed from an aggressive company to a flat-out dangerous one. Was that Carlos in the vat? Had they killed others? My suspicion of their involvement in my father's death rose by a magnitude. I hoped no one had seen me enter the building or noticed the light that had escaped through the space around the doors. I was surrounded by fields, the house the only inhabited structure nearby, so my visit to the still was probably unnoticed. Once my queasy feelings dissipated, I was eager to get back to the safety of my home—or what used to be my home.

I was about to stand when I heard footsteps in the distance. Or was that an animal? Thoughts of the man in the vat were replaced by my immediate concern about imminent danger. Upon hearing voices, I knew people were approaching. I left the lights off and listened intently. As they came nearer, the sounds of a man and woman talking and laughing became clear. A night patrol at a farm was highly unusual, but so were bodies dissolving in chemicals. I strained to understand their words, but they weren't English. To be more exact, they sounded Chinese.

My heart raced as the pair approached. They appeared to be headed to the structure I was in, and I dreaded what they would do if they saw me. I had to think quickly. I used my phone flashlight to locate the brooms, hoes, shovels, and rakes leaning against the back wall, left there by my dad. I hurried to hide behind them. No sooner had I slithered into my hiding place, thankful I hadn't knocked anything over, than I heard the door open. I turned off the light on my phone and started the recording app. I wanted to learn as much as possible about this mysterious company. I'd find someone who could translate Chinese for me later. The light was switched on, and my eyes hurt from the brightness.

I watched as a young Asian man and woman in their early twenties wasted little time disrobing and getting down to business on the hard concrete floor. They weren't on a nighttime patrol—they were a couple who wanted to spend time together in the seclusion of the shed. The woman was pretty, with short hair. The man was thin yet muscular. I noticed his left fourth finger was missing, but that didn't slow him down. For the next ten minutes, little was said. I kept as still as I could, in fear of being discovered. Although my view was obscured by equipment, it was clear what they were doing. I looked away, not wanting to invade their privacy, but continued recording them. A few loud moans later, the couple began talking, although they remained on the floor. I could see enough to know they were affectionately caressing each other as they spoke. I was frustrated, hearing them run the gamut from laughter to speaking in heated tones. They may have been discussing their feelings for each other, future plans, or the goings on at Happy Sun Farm. Since they were young and sneaking around, I concluded they weren't high up in the organization.

As the conversation died down, the couple fell asleep in each other's arms. I feared I would be stuck uncomfortably hiding behind the brooms and hoes until the morning, but the woman eventually stirred and woke her boyfriend. Ten minutes later, they had dressed and left.

I sat in the darkness several minutes after they exited, afraid they would notice if I left too soon. It was still dark outside when I headed back to the house. I again lit the way with my cell phone, thankful when I finally reached the back door. I rushed inside and lay on my bed. I had a lot to think about, but the next thing I remember was my phone ringing at eight in the morning. CJ asked how I was and reminded me he'd be by to pick me up in two hours, not that I needed reminding.

I showered and looked in my mom's closet for something black to wear as I tried to keep all other thoughts out of my head. I wanted to devote the day to remembrances of my father, and the good times we had shared. I found black pants and a long-sleeved navy top. Not fashionable together, but I wanted to look like a family member in mourning, which is exactly what I was, and that was the closest I could get.

At ten sharp, CJ was at the door. "You're going to be hot in that," were his first words after I let him in.

"I'm in mourning. This is the best I could find in my mom's closet."

"I think you'll be sorry. It's going to be super hot today. Doesn't your mom have a dark top with short sleeves?"

"No," I said as I pulled down on one of my shirt sleeves.

"You could wear a lighter color. It's not as if anyone will be there to judge you."

"Let's just go," I said impatiently.

"Sorry, I was just trying to help."

I looked down, embarrassed I had been so dismissive of CJ. I believed he was sincerely offering sound advice, but I felt I had no choice but to ignore it. He opened the passenger door to his truck, and I hoisted myself in. When he got into the driver's seat, he reached to the back and lifted a box. "Your dad's flag is in here."

With all that had happened the night before, I'd forgotten about the flag. "Thanks."

As we drove to the cemetery, CJ pointed out some of the changes that had taken place in the neighborhood, and there were a lot. Almost all of the farms had been taken over by Happy Sun Farm. The houses were gone, replaced by fields of crops. A high barbed-wire fence surrounded most of the land, in contrast to the lack of fencing when I'd lived there.

Fifteen minutes into the drive, CJ turned in a direction I wasn't expecting.

"I have to turn here," he explained, "because the road is closed ahead. Happy Sun has blocked all the roads through areas where they own land on both sides. I wouldn't be surprised if they do that to your street as soon as your two weeks are up. They own everything across the street."

"No, I didn't know that," I said. "I haven't seen the Sandborns, but it looks the same, and their house is still there."

"Happy Sun just hasn't gotten around to tearing it down. I suppose they're planning to plow new fields over the space occupied by your farm, the Sandborns' farm, and the street between. Once you're gone, they'll complete their plans pretty quickly."

I covered my face with my hands, not wanting CJ to see my tears. Despite his talking, I tried to pretend I was alone. Hearing about the planned complete destruction of everything I'd held in the memories of my youth depressed me more than I expected.

CJ squeezed my thigh gently. "Sorry, I thought you already knew, but of course, you didn't. It doesn't seem as if your mom told you much of anything.,

Chapter 14

I WAS SILENT FOR several seconds, then sniffled and wiped my eyes with my shirt sleeve. "I should have figured that out. It was pretty obvious, but I suppose I didn't want to know. Thanks for being my reality navigator."

As we made our way to the cemetery, CJ filled me in on more of the families that had left the area. When he pulled into the parking lot, he finished by saying, "Now that the Browns died in a car crash and their kids sold their land, I think the only farms left in the area near you Happy Sun wants to buy are the Kendals' and the Uptons.'"

"The Browns died?"

"About three months ago. Hit and run. They never caught whoever did it."

I'd always liked Linda and Dennis Brown. My mom hadn't told me they had died. She hadn't said much about what was happening locally, so the changes I saw were surprising and unsettling.

CJ must have sensed how disoriented I felt from my dad's death and all that had transpired when we reached the cemetery. I was happy to let him go into the office and get directions to the gravesite. He parked the truck near the hearse that had carried my dad's body. The casket was already resting on metal supports over the grave. With the help of one of the cemetery employees, CJ made sure the American flag he had brought was neatly draped over the top.

CJ and I were the only mourners present at the gravesite. I stood with my head bowed and assumed CJ did the same. I didn't have words to express everything I was feeling. Finally, not knowing what to do, I asked one of the employees nearby to begin. Using thick straps placed under the casket, he and his coworker lowered the wooden box into the grave.

It all happened so quickly and efficiently. I declined the offer to shovel dirt on the casket, but we remained standing while it was covered in the dark brown earth. Looking down in the hole, I couldn't help but think about the dead man dissolving in the building with the stills. CJ kept his arm around me as I cried silently, my shoulders shaking.

When we were back in the truck, he asked, "Are you up to looking for those girls at the Gypsy camp?"

I wasn't up for it at all. I couldn't even bring myself to tell CJ about the man in the drum. I didn't know how long it would take me to feel up to anything, but I needed to persevere, no matter how difficult. "I think it would be good for me to go there. I need a distraction."

We drove close to an hour before we came to the campsite. Along the way, CJ talked about some of the locals who wanted him to run for state assembly. The more he met with them, the more he felt most had separate agendas regarding what he could do to promote their individual interests, in addition to helping the other people in his district. He still hadn't made up his mind about running.

Located on the outskirts of a small town of about 200 people, the camp was demarcated by a row of ten dilapidated trucks and cars, separating the Gypsies from the town. CJ led me between two of the vehicles, to a large patch of dirt with fifteen shacks and tents. A group of children ranging from approximately three years old to early teens were running around, squealing and laughing as they chased each other and rode one of the two rusty bikes. If they were bothered by the layers of dirt on their skin and their filthy, tangled hair, they didn't show it. Four adults, three men and a woman, sat on crates nearby. Two were holding a can of Pabst Blue Ribbon.

I looked from one kid to the other, hoping to recognize at least one of the girls on the video, wondering if I'd be able to since they were filthy and unkempt. A man exited one of the shacks and approached us. He held a double-barrel shotgun, which was thankfully pointed towards the ground. We assumed he was the leader of the group.

"Help you?" he asked when he was close.

"We're looking for two girls," CJ said. The man raised his weapon and pointed it at CJ. "Hold on!" CJ exclaimed, raising his arms. "It's not what you think. We're looking for two girls who visited someone we know a few days ago. We just want to talk to 'em."

"What're their names?" The man's firearm was still raised.

"We don't know. We know what they look like because we saw them on a video." CJ relaxed a bit, lowering his arms.

The leader raised the shotgun a bit higher as he yelled, "None of our girls are in those sorts of videos."

"No, no," CJ protested, holding his arms up again. "It's just a video of two girls, around eight years old, dressed very nice. They were giving a small box to a fellow at his front door."

"Why you want to talk to them girls?"

CJ thought for a moment. "We want to know what was in the box, and how they got it, because we can't find that guy. That's the last time he was seen."

The man lowered his weapon. "I don't know how I can help you. These kids ain't been off this property for over two weeks."

"Are there any other kids here?"

"We got some babies and toddlers who cain't talk yet. And a fourteen-year-old boy. No one else that fits yer description."

"Could we look at the kids up close to see if any of 'em look like the girls on the video?"

"I told you they ain't left our camp." The leader turned to walk away.

"How about if I give you some money?" CJ asked in a loud voice.

"Okay, for a hundred bucks."

CJ got his wallet from his pocket and counted out five twenties. The man started to grab it, but CJ pulled the money away. "Let us see the kids. Then you get the money."

The man looked disappointed but turned and yelled at the kids. He told them to be quiet and come over to us. They quickly obeyed and formed a line in front of us. I looked at the group of fifteen girls and boys, mostly girls. In my mind, I immediately eliminated the boys who all had short hair. That left nine girls, all of whom had long hair. Three were too young, one was too old, and another had straight red hair. Four girls remained that I needed to examine more closely.

I studied their faces, trying to imagine what they would look like cleaned up with their hair washed and combed. Between the crooked teeth and facial features, as much as I wanted to, I couldn't convince myself that any of the girls were the ones I'd seen on the video. I conferred with CJ, and he concurred. We thanked the man who grabbed the twenty-dollar bills still in CJ's hand and left.

Defeated, we sat in the truck a few minutes. CJ noted how much I was sweating and commented that I would have been better off wearing something cooler, although he didn't rub it in. I knew he was right, but I'd learned to bear hot weather in long-sleeved shirts and wasn't about to change.

Switching the subject, probably thinking it would cheer me up, CJ suggested we stop at his favorite coffee shop, not too far from my farm. Or, I should say, from the farm owned by Happy Sun, where I was living.

The ride seemed long as I mulled over how I could find those girls in the video. CJ pulled the truck into the parking lot of Fine Java. Despite appearing to be in the middle of nowhere, surrounded by dirt fields, the café was clearly quite popular. The parking lot was full of vehicles, mostly trucks and motorcycles. Several people were talking by their cars.

"It's time you met some of the folks around here," CJ said as he grabbed my hand. I was hesitant, but he tugged on my arm, and I followed him inside. We ordered drinks at the counter, which CJ insisted on paying for. He introduced me to the barista, a pleasant-looking young woman who poured our brewed coffees. After a bit of small talk back and forth, we walked towards an empty table near the back. As we passed by other customers, it seemed CJ had something to say to everyone. He introduced me as we went along, but I didn't remember many of their names. I didn't recall any of these people, most of whom were about my age, from before.

CJ pulled out a chair for me when we reached our table, and we both sat. I started thinking of the best way to tell CJ about what I'd seen the night before. He began to talk about finding a storage unit for the things in my parents' house, when he looked up and said, "Uh-oh."

Chapter 15

I LOOKED IN THE direction CJ was focused, expecting to see a burley biker in black leathers approaching. Instead, I saw a thin, attractive blond woman walking our way, all smiles. She looked vaguely familiar, but I couldn't place her until I heard her raspy voice. Danielle Johnson. I hadn't thought of her in years but remembered her being what is now called the queen bee. Even at a young age, she exuded confidence and a bit of cruelty, as she sat atop the social pecking order in our school. I doubted she would remember me, since she acted like she never knew I existed when we were classmates. Back then, I thought of myself as pathetic and unattractive, not someone anyone would want to be friends with. I never would have dared to speak to someone like Danielle. That was no longer the case. Through therapy and living in the real world, I'd learned I was intelligent, likable, and, yes, very attractive to members of the opposite sex. Still, seeing Danielle brought back some of my childhood feelings.

As soon as she was close to the table, Danielle gushed, "CJ, so good to see you. Who's your friend?" She smiled at me with that large fake smile I remembered.

"Don't you remember Strawberry Fields? She went to school with us."

I braced myself for a snarky comment, determined to let it slide off me as if I were Teflon. Instead, Danielle's expression quickly morphed into a look of surprise. "OMG! Sorry, for a moment I didn't recognize you. It's been years since I've seen you."

"I moved away about ten years ago."

Danielle was surprisingly friendly. I figured since leaving high school and perhaps going to college, she had matured and realized she wasn't the center of the universe. Although her affect appeared phony to me, I felt I shouldn't be judgmental. I needed to give her a chance.

Without an invitation, Danielle made herself comfortable in one of the empty seats at our table. "You must tell me what you've been doing all these years, Strawberry. I admire you so much for leaving this shithole. I wish I'd had the brains to get out of here. Now I feel stuck. Maybe you can give me some advice about moving away."

By all appearances, Danielle really had changed. She seemed a bit helpless. Despite still being beautiful, she wanted my advice about improving her lot in life.

CJ interrupted. "Danielle, we were having a private conversation."

"Geez, CJ, are you asking me to leave?"

"Glad you could take the hint."

Danielle shot CJ a disdainful look, then smiled and focused her attention back on me. "I can see CJ wants you all to himself, not that I blame him. Why don't you give me your number so we can talk later?"

CJ looked uncomfortable as Danielle and I exchanged numbers. She walked away, and when she was at a safe distance, CJ confided, "Watch out for that woman. She's always up to no good."

"I could tell you don't like her."

"Don't like doesn't begin to cover it. I'm ashamed to admit it, but we dated for a while after high school. I broke it off with her when I saw up close what a terrible, underhanded, scheming bitch she is."

"I thought maybe she'd changed for the better."

"She'll never change." CJ paused, then continued, "Now, let's talk about something important, like what you're going to do with all the stuff in your old house and where you're going to stay after you've moved out."

The subject caught me by surprise. I hadn't given it much thought but had planned to go back to my apartment at Purdue. There was plenty of time before I needed to return for my last semester of school. I envisioned staying until my parents' things were taken care of, which shouldn't have taken more than five days or so. But there was also the question of finding the girls and possibly looking into the death of

Carlos or whoever was dissolving in that plastic drum. Maybe even the car accident that had claimed the lives of the Browns deserved looking into. All of that was potentially dangerous, and I was ill-equipped to carry out any sort of investigation by myself. Nevertheless, I wanted to do what I could. One thing was certain: in ten days, I'd have no place to live in the area.

CJ offered to buy boxes and help me pack things, perhaps ship some items back to my apartment. Once I knew what I wanted to store, he'd deliver everything to the storage facility. He knew of one about fifteen miles away. After we finished our coffee, we waded through the tables where CJ again spoke to almost everyone we came across, and we left.

We picked up boxes and bubble wrap, went to the house, and began packing. As I loaded boxes with my mother's clothes, I heard the clanging of pots and dishes from CJ packing up the kitchen. I was about to turn on the air conditioner when he appeared in the master bedroom.

"It's been a long, tough day," he said, "and I suggest we call it quits for now. Let's go out for dinner and unwind."

"Are there any decent restaurants around here?"

CJ laughed. "You're quite the city slicker snob now. Yes, we do have decent dining establishments in the area. Chinese? Thai? Mexican? Indian? Japanese? Italian? American? Vegetarian? We have everything, depending on how far you want to drive."

"How about Italian?"

"Roger that. There's a great Italian restaurant about forty-five minutes from here. I'll make reservations."

When we arrived at Ristorante del Sole, I was amazed at how crowded it was. The maître d escorted us to our table, which was covered with a white tablecloth—fabric, not paper. I opened the menu and was surprised by the prices. I hadn't planned on spending that much for dinner.

"By the way, dinner's on me," CJ said. "Don't even try to argue. Now, you need to decide: white or red?"

"What?" I struggled to make sense of the question.

"I have the wine list here. Do you want white or red? Or rosé? They have lot's of choices here."

"I'm in the mood for fish, so how about white?"

"You got it."

"Order something that comes in a half bottle."

When the waiter came around, I ordered the sole almondine, while CJ chose the pasta with mussels in a creamy garlic sauce, along with a bottle of Italian Pinot Grigio. I wondered when his tastes had become so refined. All I remembered him eating were two burgers at a time and a large order of fries at the local Dairy Queen.

The waiter made a show of opening our Pinot Grigio—a full bottle, not the half I had requested—and CJ had me do the honors of tasting and approving it. After the waiter left, I chided CJ for ordering a whole bottle. He assured me he'd finish whatever was left at the end of dinner.

I sipped on my wine, waiting for my entrée. By the time it arrived, I was feeling a bit tipsy and started to relax. The dinner was delicious, and the conversation interesting. CJ talked about taking over the family's pasta sauce business. He'd mechanized several steps in the process, utilizing AI where it made sense to lower his payroll. Recently, he'd found it difficult to get the needed supply of tomatoes. I'd never thought the pasta sauce business was interesting until he spoke of his own experience. Not that he spent most of the time talking about himself.

He asked me about my move to Indianapolis, the high school there, my aunt and uncle, and my experience at Purdue. He seemed knowledgeable about agricultural economics, at least knowledgeable enough to ask intelligent questions. I must have lost track of how many times he refilled my wine glass. By the time we were done with dinner, I was feeling soused. Soused and happy. He steadied me when I stood up and couldn't keep my balance.

"Why don't we go to my place?" CJ suggested when we were back on the road. "I'd like to show you my etchings."

He looked at me and smiled. I understood exactly what he meant. "I'm not sure that would be a good idea."

"It's only fair. I've been to your place, but you haven't been to mine."

I wanted to get to know CJ better. More accurately, I wanted to get down and dirty with him, but I thought about Perry and felt guilty.

CJ continued, "I'm not like those college boys who I'll bet give you plenty of attention. I'm out in the real world every day, doing the things they are only dreaming about doing in the future. I'm not worried about my grades, or what some professor thinks of me, or if I'll get canceled for saying something some asshole thinks is politically incorrect. I don't like to play games, so when I tell you I like you, it's the truth. I think you like me, too. You may have been gone for ten years, but I feel like I still know you, almost as if you just returned from a long vacation where you visited some place I've never been to. You were planning to come back here and help with your parents' farm. Now you may be thinking you want to take care of their stuff and get the hell out of here, because that's no longer in the cards. But I sense that farming is in your blood. Look, you could still return to the area and use your fancy education here. You might even think about working for Happy Sun Farm. Maybe they're not as bad as you think they are. Then, in a sense, you'd be working on your old farm."

"I'll never work for those Happy Sun assholes."

"I didn't mean to offend you, and I'm not saying you'll want to stay here or come back here after you graduate. Just think about it. If nothing else, I bet we'll have a good time if you come to my place."

CJ had a way about him. I'm not sure if it was his charm or the alcohol that caused me to cave, but I put Perry out of my thoughts and agreed to see CJ's etchings. He wasn't like someone I'd just met. The connection I'd had with him ten years ago was very much alive.

His home was a traditional farmhouse style, although there was no surrounding farm. Instead, there were around ten other houses in the vicinity. Walking through the front door, I was surprised at how well it was furnished. Nice furniture, pictures on the wall, recessed lighting.

"This is not what I expected," I said, looking around.

"I hired a decorator after my parents passed. Got rid of all the old furniture. I wanted a new start. Told her I wanted something comfy and homey and let her do the rest."

"I hope you left her a great review on Yelp. She did a wonderful job making this comfy and homey."

"Danielle was the decorator, if you must know. No way am I going to leave that bitch a good review."

I had obviously opened up a sore wound. I was left wondering if his hatred stemmed from a relationship gone bad or the price she charged for her decorating expertise. I favored the former. The alcohol was wearing off, and my inhibitions were starting to kick in again.

"Let's go into the kitchen. I'll fix us a nightcap," CJ said.

I've never been a big drinker, but I needed something to help me get through whatever guilt or awkwardness I felt. I wanted to have a good time and forget all the troubling thoughts that were trying to rise up and make their presence known. I followed CJ into the kitchen, where he poured two generous glasses of Irish Cream. Looking around, it was obvious the kitchen had been overhauled recently. I loved it—maybe he paid too much for it, but there was nothing not to like.

We stood in the kitchen next to the counter of the central island and made small talk for a short time. I was feeling pretty woozy when CJ said, "Enough of this." He took me in his arms and kissed me deeply.

I liked his directness. There was no awkward fidgeting or word games. Our kiss lasted a long time. My heart was racing, and I longed for something more. When we came up for air, CJ grabbed my arm and led me to the bedroom. The queen-sized bed was made up. A pair of jeans and boots in one corner were the only items out of place. He took off his shirt and started to remove mine.

"Lights off," I said.

He looked a bit surprised, maybe hurt, but turned off the lights, the dim moonlight coming through the window providing the only illumination. After that, he deftly removed his clothes and mine in the almost total darkness—I don't remember the order—but we were soon under the covers, including his expensive-looking grey quilt, that were quickly kicked to the floor. Despite his rough hands, CJ's fingers were gentle, and knew where to go and what to do. His tongue and lips were equally talented. It was a night to remember. I must have fallen asleep in his arms because the next thing I recall was sensing a light. I opened my eyes and saw sunlight streaming into the room at the same time I heard songbirds outside. At some point, the covers had been pulled up, and I felt warm and cozy. I heard CJ's gentle breathing and felt his loose, yet soothing, embrace.

I intended to slide out of the bed quietly and find my clothes before he woke up. As I began to stir, I heard, "Hey, where do you think you're going?"

"I just want to find my clothes."

"You're not getting off that easily," CJ said playfully as he tugged on my left arm. He started kissing my hand and working his way up to my arm before I could pull away. "What the fuck is that?" he asked in a loud voice.

Chapter 16

I BEGAN TO CRY. I didn't want him to see it. My long-sleeved shirts and lights-off policy hadn't gone far enough.

"Sorry," he said, wrapping his arms around me. "I didn't mean to upset you. It just took me by surprise. You seem so put together I never expected that, but I recognize the scars of someone who slashed their wrists."

I continued to sob as CJ comforted me. I knew I wouldn't be able to hide my scars from him forever if we became intimate, but I could certainly do it for a short time if I were vigilant. My guardrails had been down the previous night.

It was a few minutes before my tears dried, and I was able to speak. "It was a long time ago. I only did it once."

"You must have been in a lot of pain. Is that why you left?"

"Uh-huh. I was severely depressed and had lost all my self-confidence. I felt guilty about everything. My dad was very difficult, with violent outbursts, and I thought it was my fault. My mother found me and rushed me to the hospital where I got I don't remember how many, units of blood. They said I almost died. After that, my mom told me I needed to get away. That's the only way I had a chance of leading a normal life."

"Your mom must be pretty smart."

"I always thought so until she decided to sell the farm. I'm thankful she sent me to live with my aunt. I had years of therapy, and now I realize nothing was my fault. It was the PTSD my dad was suffering from. It had to be terribly difficult for Mom. They never had much money, and my father refused therapy from the VA. Years ago, mom was able to get him to take some medications that helped a little, but he was never what you'd call normal."

"Sorry. I had no idea. That only makes me admire you more. In my work with troubled youth, I've seen a fair number who have attempted suicide. That's why I knew right away what those scars were from. You'll let me know if you ever get close to that point again, won't you?"

"I'll never be in that space again. Sure, I get upset like everyone else, but in a normal way. I cope."

CJ kissed me again, and we had an abbreviated version of our activity from the night before. "Time for breakfast and coffee," he said. He got out of bed and started to pull on his clothes, exposing his muscular back, broad shoulders and powerful arms. Only that one tattoo, the Chinese character I'd seen previously, decorated his skin.

I was impressed by how well CJ knew his way around the kitchen. He made a pot of strong coffee, then whipped up French toast. He fried four strips of bacon, which I declined, so he ate them all without complaining.

Feeling relaxed and close to CJ, I was finally ready to tell him about what I'd seen. I told him about finding my dad's still, and the young lovers I'd recorded.

"What did they say?" he asked,

"I have no idea, but I'm going to find out. When I get a chance, I'll find someone in a Chinese restaurant who can translate it. It's probably nothing important—just banter between two young people wanting to get it on—but I want to know if they said anything about what's happening inside that company. I'm sure there's more than meets the eye."

"Seems like a waste of time to me," CJ said. "Probably nothing more than two people flirting and talking dirty, if Chinese do that sort of thing."

I was disappointed in CJ's lack of enthusiasm but not dissuaded. "That's not all I saw," I said. "In the building with the stills, I found a dead man being dissolved in a vat."

CJ's mouth fell open as he seemed to be searching for words. "WTF? A dead man? Dissolving? Are you sure that's what you saw?"

"Absolutely."

"Have you told anyone?"

"I haven't had time, but I need to notify the police."

"Of course. But let me think about this. It might be best if I see it first. I hate to say it, but the cops out here don't give much weight to what women say. You can show it to me tonight."

"We better go late. We'll have to sneak into the still building because they guard everything."

"Okay, we'll go after dark."

CJ was cleaning up the kitchen, leaving me awkwardly unoccupied. I offered to help, but he insisted I relax. I walked around the kitchen, looking out the window with a garden view. I wondered how CJ could afford the expensive kitchen remodel and dinner at the Italian restaurant if his income depended on his failing company. My eyes drifted to some papers on his small kitchen desk. I didn't want to pry, but couldn't avoid seeing what looked like a paystub for twenty-thousand dollars from a company called Acker Enterprises. I wondered if Acker Enterprises was the accounting firm for Mama Baroni's and issued checks for the profits to him. If that was a monthly payment, he was doing better than he let on.

As he was finishing up, I got a call from Danielle. I held up my phone and showed CJ her name displayed on caller ID.

"You shouldn't answer that or any other call from that bitch. I don't know what she wants, but she's up to no good."

I ignored the call.

"Tell you what," CJ said as he started the dishwasher, "I've got some things I need to do this morning. I'll drop you off at your house so you can do more packing. I need to go by Mama Baroni's, then the school. There's a baseball practice I need to run at 3:30. After that, we can have dinner. I'll pick up some Chinese food and come by your place around six-thirty. You can show me the dead guy after dark."

I had no desire to lay my eyes on that horrible sight again. As it was, I was having a hard time trying to erase the memory. "You know where the still is, don't you?" I asked.

"Sure, I know where it is." He must have read the distress on my face. "You don't have to come with me. I'll bet you don't want to see it again. How does that sound?"

So organized and considerate. Again, I was impressed. "Sounds good to me. We may be eating on paper plates tonight if I get all the dishes packed."

We drove to my house, about ten minutes away, and I got busy filling more boxes. The house wasn't big, but it was so stuffed with odds and ends, I felt I would never finish. After an hour, I was hot and thirsty and decided to take a break. I poured myself a glass of ice water and sat in front of my dad's computer. I ran the video segment showing the girls several times, studying their faces as well as I could in the grainy video. Something about how the dark-haired one moved her head and her ponytail swayed reminded me of something I'd seen. I tried to remember where I'd come across that before. Then it hit me. The Happy Sun Farm commercials. The girls had been in every commercial I could remember. They were hired actors. I smiled to myself, thinking there was a good chance CJ could help me locate them. He had a lot of practical knowledge I lacked.

I was drenched in sweat and wanted to change to a cooler top. I hadn't packed much, so I went to my parents' room to pick out a shirt my mom had left behind. Walking to her corner dresser, I was surprised by a squeak in the floor. My dad was good at keeping the house in tip-top shape if he was good at anything. I walked over the squeaky area several times. The floor was carpeted wall-to-wall, and I recalled my dad telling me about building the house. He had used a cement foundation because wood was so expensive. Cement doesn't squeak.

Chapter 17

CURIOUS, I MOVED MY foot around on the carpet near the noise. For some reason, my parents had replaced the short-haired wall-to-wall carpeting I remembered with an outdated long-haired shag carpet, an impractical reservoir for allergens, dirt, and small objects, sometimes sharp. Several sweeps with my foot revealed a seam that didn't traverse the whole floor. I figured someone had made a mistake when installing the carpet and started to make a cut where there didn't need to be one. As I examined the area more closely, it was apparent the cut hadn't been stitched together. I was surprised my father would have accepted such shoddy workmanship.

I was about to continue my walk to the dresser when my eye caught a fiber a bit off color. The rug was a mixture of shades of brown and beige, but one strand, slightly thicker than the others, had a greenish hue, made noticeable by one of the four ceiling lights almost directly overhead. Looking closer, it was apparent the fiber was a loop. Pulling on it, it became longer, as if most of its length had been tucked under the carpet.

I stood bent over with the loop between my feet and pulled up. Nothing. I rotated my feet forty-five degrees around the fiber and pulled again. Nothing. The third time I repositioned myself and pulled, I gasped. A trap door under the carpet started to rise up. It was about two feet wide. I straddled it and pulled hard, lifting the door, then flipping it back.

I walked around the opening in the floor and stared down into the space I had revealed as I caught my breath. All that was visible was a steep staircase that led down into blackness. I thought about closing the trap door without exploring further but quickly discarded that idea. I had to know what was down there.

With my back to the threshold, I crouched and grabbed wads of thick carpet with both hands before placing one foot on the second stair from the top. I slowly straightened my back, transferring my weight to the step. The staircase felt solid—it didn't budge. I set my other foot down on the next step and stood upright, my full weight on the ladder. With no railing, I cautiously descended into the darkness. When I reached the bottom, I noticed a dim blue light. Looking closer, I was relieved to see a light switch. I turned it on, and the room lit up. I felt like Dorothy when she landed in the Emerald City. The space was large, with shelves against each wall filled with food, water, and ammunition. Two electrical outlets would allow for charging electronics. A laptop was on a small desk, but I saw no evidence of an internet connection. My phone had no bars down there. The only way to communicate with the outside world was by way of one of the two ham radios I saw on a shelf.

Two cots were folded in the middle of the floor next to two chairs on rollers. When I flipped the switch labeled "AIR," the hum of a motor was accompanied by the sensation of cool air moving past me.

I walked to the bathroom and shower at the end opposite the stairs. Four five-gallon water carboys were secured on a sturdy shelf high up. Tubing connected the spigot on one of the vessels to the toilet. The tubing could be moved from one carboy to the next, or from the toilet to the shower. With judicious use, the occupants could have indoor plumbing for weeks, if not months.

A small kitchen area was next to the bathroom. A microwave and hotplate were on the counter, waiting to be plugged into wall outlets behind. Below the counter were plastic dishes, cups, and cutlery, as well as paper supplies and sanitary wipes. My dad must have spent years planning, building, and supplying this space, which would have been large enough for him and my mother to survive in when the imagined enemy came to kill them.

After I'd finished looking through the cabinet, I noticed an envelope on the counter addressed to Mr. Randall Fields, my dad. Inside was a thumb drive and a hand-made card congratulating the recipient for completing his dream underground home, and saying he was honored to have been able to help. The card was signed "Diego." A note beneath the signature read, "Banda music to pass the time if you need to stay a while." It made sense that Diego knew about this place. After all, my dad couldn't have built all of this and lifted those carboys full of water by himself.

I turned off the circulating air and the light before ascending the stairs. I could have pulled on the rope attached to the underside of the trap door to close it from inside the bunker, but decided against it, unsure I'd be able to open it back up. It was a nice space, but I didn't know how to operate a ham radio and didn't want to be stuck in there forever.

Once I was standing on the carpet in my parents' bedroom, I closed the trap door. As I ran my foot over the area outlining the opening, I was sad thinking about all the work my dad had done for something that would never be used. I was impressed by his accomplishment, misdirected as his efforts were.

I rummaged through my mother's clothes and found a long-sleeved shirt made of thin material. Perfect for the weather. I changed quickly, thankful we wore the same size. Before I got back to the task of going through my parents' possessions, my phone rang. Checking the caller ID, I saw Danielle's name again. Should I answer it? Was she as dangerous and nasty as CJ had indicated? I was never fond of her when we were in school together, but found it hard to believe she was as toxic as CJ thought. I didn't blame him for disliking her, or even hating her, after their breakup. I'd seen strong emotions like that surface after couples parted ways. But what did I have to lose? I answered the call.

"I'm so glad you answered!" Danielle gushed. "I really want to talk to you. There are so few women my age around here, I get so lonely. I didn't know you well when we were younger, but I remember you were one of the smart kids."

"I didn't think you ever noticed me."

"Of course I noticed you. Me and my friends, we were a bit intimidated by you. You didn't seem to like us."

I didn't want to argue. She and her friends were quite snobby and not afraid to express their disrespect. I had learned that people change. Perhaps she had, too, and was trying to make amends. There was no use carrying a grudge.

"I'm so sorry about your dad. Someone just told me about it. Is there anything I can do to help?"

I sighed. "Thanks for the offer, but I think I have everything under control. CJ is helping me a lot."

"I'm glad you mentioned that. I don't like to cause trouble, but I feel I must warn you about him. He probably told you we were a couple once."

"He did mention it."

"Did he tell you why I broke up with him?"

He'd told me he broke up with her, but the reason didn't matter to me. The last thing I wanted to do was get into a discussion about what a terrible person he was with his ex. "I suppose you two just didn't get along."

"If that's what he told you, it's a lie. He's a very dangerous man. Can I come over? It's important that you hear what I have to say."

"I'm really busy now, packing up my parents' stuff. Unfortunately, I simply—"

"You need to know about CJ," Danielle interrupted. Then she burst into tears. After a few moments, she sniffled and said, "Sorry. I just know I'll never be able to forgive myself if I don't tell you about CJ and something terrible happens to you. Please, please let me come over. "

To say I was surprised would be an understatement. Danielle was clearly quite upset and worried for my safety. I didn't have time to visit with her but couldn't ignore her tears. "Okay, I didn't know how important you thought this was. Sure, you can come over."

I gave her my address. Twenty minutes later, there was a knock on the front door.

Chapter 18

I WIPED THE SWEAT that had accumulated on my forehead and opened the front door. There stood Danielle, her hair and makeup perfect, her hot pink shorts and white tank top displaying her figure to the fullest extent. She carried a bottle of wine in her right hand.

I invited her in, and we sat in the living room. Before we said more than hello and it's hot outside, Danielle asked for two wine glasses. "I can open the bottle. It's one of those screwtops. It's an expensive wine, though. You like Pinot Grigio?"

"I do," I answered, "but I wasn't expecting to drink. It's pretty early—"

Before I finished my sentence, Danielle broke down in tears. So fragile. She must have been through some hard times.

"Okay," I said. "I'll get us some glasses."

I went to the kitchen to get them. By the time I returned with the stemware, Danielle had perked up. "Sorry I'm so emotional," she said as she poured two generous servings of Pinot Grigio. "I need some wine so I can get through everything I need to tell you, and I hate to drink alone. Although, honestly, since breaking up with CJ, sometimes I do just that."

By then, she had my attention. I wondered what terrible things she would tell me about him.

"First of all," Danielle said, "I have to ask, what are you going to do with the farm? Are you going to keep it and run it yourself?"

"I would have liked to, but my mom sold it to Happy Sun Farm against my wishes."

"Sorry to hear that. Is there anything you can do about it?"

"Not that I know of. I can't even talk to my mom about it because she left to take a long vacation with a man she's been seeing. Now I'm left to take care of everything. I've got a lot to do, but I'm thinking of contacting an attorney about contesting the sale. CJ, however, doesn't think that's a good idea."

"Of course he doesn't. He doesn't want you to cause any trouble for Happy Sun. He's on their payroll, you know."

Her words sent my head spinning. "He works for Happy Sun? I find that hard to believe."

"I'm not surprised he didn't tell you. He's pretending to be on your side, but he's not. He did that to my parents. CJ and I started dating around the time Happy Sun Farm started buying up the farmland around here. They offered to buy my parents' farm, but they refused to sell. CJ told them they should consider their offer, as they were getting older and should enjoy their golden years in a retirement community. They weren't even that old."

"Maybe he thought that would be best for them, even if he was wrong."

"He kept pestering them until they agreed to look at one of those places for retirees in Bakersfield. They weren't interested, but he set up an appointment for them to get a tour. He was so insistent, they felt they couldn't turn it down although they were dead set against moving there. On the way to Bakersfield, their car was in a head-on collision with a large truck. They both died instantly." Danielle teared up and stopped speaking for a moment before composing herself. "Sorry," she said. "I still get choked up when I think about it. Witnesses said the truck that hit them had no markings on it. Not even a license plate. Needless to say, it was never found. I'm sure it was no accident. Whoever was driving that truck knew when my parents would be driving through that area."

"What about the police?"

"They were no use. There was no real investigation. They never do anything when it comes to Happy Sun. They're probably all on their payroll. Of course, Mr. Chen had the paperwork ready for me to sell the farm. I had never intended to take over the business, so I sold.

After I thought about it, I could see they killed my parents so they could get their hands on it. If I had it to do over again, I never would have sold it to them, but it's too late now."

"You don't think CJ had something to do with your parents getting killed, do you?"

"I'm positive. He made the appointment, and I'm sure he told the Happy Sun people when my parents would be on that country road."

"What's his job at Happy Sun?"

"I don't know what his job title is. He never told me he worked there, but I saw some pay stubs from the company when I went through his desk one day, looking for a ruler. That's after my parents were killed. I was shocked. Then I thought about some things he said about the company. He was always on their side. Also, he has that tattoo—the one with Chinese writing. I saw the same tattoo on one of the Happy Sun people. I think it's for some kind of Happy Sun Farm cult, and CJ is a member."

"I did see a pay stub from Acker Enterprises on CJ's desk."

"See? Acker Enterprises is the name of a holding company Happy Sun Farm uses."

I was silent as I tried to process her words. Had I been conned into trusting CJ? From what he'd told me, the tattoo seemed innocent enough, but maybe it was something required of all the members of their organization, or cult. I was at a loss for words, disgusted with myself for being such an idiot.

"Like I said," Danielle continued, "I'd feel terrible if they did something to you."

"I've been suspicious of Happy Sun ever since I came here. I think they had something to do with my dad's death. I want to stay here long enough to investigate them."

"How are you going to do that?"

"I recorded a conversation between two of their employees who were in the building where my dad's still is."

Danielle chuckled. "I guess it didn't take you long to find the still. Very popular around here."

"So I've been told."

"What did the Happy Sun Farm people talk about?"

"I don't know, since they were speaking Chinese. I think they just wanted some privacy, but I'm going to find someone to translate it, even though CJ thinks that will be a waste of time."

"I hate to say it, but CJ is really taking you for a fool. I understand. You thought you'd finally found the perfect guy. There aren't many out there. Now you find that he's an asshole like all the others. Your mom must be happy to leave this place. She'll probably start a new life with the man she's traveling with."

"That's what she seems to want."

"She likely won't have much time for you, I'm afraid. You must be disappointed, losing your dad and mom at the same time." Danielle poured more wine into my glass. "Drink up. I've found that wine is the best remedy when you're feeling down."

I didn't pick up my glass as I felt I'd already had too much to drink, but Danielle wasn't going to let me stop. She grabbed my glass and shoved it into my hand. She seemed so concerned about me, and felt I needed that drink. I wanted to feel better, so I took a few more gulps.

"That couple in the shed," I said. "That's not all I saw. I saw a dead man. He was in a large drum, and they were dissolving him." I started crying uncontrollably.

"There, there," Danielle said. "Sounds absolutely horrible. No wonder you're so upset. You are dealing with something very dangerous. Did you tell CJ what you saw?"

I felt so stupid trusting CJ. I didn't want Danielle to think I was a complete moron and was too ashamed to tell her the truth. "No, I didn't tell him about it."

"That's for the best. He'd warn them, and who knows what they would do then. Maybe they'd go after you. You need to watch out for yourself. Break up with CJ right away, get all your parents' things in order, and go back to where you were living ASAP."

I looked at my watch. "CJ will be here in about an hour. He said he'd bring dinner."

"OMG. You better hurry. I wouldn't be surprised if he tries to poison you. Don't eat anything that man tries to feed you. Call him and tell him not to come."

I was distraught. "I can't believe he's as bad as you say."

"Girl, you may have moved away to a big city, but you sure are naïve. Don't wait until it's too late."

I was so drunk, Danielle probably could have talked me into anything, but everything she said made sense. I phoned CJ and put the call on speaker.

He answered by saying, "Don't think I forgot. I'll be by with dinner in about an hour."

"Don't come," I said. "Something's come up."

"Like what? Is someone from Happy Sun giving you a bad time? I'll come over right now and kick his ass."

Danielle motioned like she was throwing up.

"No, it's just that I'm not feeling well. I've been vomiting."

Danielle nodded her approval.

"Sorry. I'll pick up some chicken soup. That should make you feel better."

Danielle shook her head "no" furiously.

"I–I don't want any soup. I made some earlier and threw it up."

"I should come over and check on you."

Danielle again shook her head, "No."

"It's nothing to worry about. This happens from time to time. It's a condition I have, but it's nothing serious."

"I didn't know you had a medical problem. What's it called?"

I thought for a moment as Danielle looked at me expectantly. My mind was blank until something I'd learned in a class popped up. "Fusarium. I have Fusarium disease."

"Never heard of it. Is there anything I can do?"

"Nothing. I'll likely be better tomorrow afternoon. These attacks never last long."

Danielle and I laughed when I disconnected the call. With all the alcohol I had on board, the laughter came easily despite the tension in the air.

"How in hell did you come up with Fusarium?" Danielle asked.

"It was the only thing I could think of. Fusarium wilt. I learned about it in one of my classes. It practically wiped out the banana crops in Panama a hundred years ago. Now they grow a different type of banana, the Cavendish, which is resistant."

We both laughed again. "Glad you were able to put your fancy education to use," Danielle said.

My mind was starting to focus again on the problems at hand. I thought of the man in the vat. CJ had told me he would bring dinner to my place and look in the shed afterward to confirm what I'd seen. I wondered if he intended to pretend to visit the shed and then kill me, or just kill me without bothering with the ruse. My Fusarium attack threw a bit of a monkey wrench into his plan, but it wouldn't stop him. I realized it was only a question of time before Happy Sun removed all the evidence. "Now I want to call the cops about the body."

"Of course. You can do that tomorrow." Danielle poured me another glass of wine. I noticed the bottle was almost empty, as she'd been quietly pouring wine while we spoke. "Don't forget, though, you absolutely can't trust CJ. He doesn't care about you."

I was feeling pretty soused by then, but her words hurt, and I tried to soothe my feelings by drinking more wine since Danielle kept pouring it into my glass. She moved next to me and put her arm around my shoulder. Her kindness touched me. I felt I could trust her with my life.

"There, there," she said. "Just cry it out. You have a lot to be sad about."

After I'd had a good cry, I was worn out. "I need to get some sleep," I said. "I'm not used to drinking so much wine, and I'm unbelievably exhausted."

"Okay," Danielle said. "Do you need some help getting ready for bed?"

"No, I'll be fine. I just need to sleep." I lay down on the couch, too tired to walk to my bedroom.

"I'll turn off all the lights so no one will think you're here," Danielle said.

Her footsteps approaching the front door to leave were the last sounds I remembered hearing before waking up in the three-bed ICU of the hospital closest to my former home.

Chapter 19

I LOOKED AROUND THE small room I was in and saw a nurse walk by the glass door. Both of my wrists were bandaged, there was an I.V. in my left arm, and a monitor near my bed was tracing my vital signs. The light hurt my eyes, and I had a splitting headache. According to the clock on the wall, it was 2:10. With no windows to the outside, I didn't know if it was a.m. or p.m.

Another nurse walked by, then looked into my room. She smiled as she opened the door and walked in. "You're awake!"

"What happened?" I asked. "Why am I here?"

"From what I know, you were brought here last night by a nice young man who found you."

"Found me where?"

"In your bathroom, I believe. If he hadn't rushed you here, you would have died."

"Was I shot? I don't remember anything."

"The doctor will be in to speak to you, but I can tell you that you had been drinking quite a bit and were bleeding from both your wrists."

"Who's the man who brought me in? Where is he now?"

"His name is CJ. He was here for hours, but I told him to go home. You were out of danger, and it was after midnight, so he's been gone around two hours. He'll be back later today."

"I don't want him to visit me."

The nurse looked incredulous. "But he saved you."

"I don't care. Don't let him near me!"

"Whatever you wish. He did seem quite concerned, though. I'm sure you have lots of questions. You can ask them when your doctor makes rounds later."

I fell asleep despite the ambient noise of voices, carts rolling, and shoes hitting the floor. I woke to a gentle shake of my shoulder and looked up to see a middle-aged man in a white coat standing by my bed, a stethoscope draped around his neck. "Ms. Fields?" I nodded. "I'm Dr. Lambert. I'm glad to see you're awake." After a cursory exam, during which he listened to my heart and checked my pulse, he pulled up a chair. "It looks like your vital signs are stable, and your hemoglobin, while still low, hasn't dropped, so you won't need any more blood."

"I got a transfusion?"

"We needed to transfuse seven units. You lost over half your blood."

"How?"

"You don't remember?"

"All I remember is having some wine with a friend, then waking up here."

"Both of your wrists were cut pretty badly. Someone found you after you'd lost quite a bit of blood. By the time you arrived in the ER, your pulse was so weak, they thought you were dead. Fortunately, your blood type was on record and they were able to start transfusing you right away. You're young and healthy, and your wounds have been patched up, so your physical health is not an issue. We do need to address the reason you did this, however."

"Did what? I didn't do anything."

Dr. Lambert's eyes widened. "I wouldn't call slashing your wrists nothing. You almost killed yourself. I understand you're under a lot of stress. Your father died recently, and you're having a difficult time taking care of your parents' estate. I'm going to have Dr. Prescott, a psychiatrist, see you in a little while. She will help you deal with your issues and prescribe medication if appropriate."

I was coming to the realization that someone had tried to kill me. It was probably CJ, and he would likely succeed on his next attempt. I needed to get out of the area and return to Indiana as soon as possible. "I don't have time for that. I want to leave. You said I was in good shape physically."

"We still need to observe you for a while to make sure you remain stable. If all is in order later today, you'll be discharged to a psychiatric hospital."

I tried to sit up in bed but the muscles in my back, chest, and shoulders ached so badly I could only lie there. "I don't want to go to a psychiatric hospital. I didn't slash my wrists!"

"Then who did? They didn't slash themselves."

"I don't know who did it. Maybe the person who brought me in."

"I think you don't want to admit to yourself what really happened. I'll let Dr. Prescott explore that with you. A 5150 is in place, meaning there is a seventy-two-hour hold to keep you hospitalized for your own good."

As my heartbeat picked up, I became aware of the monitor beeping rapidly. "I can't waste three days in a hospital. I have too much to do."

"You'll have to discuss that with Dr. Prescott."

Shortly after Dr. Lambert left, the psychiatrist paid me a visit. Dressed in street clothes, with a face memorable only for thick black glasses, Dr. Prescott appeared about ten years older than me. She pulled up a chair next to my bed and introduced herself. She started to ask me a question when she was interrupted by a nurse who came to check my I.V. bag and take my vital signs.

That gave me a few moments to think. I racked my brain, trying to remember the previous evening. I'd had more alcohol than I remember ever drinking before and now had the headache to prove it. CJ brought me to the hospital, but I had no memory of it. Perhaps he had let himself into my house, intending to kill me on orders from Happy Sun. Of course, they wanted me dead after CJ told them I had found the man in the vat and recorded two of their workers. When he found me passed out, his job was that much easier. I'd stupidly told him I'd cut my wrists before, so it wouldn't be hard for people to believe I'd done it again, only better this time. If so, why would he bring me to the hospital?

It didn't take me long to figure it out. He knew my dad had cameras outside. Not knowing the password to access his computer, he couldn't have deleted the recording. If I'd died at home, police experts would have found a video of him entering the house and suspected him of murdering me. If he brought me to the hospital in such bad shape they couldn't revive me, his appearance on the video would appear innocent, and he would be a hero for attempting to save me. Unfortunately for him, the hospital staff was able to bring me back from the brink of death. Next time, I might not be so lucky. I didn't dare divulge my thoughts to the psychiatrist for fear she would diagnose me with paranoia.

When the nurse finished checking on me and left, Dr. Prescott began speaking again. "How are you feeling now?" she asked.

"I have quite a hangover and don't remember what happened to me. I understand I was found bleeding in my home."

"Yes, you slashed your wrists, but you were found by a man named CJ."

"Thank goodness he found me! If he hadn't, I could have died."

"Isn't that what you wanted?"

"Heavens, no. I don't know what happened. I drank a lot of wine with a girlfriend. I don't usually drink much, but she encouraged me. I don't remember cutting my wrists, and I certainly didn't want to kill myself. I'm not at all suicidal."

The psychiatrist tilted her head. "You've cut your wrists before. It's in your chart."

"I was much younger, and my home life was very difficult back then. Since that time, I've had a lot of therapy. I honestly don't know how my wrists were cut. Perhaps it was some sort of freak accident. I didn't even know there were razor blades in the house. Maybe I was looking for some and tripped when I found them."

"You were found in your bathtub full of warm water, and your wrists had been cut with a large kitchen knife."

Chapter 20

THAT INFORMATION SHOCKED ME. How could CJ be so cold? I didn't have much time to think about it as our conversation was interrupted by a loud argument at the entrance to the ICU. I recognized CJ's voice. He was yelling at a nurse, who refused to allow him access. "The patient left strict instructions not to let you visit her. If you don't leave now, I'll have security here in less than sixty seconds."

More heated words were exchanged before I heard heavy footsteps walking away.

"Is that the young man who brought you here?" the psychiatrist asked. I nodded in the affirmative. "You told the staff not to let him in?" Again, I nodded in the affirmative. "Looks to me like you're mad at him for finding you."

"That's not it at all."

"I understand you don't want to talk about this now. You need time to process everything, but I hope you'll be able to share your feelings with the staff at the hospital where you'll be going next. If you have alcohol and drug problems, they'll help you with rehabilitation."

My head jerked back reflexively. "I drank way more than usual, but I've never done any drugs."

"That's not what the lab testing showed. You had a high level of alcohol, as well as a benzodiazepine in your blood."

The heat in my cheeks told me my face was red. "The lab is wrong."

"I doubt it. I don't know if you are addicted to alcohol and benzos or if you just loaded up so you would have the nerve to slit your wrists."

"I'll admit to the alcohol, but not the drug."

"Confirmatory testing will be done in twenty-four hours, but I doubt the result will be any different."

"Is there any way I can get out today? I'm really not a danger to myself or others. Please."

"I'm afraid you don't have sufficient insight into your situation to be released. Don't worry, though. There are good therapists where you will be going. They'll do a thorough assessment and give you the medications you need. They're still looking for a bed for you, but it shouldn't be long." She patted me on the shoulder and left.

I was relieved when, fifteen minutes later, I heard Danielle's voice. She was taken to my room right away.

"OMG," she said as soon as she saw me. "I came as soon as I heard what happened. I don't understand. We had such a good time yesterday. You were tired when I went home, but you seemed to be in a good mood."

"I think I fell asleep right after you left."

Danielle chuckled. "I'm not surprised. You were pretty wasted. You seemed happy, though. What happened? I heard CJ brought you here. You were practically dead. It's a miracle you survived." Then, she lowered her voice to a whisper, "Did that asshole CJ do this and try to make it look like a suicide?"

I was confused thinking about the night before. I barely remembered Danielle leaving and had no recollection of seeing CJ. "He must have come by after you were already gone—"

"I told you he was no good. You can't trust a guy like that. If it weren't for him, you wouldn't be here." Danielle looked at one of my bandaged arms. "Did he say something that made you do that, or did he do it himself?"

"That's the thing, I don't remember. I certainly don't remember trying to hurt myself despite the fact that he made a fool of me."

"Don't feel stupid. You're not a fool. Anyone in your position would have trusted him. CJ's a good-looking guy, and lots of girls would be happy to get the attention of someone like him, someone out of their league."

Her words stung, but I didn't have time to dwell on them.

She continued without pausing. "He must have gotten you even more wasted than you were when I left. I wouldn't doubt if he gave you more alcohol, maybe even drugs so you wouldn't resist. Then he cut your wrists and tried to make it look like you killed yourself. Trust me, he'll try it again. He has to do what Happy Sun Farm orders him to do. If he doesn't, they'll go after him."

"Everything you're saying makes sense. They told me I had benzos in my system, but I've never taken any—don't even know where to get them. It's still hard for me to believe CJ works for those horrible people and tried to kill me. He seems so considerate and concerned."

"That's what I thought, but learn from my mistake, girl. He's nothing but a lying, two-faced SOB."

"They're planning to ship me off to some nut house. Said they can hold me for seventy-two hours, but I don't feel safe here, and I won't feel safe wherever they want to send me. I have to get out of here and go back to Indiana. Once I'm there, I plan to cause Happy Sun Farm a whole lotta trouble."

"These doctors can legally hold you for three days if they think you're a danger to yourself or others. I might be able to help you get out, but I need to be sure you didn't try to kill yourself."

"Honest, I didn't. That's just not something I would do. Not since I was a kid."

"Okay, I believe you. You're in luck because I know of a good lawyer who can probably get you out, especially if I tell him what I know."

"I can't afford to pay for a fancy lawyer."

"Don't worry. He does lots of work pro bono. A case like this will be easy for him. I'm positive I can get him to do this for free."

A sense of relief washed over me. "You're the best."

"I'm totally in your corner. Just be sure you stay away from CJ no matter what. I better phone that attorney ASAP. Call me when they discharge you. I'll pick you up."

"You sure are optimistic."

Danielle must have contacted the attorney right away because two hours later, I was told that I'd be discharged that afternoon, after the doctor checked my wounds and my dressings were changed. Shortly before 5:00 p.m., my wounds had been examined and rebandaged, and

I'd been instructed how to take care of that myself. I phoned Danielle, who arrived to pick me up thirty minutes later.

She was all smiles as she drove me to my house and asked me several times if I was sure I was okay being by myself. She had some errands to run but promised to return in a little while to keep me company.

"I'm absolutely fine," I assured her. "I don't need a babysitter."

"I'm mostly worried that asshole CJ will come by and you'll cave."

We reached my house, and I exited the car. "Don't worry, I won't let him in even if he bangs on my door. In fact, I'll get one of my dad's guns and blow his head off if he breaks in."

Danielle smiled and said, "Girl, you've got more grit in you than I thought. I think you'll be okay 'till I get back."

I let myself in and checked the front door video recordings from the previous day. I saw Danielle come and, hours later, go. Around 10:00 p.m., CJ came by and knocked several times. He checked the front door, which was open, and let himself in. I remembered unlocking it when Danielle came earlier in the day. She couldn't have been familiar with our peculiar lock and left it unlocked when she left. Ten minutes later, CJ was carrying my limp body outside, my arms wrapped in bloody towels. I must have been an easy target for him to have found a knife and slashed my wrists that quickly. If I didn't know better, I'd think his were the actions of a hero.

I made sure all the doors and windows were locked and retrieved a 9 mm Glock pistol from my dad's collection. I checked to ensure it was loaded with a bullet in the chamber and practiced aiming it a few times. I'd fired that gun before, but it had been many years. I was confident I would be able to use it. Once I had it secured in a bellyband holster I found on a shelf, I felt safe. I grabbed an extra clip full of bullets and slipped it into the belt's clip holder.

I looked for my cell phone, which had been left behind when CJ took me to the hospital. I hoped he hadn't stolen it to read my messages. I was thankful to find it between the two cushions on the sofa where it had fallen, away from CJ's prying eyes. It was out of juice, so I charged it for several minutes before turning it on and checking my messages. My mother had texted me a note telling me she was having a wonderful time on the Hawaiian island of Kauai and sent me several pictures of the ocean and palm trees. She was oblivious to the difficulties she'd left behind.

The image of the man dissolving in a vat invaded my thoughts. I felt terrible about him and wanted the responsible parties to pay for what they did.

Learning what the couple in the shed had been talking about could wait until I was safely back in Indiana. I appreciated having Danielle on my side, but there wasn't much she could do to protect me here. I would be killed if I didn't leave soon.

Chapter 21

General Bai looked sternly at his subordinate. "What are you saying?" he asked. "She can't be killed?" He leaned across his desk and stared into the face of the young man with closely cropped black hair before him, taking pleasure in watching the beads of sweat run down his face.

"That's not what I mean, General. I don't have specific details. We had an excellent plan, but it failed. Due to unforeseeable events, she survived."

"This is extremely disappointing. Your job is to foresee the unforeseeable. Everything else is going as planned, even ahead of schedule. We can't allow the whole operation to be jeopardized by one incompetent American on our payroll. If our comrades in The People's Republic of China hear of this difficulty, they could pull their support. We can't finish the job on our own, and if we fail, we won't be rewarded with their warheads."

"I understand, but I was told everything is under control now. Our American agent has proven to be outstanding and has almost complete access to her. The previous action almost worked. All the steps were carried out flawlessly, but they had some bad luck. They have come up with another plan. They are sure this one will succeed."

"How soon can I expect to hear that this new plan, the one they are confident in, did, in fact, work?"

"It could be as early as tonight."

"If she is not dead by the end of the day tomorrow, be prepared to suffer the consequences. I can accept failure due to bad luck once, but not twice."

The young man swallowed hard. "Please remember, I'm just the messenger. I didn't make the plan, I only approved it. Since I'm here, I need to trust the judgment of others on the ground there who have more precise knowledge of the situation. It's really out of my hands."

"Is that what you think?" General Bai yelled as he pounded the desk with his fist. "You think you have no responsibility? That kind of talk makes our Supreme Leader furious, and you know what happens to people he's not happy with."

"Yes, General."

"I suggest you talk to our people in California and review the plan's details again. Make sure it is foolproof because we seem to have fools over there. For your sake, I hope the operation is successful."

The subordinate backed away. In a shaky voice, he said, "I will do my best." His legs wobbly, he turned to leave the room just before tears of fear flowed down his cheeks.

Chapter 22

I MUST HAVE DOZED off, because I was awakened by a loud knock at the front door. I checked the feed from the front door camera on my dad's computer and saw it was CJ.

"Look," he yelled, "I know you're in there. Just open the fucking door and hear me out."

I remained silent, grabbing the gun from my holster and sitting on the sofa. I was prepared to shoot him if he broke through the door but hoped it wouldn't come to that. I picked up my phone and stared at it, wondering if I should call the police. If I did, who would they believe? CJ was charming, knew them all, and was a good liar. They didn't know me and would think I was unstable. After all, I had just left the hospital after what appeared to be a suicide attempt.

"I want to help you find those girls," he yelled through the door, "the ones in your dad's video."

I no longer wanted to find them. For all I knew, he was the one who hired the girls to kill my dad, and they were innocent participants. He was trying his best to get me to trust him and let him in to avoid leaving evidence of a forced entry before killing me. I figured he would get tired of yelling and either leave or bash the door in. Probably bash the door in, but I was ready.

"I don't know what kind of poison Danielle has been feeding you," CJ yelled. "I can't think of another reason you won't talk to me. Remember, I warned you not to trust her. I have good reason to believe she's dangerous. I'm going to leave now. Please think about what I've told you. When you realize who the real enemy is, give me a call. I won't be mad at you. Promise. Meanwhile, don't turn your back on her."

I heard CJ's heavy footsteps retreat. I looked at the video feed on the computer and saw him walk towards the street, then veer off to the side before reaching the road. My heart raced as I switched the feed to different cameras. I wasn't familiar with the labels on my father's computer, so I clicked from one camera to the next in a panic.

The fourth camera labeled "side right back" showed CJ. He was crouched low, walking to the back of the house. I switched cameras again and saw him removing the screen on the window in the master bedroom. He wasn't giving up.

Still holding my firearm, I ran to my parents' room and faced CJ through the window as I pointed the gun in his direction. Did I have the guts to shoot him? You bet I did. I wasn't about to let him kill me. My dad went down without a fight, but I wasn't about to. My hands were shaking, but the clip had ten bullets, and I was prepared to fire all of them. Surely at least one would hit him.

CJ must have seen the determination on my face. He looked surprised, raised both arms, palms open, and backed away. For good measure, I fired a warning shot over his head. My ears rang uncomfortably as rays of cracked glass surrounded the bullet hole. I looked at the damage to the window for a moment. When I moved my gaze back to CJ, he was gone. I was a bit surprised but thankful I had scared him off so easily. I shut my eyes, took a deep breath, and let it out. It was good to be alive still. It was only then that I realized how tense my whole body was. I closed my eyes again and systematically relaxed every muscle group. To be sure he had left, I checked all the camera feeds and confirmed he was gone.

With CJ's betrayal, the sphere of people I could depend on had shrunk considerably. Sure, I could trust my mom, my aunt, and my uncle, even Perry, but they were too far away to respond to an emergency. Could I depend on the local police, or were they in the pocket of Happy Sun, too? I realized I was becoming paranoid, but I had good reason to be. Danielle had told me she would be coming back soon, and I waited anxiously. She was the only one in the vicinity I trusted, but there was little she could do to protect me.

I opened the Expedia app on my phone and looked for the next flight out. Nothing that night, but I reserved a seat on a United flight the following morning. I hated leaving all of my parents' possessions for Happy Sun to dispose of unceremoniously, but I had no choice. I wanted to live.

The sun was low in the sky, and I scanned the fields around the house. I saw no workers, so I figured it would be safe to walk around without being confronted by one of the Happy Sun goons. In case I was wrong about that, I carried the Glock in my holster. I went to the strawberry fields, hoping to scavenge more of the unpicked fruit as I lay between rows of strawberry plants. To my horror, every last one of the plants had been removed. Yet more evidence of their ridiculous, nonsensical farming practices. Those strawberries were not only delicious, they were certified organic and non-GMO. They would have been good for a whole other season and would bring in top dollar. I was partially satisfied knowing the people running the company were incompetent and would probably go out of business shortly, but I took the removal of the strawberries personally.

I returned to the house and sat on the couch to think. It was almost dark, but I didn't turn on the lights. Would someone else come to kill me now that I'd scared CJ off? Would he return with a bulletproof vest and five other assassins to take me down? I went to my dad's inner sanctum and located several grenades. I'd seen how they work in movies. You pull the pin and throw it, but was there something else I needed to know? Does the pin come out easily? What if you can only get it out halfway? Would it explode? How far could I throw it? Could I hurl it far enough away from me that I wouldn't be injured? These were the sorts of questions stirring in my mind as I looked through my father's survival manuals for instructions on the operation of grenades.

A loud knock on the door removed me from my thoughts. My shoulders tensed and my heart raced as I checked the front door camera feed. I relaxed immediately. It was Danielle. I removed my holster still holding the pistol, and placed it next to the computer.

There were no hotels around. I thought about asking my new best friend if she'd spend the night or, even better, if I could stay at her place. I'd never been there and didn't know if she had room for another person. I only knew I didn't want to spend the night alone, especially not in the house I was in.

I rushed to let her in. "I'm so glad to see you," I said.

"What took you so long? It seems I've been banging on the door forever."

"Sorry, I was lost in my thoughts. You'll never guess who came by a little while ago."

Danielle cringed. "Don't tell me CJ was here."

"He was. But I scared him away with my gun."

"So you didn't talk to him?"

"I'm never going to talk to that asshole again. Not after what he did to me."

Danielle relaxed as she walked inside. "I think you need some of this," she said as she held out a wine bottle I hadn't noticed until that moment.

"Although I feel I could sure use a drink, after what happened last night, I think I'd better lay off wine or any other liquor for a while. I was going to ask a favor, though."

"Anything," Danielle assured me, as she comforted me by lightly squeezing my arm and gazing caringly into my eyes. "What do you need?"

"I'd rather not stay here alone tonight. I was wondering if you could spend the night, or, if you have room, if I could sleep at your place."

Danielle paused momentarily as if she was recalculating something in her head, then smiled and answered, "Of course. Mi casa es su casa." The Spanish expression, meaning my house is your house, is well known in areas such as California with a large Hispanic population. "How soon do you want to go?"

"How about right now?"

Again, Danielle thought intently before speaking. "Sure, but I'm a bit tired right now from everything I had to do earlier. I came straight over here and haven't had a chance to rest. Mind if I sit for a bit and get my energy back before we leave for my place?"

"No problem. I'll just get some of my things together."

"Before you do that, let me give you something I bought for you to celebrate your recovery from CJ's attack."

"Goodness! You didn't need to get me anything."

"I wanted to. I consider you a dear friend now, even though we haven't reconnected for that long. I've been told that sometimes I can be a bit too pushy with my friendships, but when I meet someone I really like, someone I feel I can connect with and get close to, I want to show it. So here, I had to drive to a special store to get this just for you."

Danielle reached into her purse and pulled out a small box. I stared at it for a few moments before I took it from her. I was speechless as I turned it around in my hand, looking closely at every detail. A shiny silver cubicle box, two inches on each side. The top flap was tucked in and secured with a gray seal.

Chapter 23

THE BOX DANIELLE HAD just handed me looked exactly like the one the girls had given to my dad shortly before he died.

Could this be a strange coincidence? My world was topsy-turvy. I needed to think. My heart pounded as thoughts swirled in my head. Danielle had been so supportive and caring in my time of need. I didn't want to believe there was any connection between her and the events that had brought me to this point. But could I ignore the silver box?

"Everything okay?" Danielle asked in her chipper voice. She must have noticed the dazed look on my face.

I tried to perk up and smile. "Of course. Everything's fine."

"Then open it up. There's a very special truffle inside. It's absolutely the best. I bought one for myself but couldn't resist eating it before I got here."

I needed to stall for time. I had to find a quiet space where I could think. I wished my heart would stop pounding. "You'll have to excuse me, but I suddenly have a splitting headache. I'd better take my migraine medicine and lie down for a few minutes." I wondered if Danielle was an innocent dupe like the girls from the talent agency.

"Maybe the truffle will make you feel better. I get headaches, too, and there's some ingredient they use that makes them go away. Maybe it will work for you, and you won't need to take your medicine. All those pharmaceuticals have terrible side effects."

I hoped Danielle didn't notice I was hyperventilating. "Sorry, but I'm in too much pain right now. I'll eat the truffle in my room and lie down. If I don't feel better soon, I'll take my medicine."

"But I want to see you eat the truffle."

I rubbed the back of my neck. "Why?"

"I want to see the expression on your face when you eat the best thing you ever tasted."

I couldn't avoid the fact that her need to see me eat whatever was in the box was odd. Maybe that's all it was—odd. Still, it was impossible to sweep under the rug. I was at a crossroads. Could I trust her? I could a minute ago, but now I was having serious doubts. I didn't want to hurt her feelings if, in fact, she was truly trying to help me. On the other hand, I didn't want to end up in a drum filled with sodium hydroxide.

"If I eat it now, I'll throw up. I'll be back as soon as I can." I took the box and hurried to my bedroom. Still hyperventilating, I closed the door gently and noticed for the first time that, thankfully, my father had installed a deadbolt. After securing the door, I became aware of gentle knocking on the door. I moved a stack of books in front of it to block entry should the lock be disengaged.

My heart raced as I tried to focus while hurriedly reviewing the video from the night before. Danielle had arrived hours before she left. As she exited the house, I saw things that had escaped me before. She looked disheveled. She was hurrying, looking around nervously. I noticed a dark stain on the side of the white tank top she was wearing. Could that be blood? I continued to watch, my wrist throbbing as I operated the mouse, but I couldn't stop.

Danielle's gentle knocking on the door became louder. "Are you okay in there?" she yelled through the door. "I'm worried about you. Can I come in?"

With my stomach in knots, I tried to block her voice as I frenetically continued to go through the recording. My concentration was increasingly rattled upon hearing Danielle gently push on the door. I redirected my attention back to the video.

An hour after Danielle had left, CJ arrived. He knocked several times, tried the door, and let himself in. It was only nine minutes later that he rushed out of the house carrying me. My arms were wrapped in towels, and a small amount of blood dripped from them. My thoughts raced as I tried to analyze the information I had. Could CJ have subdued me, slashed my wrists, and wrapped them in towels in such a short time? I thought about his tattoo. Lots of people have tattoos with Chinese symbols. By itself, it was nothing out of the ordinary.

Was being on the same bus as him from the airport a set-up or just a coincidence? Had he really flown to and from Sacramento that day? Was he really considering running for office? Was it possible he really was attracted to me? I wanted to think so, but nagging doubts resurfaced in my mind as painful events from my childhood, when I was considered uncool and I thought of myself as ugly, reemerged.

It had taken years for me to gain self-confidence, but maybe that was misguided. Thinking back, it was Danielle who, in her own subtle way, made me feel CJ couldn't possibly care about me. Cunningly tried to convince me I was unattractive and undeserving of having a relationship with someone as desirable as CJ. Being liked, or thinking I was liked, by one of the popular mean girls from my past had invaded my subconscious and eroded my usual level-headed analysis of the situation.

Thoughts continued to dash around in my head. Danielle was the one who pushed the alcohol on me. It made me extremely tired, but now I wondered—could she have added a benzodiazepine to my glass?

My concentration was interrupted by the sound of Danielle trying to open the door forcefully, followed by loud pounding. "We need to talk," she yelled. I didn't respond.

She crashed into the door, but it held firm. It was only a question of time before she would break the door down or call someone who would break it down for her. I turned off the computer, grabbed several tasers and grenades, and fastened the holster around my waist again. After quietly opening a window to the outside, I removed the screen and silently dropped down. The silver box Danielle had given me and my phone were in my purse, which I carried over my shoulder.

I landed on the dirt harder than I thought I would and collapsed to the ground. The moon was almost new, so there was little light. I couldn't see where I was going and moved slowly away from the house.

My outstretched hands were ready to detect any obstacle blocking my way.

I don't know how long I was wandering in the dark—probably less time than I thought—before I ran into a tree. I realized it was the crepe myrtle near the house. That meant I wasn't far from the gravel yard where my dad kept farm equipment and a diesel fuel tank. Taking my time, with my arms still outstretched, I felt a tractor in front of me. I walked around it carefully and slunk to the ground.

I had to think of something quickly. Whatever I decided would be the most important decision of my life. I was in a life-or-death situation. Hoping I'd made the right decision, I pulled the phone from my purse and called CJ.

"Berry?" he answered after a few seconds. "What's happening?" He sounded anxious.

Hearing his voice, I was powerless to speak. Instead, I cried uncontrollably. My body was shaking as tears and snot ran down my face. CJ was quiet until I started to get a handle on myself.

"Don't try to talk," he said. "I'm glad to hear your voice. I'm glad you're safe." He paused. "You're safe, aren't you? I hope nobody has a gun to your head right now."

Finally, I could speak. I didn't know if anyone was outside looking for me, so I kept my voice low. "I'm really sorry. I see now that I should have trusted you. I think Danielle is trying to kill me."

CJ was quiet a moment before responding. "Are you in danger right now?"

"I think so."

"Where are you?"

"I had to sneak out of my house. I'm behind a tractor in my dad's gravel yard, where he kept all the farming equipment. I don't think I have much time before Danielle comes out looking for me or calls someone for help. Shit! I see some vehicle lights coming across the field in the back. People from Happy Sun are coming to help her."

"Okay. I'm leaving right now to get you. Try to stay in the area so I can find you, but leave if you have to. I can be there in fifteen if I rush."

Before I could respond, CJ disconnected. The night was warm, but I was shivering. The vehicle lights came closer, accompanied by the roar of engines. Moments later two trucks and a motorcycle arrived at the back of the house. I heard male voices, mostly yelling, but couldn't make out the words, which sounded Chinese.

A door slammed, and I heard Danielle yelling excitedly. Peaking from behind the tractor, I saw three beams of light from flashlights or similar devices moving away. Two beams went down the road in front of my house in opposite directions. The third light was slowly making its way around the house. I felt I'd be safe for the next few minutes. Hurry up and get here, CJ.

I wondered if the men looking for me had guns or truffles. Would they try to force me to eat poison or shoot me and dissolve my body in a vat? The man looking around the house had completed a 360-degree search and was slowly walking toward me, shining his light in all directions. I didn't think my heart could beat any faster, but it did. I walked from behind the tractor to the seed spreader, near the diesel tank.

My pursuer came closer. I picked up a rock and threw it as hard as I could toward the street. The soft thud it made hitting the dirt was enough to cause the person to turn and aim the light in the direction of the sound. The ruse, in retrospect, wasn't a good idea. The distraction was short-lived but provided assurance I was somewhere in the vicinity. I saw a glint of metal as light bounced off something in my stalker's left hand. In the light supplied from his flashlight, I barely made out the form of a gun. Poison was off the table. They planned to make quick work of getting rid of me.

The footsteps were getting closer, but strain as I might, I saw nothing but a bright shaft of light. Out of the darkness the faint rumble of an engine floated in the air. As it got louder, I shut my eyes and hoped it was CJ and not more reinforcements from Happy Sun. The engine sound became a roar and I saw headlights approach, but I couldn't make out the vehicle type. It drove down the road, just past where I stood facing it, and screeched to a stop. I was almost giddy when I recognized CJ's truck. He made a U-turn, causing the vehicle to point in my direction momentarily.

I waved my arms furiously in the light of the headlights and saw him open his door and jump to the road. He yelled for me to hurry. I turned towards the sound of the footsteps quickly approaching, just on the other side of the diesel tank. I made a split-second decision. In retrospect, I should have grabbed one of the grenades in my pocket. Instead, I ran toward CJ and shot in the direction of the diesel tank several times, anticipating a huge explosion.

Chapter 24

"WHAT WERE YOU SHOOTING at?" CJ asked when I reached the truck despite the volley of bullets coming from behind. As soon as I was in my seat, he peeled away.

"The gasoline tank. I thought it would explode and protect me from the guy chasing me."

CJ chuckled. "That only happens in movies and TV shows. We're a hundred miles from Hollywood so that sort of stunt doesn't work here. Actually, it was debunked years ago on MythBusters."

"I guess I missed that episode." After a few moments of silence, I said, "I sure am glad to see you. I guess I have some explaining to do. "

"There's plenty of time for that, but I can figure out the gist of it."

"Where are we going now?"

"I don't think it will be safe to take you to my place, so I'm heading to my cousin Melinda's house. We'll be there in about an hour." I noticed CJ checking his rear-view mirror. "No one is following us so they'll never find us there."

"Right now, I'm so confused. You're the only person around here I can trust. At least I think I can trust you."

"You can. Once we're settled, you can tell me everything, and I'll try to help you decide what to do next."

"Since we won't be there for an hour, why don't I tell you everything now?"

"Okay. I'm listening."

I took a deep breath. "First, I have to know. Are you on Happy Sun Farm's payroll?"

CJ leaned forward and took his eyes off the road a few moments to look at me, his eyebrows furrowed. "Me? Of course not. Why would you think that?"

"Danielle said you were, and, well, I'm ashamed to say it, but when I was at your place, I saw a check lying around from Acker Enterprises. When Danielle said Happy Sun was paying you, I told her about that check. She said Acker Enterprises was a holding company Happy Sun uses."

"Why, that little bitch. . . she made that up. Acker Enterprises is a firm I use for my business. It has nothing to do with Happy Sun Farm. Go ahead and Google them if you don't believe me."

Danielle was the only one I was sure had tried to kill me. Surely, she wasn't too principled to lie about Acker Enterprises. I wanted to believe CJ but did a search on my phone to be certain. Once I saw that it looked legit, I felt better.

"I probably should have told you more about Danielle earlier, but didn't think you'd believe me. I have no proof, but I believe she was involved in having her own parents killed in an accident with a truck."

"She said you arranged it."

"Figures. Truth is, she never seemed truly surprised when they died. After their funeral, she took a nap, and I wanted to cheer her up by surprising her with pancakes. Everyone loves my pancakes. When I looked through her pantry, I found two cans of Calumet baking powder, both opened. One contained a baggie holding white powder. The other was half-filled with what appeared to be normal baking powder. I knew she had been a drug addict previously but thought she had kicked the habit. Since I started running my school, I've been carrying around fentanyl test strips, so I tested the powder in the bag. It was positive."

"Goodness," I said. "I never would have suspected it."

"I checked on Danielle, and she was fast asleep on her side, pillows wedged under her head and shoulders, the way drug addicts sleep after shooting up so they won't roll on their back and choke to death. That's the moment I put the pieces together. She was a drug addict and had a huge amount of fentanyl she couldn't possibly afford. Her parents were killed in an accident when they were driving to visit a senior living facility in Bakersfield at her insistence, and she had sold the farm to Happy Sun before the funeral. To this day, I'm convinced she got the fentanyl from Happy Sun as payment for helping to arrange her parents' death and selling the farm."

"Wasn't she upset when her parents died?"

"She cried a lot when people were around, but I knew the woman could cry buckets of tears whenever it suited her. I figured if she killed her own parents for drugs, there was nothing she wouldn't do. Drug addiction makes people do terrible things. I left before she woke up and hadn't spoken to her until she showed up at Fine Java."

I sat in stunned silence for several minutes. Finally, I said, "I wish you had told me all that before."

"Like I said, you wouldn't have believed me."

"You're right, but now I know you were telling the truth about Danielle. She's a nasty, lying, manipulative, evil—"

CJ interrupted me, "We'll be here all day if you list all of her characteristics, but I agree with everything you have to say."

I proceeded to tell CJ about what, in retrospect, was a carefully planned scheme whereby Danielle gained my trust and convinced me he, CJ, was working for Happy Sun. That scheme came to a screeching halt when she tried to get me to eat the contents of a small box identical to the one my father had received. I knew she wasn't an innocent chump after I reviewed the front door video of the night I almost died, and she insisted I eat the candy right away.

"I'd sure like to know what's in that candy," CJ said. "They might try to use it again."

"We need to find a place to test it."

"Do you have it?" CJ asked, turning to look at me.

"It's in my purse. I wasn't about to leave it behind."

"Awesome. Once it's tested, it should be enough to put them out of business and in jail."

We arrived at Melinda's house, a large ranch house in a suburban area. Melinda was older than CJ—about forty-five—and lived alone, having been divorced several years earlier. She'd never had kids and seemed happy to have company. After showing us the guest room, she turned to CJ and said, "You can sleep here." Then she looked in my direction and added, "I'll set up a cot for you in my study."

"I don't think that will be necessary," CJ said, looking to me. "Will it?"

"Not at all," I replied.

I was glad to be someplace safe, but my mind was still racing from recent events. For the first time in hours, I remembered that both of my wrists were bandaged and needed to be tended to. With the first aid supplies Melinda had on hand, CJ changed my dressings. We were happy to see I hadn't bled from my wounds since the last dressing change.

After a glass of wine, I felt more relaxed. My mind drifted from the horrors of the day to the light conversation CJ was having with his cousin, reminiscing about the days their families would get together when they were kids. After scarfing down leftovers Melinda found in the refrigerator, we retired for the evening.

I slept surprisingly well despite being in a strange house and a strange bed, without any of my things aside from my purse, cell phone, and gun. When I woke up the following morning, I was snuggled against CJ, his arm under my head, around my shoulder.

I put my clothes from the day before back on, as did CJ. Melinda had already left for work, and we helped ourselves to coffee and toast.

"Before we do anything else," CJ said, a concerned look on his face. "I want you to tell me about Fusarium. I know you said it's not serious, but I don't believe you. I want to know everything about it."

I had to think a moment before I remembered telling him I was suffering from a Fusarium attack. Then I laughed. CJ looked bewildered as I explained. "You have to understand. Danielle had me so confused, I thought you worked for Happy Sun Farms. I made that up so you wouldn't come over. I don't have Fusarium or anything else. Fusarium is a plant disease, but it was the first thing that popped into my head that sounded like an illness."

We both laughed. "Well, you sure had me worried," CJ said.

"We have a lot to do so let's plan our day."

We decided to stop by Target to buy clothes, then contact the police station near my parents' farm. I asked CJ if he had any idea how to locate the girls in the Happy Sun Farm commercials.

"I used a production company in Bakersfield when I made commercials for Mama Baroni's," he said. "That was over a year ago, when I had enough product to sell in other areas. I would start with them. They're the biggest around. I'll give them a call and tell them I'm interested in using those girls in another commercial."

I listened as CJ called the production company. He had a way of talking people into anything, including giving him the contact number for the agency that represented the girls who, he learned, were twin sisters.

After calling the All Seasons Talent Agency, we had an appointment to meet the girls at 4:00 p.m. that afternoon, when they'd be home from summer school.

Buying new clothes when you're too hurried to try anything on isn't much fun. CJ swore about the high cost of everything. We didn't buy much, but between the two of us we spent north of $250.

Back at Melinda's, CJ called the police. We thought he should do the talking, knowing the police in the area were more receptive to male voices. After several transfers, he put the phone on speaker and spoke to an officer who took our complaint. He remained calm, calmer than I could have been, when he explained the chronology of events, starting with my mother being coerced into selling the farm, the suspicious box given to my dad, the dead man in the vat, and ending with my attempted murder.

The officer sounded weary when he told CJ they'd had complaints about Happy Sun from neighbors who didn't like a foreign company moving in and buying up American land, but that wasn't against the law. The persuasive techniques used to get my mom to sign over the farm weren't illegal to his knowledge. He explained that he wasn't a lawyer, as if we didn't know, and we were welcome to consult one. He seemed mildly interested in the man in the vat but not in the contents of the silver box or my attempted assassination.

When CJ finished, the officer sighed. "You've said quite a bit, but there really isn't much to go on here. I understand your girlfriend is upset, but it doesn't sound like you can prove anything."

"I'd say finding a dead body dissolving in a drum is proof of something," CJ yelled.

"Tell you what," said the officer. "We can search the building where your girlfriend claims she saw a body, but other than that, there's not much I can do."

"What about the poison? Can you test for that?" CJ asked.

"That's not something we do here. It's not like your girlfriend died and became a coroner's case."

I could no longer stop myself from speaking up. "Excuse me, officer. My father was Randall Fields. I think those people gave the same poison to my dad, and he died."

"Sorry for your loss, ma'am, but your dad was known around these parts. I had nothing against him, but he was a bit of an odd character. I wouldn't be surprised if he were experimenting with drugs of some sort which could have been delivered in a box. No matter. According to the coroner, he died of a heart attack. I think you're letting your dislike of Happy Sun, which I understand, cloud your judgment. I'll tell my sergeant about that dead body you think you saw, and if he considers it worthwhile, he'll get a warrant to search the place."

"I don't think I saw a dead body. I know it."

"Of course, ma'am."

Once we had disconnected, I turned to CJ. "That sure was disappointing. Doesn't seem like the police are concerned."

"I'm sure the sergeant will get a warrant and look for that body. He has to. Then things will happen."

Chapter 25

AT 2:30 P.M. WE were on our way to the city of Taft, approximately thirty minutes past Bakersfield. As we approached the town, the number of oil derricks that dotted the land increased. Once we'd passed the sign reading "Welcome to Taft, the Best of Places," I knew we were close, although I wasn't convinced it was the best of places. We found the girls' house with little difficulty: a ranch house with an oil derrick in the back. We figured the family had a steady income from leasing the land to an oil company.

The girls' mother, a pretty woman in her thirties, well-dressed with manicured nails, welcomed us. CJ introduced himself as the owner of Mama Baroni's, and me as his assistant.

The mother told us her girls would be out momentarily, then sat with us for several minutes, showing pictures of them in various ads and boasting about their success and professionalism. "The All Seasons Talent Agency told me you have commercials you would like my daughters to star in," she said after her presentation. She was clearly eager for them to land another lucrative commercial acting job. "Selling your pasta sauce will be easy for them. We all love Mama Baroni's pasta sauce. We use it at least once a week."

"I'd sure like to meet them," CJ said. I followed with a similar comment.

The mother left to fetch the girls, and I whispered to CJ, "I feel terrible lying to this woman about having a commercial for the girls."

"I wouldn't worry about her," CJ said. "She looks like a woman who can take care of herself."

We heard giggling, followed seconds later by the arrival of the twins, who I immediately recognized as the youngsters in the video giving the box with the deadly truffle to my dad. Their hair was exactly the same: the dark-haired one with a ponytail and the light-haired one with loose curls.

CJ and I both stood and greeted them. We all sat, and I got right to the point. "I understand you were in some commercials for Happy Sun Farm."

"That's right," the mother said. "They were so impressed with my girls, they asked them to cheer up a farmer who was an important client of theirs."

I was relieved that the mother volunteered this piece of information because I still hadn't figured out how to ask about their interaction with my dad.

"That's very interesting," I said. "What did you have to do to cheer him up?"

"All they had to do was hand the man a truffle beautifully wrapped in a silver box and tell him Mr. Kendal wanted him to have it as a sign of his appreciation."

"Didn't the man wonder why Mr. Kendal didn't give it to him instead?" CJ asked.

"He did," the pony-tailed girl said. "We did just like Mr. Chen told us. We said Mr. Kendal was ill and couldn't come himself, but we were his nieces and were visiting for a week, so our mother drove us." The girl sat back proudly when she was finished describing their acting expertise.

"What did I tell you?" their mother said. "Very professional. You can depend on them to exceed your expectations. Now, did you bring a contract with you? I can send it right to our agent."

"We're not ready to make an offer at this time," CJ said.

"Didn't the agency tell you to bring it?"

"Yes, but I wanted to meet the girls first."

The mother became furious. "Sure you did," she said sarcastically. "I can see we're wasting our time. This wouldn't be the first time people have come around here, wanting to meet my celebrity daughters so they can brag about it later. No contract, no more time with us."

"We'll see ourselves to the door," I said as we got up and started walking towards the entryway.

"Don't let the door hit you in the ass on the way out," the mother said. When we opened the door to leave, she yelled, "We hate your shitty Mama Baroni's pasta sauce."

By the time we were sitting in the truck, I was tense and sweating. A few seconds later, CJ and I both burst out in laughter.

"Well, that didn't go exactly as I had wanted," CJ said. "But we got the answer to our question. Those girls were hired by Mr. Chen to poison your dad."

Chapter 26

"YOU TAKE RILEY HERE and go check out this complaint about Happy Sun. Seems pretty ridiculous, but we need to be able to document that we followed through." The sergeant was speaking to Officer Chapman.

"What the hell, Sarge. I thought we were friends. I don't wanna babysit the new kid. She's only worked here a week and will only get in my way."

"I'll talk to her and explain the way we operate. As you know, we're going to be watched, see how we treat the first woman we were forced to hire. I'll make sure she stays out of your way and doesn't cause any problems, but we're stuck with her, and she needs to be brought up to speed. I'm counting on you to make sure you don't upset the Happy Sun people. They've gone out of their way to support us. Those Chinese love law and order."

"You bet."

Twenty minutes later, Officers Chapman and Riley were on their way to Happy Sun Farm. Chapman, a twenty-five-year police veteran, appeared crusty on the outside. Once that outer crusty shell was peeled away, there was more crustiness underneath. He was putting in his time until his retirement in six months.

Officer Riley was a twenty-six-year-old rookie. She had graduated with honors from San Diego State University with a degree in criminal justice. Originally planning to become a lawyer, she switched gears to become a police officer after her father's murder. He'd been working at a convenience store one night when a man shot him and took off with a hundred twenty dollars. The investigating detective had bungled the case by failing to read the chief suspect his rights before he confessed.

Charges were dropped, and the guilty man was freed. Riley didn't want to see that sort of error repeated.

The two officers drove to their destination in silence, Chapman at the wheel. They turned at the small sign reading "Happy Sun Farm" with an arrow pointing to the driveway, and passed a company truck that was exiting, no doubt full of produce. Soon, they passed a large sign reading "Happy Sun Farm," which partially blocked the view of the large metal sculpture of a smiling sun, and stopped in front of the yellow arm extended over the road. Moments later, a guard emerged from the nearby kiosk and greeted them politely in heavily accented English.

Chapman explained that they had a warrant to search the shed used by the previous owner for distilling alcohol.

The guard had a brief conversation through his walkie-talkie in a foreign language, then lifted the arm and directed the officers to park in front of the main building, a large, stucco structure just beyond the busy loading dock a hundred yards away.

“I'll do all the talking,” Chapman said to Riley. “Remember, you're here just to look and learn. All you have to do is be quiet and follow my lead.”

“Understood.” Riley had felt disrespected from day one. Her petite size didn't help her fit into the boys' club. For now, her goal was just to keep her job. Later, when she felt more comfortable, she'd tell those assholes she worked with what she really thought.

As they approached the building, Riley thought it was strange to have a sentry gate and such a large office-type building at a farm. Once the cruiser was parked, Mr. Chen emerged from the building, dressed in a blue suit with a white shirt and navy tie. He bowed politely and introduced himself after both officers had emerged from their vehicle.

Chapman introduced himself and his accompanying officer, then began to chat about the weather as well as how much the local police appreciated all of Happy Sun's contributions to their department for equipment, public relations, and restaurant vouchers. A few minutes later, Chapman looked apologetic as he produced the emergency warrant he had to search the building on the old Fields' farm.

Mr. Chen waved over a nearby worker driving a cart and directed him to take himself and the officers to the building in question. The ride took several minutes, minutes that were filled with Mr. Chen's words of appreciation for the local police department. Once they reached the shed, they all looked inside. The inspection took little time, as the structure was completely empty. The stills were gone, as were all the supplies and shelving. Rather than the sweet smell of alcohol, they were exposed to the caustic smell of bleach.

"No evidence of anything here," Chapman said.

Mr. Chen chuckled. "I could have told you that, but of course, you needed to see for yourself. This must be some sort of practical joke. I know there are some people who don't like foreigners and would like us to leave, but my company is dedicated to growing superior, inexpensive produce for your country." He paused and grinned. "While still making a profit."

"Of course," Chapman said. "I'm sorry to have bothered you."

"Don't you think we should look around a little more?" Riley whispered to her fellow officer. "It looks like they just cleaned this place. If there's a dead body, they could have moved it."

"Typical rookie move," Chapman shot back. "We can't look beyond what is designated in the warrant."

"But we could ask to see other areas or use the restroom. This hardly seems like a complete investigation."

"Something wrong?" Mr. Chen asked.

Chapman turned to their host. "No, nothing. I think Riley here is on the rag."

"On the rag? I don't understand."

"Just an American expression. I think we've seen enough."

They rode the cart back to their car, where Chapman thanked Mr. Chen and the officers got back in their vehicle. While returning to the police station, Chapman chided Riley for her insubordination and bad judgment. She said nothing as she fought to control her anger.

Chapter 27

"SINCE THE COPS WON'T do it, we'll have to get that candy analyzed some other way," CJ said. "I also think there's a few people we should warn. From what I know, there are still a couple of more holdouts—two more farms for Happy Sun to acquire so they can have a complete rectangle of farmland under their control. They may go after more land in the future, but for now that rectangular area seems to be the focus"

"I can't understand why they want so much land, especially since they don't seem to know what the hell they're doing. I don't see how they can possibly make a profit."

"I agree," CJ said. "It's hard to believe a Chinese company would invest so much money in something they knew so little about. I hate to stereotype anyone, but they're usually such good businessmen."

"Maybe we're missing something," I said. "Maybe they know exactly what they're doing."

"You think the farming is just a coverup for some criminal activity?"

"It's possible. They could be making counterfeit money, selling fentanyl, or spreading ransomware."

"There's a lot of things they could be doing, but they wouldn't need to spend millions on all that farmland."

"I don't suppose we'll know until we figure out what's going on."

"One thing I'm sure about," CJ said, "is that they're shipping their produce all over the US. I've been told they've been undercutting the prices of just about every other grower."

"How do you know that?"

"Folks around here have been concerned enough to look into the company and find out where they ship their produce. I see all the data they've collected when I meet with my supporters. They want me to go to Sacramento to stop it, although I'm not sure I could, even if I were elected. A lawyer is looking into that now."

"Maybe they're prepared to lose money until they drive other farms out of business," I said. "Like Chinese furniture companies. The government subsidized furniture manufacturers in China. They sold their furniture here at a loss, and many US companies went under because of that."

"A few of my backers have brought up that very issue," CJ said. "They think China wants to bankrupt all our farmers, but I don't think that would be possible. They'd need to buy up a helluva lot more land to do that. That's not going to happen anytime soon. Probably never."

"Meanwhile, do you suppose we should notify the other holdouts they may be in danger? Maybe pay those farmers a visit?"

CJ thought for a moment. "Too dangerous to visit them until we know what we're dealing with. For now, I'll give 'em a call and warn 'em to watch out for anything suspicious. They shouldn't eat anything from someone they don't know well."

"After you do that, let's look for a Chinese restaurant in the area. Maybe someone who works there can translate that recording I made."

Thirty minutes later, after CJ had warned people in the two households he thought were at risk, we were on our way to find a Chinese restaurant. Our timing was sub-optimal, to say the least, as it was rush hour.

After parking and walking from the opposite end of the strip mall parking lot, we were hot and sweaty by the time we arrived at the Pagoda Palace, a Mandarin Chinese restaurant. CJ and I entered and sat at a table. I had imagined all sorts of conversations the young couple I recorded might have had. It was early, so the restaurant wasn't crowded. Neither of us had much of an appetite, but we ordered several dishes. I used chopsticks, while a fork was CJ's choice of utensil. Our waiter, a middle-aged man, had a heavy Chinese accent. We agreed that we'd ask him to listen to my recording when he came to refill our glasses.

He didn't come by our table again until he presented us with the bill. The restaurant was getting noisy by then. Nevertheless, CJ seized the opportunity.

"I'll give you twenty dollars if you can translate a recording for me," he said.

The waiter seemed to perk up. "Sure, sure. You have money now?"

CJ put a twenty-dollar bill on the table. The waiter wasted no time grabbing it and securing it in his pocket. "Still must pay for food," he said.

"No problem," CJ answered as he put down his credit card.

"Okay, let me hear recording."

I placed my phone on the table and played the recording on speaker. The waiter looked puzzled. "I not understand this."

"Is it Cantonese?" I asked, knowing that the Cantonese dialect, spoken in Hong Kong and other areas, is not understood by most who speak the more common Mandarin dialect.

"Let me listen again."

The man strained to understand the recording as I played it for him several more times. Finally, he shook his head. "Sorry. Not Chinese. Korean. The language Korean."

I wasn't expecting that. "I just assumed it was Chinese, since Happy Sun Farm is a Chinese company," I said.

It seemed odd that South Koreans would be brought here by a company headquartered in The People's Republic. I asked if he knew someone who spoke Korean, and he said he didn't. He retrieved the twenty-dollar bill from his pocket and held it out.

"Keep it," CJ said. "We'll drive into Bakersfield and look for a Korean restaurant. They probably have a lot of them there." After settling our lunch bill, we departed.

"That doesn't make any sense," I said as we walked towards the truck. "I thought the company brought all the employees from China."

"That's the case as far as I know. Other than the field hands from south of the border, word is they haven't hired anyone else. Seems they brought over more personnel with them than necessary. Their people do a lot of supervising—they keep a close eye on the workers doing the hard manual labor. Other jobs, such as loading and driving the trucks, are done by the folks they came here with."

"The whole operation is very curious," I said. "I wonder if they have some secret they don't want outsiders to learn about."

"After what you told me about Diego, I'd say they sure act like they do."

When we reached the truck, CJ checked his messages. "Damn," he said, staring at his phone. "I got a message from a buddy of mine. It's about Danielle." He paused and looked up at me. "She's dead."

What had originally been feelings of hatred when I heard her name quickly changed to forgiveness and curiosity. "What happened?"

"They think she overdosed. She was found in her apartment with a needle in her arm and a lot of needle marks, both old and new. They're going to run toxicology tests on her, of course, but it looks pretty clear."

"I don't know what to say. She was a horrible person. I'm sure she was trying to kill me. Now that she's dead, I don't know how I should feel." A thought crossed my mind at that moment. "You don't suppose they murdered her, do you?"

"The Happy Sun people?"

"I believe she was supposed to kill me for them but failed. They killed Carlos, I'm sure. They don't like people who might be disloyal or disruptive. Maybe they feel the same about those who fail them."

"We'll never get that figured out talking about it here," CJ said. "Let's see what we can find out when we get your recording translated in Bakersfield. Maybe we're on a wild goose chase. Maybe that couple was just talking like two people in love, or at least in lust."

"Possible, but why were they speaking Korean?"

"Good question."

Once we were on the road, we listened to country music over CJ's sound system. Not my favorite music, but I didn't complain. As he filled up with gas near Bakersfield, I checked my phone for Korean restaurants in the area. The name "Best Korean BBQ" caught my eye. Google Maps directed us there, and we arrived at 8:00 pm. The place was half-full. A third of the clientele looked Asian, which I took as a sign the food was good and authentic. We were seated immediately and given menus.

Neither of us had eaten Korean food before, so we were left to read the descriptions of each item. CJ chose a beef dish, while I opted for seafood. When the waitress took our order, we were disappointed that the Asian-looking woman spoke perfect English without an accent.

Despite all the anxiety and sadness I was experiencing, the restaurant was one bright spot. If we hadn't been looking for a Korean translator, we never would have tried Korean food. Having eaten recently, we weren't hungry, but it was so delicious and flavorful we scarfed it up. For a few moments we both forgot about the predicament we were in.

Halfway through our meal, the waitress checked to see if everything was okay. After telling her we loved the food, I revealed that I had something recorded in Korean I needed to be translated and asked if there was someone there who could do that.

"My Korean is pretty bad," she said. "but my dad could do it. He's busy in the kitchen now, but we close at nine, and if you stay until nine-thirty or so, he might be willing to help you out. I'll go ask him." She returned a few minutes later and told us to wait around. He'd come out when he was through cooking and straightening up.

We sat patiently as more diners ambled in and ordered food. Knowing that each new customer would require her dad to be tied up in the kitchen, we resigned ourselves to waiting around. We ordered sticky rice cakes for dessert and ate slowly.

"I hope he doesn't tell us it's not Korean, but Vietnamese or Japanese," CJ said when we were finished.

Finally, a diminutive Asian man with salt and pepper hair, around fifty years old, emerged from the kitchen wearing a stained white smock and a chef's hat. Our waitress pointed to us, and the chef approached.

He greeted us in heavily accented English, bowed slightly, and took a seat. We introduced ourselves, and I learned his name was Kwan.

"I recorded a young couple who I think are speaking Korean," I said, "and suspect they are involved in a crime. I would appreciate it if you could translate the conversation for me."

"No problem," he said. "I've have lots of experience translating between English and Korean for my mother. She never learn English in the ten years she live here."

I played the recording on speaker. At first, he smiled as he listened, but his expression quickly changed to one of concern. I hadn't realized how long the conversation had lasted, including the embarrassing interludes of moaning and groaning when the couple was engaged in the physical manifestation of their attraction for each other. I noticed the chef smile during the most intimate moments. When the recording ended, he was silent.

Confused, I asked, "Was that Korean?"

"Yes, Korean," he answered. "But not the Korean I speak. Different accent, different way of talk."

"Did you understand it?"

"I understand, but these people not from South Korea."

"Then where are they from?"

"North Korea. Definitely North Korea."

Chapter 28

THE NEWS WAS SHOCKING. CJ and I looked at each other. "Do you think—" I said.

"Yup," CJ interrupted. "I think everyone at Happy Sun may be from North Korea. Maybe they're a mixture of North Koreans and Chinese, but this is very strange." He turned to the chef and asked, "What did they say?"

"So long, I need to listen again." He smiled and added, "Some of the time they stop talking. Sound like they very hot for each other."

"Yes," I said. "I forgot to mention I think they had sex part of the time." I hadn't forgotten. I didn't want to mention it ahead of time, not knowing how he'd react, but I think he enjoyed that part of the recording. "What I'm really interested in, though, is what they were saying to each other. It could be important."

"Okay. I listen again. Stop many times so I can translate as I hear more."

"Good idea," I said as I played the recording, now more eager than ever to learn what the couple was discussing.

After listening a short time, Kwan raised his hand, and I stopped. "They say they miss each other when they are apart. Love each other. The man say he glad he meet her. She glad, too."

He nodded, and I played another segment until he raised his hand again, and I stopped. "He say he hate wife back home. Only come here to escape her."

He nodded again, and I played more. We continued like that for some time, stopping so he could translate, then starting again. When we reached the X-rated portion, there was no stopping for ten minutes while Kwan sat patiently and smiled. After going through the whole tape, I learned that the man with the missing left fourth finger hated working at Happy Sun, where they were constantly watched and prohibited from leaving the property. Only those very high up in the organization were free to come and go as they wished. They were planning to transfer him to the facility in Tulare, but he didn't want to go. He told her he was going to try to escape and wanted her to come with him. She responded that she was too afraid. He asked her to wish him luck, which she did. He had heard about a Korean temple in Los Angeles that takes in Koreans who need help. He would try to reach it and hoped she would meet him there one day.

When our translator had finished, we sat in silence until he said, "I know about the Korean Buddhist temple in Los Angeles Koreatown that he talk about." He paused, then asked, "What will you do with this information?"

"I don't know," I said. "The company, Happy Sun Farm, doesn't sound like a good place to work, but that's not a crime."

Kwan leaned towards CJ and me. "The people you recorded are not allowed to leave, like prisoners. I think this is not a Chinese company. This is a North Korean company. North Korea very dangerous. You must stop them."

I wasn't sure how much I should share with Kwan. "I saw some suspicious activity on the farm and reported it to the police," I said. "I'm hoping to hear soon that they found illegal activity there, but until then, there's not much we can do. I was hoping the couple I recorded would say more about the company, maybe even serious crimes like murder."

The translator shook his head. "They may murder a few people, but that's nothing unusual for the North Korean government. They have something big planned. I don't know what, but it's more than killing a few people." He told us he would be available to translate more recordings if needed. He was not afraid of the North Korean government as long as he was here, on American soil.

We thanked Kwan and offered a payment of twenty dollars, which he refused. We left the restaurant and sat in the truck where we could talk in private.

CJ began. "Now that I think of it, I've occasionally seen Happy Sun truck drivers at truck stops eating lunch, which looks like a mixture of rice and vegetables, topped with a fried egg, like the pictures on the menu in Kwan's restaurant. I've never seen a Chinese restaurant serve food with a fried egg on top. Makes me think they're all Korean. Kwan is probably right—this is a North Korean company, pretending to be Chinese."

"What about Mr. Chen? That's a Chinese name. Do you think that's not his real name?"

"Quite possible."

"If this is part of a North Korean plot to do something terrible, Kwan is right," I said. "We can't just sit around and wait for it to happen. He seemed pretty convinced they have something horrific planned. Being from South Korea, he's well aware of North Korea's evil intentions."

"We can't figure this out on our own. The local farmers don't like them, but being an asshole is perfectly legal. Until now, they've avoided any serious investigation by the cops. Even if they search the shed for the body you saw, I'll bet Danielle warned them, and they moved it."

"Damn," I said. "You're right. I was hoping they'd bring in the FBI once they saw the murdered man. Instead, they're going to think I'm a nut job."

We returned to Melinda's house and slept. More accurately, we tried to sleep. Neither of us felt well-rested the next morning.

After breakfast, I must have checked my watch a hundred times, anticipating a call from the police. When noon arrived, I phoned the precinct office. After being transferred several times, I spoke to an officer who informed me they had found the shed where my dad's still had been, but it was empty. Not a single drum containing a dissolving body had been found. That confirmed my expectation that they removed all the evidence after I told Danielle about it.

"Did they look around outside the shed?" I asked, hoping they might return to Happy Sun and explore the area more thoroughly. "The body was there. I saw it. They obviously moved it."

"The search warrant was very specific. The officers who went there looked around as much as they could legally and saw nothing. Are you sure you didn't imagine what you saw in a bad dream?"

I felt like slamming the phone receiver down, but I was talking on my cell phone, so that wasn't possible. At any rate, I didn't want the police to think of me as hostile. "I'm quite sure of what I saw, but the Happy Sun Farm people got rid of the evidence. I hope you'll keep an eye on that place. There is something fishy going on there. Can you check Mr. Chen's passport and confirm his identity and country of origin? I believe he's in this country illegally."

"I can't do that. We can't go around harassing people who we suspect are undocumented, certainly not without a good reason."

I wasn't going to get anywhere with that guy, and wondered if the local police were purposely avoiding any meaningful investigation of Happy Sun Farm. It's not as if they didn't ever ask Hispanics in our community for documentation of citizenship or legal residency. I thought about asking again if they would analyze the candy I received from Danielle but decided against it. I didn't trust them to do anything. Worst case scenario, they would connect me to her death. I held back what I was thinking, thanked him politely, and disconnected. Turning to CJ, I said, "We have to do something. The shed was emptied out, so the cops didn't find anything. They think I'm an unreliable flake, and the police aren't going to pursue this. Maybe I'll have more luck with the FBI. They might be more interested in looking into this."

"It's worth a try. They could analyze the candy."

I contacted the nearest FBI office and gave a summary of what had transpired. I sensed the clerk I spoke to was used to brushing people off. They probably got lots of calls from people who were mentally ill or had a beef against a neighbor or co-worker.

"Can you at least test the candy?" I asked.

"No, they only analyze specimens related to an active investigation. Call your local police office and request they look into it. They'll contact the FBI if needed."

I already knew contacting the local police was a dead end.

Undeterred, I searched on my phone for a way to contact Homeland Security. I was surprised by how difficult it was to find a phone number or online information on how to alert them to a problem. I sat for a moment in shock. I supposed they relied on local law enforcement to handle all the preliminary work that needed to be done. Only problem was, the local law enforcement agency wasn't interested.

Looking around the website, I found the Homeland Security division that oversaw Kern County, where Happy Sun Farm was located. I dialed the number to report suspicious activity and was greeted by a phone tree. There was a list of options, including technical help and personnel questions. Finally, I was instructed to press "eight" to report suspicious activity. I touched the appropriate digit and was pleased to hear an actual human's voice. I started to explain my concern but was interrupted when the person on the other end asked me if this could wait until Monday. It was Saturday, and Homeland Security Intake was closed. He could take a message, but it was best to call on Monday. I insisted on leaving a message which included my name, phone number, and a description of some of my concerns. I was assured someone would look at his note the morning of the next workday.

I didn't want to wait around for law enforcement to become interested while something dangerous was brewing. Next on my agenda was finding out if everyone at Happy Sun was Korean, or only the young couple I had recorded. We returned to The Pagoda Palace, the Mandarin Chinese restaurant we'd visited before.

I spotted the waiter we had spoken to previously on break near the front of the restaurant, just as he disconnected a call on his cell phone.

"How would you like to make two hundred dollars?" I asked.

His eyes lit up. "Just tell me what I have to do."

"Visit Happy Sun Farm. We'll give you the address. Say you're lost, but pretend to speak only a little English. All you have to do is find out if the guards, and other people you see, speak Chinese."

"Sounds easy," he said. "I can go tomorrow morning, before my shift. But pay me half now."

CJ retrieved five twenty-dollar bills from his wallet and handed them over. “We’ll come back tomorrow around the same time to learn what you found out. Then I’ll give you the rest.”

CJ and I left the waiter smiling and counting his money. We returned to Melinda’s house, where we waited for a call from the FBI. No call was forthcoming. When my phone started playing “Strawberry Fields Forever,” I looked at the familiar number on my caller ID.

Chapter 29

I TOOK THE CALL outside, away from CJ. It was Perry, wondering when I'd be finished cleaning out my parents' house and returning.

"You should be done in a day or two," he said.

"It'll take longer than that to go through their things. Also, I want to look into the cause of my father's death. The circumstances are suspicious, and I think he may not have died of natural causes, like the coroner said." I didn't want to tell him people had tried to murder me. If he believed I was in danger, he might insist I return to Indiana. I would feel even worse if he questioned the validity of everything I said, as he often did. I desperately wanted to get to the bottom of things, no matter how foolish it was, and didn't want any push-back.

"So you think you're some sort of detective now?" he asked sarcastically.

"No, but I have evidence someone poisoned him."

"You have to trust the people who know what they're doing. If he were poisoned, the coroner would have found out."

"Not if he didn't look into it."

"You need to get your head screwed on straight."

He'd said that to me countless times before. It had always made me feel foolish, but this time his words only angered me. "Listen, Mr. Know-It-All. You don't know what I've seen here, and I don't want to take the time to explain it all to you right now. Just trust me. My concerns are based on solid evidence."

Perry chuckled. "Trust me. Famous last words. Just don't do anything ridiculous."

"Like I ever do ridiculous things?" Being away from Perry made me realize how much he put me down in subtle and not-so-subtle ways.

"You know what I mean."

"I think I do." We ended our call on a sour note, and I spent the next fifteen minutes reflecting on our relationship. My thoughts were interrupted by CJ, who suggested we shop for dinner. He wanted to cook pasta for me and Melinda. We headed off to the closest Ralph's supermarket, where CJ picked out his favorite brand of spaghetti and, of course, Mama Baroni's Delizioso sauce. He chose the basil flavor.

Back at Melinda's house, CJ started preparing dinner so it would be ready when our hostess arrived. Trying to help, I reached for the jar of pasta sauce.

"Ever have trouble opening glass jars?" CJ asked as I grasped the lid tightly and was preparing for my usual struggle to twist it.

"How did you guess?"

"Lots of people have trouble with that. Especially if they have arthritis." I wondered what he was getting at. "My mom had arthritis. That's why I invented my lid popper."

"What are you talking about?" I asked.

"The lid popper. See that little indentation on the side of the lid, with the button in the middle?" I looked and nodded when I saw it. "Press on it. That will release the vacuum. The vacuum is what makes it so hard to take off the lid. Once you let air in, the jar will be super easy to open."

I pressed the button, heard a soft whoosh, then smiled as I easily turned the lid. "That's phenomenal," I said. "You should patent this."

"I did. I use it on all our jars, and a number of manufacturers in the Bakersfield and Los Angeles area are using it, too."

"Are they paying you?"

"Sure are. That's where Acker Enterprises comes in. They handle the licensing and collection of royalties. I'm already making plenty to live on, which is good because, like I told you before, the pasta sauce factory isn't doing well right now. I've hired someone to promote the lid popper nationwide, and they predict I'll make quite a bit from the proceeds."

"I wondered how you got that big check I saw, when your business isn't doing well. Seems like a win-win. You get paid, and people can easily open jars." I smiled and kissed him. "I'm impressed."

Melinda came home at the usual time and was happy to see the evening meal ready. We enjoyed dinner and a lively conversation which touched on many things, but not our concerns about Happy Sun Farm. We didn't want Melinda to worry.

The following morning, CJ and I waited at the Golden Pagoda for our spy to arrive. Nervous he might not show up, I paced back and forth in front of the restaurant. Five minutes before his shift was scheduled to start, he arrived in a twenty-year-old compact car. We followed him to the rear of the restaurant, where he parked. "Only one person there speak Chinese," he said as he exited his car. "Guards and truck drivers don't speak Chinese. All sound Korean. They get man in suit, Mr. Chen. He speak Chinese, but with accent. He probably Korean, too." He held out his hand immediately when he finished talking, and CJ gave him five more twenties. Well worth it, in my opinion. I was now sure everyone at the company was Korean. At least two of the people, the young lovers, were North Korean. Most likely, they all were.

I didn't want time to go by without doing anything. "I wonder if we could find the Happy Sun Farm in Tulare the man in the recording spoke about," I said to CJ.

"We don't know where it is."

"We could drive there and look around."

"Tulare isn't that small. There's a population of more than fifty thousand."

"We could ask people there if they know of a Happy Sun Farm around there." I paused, then added, "How about we visit all the Korean restaurants in the area—there can't be many—and look for people who work for Happy Sun? Then we could follow them to their workplace."

"How will we identify them?"

"Good question." I thought for a moment. "I've noticed they all drive cars or trucks with their Happy Sun Farms logo on the front doors. We'll drive around to find Korean restaurants and look for vehicles with their logo."

"We have nothing else important planned," CJ said, "so okay, let's try to find their Tulare farm. What do you think we should do once we find it?"

"Let's start by observing as much as we can from a safe distance."

"Roger that."

We headed out of town and drove north on Route 99. Tulare was about ninety minutes away. As it was dark, we didn't see much of the surroundings, which were mostly farmland. When we were close to our destination, we pulled into a truck stop to sleep. CJ unrolled a thin mattress, which he kept behind his seat, and placed it in the truck bed. After spreading a quilt on top, we slept under the stars. Despite the mattress's thinness and the truck bed's hardness, I slept better than I had the night before.

I woke up at 5:30. CJ handed me a cup of hot coffee he had just purchased from the nearby fast-food joint.

"I must look a fright," I said.

CJ smiled. "You've looked better, but you still look great."

I wondered if I could trust a man who said I looked great when I knew I didn't, but decided I could overlook a lie like that. We located pay showers and washed up. I removed my bandages and cleaned my wounds. My wrists were healing nicely and no longer needed to be wrapped. I felt good—ready for the day.

Only a short drive away, we were in Tulare well before lunch. We got breakfast at a fast-food joint and mapped out the best route to visit all five Korean restaurants in town. At 11:30, we pulled up in front of the first eating establishment on our list. Few cars were in the parking lot, but as noon came, more customers arrived. No Happy Sun logos. We reached the second restaurant at 12:20. Again, no Happy Sun logos. The small parking lot of the third restaurant was full when we got there at 12:45. Driving past the hole-in-the-wall, I noticed a car with the Happy Sun logo on the door. We found a nearby parking space and waited.

CJ played more country western music while we waited over a half hour, lowering the truck windows as the heat became unbearable. The music complemented the weather, and I started to appreciate it. Forty-five minutes later, a diminutive Asian man wearing a suit entered the car we were focused on. After making a call, he pulled away from the curb. We tailed him from a distance to a small Asian market and parked down the street while he shopped.

Fifteen minutes later, the man emerged with a bag of groceries and drove to a main street leading out of the city. With several cars between us, we followed him several miles out of town to an area with large warehouses and a lumber yard. He pulled into the driveway of a large, unmarked warehouse.

No windows faced the front, just a long gray stucco wall with an unremarkable brown entry door at the end closest to us, and a three-bay loading dock at the other. Two trucks were parked in front. Our view of them was partly obscured by bushes close to the street, so we were unable to determine if either had the Happy Sun logo. We pulled to the side of the road and watched as the man we were tailing followed the driveway around back and disappeared.

Not wanting to raise suspicion, we pulled into the parking lot of the lumber yard next door and parked near the street, ready to continue our pursuit when the man we'd been following emerged. After listening to CJ's country western music for an hour, I became restless.

"I wonder what's taking him so long?" I asked.

"Good question. There's no sign on the building, so it could be anything from a place that sells fertilizer to a whore house."

"Have you noticed there's been no traffic in or out of that place since we got here? Several trucks have come and gone from this lumberyard while we've been waiting. Do you suppose he knows we're waiting for him?"

"I was way behind him, and there were at least two cars between him and us for most of the drive. Hard to believe he noticed us."

"How much longer do you think we should stay here?" I asked.

"It's three o'clock now. Whatever that business is, they probably close at five. I expect he'll leave before then."

"Okay, let's wait."

We were still there at 5:15. Both of us were hot and sweaty as we sat in silence. I asked CJ to turn off the music, which he did. I was hungry and irritable. CJ must have sensed my discomfort, because he asked, "Fusarium acting up again?" We both laughed, relieving the tension, but that provided only temporary relief.

Workers in the lumber yard started draping the stacks of boards outside and closing the roll-up doors leading inside. Most of the trucks were gone. A man in overalls walked to us and told CJ he'd have to leave as they would be locking everything up. Someone was already starting to close the parking lot entrance, securing the whole lumber yard in chain link fencing.

CJ drove out of the lot as the gate was locked behind us and pulled to the side of the road. Again, we sat in silence.

"You think we should enter the warehouse like we're customers or lost?" I asked.

"Let's wait a little longer. There's something funny going on. I'll bet not everyone in these parts loves Happy Sun. Maybe our guy walked into a trap, and they killed him. Far-fetched idea, I know, but I sure wouldn't want to stumble into a murder scene."

"We haven't even seen anybody leave, so they aren't in a hurry to dump the body someplace if they did kill him."

"Let's get something to eat," CJ said, "then come back after dark. The place should be empty by then, and we can look inside."

CJ made a U-turn and drove back to town. We checked into an inexpensive hotel next to a diner and got burgers for dinner. By the time we were finished, it was almost dark. We drove back to the nameless warehouse we had watched earlier. The same trucks were parked in front. It appeared that no one had come or gone.

CJ parked on the road in front of the warehouse, and we stared. It was dark for the most part, but lights emanated from cracks near the building corners and from below one of the loading dock doors.

"I thought the place would be deserted by now," CJ said.

"Do you think people live there?" I asked.

"Anything's possible. As you know, people who work on farms often live nearby or on the property, but I don't see any farms around here."

As we spoke, a box truck approached. Afraid it might barrel into us since CJ's truck was a dark color and the shoulder was narrow, I told CJ to turn on his lights. Before he did so, the approaching truck braked and pulled into the parking lot of the warehouse we were watching, next to the trucks already there.

The driver exited his vehicle and knocked loudly on the warehouse door—loud enough for us to hear from across the street.

Outdoor lights lit up the area outside, revealing the Happy Sun logo on the truck door. The driver was an Asian man, who was greeted by a woman in a lab coat, also Asian. They had a short conversation, and the woman pointed to the loading dock to her left. After hopping back in the truck, the driver maneuvered around the other vehicles, then backed into the middle bay of the loading dock, opened the back of the truck's cargo area, and waited.

I wondered if he was about to unload several large drums containing dead bodies. I wasn't sure about the size of a nuclear warhead but thought a few might fit into the truck. Several minutes later, the door in front of the truck rolled up, revealing a well-lit space filled with boxes and equipment.

An Asian man driving a forklift carrying black trays stacked in a sturdy frame emerged. Straining our eyes, we could see that each tray contained many seedlings planted in dirt. The frame holding the trays was transferred to the truck, and the forklift driver went back into the building. He returned a few minutes later with another stack of seedling trays. Several trips were made, and I estimated about eighty trays in all were loaded onto the truck, each having a different colored label. We were too far away to read the writing, but we figured it was Korean.

After the seedlings were loaded, the truck driver signed a sheet on a clipboard the woman in the lab coat brought him, closed the back of the truck, and drove off, headed in the direction he came from.

Once the truck was gone, the others returned to the building and closed all doors. CJ turned to me and asked, "What the fuck was that?"

Chapter 30

WE SAT IN THE truck and discussed what we'd just seen.

"Obviously, the guy we were following isn't the only one in the building," CJ said.

"It's so huge, there could be a hundred people in there."

"They probably live there."

"I'd sure like to know what's going on inside."

"Any ideas?" CJ asked.

"Maybe it's because of the classes I've taken, but the only thing I can think of after seeing all those seedlings is that this has something to do with crop genetic engineering."

"All their stuff is labeled non-GMO. The government oversees testing before anything can get that label," CJ said.

"I know, but I'm trying to make sense out of this. I've learned a bit about the GMO process in school. It's obviously very important in agriculture these days. I wonder if they've figured out a way to get genetically modified seeds certified as non-GMO."

"You think they're paying the inspectors off?"

"That's one possibility, but they may have thought of something else."

"Say they wanted to genetically modify their plants and get around the certification inspection," CJ said. "So what? They wouldn't have to pay the exorbitant prices charged by seed companies. Can't say I have a big problem with that. It's unfair to the other farmers, but I don't have much sympathy for the seed companies that are getting cheated out of their exorbitant profits. Still, I don't know why Happy Sun would want to spend so much money over here just so they could do that."

"I don't either. But what if they were modifying genes that make the food dangerous?"

"I haven't heard of anyone dying or even getting sick from their produce. They sell it all over, so it would be big news by now."

"You're right. I've even eaten some of their food myself and haven't gotten sick. I don't suppose my theory makes sense, but I can't escape the feeling that they're doing something involving genetic modification."

"What kinds of genes do seed companies modify to improve crops?" CJ asked.

"There's a variety of characteristics they go after. Typically, they insert a gene to make a protein that will generate the desired effect, such as disease prevention or insect resistance. Sometimes they eliminate genes like the one in peanuts that encodes for the protein many people are allergic to."

"Is it easy to do?"

"No. It requires a lot of expertise. I haven't done it myself, but I've learned about it in some of my courses. Before they begin, they need to isolate and modify the gene they are interested in. Next, they need to get that gene into the plant. They start by growing cells from the plant they want to change in tissue culture. Once there are enough cells, they insert the new gene into them. Then they test the cells to determine which ones have been successfully modified. The cells that pass the test are then grown into seedlings. After the seedlings are planted and mature into plants, they collect the seeds, which will have the modified DNA. After that, all they have to do is grow more plants from those seeds, and sell them to farmers. Sounds simpler than it is."

"I suppose it takes a lot of highly trained people and lots of time to get all that done."

"Right. Each step I described, up to planting the seedlings, requires highly trained people." I thought a moment before continuing. "Something's going on, or they wouldn't be so secretive. I don't know what kind of seedlings they're shipping, or where they're going, but I think it's important we find out. It doesn't look like we're going to get help from anyone in law enforcement until we have something solid."

"Right."

"We need to learn more about what they're doing. I doubt they're getting genetically modified seeds from North Korea, even if they're sent through China. If they were confiscated and tested, their operation would be discovered. I'd sure like to be a fly on the wall in there."

CJ's expression changed to one of excitement. "Speaking of flies reminds me—I have a friend with a drone. It's new and top-of-the-line. I'll ask if we can borrow it. We can fly it around here after the sun goes down. If we can see what's going on inside, we might be able to figure out what they're doing."

"Good idea," I said.

"I'm beat. Let's get some sleep. I'll call Adam in the morning."

We arrived at our hotel at 11:00 p.m. I imagine it was two stars at the most, but the small room and adjoining bathroom provided all we needed. I fell asleep as soon as my head hit the pillow.

The following morning, we had breakfast at the next-door diner, then returned to our room. CJ phoned Adam and asked to borrow his drone. After a long conversation, CJ told me he had some good news and some bad news. The good news: we could spy on the facility with his drone. The bad news: he insisted on giving us a long lesson on how to operate it.

"Did you tell him what we're going to use it for?"

"I just said we were worried a woman was being held against her will in a house down the block. I wanted to use the drone to look inside so I could be sure before calling the cops."

"Good idea," I said. "Right now, I think the fewer people who know about this, the better."

"Unfortunately, Adam is busy with work today and tomorrow, so we can't pick up the drone for two days. We can go back to my cousin's house and wait." CJ warned me that his friend was depressed, as he was still getting over a painful breakup with his former girlfriend six months earlier. He'd refused to meet several eligible young ladies CJ had tried to introduce him to.

We checked out of the hotel and decided to drive by the Happy Sun warehouse one more time before heading back to CJ's cousin's house.

The traffic was light, and we arrived at the warehouse in half an hour. As we passed by slowly, we noticed another truck being loaded with seedlings, similar to what we saw the night before. The door of the truck displayed a smiling sun. A quarter mile down the road, CJ pulled over.

"What do you think we should do now?" I asked.

"How about if we follow that truck when it leaves?"

"I was hoping you'd say that."

CJ made a U-turn and parked on the shoulder. We waited ten minutes, until the Happy Sun truck started up again and headed down the road. The road was flat, so CJ could see a long distance ahead and follow from far enough away to be unnoticed. A few miles down the road, the vehicle we were pursuing turned left onto a dirt road. When we got to the turnoff, we saw a cloud of dirt trailing behind the truck in the distance. On either side of the road were grape vines.

"You think we should follow?" I asked.

"Probably not a good idea. If someone's watching, they'll see the dirt we raise."

"How about we walk for a bit?"

It was mid-morning, but was already hot when we started walking. The Happy Sun truck had disappeared, but after covering about a half mile, it came into view in front of a warehouse, smaller than the large one we had just left farther up the road. Again, the building was gray, nondescript, windowless from the front, and had no sign. A brown entry door was at one end, a single loading dock was at the other. The roof of a second building in the rear peaked above the flat roof of the main building. We had a limited view of the edge of a field behind the warehouse. Several people were tending small plants growing there. I wished I had binoculars to see what was happening in greater detail.

"I think we should leave now," CJ said. "We can fly the drone here, too."

"Are you worried they might see it?"

"Unlikely, because it'll be dark. We'll have to take our chances." He paused a moment before continuing. "I don't think these guys would report illegal drone activity around their property to the police. But if they have guns, I wouldn't put it past them to shoot it down. I won't mention that to Adam. He'd refuse to let me borrow it. He seems to have an unnatural attachment to his beloved drone."

We drove back to Bakersfield and picked up several dishes to go from Best Korean BBQ. We reheated it for dinner, surprising Melinda with the inviting smell of charcoal and meat when she arrived home.

Although she'd never tried Korean barbecue before, Melinda enjoyed the dinner as much as CJ and I. While we ate, Melinda complained about her day at work, when she had to deal with a co-worker who was a jerk. We told her we'd been to Tulare to visit a friend.

Chapter 31

ALL ROSE AS GENERAL Bai took the podium. The room was large with white walls. Prominently displayed on the stage next to the speaker was a red flag with a central white circle surrounding a five-pointed red star. Blue and white stripes formed borders at the top and bottom. It was the flag of Ramhongsaek Konghwagukgi, or the Democratic People's Republic of Korea. Westerners refer to the country simply as North Korea. A large portrait of Kim Jong Un was on the wall behind the speaker. Several honored guests, one in a long white lab coat, the others in decorated military uniforms, sat on the dais on the side opposite the flag.

The general gestured for everyone to sit before he began speaking. "We are gathered here to honor a great man. His dedicated work will be rewarded with the highest honor our government can bestow on a great scientist.

"At first, we were led astray by our previous team of inferior scientists who followed in the footsteps of their predecessors, never coming up with an original idea. Their minds were stuck on old, worn methodology—chemical warfare. Every substance they recommended was shown to be incapable of fulfilling our goal. They repeatedly presented scenarios using primitive gasses like phosgene and mustard gas, poisons such as cyanide and sarin gas, and the most advanced chemicals, neurotoxins including VX and Novichok. Each had countless unsurmountable problems.

"All would have to be synthesized in the United States in large volumes, as importing them in sufficient amounts would be impossible. For many of these chemicals, the manufacturing precursors are tightly regulated by the American government, making it unfeasible for us to make them there. Lingering contamination with many of them is a problem which would make buildings and land unusable. Rapid chemical distribution in lethal concentrations is another area our scientists could not overcome. However, perhaps the biggest drawback of all of these chemicals is that they would kill all animals indiscriminately, including livestock. Instead of supplying us with an enormous supply of consumable protein, all the cattle, poultry, pigs, dogs, and cats would only present a huge disposal problem.

"Dr. Gang had a fresh approach, one that is sure to succeed. We are now poised to inflict great damage on the imperialist country of the United States. We are ahead of schedule for Operation America Takeover and will be ready to unleash our great destructive weapon in less than six months. Once the enemy is under our command, the rest of the world will follow, one country after the next. They will all see the futility of resisting and will quickly surrender without a fight. And now, I'd like to present the Hero of Labor Award to Dr. Hoon Gang."

To great applause, the man wearing the lab coat rose from his chair on the stage and maintained a serious demeanor as the general presented him with the Korea Hero of Labor medal. Dr. Gang bowed politely, then stood before the microphone. The revered scientist praised the Supreme Leader of the Democratic People's Republic of Korea, and spoke of the great honor bestowed upon him simply for doing his best to help his beloved country. He hoped that, in his small way, he had significantly advanced the cause of worldwide domination.

He resumed his seat to great applause, followed by rousing speeches from the other luminaries on the dais.

This was the happiest day of Dr. Gang's life.

Chapter 32

THE FOLLOWING DAY, WE needed to stay busy as we waited for our drone lesson. CJ phoned a friend with connections to the police department.

"Find out anything interesting?" I asked when the call ended.

"Looks like they've confirmed that Danielle's death was from a fentanyl overdose. No surprise there. But he also told me that one of the farmers I'd warned about Happy Sun died yesterday. His wife had left him home alone watching a baseball game while she went shopping. When she returned, he was dead on the kitchen floor. He was a bit overweight and had a history of untreated high cholesterol, so the coroner is saying he died from natural causes."

"I'll bet that's bullshit. Sounds just like my dad. Despite your warning, they got to him somehow. Probably arranged for a person he knew to give it to him."

"Sure looks like it. The widow is expected to sell the farm to Happy Sun."

CJ and I spent the rest of the day trying to occupy our minds by visiting a park and two different coffee shops, although we couldn't help but think about the following night when we planned to carry out our fact-finding mission using the drone.

The next morning, we drove to Adam's residence, a small farmhouse five miles from Happy Sun. As we rode over the gravel driveway leading to his front door, I noticed plenty of fields around to demonstrate the capabilities of the drone. Adam met us outside as we were getting out of the truck. He was around CJ's age, of average height, and noticeably muscular. His hair was dirty and unkempt, his beard several days old, and he smelled slightly of body odor. He was in no shape to meet available women.

CJ introduced us, and we exchanged a few pleasantries. Adam didn't smile much but was congenial, if not overly friendly. He struck me as someone who was looking for a reason to get up in the morning. That morning, his reason for getting up was us.

He showed us how to manipulate the drone, which looked like a black four-legged crab with a propeller on each leg. Its small size and dark color would allow it to easily escape detection by a security camera in an unlit environment. We learned to direct the small craft in all directions: right and left, forward and backward, up and down. I was surprised by the impressive resolution on the Wi-Fi-connected color screen.

Once we'd gotten the hang of coarsely operating the gadget in the wide-open space, Adam homed in on operating the zoom lens, fine-focusing details, and lighting. That's when I realized we would need a drone equipped with night vision. As I thought about that, CJ asked, "Does this thing work at night?"

Like a proud father, Adam answered, "I'm glad you asked. This baby is equipped with thermal and infrared imaging capabilities. She's got everything. Are you planning to do your investigation after dark?"

"Most likely."

"Your picture won't be as sharp, but you'll be able to see if there's someone in the house being held captive. Now that I think of it, I better show you how to guide her through a window and around a room. That's going to be more important to you than how to control the fine focus."

We spent several hours flying the small aircraft in and out of open windows and around Adam's house while we controlled it from the outside. We discovered that Adam had a crucifix on the bedroom wall across from his bed but left his bed unmade. The kitchen was surprisingly clean, so I assumed he didn't cook. On the kitchen table were several pistols he appeared to be in the midst of cleaning. We were pretty tired after our training.

"Thanks for being such a great teacher," I said as we were getting ready to leave.

"We'll keep your baby safe," CJ added.

"She's fully charged now," Adam said, "but don't forget—the battery life is only about forty-five minutes."

Back in the truck, we drove to Tulare and ate an early dinner at a restaurant rated four stars on Yelp. It would be hours before dark, so after CJ reserved a room in a local motel, we killed some time by exploring the local sports park. We happened upon a children's soccer game, which kept us occupied for an hour. Then, we walked around until it was almost dark before leaving.

Brimming with curiosity, anticipation, and a bit of fear, we drove down the highway to visit the first Happy Sun facility we'd found in the Tulare area. By the time we reached it, the sun was completely down. The building was dark. CJ parked the truck next door, in front of the lumber yard's locked gate. The quarter moon provided some ambient light, but not much.

We started to exit the truck when we saw headlights approaching.

"Duck!" CJ yelled.

Together, we ducked behind his pick-up and waited as the vehicle approached. When it was close, it slowed and turned into the driveway in front of the Happy Sun building. In the moonlight, we could see that the vehicle was a UPS truck. The driver exited and rang at the door. The same woman we'd seen before turned on the outside lights and stepped outside. She directed the driver to the loading dock to her left, and the driver, a young Black man, backed his truck into one of the bays.

The warehouse door rolled up, and a man driving a forklift emerged. He and the UPS driver loaded boxes from the truck onto a palette. After delivering them inside, the forklift driver returned for more boxes. They were a mixture of large and small, square and rectangular cartons. Without binoculars, I was unable to read any of the labels. After delivering the goods, the truck departed. The woman walked in our direction, then closed and locked the fence to the driveway entrance. We remained crouched and held our breaths until she returned to the building and turned off the lights.

A few minutes passed before we thought it was safe to deploy the drone. We quickly set it up, with CJ at the controls. First, he flew it around the building perimeter. Five cars were parked in the back, including the one we had followed from the Korean restaurant. The drone soared over the land around the building and revealed only uncultivated fields of dirt and weeds. Lights were on in the rear, hidden from the road. We concluded people lived there. From what we'd already seen, it didn't appear that the residents left the facility often. Although there weren't a lot of cars, many people might have been inside.

After gleaning what we could from the outside assessment, it was time to explore the interior of the building. The drone was quiet, but not silent. We needed to keep it away from the people inside if possible.

"I can't find any open windows," CJ said.

"Damn," I said. "Try the roof."

CJ maneuvered the drone over the top of the building. With the camera pointed below, a large skylight came into view. It was open, the glass panel raised approximately thirty degrees. Only a faint light was visible in the room underneath it. CJ maneuvered the drone through the opening, clearing the edges. I hoped our practice earlier in the day adequately prepared us for controlling our spy craft inside.

As much as I tried to relax, my shoulders tensed, and my heart raced as I watched the screen CJ was holding. The flying gadget was in a dimly lit room that looked like a lab. A small amount of light emanated from the glowing buttons on the electronic equipment. That illumination, combined with the drone's night vision technology, allowed us to visualize lab benches with incubators, microscopes, scales, glassware, and other equipment occupying much of the counter space.

"You know what all that stuff is?" CJ asked.

"Most of it," I answered.

I took over the controls so I could look in more detail at the items that interested me, and narrated what was in view for CJ's benefit. An open notebook was on one bench, but I couldn't read the writing even at a close distance. That was partly due to the low resolution from the dim light, and the fact that the writing appeared to be in Korean. A large picture of Kim Jong Un was affixed to the wall. "That nails it," I said. "This is a North Korean company."

I navigated the small aircraft to more rooms filled with laboratory equipment. Although I couldn't discern colors in the low light, the objects in view were sharp. Stacks of trays growing seedlings occupied almost all the space in one of the labs. Light for growing the seedlings was supplied by towers of LED's adjacent to the trays.

Another room housed fifteen motorized countertop platforms, each approximately two by three and a half feet in size. Every platform held eight Erlenmeyer flasks—the triangular flasks often used by chemists and other scientists—partially filled with liquid. They were bigger than any flask I'd used in my lab classes and suitable for industrial use. Each was secured in place by clips affixed to the underlying platform, which gently moved, swirling the contents.

A nearby laboratory had large incubators with glass doors. Inside were numerous roller bottles, two-liter bottles containing a pink fluid. The bottles rested on their sides and were held by racks made of slowly rotating cylinders, gently turning the vessels they supported.

Hurrying along, the drone entered a room where half-liter bottles stood on a conveyor belt which was idle at the moment. It appeared that when operating, the bottles passed under a reservoir, where they were filled with liquid, and then a spray nozzle was screwed on. A box nearly full of assembled spray bottles was near the end of the conveyor belt.

In another room, small canisters holding approximately one hundred milliliters were being prepared in a similar way. Small nozzles were attached after they were filled.

Traveling down a hallway, the spy craft discovered several large rooms that opened to the loading dock bays. Boxes of supplies were stacked. Printing on the outside of the boxes was written in English. I could make out a few words like "Fragile" and "Caution" on the outside of some of them. I assumed this was where they stored their laboratory chemicals and supplies, purchased here, in the US.

"Damn," I said. "I've already used up thirty minutes of battery time."

"Better bring her in," CJ responded.

I maneuvered the drone back through the skylight and brought it to rest at our feet. We hurried back to the truck and drove to the facility where the seedlings had been delivered. After turning on the dirt road leading up to it, CJ parked a safe distance away. With the help of our flashlights, we walked towards the compound. CJ carried the drone in a backpack.

A few rays of light escaped small openings near the roof of the warehouse. What we could see of the second building and the fields was dark. No one was visible when CJ directed the airborne gadget to fly low around the area behind the warehouse. Looking at the screen, we learned there was a field divided into six relatively small areas, each with a different crop. Some of the plants were tiny, the size of the seedlings recently delivered. Others were large, past their prime for harvesting, and had gone to seed. A tall wire fence surrounded the back and sides of the field. On one side was a dense growth of bushes just inside the fencing. A harvesting machine stood idly nearby.

The unlit building behind the warehouse was a barn-like structure fifty yards away.

"We're in luck," CJ said. "No windows, but the sliding door is open."

He directed the drone inside. Lighting from instrument LEDs provided enough illumination for me to identify several pieces of equipment that looked similar to seed harvesting machines I'd seen at Purdue. Large bins of seeds stood near some of the equipment. Time was of the essence, so after the small aircraft flew around the interior space, CJ brought it out and circled the warehouse.

A high window in the rear, near the end with the loading dock, was open. CJ steered the drone through it, into a dark hallway. Light came from one direction. The other direction showed only darkness. CJ guided the spy craft away from the light, then through an open doorway that came into view. Seeing a large, roll-up door ahead, we knew we were looking inside the storage area behind the loading dock. CJ directed the drone to sealed bins stacked against one wall. They looked like those partially filled with seeds we'd seen in the other building and were neatly labeled in Korean.

"What do you make of all of this?" CJ asked me.

"It looks like they're planting seedlings for the sole purpose of harvesting their seeds. These bins are most likely full of seeds they've produced here and are ready to be shipped to the main farm near what used to be my home." Just saying used to be my home made me sad, but I couldn't dwell on those painful feelings.

"You think those seeds have been genetically modified?"

"I can't tell by looking, of course, but I can't think of another reason they're collecting seeds. There's a lot going on in that lab at the other warehouse, and—"

"Damn!" CJ interrupted, "there's less than five minutes of power left." He started to direct the spy craft up, preparing to steer it back to us. We were stunned when a bright light suddenly lit up the room.

Chapter 33

CJ REACTED QUICKLY AND directed the drone to hover as high as possible near the ceiling. A man, Asian of course, entered and looked around nervously, then stood with his back against the wall near the storage room entrance. Dressed in pajamas and slippers, he was holding a cell phone. After entering a number, he began speaking as he gestured with his hands. I would have given anything to be able to record the conversation. The secretive nature of his actions led me to conclude he was breaking protocol. As important as the call was, I wanted him to keep it short so the small aircraft hovering above wouldn't run out of power and crash to the floor before he was through.

I was relieved when the fellow ended the call in less than a minute. He turned and reached up to shut off the light. That's when I realized he was missing his left fourth finger. "Holy cow," I shouted. "Did you see that?"

"See what?" CJ asked.

"That man has a missing fourth finger."

"I saw it. Probably a bad encounter with farm machinery."

"The couple I saw in the still—the man had a missing fourth finger. This is the same guy. He said he was going to be transferred to Tulare, and here he is."

"Are you thinking what I'm thinking?" CJ asked as he steered the drone down the hallway.

"Sure am. He didn't want to be transferred here, away from his girlfriend. That's who he most likely called. He's got to be mad. He wanted to defect before, so he'd probably cooperate with us if we could help him arrange for that."

CJ maneuvered the flying gadget out the window where it had entered, as we held our breaths. We both whooped in excitement, quietly of course, as it emerged above the building. Less than a minute later, it landed at our feet. According to the gauge, it had about thirty seconds of power to spare.

"Adam would have killed me if his baby crashed," CJ said as he folded the device and slipped it into its carrying bag.

We wasted no time getting back into the truck and driving to the motel CJ had reserved in Tulare. By the time we checked in, all the restaurants were closed. We quickly plugged the power cord into the drone to recharge it, then went to a nearby grocery store and loaded up on snacks. We brought them back to our room, where we sat on the queen bed, eating chips and drinking beer. We needed to come up with a plan to extract the man missing his left fourth finger and convince him to cooperate with us. He appeared to be a low-level worker and might not know much, but he could likely point us in the right direction.

"We've got to find a way to connect with this guy," I said.

"Sure, but how? He seems to be locked up in that fucking building where we can't possibly get to him. On top of that, he doesn't even speak English."

"That's why it won't be easy." We sat in silence for a while, thinking. A few minutes later I had an idea. It wasn't well-formed, just a seed. "We could make a small sign. I'm sure Kwan would help us."

"What'll it say?"

"Something like 'Want to defect?' or 'Need help?' What do you think? If we see him in a field or someplace outside when no one is around, we can hold it up so he could see it."

CJ thought a moment. "I don't think he's going to go for something like that. If I were him, I'd feel it was too risky, even if I did want to defect. Those North Koreans don't fool around. One false move, and you're dead."

"Do you have another suggestion?"

"I do, but you're not going to like it."

"Try me."

"We kidnap him."

His answer surprised me. "How are we going to do that?" I asked.

"I haven't worked that out yet. But I think if we can get him alone, just you, me, and a translator, we could convince him to help us. He could get asylum and live here happily ever after."

We decided to sleep on it. Maybe we'd come up with a good idea for kidnapping the man in our dreams. But when morning came, we still had no plan. We drove to Adam's house and returned his drone. He asked if we'd found evidence the woman up the street was imprisoned. I'd forgotten about the ruse we'd used to borrow his precious toy. I let CJ answer, not wanting to risk us speaking at the same time with conflicting answers. CJ assured Adam the woman he had worried about was safe and free to come and go as she pleased.

CJ hooked the drone up to the USB port on Adam's computer so I could download the video from the previous night to a thumb drive I had brought. While I was occupied with that, CJ took Adam to another room to talk. We didn't want him to see what we had really used the drone for. Once the files were downloaded, I put the thumb drive in my purse, then went outside where CJ and Adam were in deep conversation. I feigned a headache so we could leave quickly without insulting our host. From there, we went directly to CJ's cousin's house.

CJ and I spent the afternoon reviewing the drone videos on Melinda's computer. First, we studied recordings from the larger of the two warehouses. Seedlings were being grown, but how? We didn't see any seeds in that facility. They could have been out of the drone's field of surveillance, but I was drawn back to the idea they were growing genetically modified plants from single cells.

Such an operation would be super costly, and I was puzzled by the fact that their produce was priced very low. Perhaps their modified crops had much higher yields than normal. If they were growing just one crop on all the land they'd acquired, it might make sense to go through the expense of genetically modifying that one plant, but they were growing a large array of fruits and vegetables. Developing genetically modified variants of all of them would be ridiculously expensive. The people in their country were starving, so I thought that if they could easily produce more food, they would first do it there.

I racked my brain as I reviewed the drone video, rewatching segments often when I needed to study a detail. Even with the microscopes, incubators, and other equipment I saw, I didn't think they could be performing genetic modification of plants right there. If I was wrong, I had no clue what the genetic modification might be. I understood that a company would want to claim its products were non-GMO even if they weren't, to attract more customers. How Happy Sun Farms could get around the testing needed for certification was, however, beyond me.

As I'd never done it myself, I didn't know details about the process of inserting genes into plants, but I did know you need a lot of highly specialized equipment and trained scientists to pull it off. Testing each gene modified is a painstaking task. Developing just a single edited gene to insert into plant DNA can take years. The modified plants need to be grown and tested. Then changes in the inserted DNA are made as needed, followed by another cycle of growing and testing.

It was possible that a gene or genes had been developed and tested elsewhere, then brought to Tulare to be introduced into plant cells there. A gene is, of course, incredibly tiny—submicroscopic. I could envision being able to smuggle DNA into the country unnoticed. It would still require a lot of expertise to successfully introduce a pre-made gene into plant cells. Could they have all the expertise needed for such an extraordinary feat living there, in that innocuous building in Tulare, right under our noses? Possibly.

None of that addressed the roller bottles. They are typically used to grow living things such as animal or plant cells. As the vessels are slowly turned, the liquid in them bathes cells which form a thin layer on the bottles' inner surface. Sometimes cells are grown to produce viruses, which require living cells to proliferate. At other times, they are propagated because they secrete a substance, usually a protein, into the growth medium. That substance can be collected and purified. To my knowledge, roller bottles have no clear role in making genetically modified plants.

Then there were the Erlenmeyer flasks, spray bottles, and canisters. Where did they fit it? I couldn't come up with a coherent way to connect all the dots.

Reviewing the video of the seed harvesting facility took relatively little time. I didn't need to rewind any portions. It appeared that seedlings growing in trays at the larger facility were shipped there and planted in the soil, where they were harvested when their seeds were ready. The seeds were collected and prepared for shipment, likely to the main farm.

I wanted to have something solid to bring to the FBI. Perhaps my video would be enough, but they'd have no reason to believe I hadn't just recorded fields at a farm and legitimate laboratories at a university or biotech company.

Thinking about a biotech company reminded me of Frangelica Grabowski, or Fran, as we called her. She was two years ahead of me at Purdue, majoring in plant biotechnology. Her studies focused on producing genetically modified plants. We had emailed and texted each other after she graduated and started working in a plant biotech firm in San Diego, California, but our back-and-forth messages fizzled out. I hadn't heard from her in over a year but still had her old contact information. As I hit "Call," I hoped she hadn't changed her number.

Chapter 34

FRAN ANSWERED MY CALL almost immediately. "How's my favorite non-genetically modified strawberry?" she asked.

"Honestly, that would be hard to answer in just a few words. I wanted to give you a call, not only because I miss you, of course, but because I'm in California."

"San Diego, by any chance?" she asked cheerily, which was her usual way of speaking.

"No, but not too far. Near Bakersfield."

"You must be visiting your family. No other reason to be in Bakersfield." Fran chuckled.

"My dad died."

Fran's tone became serious. "I'm so sorry to hear that. How are you and your mom doing?"

"My mom left town to be with a friend, so I was left here to take care of everything. Mom sold the farm."

"Dang. Sorry to hear that. I remember you wanted to help out with the management and turn things around for them."

"Good memory. Now I have to change my plans."

"Any chance you can make it down here for a visit?" Fran asked.

"I can't get away right now. In fact, I was hoping you could come here for a day or two to help me understand something."

"You need help with a class?" Fran asked. "I don't remember you needing help before."

"This isn't about a class. This is about a real-life situation that's very troubling."

"You know I'd love to help you, but I'm just a plant geneticist. What could I possibly help you with?"

"Plant genetics."

Fran laughed. "Now I know you're bullshitting me."

"Actually, I'm not." I explained that a foreign-owned company bought my parents' farm, and most of the surrounding farms. They were ripping out many of the good crops and replanting with seeds that I believed were genetically modified.

"That's not unusual. Many farmers like the improvements genetic modification makes in plants."

"But they label their produce 'non-GMO.'"

"Definitely dishonest, but I'm not surprised a foreign company might try to do that. I know a lot of the public is worried about genetic modification of plants, but I don't have to convince you that I'm confident all the approved modifications are safe. You can expect the company to run into problems when they're inspected. Others have tried and failed certification when they use genetically modified seeds. You don't need any help from me. Just wait for their inspection. They'll get caught."

"Not likely. They haven't been caught yet. They've already been inspected and certified. I don't think they're buying their seeds here."

"You think they're trying to illegally reproduce patented US genetically modified seeds? Now that I think of it, I wouldn't be surprised if a country like China tried to do that. They steal so much intellectual property it would make sense. I imagine government people are looking into that already. Is this country owned by China, by any chance?"

"That's what I thought at first, but now I think it's owned by Korea. North Korea."

Fran was silent for a moment. "I don't think our government would allow a North Korean company to do business here."

"The people operating the farm are pretending to be Chinese, but they're really North Korean."

"Sounds pretty wild. Even if what you're telling me is true, how can I possibly help? The company whose intellectual property is being stolen will take action if they learn about it. They make a lot of money and don't need my help."

“It’s not as simple as that. They’re doing things I don’t understand, and I was hoping you could visit me and look at the videos I have of their lab.”

“They have a lab, and they let you tour and record it?”

“They have a lab, but they didn’t exactly let me tour it. I got the videos surreptitiously. Now I need someone with more knowledge than me to help me figure out what’s going on.”

“Can you bring your videos here or email them to me?” Fran asked.

“I was hoping you could go over them with one of the workers at the company. He might be able to explain things that aren’t clear.”

“If you have someone who knows all about it, why don’t you just ask him directly? You don’t need me.”

“He’s not a scientist. I don’t think he’d understand what you would.”

"What has he told you already?"

I was glad Fran couldn't see me, because I'm sure I looked flustered. "Nothing yet."

Fran was silent a moment before continuing. “Have you spoken to him?”

“No, but I plan to very soon. With a translator.”

“I can’t get away to Bakersfield but let me know when you have everything lined up—your North Korean and your translator. Maybe we can work something out with a video chat. I have to admit, although this sounds a bit far-fetched, you’ve piqued my curiosity.”

We ended the call, and I turned to CJ. “We have to figure out how to get that guy out of there.”

“You didn’t like my kidnapping idea. Got a better one?”

“My best idea is I think we should brainstorm over coffee.”

We went to a nearby café and ordered coffee and pastries. Nothing like sugar and caffeine to get our brains working. We had no dearth of bad ideas. We quickly realized starting a fire wasn’t a good plan. Neither was reporting a kidnapping in progress to the local police. Pretending to be door-to-door salesmen wouldn’t work if none of them spoke English. It was more likely we’d raise suspicion and be murdered than succeed in smuggling our guy out. If we did manage to get him out, we’d need him to cooperate, but if he didn’t know who we were, I expected he would fight like hell. They likely had security cameras, so we doubted we could sneak into the building without being found.

Yet, after much debate and two cups of coffee each, we had a plan.

Chapter 35

THE FOLLOWING MORNING, WE went to several strip malls in the area to pick up what we needed. Next, we drove the truck down a dirt road that took us behind the side of the Happy Sun Farm fence, which was hidden by shrubs. CJ retrieved a trowel and a large bolt cutter from behind his seat. I brought two six-inch pieces of wire. Using the bolt cutter, CJ began clipping the wire fence to create three sides of a thirty-inch-wide square opening. The vegetation hid him from the scattered farm workers in the fields. Once he'd made the final cut, CJ bent the cut fence back, making a door large enough for a person to fit through. Then he put the trowel to work, creating a short, six-inch-wide tunnel under the fence.

He stood up to stretch his legs. "You ready?" he asked, looking at me obliquely, a sly smile on his face.

I took two deep breaths to clear my mind. "As ready as I'll ever be. Let's do it."

We both began hauling cages out of the truck bed, placing them on the ground as close as possible to the fence door CJ had created. There were twenty cages in all. One by one, we opened them and guided the three bunnies inside each through the bushes on the other side of the fence, into the field where young, tasty crops were growing. In no time, the fields were swarming with bunnies, devouring everything they came upon.

I couldn't help but smile as I looked through the thick foliage and saw the workers running around, trying to scare all the cute little furry animals away. I'd read that bunnies aren't found in North Korea. Farmers there don't take measures to protect their crops from them, so no protective fencing was in place to protect the Happy Sun crops.

The field workers started yelling for help. We watched as fifteen men and women poured out of the building, onto the field. The man with the missing left fourth finger was amongst them. We waited patiently, or at least tried to be patient, as we watched him pick up bunnies and hand them to one of three men walking around with a large pail.

After collecting four of the cute little cuddly animals into their buckets, the men walked around the building towards the front, then returned with empty buckets to collect more. We hadn't given much consideration to how the workers would ultimately get rid of the bunnies. As the scene unfolded, I wished we had thought about that aspect of the operation. I hoped they let them loose on the long driveway in front of the building. I heard no gunshots but couldn't rule out the possibility they did away with them using knives or other means.

About half the bunnies had been cleared when our intended target, the man with the missing finger, neared the fence door CJ had created. I had put two cages still containing bunnies to the side and lay in wait until he was close enough to see three bunnies come through when I opened one of the cages.

As they scampered through the fence opening, the man dropped to all fours and looked at the ground between the bushes from where they had emerged. CJ immediately flung his arm through the opening, dropped a piece of paper in front of our target, then grabbed one of his arms. The man emitted a faint startled yelp, then looked at and read it.

We had driven to Bakersfield the day before and engaged Kwan's services to compose a series of questions for the potential North Korean defector. The first question we presented asked, "Would you like to become an American?"

The man looked confused. I imagined he was wondering if this was a trap set up by his superiors. He looked around and appeared ready to forcibly free his arm and dart away. I retrieved the taser I was carrying and zapped him, the very person we needed to trust us. The prongs landed on his arms, and he went down. Fortunately, being on all fours, he didn't have far to fall. CJ raced to drag the limp body between the bushes and through the fence hole. The man began to stir almost immediately. Looking around, he must have seen the opening in the fence, as his colleagues were noisily chasing down bunnies.

I held up another sign. "We want to be your friend."

The man stared at us, wide-eyed.

I had hoped he'd immediately see that we could help him escape North Korean control and live happily ever after as a free man in the United States. I should have anticipated his more circumspect reaction. If I were born and raised in a country where I wasn't free to go against authority or express my true thoughts, where spies would turn me in if I said the wrong thing, I wouldn't trust someone I didn't know. It could easily land me in a prison camp.

I held up the next sign: "What is your name?"

The man thought a moment, then said, "Bong."

We were making progress. Now we had a name. I was tired of referring to him as the man with the missing left fourth finger. I realized seconds later that my sign should have specified he answer with his name only. Fortunately, he simply said "Bong," not with a sentence such as "my name in Bong. Nice to meet you." I'd never be able to fish his name out of such a massive number of Korean words.

I held up another sign. "We want to make you an American. Would you like that? Point to your answer." Below were the Korean words for "yes" and "no."

Bong looked around. He seemed hesitant, then closed his eyes a few moments as if praying. Seconds later, he opened his eyes and pointed to the word for "yes."

We both smiled. I didn't remember breathing for the previous few minutes, ever since I'd tasered him, but I was breathing easily now, the muscles in my chest and arms relaxed.

I held up another sign. "We are sorry we used a stun gun, but there was no other way to talk to you."

Bong appeared to be awaiting our next move, preparing to scoot backward through the fence if need be. I held up another sign. This could make or break our plan. "We need five seeds from here, five milliliters of fluid from a flask on a shaker platform, and five milliliters of fluid from a roller bottle in the lab building. If you agree to give us that, we will take you with us and hide you."

Bong smiled and vigorously shook his head from side to side. Kwan had warned us that Koreans shake their head from side to side when they mean "yes."

Using a combination of Google Translate and pre-printed signs, we arranged to meet at the same place in three days at noon. Before he crawled back through the fence, we gave Bong the three bunnies I had held in reserve to carry back through the fence. He could tell others he found a hole where the bunnies were getting through. We quickly closed the fence door and held it in place with the two wire segments I had taken with me. If someone from the facility investigated, they'd figure the bunnies had come through the tunnel under the fence and fill it with dirt.

I was optimistic as we drove away. There was no guarantee Bong would be able to collect the samples we wanted and escape with us, but we had to be prepared. CJ and I drove to Bakersfield to meet with Kwan. We needed to determine how much time he could commit to helping us.

Chapter 36

OUTSIDE BAKERSFIELD, CJ SPOTTED a self-service car wash. We unloaded the empty bunny cages in a nearby dumpster and thoroughly cleaned the truck. The bed was filthy with bunny urine and droppings pooling in the gutters between the ridges. After several washes, CJ was satisfied that his pick-up had been restored to its pristine condition.

We arrived at Best Korean BBQ around 4:00 p.m. Business was slow at that hour, and the dining room was almost empty. We found Kwan in the kitchen.

"We expect to have a defector from North Korea with us in a few days. He doesn't speak English, so we're hoping you can translate for us."

"I would be most happy to do that, but I need to work. Come back here when you need me, and I'll get away from the kitchen as much as I can."

"Hope to see you soon," I said.

We were driving back to Melinda's house when I received a call from Martina. "I can't reach my dad," she said, foregoing any sort of greeting. Her voice wavered in a way that revealed she was crying. Her sniffles confirmed that impression. "He hasn't met me at our meeting spot two times in a row."

"When's the last time you spoke to him?"

"Four days ago. We met every other day. He missed our last meeting, and when I went to see him this morning, he wasn't there. I'm very worried. I drove into the main entrance of the farm earlier today, but they told me he was busy working and couldn't be interrupted. They wouldn't let me past the guard gate."

"Did you call the police?"

"I did, but I know they won't do anything. They never look into complaints about Happy Sun. I'm calling you out of desperation, hoping you'll have an idea."

"Did he say anything unusual the last time you spoke to him? Anything to make you think he felt unsafe?"

"He never felt safe after Carlos was killed. He would have left but thought he would be murdered, too, and they might even come after me."

"Let's think about this," I said. "Your dad's a smart man, and I don't see him doing anything foolish. He's also a good worker, and that's exactly what Happy Sun needs, so I don't think they would harm him without good reason. They killed Carlos to make an example of him so no one else would leave. It doesn't make sense they would harm people like your dad who stayed. There's got to be a reason we don't know about."

"I know, but I don't trust them. If they didn't harm him or—" Martina started to cry before she was able to force her next words out, "or kill him, then where is he?"

"Do you have a picture of him you could send me?"

"Only about a thousand."

"Text me one or two recent ones. If your father felt he was in danger, he's probably hiding out."

Martina stopped crying. "Where would he hide? If he left Happy Sun Farm, I know he would have contacted me. If he's still there, I don't think he could avoid being found by the people who run the place."

"If I were him, I'd be hiding in my dad's underground bunker."

Martina gasped. "He had an underground bunker?"

"I guess you didn't know about it. I only learned of it when I was going through my parents' things. Your father helped build it. He was one of the few people my dad trusted. Most likely, Dad told him to keep it a secret."

"Dad was always good at keeping secrets. He kept plenty of things I did from my mom," Martina said. "Otherwise, I would have gotten in a whole lot more trouble."

"I imagine if your father felt he was in imminent danger, he would have thought he could go through my parents' house and escape from Happy Sun out the front, then run down the road to safety. Unfortunately, with the house now surrounded by Happy Sun people, he wouldn't be able to leave."

"Could he get to the bunker from the house?"

"Yes, it's accessed from the master bedroom. If he's there, he's going to need help to get out safely. I can't go back there myself without being killed, but maybe CJ can get one of his friends to do it."

"I don't think he's there because he hasn't contacted me." Martina started weeping again as soon as the words were out.

I waited for the sobs to stop before speaking. "There's no cell phone or internet service in the bunker. Unless your dad knows how to operate a ham radio, he'd have no way to contact you from there. He could stay safe there for a long time because there's enough food and water to last months."

"What if he's not there?"

"Let's find out and worry about that if we need to. There's every reason to be optimistic. I'll talk to CJ and come up with a plan, then call you back."

"Thanks, Berry. I hope to hear from you soon. This can't wait."

As soon as we disconnected, I turned to CJ and relayed Martina's concerns. "I hope you can get a friend of yours to look in my old home. He could pretend I hired him online to deliver some items from the house to a storage unit in Bakersfield. I'll have to explain where the entrance to my dad's bunker is."

"This would be a perfect job for Adam. He needs something to focus on, and he's strong as an ox. I'll call him when we get back to Melinda's. Adam works for a small moving company, so he'll look totally legit when he arrives with a moving van. I know he's been a bit off since his girlfriend dumped him, but underneath it all, he's a good guy, and I trust him. Hell, we went through catechism together. I've known him that long."

"Are you Catholic?"

"Is the pope?" He chuckled. "My mom's Italian, so of course, I was raised Catholic. Don't really practice it now, but Adam still does."

"As long as he can be trusted, sounds perfect. We can get him a large chest to bring on the moving van. Diego isn't very big, so he could fit inside. I just hope he's there."

When we were in Melinda's kitchen, CJ called Adam, who agreed to rescue Diego the next day. CJ put the phone on speaker, and I explained exactly how to find the door to my dad's bunker under the floorboards in the bedroom.

"Looks like it's all set," CJ said after the call ended. "We can drop a chest off at his house tonight. He's got a dolly, so it will be easy for him to wheel Diego out if he's there."

"Did you tell him to bring a gun, just in case?"

"You have to ask?"

I called Martina and told her about the plan. She'd have to wait until about noon the next day to find out if her dad was there, and if he had been rescued.

I was tired, as was CJ, but we had much to do before we could sleep. We went to the closest Target and bought the largest trunk they had. I had a copy of my old house key made at a hardware store, and we drove to Adam's.

Adam was cleaning a revolver in the living room when we arrived. CJ was carrying the chest we had just purchased. He plopped it down on the rug and turned to his friend. "Things may get a little rough," he said. "Can I borrow one of your guns?"

"Sure. What would you like? Pistol or long gun?"

CJ thought a moment. "How about a shotgun. Got one you can spare?"

"Sure thing."

Adam disappeared for a few minutes, then returned with a double-barrel shotgun and a box of shells. CJ loaded the gun and pocketed the remaining cartridges. Following that, we sat in the living room and went over details of the plan. When we were done, we answered all of Adam's questions, which weren't many, and I texted him one of the pictures of Diego that Martina had sent me earlier.

Adam wanted us to stay longer and visit. He seemed so desperate for company, I agreed to stay for a while despite being exhausted. We each had a beer and talked about what CJ should do once he won the election to the statehouse. CJ gently reminded Adam he would be a junior state assemblyman, not king of the nation, but he would do his best to address Adam's concerns.

It was almost eleven by the time we left. CJ thanked Adam for the shotgun and placed it behind his seat, under a folded tarp. Melinda's house was dark when we arrived, so we let ourselves in with the key. It was hours before either of us fell asleep. I had a lot on my mind. I was still grieving over my father's death and reeling from the disappointment I felt when Mom sold the farm. There was Bong, and all the goings-on at Happy Sun. On top of that, I was now worried about Diego. I hoped CJ didn't have more confidence in Adam than he should. I desperately wanted to have good news for Martina, but I wasn't optimistic.

When I woke at 7:30, CJ was up and dressed. He brought me a cup of coffee which I nursed as I put on the same clothes I'd worn the day before. By the time we arrived in the kitchen, Melinda had already left for the day. CJ had a breakfast of cereal, toast, and orange juice, but I couldn't eat. I jumped when CJ's phone chimed.

"I better get this," CJ said. "It's Adam." I nodded, and they spoke for a short time. CJ shook his head after they'd disconnected. "I told you this guy is a little off. He wants to know about Diego's daughter. What do I tell him?"

"What does he want to know?" I asked.

"Is she single?" CJ asked, sounding exasperated.

"She's single, and adorable, and I'm sure she'll be forever grateful to him if he rescues her dad." I paused and added, "But that doesn't mean she'll want to ride off into the sunset with him."

"I'll call him back and tell him. The first part—not the part about riding off into the sunset. A little extra motivation never hurt."

After CJ called Adam back and relayed the information about Martina, we passed the time pacing and watching morning game shows. Two hours later, Adam phoned. CJ put the call on speaker.

"I just drove by the house," he said in a hushed tone as if someone were listening. "There's a man sitting in a chair by the side of the road across the street. He's watching the house."

"Where are you now?"

"About half a mile down the road."

"Why are you whispering?" CJ asked. I'd been wondering the same thing.

"I dunno, it just seems a bit dangerous."

"Was the guy carrying a shotgun or something?"

"Not that I could see, but he could be armed."

"Is he Asian?"

"Yes, I think so."

"I'll bet he works for Happy Sun Farm," CJ said. "He's not going to go around shooting people. If he asks you, just stick to the plan. Tell him you're there to pick up a few things. If he asks if you met either of us, tell him 'no.'"

"What if he wants to follow me inside and watch?"

I had to admit that was a good question, and we hadn't planned for it. CJ and I conferred quietly while we considered options.

Once we'd agreed on a plan, CJ conveyed it to Adam. "Tell him you have COVID. You're only working because you need the money. Then cough loudly and make it sound wet."

"What if he insists anyway?"

"Let him in the house with you, then beat him up before he has a chance to call for help. Bring some rope or zip ties if you have them. Take his cell phone away. Whatever you need to do."

"Got it. I've got some rope. No zip ties, though."

We wished him luck and disconnected. I felt queasy. "You think he can handle this?" I asked CJ.

"Adam can handle himself in a fight, if that's what you mean. My biggest worry is that Martina's dad isn't there."

Chapter 37

WE WERE BACK TO waiting. I checked my watch every few minutes, but that didn't make the time go by any quicker. Pacing and watching daytime TV didn't lessen the tension. The next call from Adam came forty-five minutes later. His voice was low and difficult to hear over the speaker. "Which room did you say it was in?"

The tension was unbearable. Was he really asking such a lame question? We'd gone over the where and how numerous times. The simplest part was remembering to go to the master bedroom, the room with wall-to-wall brown shag carpeting. I felt like pulling my hair out.

"The master bedroom, don't you remember?" I answered. "Brown, shag rug? There's only one other bedroom, and it's filled with survivalist gear."

"Oh, yeah. Well, I'm in the house now. Got in, no problem. But the guy's watching me through the window. What should I do?"

I thought for a moment before answering. I was glad I hadn't packed up everything yet. "Take the trunk into the kitchen. Pretend to be looking at a list of stuff to collect on your cell phone. Look carefully through the cookbooks and pick out a few to put in it. Then, go to the master bedroom and close the shades. Go back to the kitchen and select a few pots and pans. Then drag the locker into the master bedroom and look for Diego."

"Got it."

By the time we disconnected, my shoulders and chest were so tense I could hardly breathe.

"I think we should go for a walk," CJ said. "You're wound up so tight I expect to see a baby alien come bursting out of your chest."

"That's exactly what I feel like."

We went around the block, about a quarter mile, half walking and half running. The exertion relieved the tension somewhat, but it was still there when Adam called again. CJ spoke to him as we walked into the house, then put the call on speaker.

"Ok, I'm in the master bedroom," Adam whispered. "I forgot what I was supposed to look for exactly."

I motioned to CJ that my head was about to explode, but he remained calm. "Remember, there's a loop made out of a thick strand of greenish carpet. Berry said it was directly below one of the four ceiling lights. You might see it better if you turn on the lights."

Adam was silent a minute, then said excitedly, "I see it, I see it. Should I try to open the trap door?"

"You bet. Leave the phone on speaker so we know what's going on," CJ said.

"There's no cell reception down there, so put your phone on the rug near the trap door," I added.

The sound of a few footsteps was followed by several heavy breaths. A loud thud told me Adam had managed to swing the trap door open and let it fall to the floor. My heart raced at the sound of shoes hitting the wooden steps of the ladder leading down into the bunker.

"Call his name when you get down there," I yelled. "Call for Diego, so he knows you're a friend."

My words were met with the sound of footsteps. Then I heard Adam speak. "Diego? Diego? I'm a friend of CJ's."

"Say Berry!" I yelled, hoping he heard me.

"I'm a friend of Berry's," he said.

More footsteps, but no reply. I felt tears well in my eyes as the stress I was feeling transformed into major disappointment. Adam was farther from the phone, and his footsteps sounded faint. Moments later, I heard what sounded like the rustle of fabric being disturbed. "Hey, you okay?" Adam asked. He was difficult to hear, but I could still make out the words.

"Who are you?" I recognized Diego's voice.

Was this real? Did I really hear Diego's voice? My eyes met CJ's, and we both smiled.

"Berry sent me here to look for you."

"Thank you Jesus and Mary," Diego said, his voice fraught with emotion. I imagined him crossing himself, teary-eyed. "I fall asleep. Then you wake me. I thought you were an angel."

"Sorry to disappoint you," Adam said, "I'm no angel, but I'm here to get you outta this place."

I yelled into the phone, "It's me, Berry! Do what Adam tells you, and you should be able to see Martina soon. She's waiting for you."

It sounded like Diego was crying when he asked, "How is she? I was afraid I'd never see her again."

"She's fine but misses you."

"How can you get me out? They have guards outside. They kill me if they see me."

"They won't see you," Adam said. "I told the man watching the house I was picking up some things to move into storage. I have a large locker upstairs big enough to hold you. I'll put you in there, close the top, wheel you out on my dolly, and load you into my truck. I should be able to drive away with no problem. It may be uncomfortable, but you can get out as soon as we're a safe distance away." After relaying more details about the plan, Adam asked, "Sound good?"

"Let's do it," Diego said. "I want to get out of here."

I listened intently to the sound of footsteps, followed by heavy breathing and the creaking of the ladder as I envisioned the two men ascending to the ground level.

"There it is," Adam said. "You still with me?"

"What choice do I have?"

The squeak of the locker being opened came through CJ's speaker.

"There's no air holes," Diego said.

"Yeah, we decided that would be a bad idea 'cause they might see 'em," CJ said. "You'll only be in there a few minutes if all goes as planned. Just keep your face as close as possible to that place over there where we bent back the inner lip. You should be able to get enough air there."

Sounds of grunting and jostling were followed by the thump of the lid shutting.

"You okay in there?" Adam asked.

Diego's voice was muffled, but he answered in the affirmative.

"Here goes," Adam said, as I heard the click from each of six clasps being secured. "I'm gonna load you onto my dolly now," Adam whispered. After that, he was silent. CJ and I heard the squeal of wheels turning, then the opening of a door as I imagined Adam wheeling Diego outside. A low rumble indicated Adam was opened the roller door on the back of the truck. The clank of the metal ramp dropping from the back of the cargo area was the last sound I heard before the voice of a man yelling startled me.

"Hey, I have to inspect that." The Asian accent was heavy.

"Man, I'm in a hurry. There's nothing to see here."

I heard the sound of the fasteners being opened. "Hey, this one stuck," the man said.

"I'm not surprised. I had a hard time closing it, but it's not my problem. The owner can open it by blowing it up for all I care. I just want to deliver it and get paid."

Loud banging ensued as I envisioned the man whacking the locker with something metal. "Okay. You go."

"Sheesh," Adam said. The sound of Adam pushing the locker up the ramp was followed by him scooting the locker to the rear of the truck, behind furniture he had loaded onto the moving van earlier that morning. When the sliding stopped, Adam whispered, "Okay, I've undone all the latches, including the extra safety on the one that was stuck. After you feel me drive away, count to ten. Then open the locker. Understand?"

The sound of a loud knock confirmed Diego had understood. I started to relax as I heard Adam walk down the ramp, slide it back into the truck, close the rear door, get into the truck cab, and drive away.

"I told you Adam would get it done," CJ said. "I sure hope Martina likes him."

We picked Martina up at a small shopping plaza near her apartment and drove her to the moving company lot where Adam worked. He arrived ten minutes after us, and parked. As he jumped out of the driver's seat, I introduced Adam to Martina.

Adam stopped and looked at Martina a little longer than seemed comfortable. He ran his fingers through his hair as if embarrassed by how messy it was.

After an awkward moment of silence, Martina said, "Thank you so much for what you've done."

"Anyone follow you?" CJ asked.

"Nope," Adam replied. "I was the only one on the road for most of the ride."

Not wanting to waste time, I said, "Better let Diego out, Adam, before he roasts to death back there."

We all stood behind Adam as he opened the back of the truck. Diego was sitting on the couch, facing us. He was drenched in sweat from the stifling heat, but was smiling. He jumped off the truck and embraced Martina, who was crying.

As soon as they separated, I handed Diego a bottle of water, which he emptied quickly.

"Thank you all so much," Martina said, looking from one of us to the next. Her eyes met Adam's. "I don't know how I can repay you."

"Yes," Diego added, "I cannot thank you enough."

Adam looked down at his feet. "Aw, it was nothin'."

"I hate to interrupt this wonderful moment," I said, "but we need to decide what to do next. I don't think it would be safe for Diego to go to Martina's apartment. I'm sure they're watching it. Once demolition of my house starts, they'll discover the bunker. They're not stupid, and will figure out that Diego hid there, and was extracted by Adam. They'll suspect Martina's hiding him so she won't be safe, either."

"I can work anyplace," Diego said. "They're probably hiring pickers in the Salinas Valley right now. Martina and I can go there."

"You can drop me off at my apartment," Martina said. "I'll get my car and pick up my dad at a safe place so we can leave later today."

"Let's not rush into anything," I said. "We should try to figure out what's really going on at Happy Sun. Your dad may have some valuable information." I turned to Diego. "Do you think they wanted to kill you?"

"Yes, but I don't know why."

CJ turned to Martina. "We'll drop you off at the shopping plaza so you can walk to your apartment and pick up your car. Then you can meet us back at the plaza and follow me back to my cousin's house. We can relax there and try to figure out what's going on."

Martina and her father rode with me and CJ. Adam had to work so he couldn't accompany us. We drove to the shopping plaza and waited while Martina walked home, collected a few things, then took her car to meet us back in the parking lot. There, she picked up Diego, and they followed us to Melinda's house.

During the drive, I got a text from my mom telling me about her wonderful trip. She'd gone snorkeling and had seen many beautiful fish at Tunnels Beach. I answered her text with a note saying I was visiting with Martina and Diego. I gave no details.

Once we arrived at our destination, we sat around the kitchen table. Diego insisted he wasn't hungry, as he had eaten well the brief time he was in the bunker. He was, however, still quite thirsty and drank two tall glasses of water.

I didn't waste much time before getting down to the subject at hand. In my mind, there were many moving parts to the mystery presented by Happy Sun. I looked forward to questioning Bong in the near future and obtaining the samples he said he could supply.

In the meantime, I hoped Diego could shed light on the farm itself, and the strange farming practices I had observed. Perhaps there were even others I didn't know about. A question that loomed large in my mind was, why were a bunch of North Koreans, claiming to be Chinese, running an agricultural enterprise in California, and what was so damn secret about the farm? Why would anyone want to harm Diego or any of the other workers?

Chapter 38

I GRABBED A PEN and paper and turned to Diego. "What exactly do you suppose is going on at Happy Sun?"

"They guard so much. They hide something, but I don't know what."

"I want to know everything you've noticed. Take your time. Even a small detail might be important."

"First, you have to know, Berry, I really love your dad. He treat me so good. I admit I think he a little odd with all his worry about conspiracies, but now I wonder if he is right. He have an illegal still, but everything else he do is totally honest. When Happy Sun started buying up all the farms, the whole area around your parents' place change so fast. Your dad, he get very upset, and when they start pressuring him to sell, he become very mad. Talk to me about it all the time. Have everything he need right there on the farm. After he spend all that time and money building the bunker five years ago, he never going to leave. Not willingly, anyway. He is also sentimental about some things, like the strawberry fields he plant for you. He don't want other people working it."

That last comment brought tears to my eyes. "He planted the strawberry fields for me?"

"He never tell you?" I shook my head no. "He don't grow them until you are one or two. I don't remember exactly when, but he tell me they are for you."

My dad probably said something about that to me when I was too little to understand or remember, but the memory must have been buried deep in my brain. That's why the strawberry fields always felt special to me, like they were my own private happy place. "I always loved those fields, but now it makes me even more sad that those horrible people have taken them over."

"They destroy everything. Once Happy Sun buy a farm, they tear down the house and plow over many of the good crops. Your dad and I talk about it. Neither of us can understand why they do it."

"What kind of crops did they plow over, and what crops did they keep?"

"I never understand, but from what I know, if they keep a certain kind of crop on one farm, they keep it on all of them. If they rip it out on one of them, they rip it out on all of them. I wasn't surprised when they plow under your strawberry fields, because strawberries are plow under at all the farms. Then they plant more strawberry seeds in the same place. Make no sense."

"What other crops did they destroy?"

"I'm sorry, it's hard for me to think right now. I'm still a little shaky from that ride over here." Diego took several more gulps of water.

"What about tomatoes?" I asked.

"Gone."

"Broccoli?"

"Gone."

"Oranges?"

"Gone. All citrus is gone."

"Almonds?"

"Gone."

"Onions?"

"Gone."

"Grapes?"

Diego paused. "They keep. I don't believe they remove any of them."

"Lettuce?"

"All gone—iceberg, romaine, arugula—every kind I can think of."

"Apricots?"

"Keep them."

I asked about twenty other crops. Some were kept, some weren't. I tried to come up with a pattern but couldn't. It seemed so random.

"The crops that were removed," I asked, "were they all replanted with the same crop, like they did with the strawberries, or did they usually plant something else?"

Diego thought for a moment. "I don't know about all of them, but they replace the lettuces with the same type of crop. They don't plant new almond trees. Same with oranges. They replace them with different kinds of lettuces, radishes, strawberries, and a lot of other crops I can't remember right now."

"Did they plant any trees?" I was asking about anything I could think of, trying to come up with a rationale or pattern for what they were doing.

I still couldn't understand why a country like North Korea, a country that can't feed its own people, would spend so much money to start a large farming company here. On top of that, their company seemed doomed to failure because the people in charge didn't know how to run a farm. I could think of a lot of bad things to say about the government of North Korea, but stupid wasn't one of them. There had to be a reason. The clues were likely right in front of us, but I couldn't figure it out. Once we knew what was behind their actions, it would probably be obvious.

"What else can you tell me about what was going on there?" I asked. "I know there are a lot of Asians working for them. What sorts of things do they do?"

"When they buy farms, they hire the same pickers, like me, and get even more using brokers, like the way I find farm work before I start working year-round for your dad. Back then, the broker would find farms that need labor and take me, Camila, and others there."

Diego teared up when he mentioned his late wife, Camila. "Now," he continued, "the broker just hires laborers for Happy Sun Farm. I never see Asians do the hard labor. Some of them supervise the pickers, or drive tractors, delivery trucks, or other equipment. Many work in dairy or the food packing facility. There's a lot that work inside, more than I've see at any other farm. I don't know what they do. Lots of the time they walk around talking on their phones, but I don't understand what they're saying because they speak Chinese."

"How many Asians do you think work there?"

Diego held his chin in his hand as the considered the question. "Hard to say. I haven't seen all of them, but at times there were over twenty-five walking around. Maybe even fifty."

That bit of information had to be important, but I didn't know what to make of it. Were these workers having meetings all day to decide what crops to plant? I didn't think so. "What do they do in the packing house?"

"They pack all the produce for shipping."

"What about canning?"

"No canning. They don't do any canning there."

"They sell only fresh produce?" I asked.

"Yes, and dairy."

"Of course. I've seen their yogurt and cream cheese, but I don't remember any of the farms around here having dairy cows."

"They start a dairy farm in the area that used to be the large almond orchard on the old Higgins' farm. I only learn about it after your mom sell the farm and I start working for Happy Sun," Diego said, looking at me. "They make cheese, yogurt, butter, and sour cream. Things like that."

"Who milks the cows?"

"Nobody. I hear they have an automatic robotic cow milking system, but I never see it. A few workers load feed for the cows, and do other hard work like that in the dairy."

"A robotic milking system makes sense," I said, "especially if starting from scratch. One of my professors described them in a class I took." I knew dairy products weren't popular in Asia, and probably non-existent in North Korea, so I didn't expect them to have expertise in dairy farming. "Where do they make the dairy products from the raw milk?"

"I believe they're made in the packing house."

"You aren't sure?"

"No, I never go inside."

His answer surprised me. "You've never been in the packing house?"

"Only Asians are allowed in. They have special badges that let them go wherever they want. None of us farm workers can get inside."

That struck me as odd. Packing up produce is hard work, although not as back-breaking as picking fruit. "Do you know if they do anything other than package produce and make dairy products in the packaging house?"

"I have no way of knowing. Some of the workers there take care of the pests. I believe they have a lot of problem with pests."

"What kind of pests?"

"I don't know. Insects or rodents, probably."

"Did one of the workers tell you that?"

"No, they don't speak English. Or Spanish. But they deliver a lot of spray cans. I know that because I walk by one day when they unload a shipment. One of the boxes open up, and a bunch of red spray cans, they fall out. I don't know what else all those cans would be for." Diego stopped and thought for a moment. "Now I remember something odd. I try to get a closer look at the spray cans because I wonder what product they were using. The cans look unfamiliar, but before I can get close, one of the guards push me way back. There is a lot of yelling. The supervisors very mad at the person who drop the cans."

I turned to CJ. "Do you have a lot of problems with pests at the Mama Baroni factory?"

"Naw. Sometimes a mouse or rat might get in, but our traps handle 'em. Spraying a ton of chemicals around fresh produce about to be shipped out doesn't sound healthy, and I can't believe any government inspector would approve if they saw it."

"I wonder if the cans Diego is talking about are the ones being assembled in Tulare."

"Interesting idea. Too bad there's no way to compare them."

I turned back to Diego. "What about Carlos? Did you ever hear any more about him?"

"No. Some police come by but don't do much. Don't talk to any of us, only Mr. Chen. They look around the shed, but it is already emptied out. Then they leave."

"Is there anyone else you suspect they may have killed?"

"Two other field workers disappear. Me and the others, we think they are murdered, too. Make everyone scared to leave, although we all want to. I never try to leave, but they want to kill me anyway. No doubt about that."

"Maybe they didn't like you seeing those spray cans. I don't know what's in them, but I have a feeling it's not a pesticide. I'll level with you, Diego. The people running Happy Sun aren't Chinese. They're North Korean."

Diego's eyes widened. "North Korean? Here? Does the American government know? I don't know much about world politics, but I know North Korea is a very bad country."

"Exactly," I said. "I've tried to notify the FBI and Homeland Security, but they seem to have ignored my information. I'm trying to collect more evidence because I'm convinced they're planning something. Something the likes of which we've never seen before. Call me if you can think of anything else."

Diego promised he would. I wished him and Martina luck as they drove off to find work in Northern California. Meanwhile, I wondered what I was missing.

Chapter 39

WE LEFT EARLY IN the morning so we'd be sure to be on time to extract Bong. CJ parked the pick-up behind the fence bordering the facility's farming area, facing the direction we drove in from so we could make a quick getaway if needed. We noticed the tunnel CJ had made under the fence was filled with dirt. Then we re-opened the fence door we had created three days earlier. Following that, we waited.

Through the foliage, we saw a few workers in the fields occasionally yelling at each other. After one exchange, there was laughter. That was quickly followed by a man who appeared to be a supervisor, shouting angrily. I imagined he was ordering them to work harder and cut out the jokes.

A rustle of leaves caught our attention. Bong had quietly walked to the brush in front of the fence, apparently unnoticed. I reasoned he had waited until the supervisor was distracted by the field workers before making his move. My heart raced as he quickly assumed a prone position and moved forward on his elbows, army style. He was halfway through the bushes before I heard loud yelling and footsteps coming in our direction. CJ grabbed Bong's arms and pulled him through the fence. We all jumped into the front seat of the truck and CJ floored it while the doors were still open. I turned to see several men chasing us, one with a hoe. They must have slithered through the fence quickly, though not quickly enough. Shots were fired, but none of us were hit.

"Damn," CJ said. "I should have had my shotgun ready."

"I think we're safe," I said a few seconds later when the sound of gunfire faded.

We were soon on the main highway. CJ momentarily slowed down so we could close both doors of the cab, then sped up again and headed toward Tulare. I took a deep breath for the first time since hearing Bong as he first approached us.

Bong was covered in sweat. He looked around as if he had just landed on another planet. It might as well have been Mars, as we were incapable of communicating with each other. My cell reception was poor, and I was unable to use Google Translate.

A few minutes later, I realized Bong's arms were fixed at his sides, and he was staring straight ahead. He looked terrified and must have been wondering if he'd made the right decision. He'd left a bad situation for one that might be worse. I tried smiling, but he wouldn't look at me. We headed to Best Korean Barbecue. The lunch hour would be over when we arrived, and we were depending on our trusted translator to bridge the huge language gap we had with our frightened passenger. I hoped he could clear up a lot of the mystery surrounding Happy Sun. Were they just bad farmers who didn't mind killing a few people they thought were in their way, or were they involved in a diabolical scheme?

CJ and I spoke little before parking in front of the Korean Barbecue. Bong stiffened even more when CJ cut the engine. Perhaps he feared we were going to torture or execute him. I pointed to the restaurant sign, but Bong continued to stare straight ahead. He finally turned his head when I tapped him on the shoulder. His eyes followed my finger as I again tried to direct his attention to the sign, which had Korean writing as well as English. I assumed the Korean characters translated to "Best Korean Barbecue" or something similar. Bong looked at the sign and relaxed his arms, but still appeared to be on high alert. I exited the vehicle and motioned for him to follow me with a sweep of my arm toward the sidewalk.

I looked at CJ, who was walking around his truck, inspecting it for bullet holes. Miraculously, he told me, his pickup had escaped unscathed. CJ, Bong, and I entered the restaurant, which had a few diners finishing their lunches. Kwan's daughter was at the cash register, and I asked her to tell her dad we were waiting for him with our new friend.

CJ and I sat at a table near a corner and motioned for Bong to sit. He slowly shuffled to the table as he looked around, his mouth agape. Then, he sat down in a daze.

Kwan burst out of the kitchen, a big smile on his face, clearly excited at the prospect of meeting someone from North Korea. He didn't wait for introductions before bowing slightly, taking a seat, and launching into a language neither CJ nor I understood.

Bong smiled and nodded. Moments later, we were witnesses to the back-and-forth conversation between the two Koreans, one from north of the Demilitarized Zone, the other from the south side, yet worlds apart. I waited patiently as they continued to speak, an outsider to an animated conversation, in which I understood not one word.

Kwan turned to CJ and me and explained that Bong was twenty-four years old. He and his wife were unskilled factory workers in a North Korean weapons manufacturing plant. The work was dangerous. In fact, a good friend of his was killed in a large munitions explosion. He wanted to leave his job, but there were no opportunities for other employment. At least the job provided enough money to pay for a roof over their heads and food, although meager.

When he heard about the possibility of promoting the cause of North Korea by traveling to America, he jumped at the chance. He had heard rumors that the enemy, America, was a land of freedom and opportunity, not the horrible, evil place it was portrayed to be. He wanted to see it for himself, hoping to defect if it was as wonderful as some said. If nothing else, he could get away from his nagging wife.

Over the course of several days, government officials asked him many questions about his love of North Korea and hatred of the enemy, America. Bong pledged his devotion to all things North Korean, his loyalty and admiration of Kim Jong Un, and his desire to see the imperialist country of America destroyed, with all the capitalist dogs killed. He remained consistent throughout his interviews, although he looked at this as an opportunity not to help his country, but to escape to America. When he was chosen to go, he was overjoyed. Lacking any specialized training, he was assigned to do odd jobs such as janitorial work, running errands, and farming.

A waitress walked by, and Kwan said something to her, which I later realized was a request for food. Soon, bowls of rice, chicken, and beef were placed in front of Bong, along with a single pair of metal chopsticks and a spoon.

Bong appeared overwhelmed as he looked from one bowl to the next, then picked up the chopsticks and dug in. As he ate, Kwan continued to speak, Bong occasionally replying with short answers, usually one or two syllables. When half the food was gone, Kwan spoke to the waitress again. Minutes later, she served Bong a cold glass of beer. Our North Korean visitor was overcome with emotion, almost tearful, as he brought the glass to his lips and sipped, his eyes closed. I imagined he was wondering if he had died and gone to heaven. Then I remembered North Korea is officially an atheist state, so he was probably just happy.

I realized keeping Bong content and relaxed was important, but I was getting impatient. Time was passing, and I had a lot of questions. My first question was, did he get the specimens I had requested? I nudged Kwan and requested he ask Bong about that.

The Koreans exchanged words, after which Bong reached into his pants pocket and produced three envelopes, each containing five seeds and labeled with Korean characters. Kwan translated the words on the envelopes: strawberries, arugula, and cucumbers. I wrote the English words on the envelopes as he translated. Next, Bong produced a capped test tube filled with approximately ten milliliters of tan fluid, as he continued to speak to Kwan. When Bong paused, Kwan explained, "This is fluid from roller bottles." Lastly, Bong pulled a Ziplock bag containing another Ziplock bag that held another sealed test tube from his back pocket. That tube contained three milliliters of cloudy fluid. Kwan listened to Bong, then told us, "This is from a flask on the shaker platform. He double bagged it while he was still in the room, wearing a head-to-toe protective covering. He said to be careful with it. It's very harmful."

I took in a deep breath and let it out slowly. Bong had delivered. There was a lot more to do, including figuring out what these samples could tell us about whatever Happy Sun was planning, but for a moment, I only felt a great sense of relief. We finally had something concrete to work with.

Bong finished the food in front of him and sat back. With eating and drinking out of the way, I had the opportunity to ask more questions. I went down a list of queries I had in my purse, asking Kwan to translate them for Bong, then convert the answers to English for me.

My first question was, "What is the goal of all the work being done at Happy Sun Farm?"

Through Kwan, Bong told us that he didn't know. Everything was a secret from lowly workers such as himself. The lab received supplies shipped from North Korea. Small items were routed through the People's Republic of China, hidden inside pillows. The occasional large items were first sent to Mexico, then smuggled across the border in trucks. So far, nothing, to his knowledge, had been discovered by customs.

At the main farm, he had worked in the kitchen, preparing food for their large staff. In Tulare, he did some food preparation, but also worked on the farm and did janitorial work, going back and forth between the two facilities.

I asked if he entered the lab areas and learned that he cleaned them three times a week. The scientists worked long hours, often late into the night and early morning, so he did his cleaning at all times of day, doing his best to stay out of their way. He had plenty of opportunities to observe what they were doing, although he didn't understand much of it.

Many of the government's top scientists, with advanced degrees in biochemistry, virology, genetic engineering, and agriculture, worked in the lab. They had frequent meetings, but unskilled workers like himself were never allowed to hear what went on in them. All he knew was there was a plan to overthrow the government of the United States, and its success depended on the work being done in the labs in Tulare and the large Happy Sun Farm in Kern County.

Chapter 40

BONG KNEW JUST ENOUGH to make me very worried, but not enough to know exactly what the North Koreans had in store. All I could do was throw a lot of questions at him and try to organize the pieces of information in my mind.

I asked about the roller bottles and learned the fluid in them was emptied twice a day, replaced with a solution freshly prepared in the lab from chemicals they received from UPS. The liquid removed was passed through a large filtration apparatus, and the residue was gently dried. Then it was suspended in a small amount of liquid and stored in small, black canisters to which nozzles were attached.

"What happens to the canisters?" I asked.

Bong told Kwan, who told me they were sent to the main farm, then shipped to various storage facilities across the country. I asked if the workers needed to wear protective clothing when exposed to the roller bottle material, and was told they did not. I concluded that whatever they were producing there was non-toxic to humans.

Next, I asked about the flasks on the shaker platforms. I learned that the fluid in the flasks was collected daily, then replaced with a solution made by dissolving the contents of a small package of powder received from North Korea in distilled water. The liquid that had been removed was taken to another room where it was evaporated, leaving behind a tan, powdery material. Some of that powder was put in vials. The rest was suspended in a small amount of the same solution used in the flasks, and packaged into red spray cans.

All the people who entered the labs housing the flasks on the shakers or where the material from them was processed, were required to be covered head to toe, including face coverings, booties, and gloves.

At no time were they allowed to touch anything in the rooms with their bare skin. They removed their biohazard gear in a small enclosed area between those labs and the rest of the building. I was glad Bong had the sense to double bag the specimen from the flasks.

I sat back to reflect on what I had just learned. Something highly toxic was being produced in the flasks on the shakers, then packaged in spray cans and vials. Whatever it was, it had to hold the secret to the North Korean's plan. I postulated it was a poison, radioactive substance, or deadly microbe. Concerned about an infectious agent, I asked Kwan to find out if the employees at Happy Sun received vaccines before or during their work in the US. After conferring with Bong, he assured me they had not.

I had to figure out what the North Koreans were concocting in the unremarkable warehouse hidden in that small farming community amongst all the other non-descript warehouses. The red spray cans assembled in Tulare were likely the same as those Diego had seen being delivered at the farm. The substance in them was probably so secret, they wanted Diego dead so he couldn't tell anyone about the cans he'd seen dropped on the ground in front of him.

"What happens to the spray cans and powder?" I asked.

Kwan translated my question, then relayed Bong's answer. "They are delivered to the packing house at the big farm. Some of the produce is sprayed with the contents of the spray cans. Some is not sprayed. The powder is mixed in with the dairy products."

I tried to make sense of all this information but couldn't. They were producing a highly toxic substance, so toxic they wanted to prevent their workers from being contaminated with it. They were mixing it into dairy products and spraying produce with it, but only some produce. Why were some crops treated differently?

My biggest question, however, was, why hadn't anyone died or gotten sick from eating the treated food? Happy Sun sold massive amounts of produce nationwide. I doubted they were making a profit, certainly not with all the laboratory work that was going on behind the scenes. I was glad no one had died, at least not in large numbers. I would have heard about that. I thought about the Happy Sun Farms yogurt I'd eaten on the plane. The company had generously donated it to the airline, but I never suffered any ill effects. Were we being exposed to a slow-acting poison? Was there such a thing? Was I in danger?

My questions continued. "Are their seeds genetically modified?" I wanted my suspicions confirmed.

"Yes," Kwan said. "He doesn't know what is the modification, but was told they grow genetically modified plant cells into tiny plants in Tulare lab. After they are big enough, they send to nearby farm where you find him. There, the plants grow in the soil until they produce seeds. They harvest the seeds and send them to the main farm."

I turned to CJ. "Now I know why they rip out many of the crops on the farms. They're replacing those crops with their own genetically modified crops."

Kwan continued, "The workers aren't allowed to eat any of produce that grows from their seeds, the packaged produce, or the dairy products they make."

"Why?" I asked.

"He doesn't know, but Bong say no one eats it. All are afraid because they know they will be harshly punished if they disobey orders." He chuckled. "He also say if anyone break rules, it will be for something important enough to risk consequences. Like escaping or sneaking cell phone from supervisor to make secret call."

I wondered if they forbade workers from eating the produce to maximize the amount they could sell. That didn't make sense, as they had to feed them anyway, and the amount of produce grown was magnitudes more than the staff could eat. Trying to think of more questions, hoping to learn something important, I asked, "What about the fruit grown on trees, like apricots and plums?"

"They are allowed to eat those, but only before they have gone to the packing house," Kwan said.

I reasoned that something happened to the fruit grown on trees when it was in the packing house. The produce grown by Happy Sun from seeds was likely already dangerous as it was genetically modified. But fruit grown on trees, which would take years to produce from genetically modified seeds, was sprayed with something after it was picked. Simple: all I had to do was figure out what genetic modifications had been made, what they were spraying the produce with, and why no one had become ill from eating any of it. In actuality, I wasn't much closer to figuring out what was going on than I had been before.

I was silent as I sorted through the information in my mind, but could only conclude they were planning something terrible, possibly catastrophic. I told Kwan to ask about Mr. Chen. What was his background? Was he the boss of the whole operation?

After some back and forth between Kwan and Bong in Korean, Kwan turned to me. "General Jeong is boss. Everyone does what he say. He very smart. Speak several languages. He also is cousin of Kim Jong Un. In the United States, he go by the name Mr. Chen. You can be sure they plan something big, just like I say."

Knowing about Mr. Chen raised a lot more questions in my mind. "What about regular, old-fashioned weapons? Ask Bong if they have a lot of guns, bombs, grenades, or other weapons."

After speaking to Bong, Kwan turned back to me. "Top people have handguns and rifles, but no big supply of guns. No rockets, grenades, or bombs that he know of. Only drones."

Chapter 41

DRONES? THAT ANSWER TOOK me by surprise. What were they doing with them? Did they have sophisticated cameras, sound recorders, communication systems? Were they armed? My imagination went wild, wondering about the spy or attack capabilities of the drones. Perhaps this whole farming operation was a front to bring spy craft into the country. Perhaps their drones were better at spying than anything our government had. If that were the case, we were pursuing the Happy Sun operation from the wrong angle. "What are they planning to do with the drones?"

Bong didn't have the answer, but he did know that General Jeong's expertise was drones. He was in charge of all drone operations controlled by North Korea.

That information was downright scary. "How many drones are there?" I asked.

After speaking with Bong, Kwan told me, "They have lots of them. Thousands. They are being sent all over US, to warehouses where Happy Sun have storage space. Canisters made at laboratory are being sent to same places."

I figured the drones and canisters were being stockpiled together, so the drones could be quickly loaded with the canisters and deployed. This sounded like more than just a spying operation. They were planning to spray vast areas of our country with whatever was in the canisters.

"Are there nuclear physicists, engineers, munitions specialists, computer hackers, or poisoners at any of the facilities?"

Kwan and Bong spoke several minutes, as Bong often paused and looked deep in thought before responding. When done, Kwan relayed what he had learned. Bong only knew of experts in the fields he had mentioned before—biochemistry, virology, plant genetics, and agriculture.

"Holy cow," I said. "They are planning some sort of biological warfare. Most likely involving a pathogen." I could imagine drones spreading a virus. If many were launched at once, emitting smallpox, Ebola, or another deadly microbe, it would be devastating. A large-scale dissemination would quickly lead to a worldwide epidemic, killing millions indiscriminately, including those living in North Korea. We'd already seen what COVID-19 did, and that virus wasn't nearly as deadly as some others out there. I wondered if North Korea would be so reckless.

"Another possibility," I said, "is they plan to attack our crops. That would explain why they have experts in plant genetics and agriculture. They could be synthesizing something in the roller bottles, like a chemical secreted by cells they genetically modified that would wipe out all the US farms. If it were sprayed from drones over California and the heartland, it would be disastrous. That doesn't explain everything, though." I wondered how that could be related to genetically modified plants, and why their produce was sprayed. Why weren't their employees allowed to eat any of those foods?

"What are the countries Happy Sun ships produce to?" I asked.

After conferring briefly with Bong, Kwan informed me that nothing was shipped out of the country. He heard some distributors in Canada had requested their products, but General Jeong refused to authorize shipment to any place outside the US.

I inquired about other people at Happy Sun whom Bong could confide in and would want to help us. I was told Bong had several people he confided in, but the person he trusted most was his girlfriend, Nabi. She wanted to defect but didn't see an opportunity for that. He hoped the two of them could live here together. Nabi primarily worked in the dairy division, where she mixed powder made in the lab into yogurt and sour cream before dispensing it into cartons. She had never been told what was in the powder. She and Bong often discussed it, imagining all sorts of things from bacteria to miniature chips. Nabi didn't understand why they had to be so careful, being fully covered while they worked. She knew of a co-worker who had put some of the powder in the drink of another worker he was very mad at. He thought the other man would die, but nothing happened. He didn't even get sick.

I felt bad for these star-crossed lovers and wanted them to be together. "Can Nabi help us in any way?"

Kwan asked Bong, who paused, his brow furrowed, before answering. He and Kwan conversed a while before I had an answer. "Bong say Nabi do occasional housekeeping in main building where General Jeong work. They never discuss it, but she can read and probably see some important information."

Bong may have been exaggerating Nabi's potential usefulness, but I wanted to rescue her for Bong's sake, even if she wasn't helpful.

I looked from CJ to Kwan, then back to CJ. "Do you have any thoughts about how we could free Nabi?" I asked. Before he could answer, I turned back to Kwan. "We'd love to help her out and question her, but coming up with a good plan will take some time. Ask Bong if he has an idea. He knows more about the operation and current layout of the farm than we do."

A series of questions and answers ensued, questions from CJ and me, translations from Kwan, and answers from Bong. After a half hour of discussion, Bong had an idea. Happy Sun trucks were continually filled with product at the loading dock, then driven off for delivery. Nabi often brought out containers to be loaded onto refrigerated trucks. She could devise a diversion, such as loosening a wheel on her cart. She'd make sure the cart tipped over and dumped yogurt or sour cream containers. Some would break, leaving a mess that needed to be cleaned. In the confusion, she could sneak into the truck when no one was looking. Once the truck was fully loaded, she would be driven out with the dairy products.

"But she'd be in a refrigerator truck. She'd freeze," I said.

"It's cold like that where she processes the dairy. She always wears a sweater under her clothes."

"How will she get out of the truck?" CJ asked.

"You would have to think of a way to do that. Bong could help."

CJ turned to me. "We'll think of something, won't we?"

"Sure," I said, trying to act confident while feeling anything but.

We asked how soon this might happen and learned that Bong would try to call her the following night. They spoke to each other by slipping the phone of a superior into their pocket and returning it unnoticed, usually leaving it in a place that person had been recently. Lowly workers like him and Nabi weren't allowed to have cell phones but had identified the most careless supervisors they worked with, ones who could easily be fooled into believing they had absentmindedly left their phone somewhere.

"We'll have a plan by then," CJ said.

His words left me feeling queasy. I wished I had his confidence. "Bong must be worn out," I said, "so we should think about making arrangements for him to stay someplace."

"Can I say something?" Kwan asked.

"Of course," I answered.

"I don't know much. I just simple cook. Since I cook, I think a lot about cooking, and when people talk about food, I think about what I can make with it."

Kwan had been so helpful, I wanted to show him respect, but didn't have time to hear him talk about recipes. We had an escape from a North Korean facility to plan. I bit my tongue and, although my chest tightened with every second of delay, I maintained a calm exterior. "Very interesting, Kwan," I said. I'm sure I sounded patronizing, because I was.

"No, no. Not interesting. But I notice something."

I sensed CJ was as impatient as me. He sighed and asked, "What did you notice?"

"All these things that Happy Sun grow. Grapes, plums, lettuce, strawberries. Also dairy. All these things usually eaten cold or at room temperature. Not cooked."

Not cooked. That means not heated. There had to be something in their produce and dairy that would be destroyed by heating. I hit my forehead and smiled. "Damn, Kwan. I think you're really on to something. I didn't see it before, but it's so obvious now that you mention it." I thought for a moment. "But what about oranges, grapefruits, and avocados? They ripped out all of those trees, but those foods are eaten at room temperature, too."

"Yes, but everyone peel before they eat. If they spray orange, whatever they spray with won't be eaten. They want it eaten."

Kwan was making perfect sense. "Of course. Now we're getting somewhere. We're not dealing with a simple poison, like cyanide, arsenic or strychnine, but we already knew that since people aren't getting sick from it. Whatever it is, it's destroyed by high temperatures."

I kept coming back to the same question. Why aren't people getting sick? "Could it be something with delayed action? I don't know of any toxins like that. I doubt we are dealing with prions, because they aren't destroyed by heating. We need to get that stuff from the shaker flasks analyzed ASAP."

Kwan offered to let Bong stay in his apartment, which was above his restaurant. He said he would take Bong for a haircut and buy him sunglasses and a Dodger's hat so he would escape the notice of Happy Sun people who were surely looking for him. I wished we could quickly get him a prosthetic fourth finger, but that wasn't possible. We asked Kwan to tell him to keep his left hand in his pocket whenever he was in public.

Bong was excited to be away from Happy Sun, free in the US. He wanted to travel with Nabi, but that would have to wait until we extracted her and started the paperwork they would need to be legal residents. Kwan offered to introduce him to a local immigration attorney many of his friends had used.

CJ and I left Kwan and Bong feeling optimistic. We still didn't fully understand what was happening at Happy Sun, but we were slowly filling in the blanks. I had the samples from Bong in my hand. I needed to be careful with them, especially the one from the shaker flasks, as it likely contained something deadly. No amount of staring at them would reveal what they were comprised of. I hoped Fran could help us figure that out.

Chapter 42

I DIDN'T WAIT UNTIL we returned to Melinda's house before calling Fran. CJ turned off his country music so I could converse with her while riding in his truck. She answered right away.

"What's up?" she asked.

"I'm very worried. I've learned a lot since last talking to you, but still have many questions."

"You still think there's some sort of conspiracy going on with a farm in your area?"

"I'm sure of it now. I have some of their seeds and samples of two of their other products which I suspect are biological agents. Can someone at your company analyze them?"

"That might be difficult. Right now, I'm working on a project to genetically engineer soybeans to make vitamin B12. Can you imagine if tofu were rich in B12? It would be a game changer for vegans. They wouldn't have to supplement their diets with it."

"That would certainly be useful, but I don't know how many vegans would be willing to eat genetically modified soybean products."

"We were wondering about that, but our marketing department decided enough would eat GMO soybeans to make it profitable."

"I suppose you could try to hide the fact that your soybeans are genetically modified."

"To be honest, the people upstairs would want to do that if they could, but they couldn't get away with it. It wouldn't make sense, anyway. No one would pay more for seeds that grew plants that make their own vitamin B12 if they couldn't advertise it, even if they could get around the testing."

"I don't know much about how they do testing and have some questions. How difficult would it be to fake it?"

"No way. To get certified, growers need to have their crops tested periodically by a licensed testing company. Certification can be checked on the testing website. I suppose a company could figure out how to make a forged butterfly label—the label on verified non-GMO products—even if they were genetically modified. Out-and-out fraud can't be totally prevented in farming any more than in other industries, but of course they wouldn't be listed on the Non-GMO Project website, or any other official testing website."

"Would it be possible to fool the testing company?"

"I see where this is going." Fran paused a moment. "Yes, it would be possible, but not if the genetic modification involved the sites where plant genes are typically changed. There are certain areas of the chromosome DNA that are normally targeted for things like disease resistance. Honestly, the testing companies only look at these areas. It's not like they test the whole genome. Maybe someday that would be practical, but currently only specific genes are targeted, and those are the areas that are tested. Testing the whole genome would be prohibitively expensive."

"So if someone were to genetically modify a plant in a totally unique way, away from the area usually targeted, that could be missed in the standard testing?"

"I suppose so."

"Is there a way to determine that?"

"Sure, but someone would have to sequence the whole genome unless they knew where to look," Fran answered.

"I have three kinds of seeds I'm pretty sure have been genetically engineered."

"Do you have any idea what genes are involved?"

"Could be anything. No one has been sickened as far as we know, so I doubt they inserted or converted a known gene to make a toxin. I'm really stumped, but I have every reason to believe they have done something harmful. They don't allow their own people to eat any of the produce that has been genetically altered."

"Maybe they've removed some things, like vitamins, from the produce. That would be harmful."

"Over the long run, I suppose it could be if people didn't eat anything else, and they didn't take vitamin pills. If they think they're going to take over the country by causing beriberi or some other vitamin deficiency disease in a few years, that sounds like a really bad plan.

"Hold on," Fran said, "you've gone from a company producing something harmful to a company planning to take over the country. Do you know how crazy that sounds?"

"According to Bong, our informant, that's exactly what they're planning."

"You've spoken to an informant?"

"Yes. He's from North Korea and he wants to help."

"To be honest, I'm finding your suspicion of a huge conspiracy involving North Korea difficult to believe. How do you know your informant is telling the truth? Wasn't your dad big on conspiracy theories?"

Fran had a point. If she was difficult to convince, people who didn't know me would be even harder to win over.

"I understand how I might sound crazy," I said, "but listen to everything I have to say. There's a large agribusiness that's buying up all the farmland where my parents' farm was. At first I thought they were just incompetent because they've been ripping out lots of good, productive crops. Also, they're selling their produce all over the country at rock bottom prices and claiming it's non-GMO. You've probably heard of them. I didn't want to mention their name because I thought you wouldn't believe me. They're pretending to be owned by people from China, but I've learned that the company is actually owned by North Korea, and they're planning something devastating. It could be weeks or years away, but I doubt they want to be pouring money into this project for a long time. I think we should assume whatever they're planning will happen sooner rather than later."

"Well, don't keep me waiting. Tell me the name of this diabolical company."

I ignored the sarcasm in Fran's voice. "Happy Sun Farm."

Fran was silent a few moments. "Dang," she said. "I must admit they've been the topic of conversation in the lunchroom. A Chinese company that's been undercutting the competition. Everyone's wondering how they do it."

"They do it by being supported by the North Korean government."

"Who is this informant of yours? Can you trust him?"

"Absolutely. His name is Bong, and we smuggled him out. He wants to defect. We speak to him through a translator, and he's given us a lot of information, as well as specimens, including seeds. If you saw our video of their secret labs, I know you'd believe me."

"I'm starting to think you might not be crazy," Fran said. "I know someone who works in the gene sequencing lab. I'll ask if he can analyze the seeds. Where are your other specimens from?"

"We have two samples from their central lab. It's very sophisticated. I think, besides the genetically-modified seeds, there are two products that are important components of their plan, and Bong got us samples from both—fluid from roller bottles which I suspect are growing cells that secrete something important to their plan, and liquid from flasks where something else is being made."

"What are they doing with these products?"

"Material from the flasks is sprayed onto produce that isn't genetically engineered. It must be highly dangerous, as the workers have to suit up to enter a room with the flasks or their contents. The roller bottles are used in the production of a substance that is stored in cartridges, which we believe will be loaded onto drones and sprayed across the country. Perhaps it's a chemical or virus toxic to plants, and they intend to attack our agriculture."

"I'll send your roller bottle and shaker flask samples to people in our company who work with proteins, carbohydrates, bacteria, and viruses. Between all those places, someone should be able to figure something out. Unfortunately, I absolutely can't drive to you to pick them up. Can—"

"I can be there tonight."

Chapter 43

AN HOUR LATER, CJ and I were on our way to Fran's condominium. It was evening when we reached her place which she shared with her boyfriend, Tyler, a local surfer and musician. Her accommodations were small, but big enough to put us up without feeling too crowded. We had dinner at a nearby seafood restaurant, then went for drinks at a local bar where Tyler and The Waves were a popular cover band, playing songs from the eighties and nineties. That's where Fran had met him six months earlier when she'd gone for happy hour with some friends. With his long, thick blond hair, tight jeans, and powerful voice, I understood why she was instantly attracted to him. After seeing how kind and thoughtful he was, I knew why he was more than a one-night stand.

We left the bar after Tyler's set was over, around 10:00 pm, and headed back to the condo. Morning would come soon, but I wanted to show Fran my drone video before accompanying her to work the next day.

We spent the next hour looking at the video CJ had saved to a thumb drive. Fran looked closely, often wanting me to replay certain segments. We were looking at a recording of a lab with microscopes, when she excitedly pointed to something I hadn't noticed before. "Those blobby-looking things are forming new seedlings. That's pretty good evidence they are growing genetically modified plants. See? They have small shoots and roots."

"I see what you mean, now that you point it out," I said.

"They may be doing the genetic modification somewhere at this site, or getting the cells from elsewhere and growing them here."

"How could they import genetically modified cells?"

Fran thought for a moment. "There could be freeze-dried cells in the liquid nitrogen tanks I noticed earlier. Back it up again."

I reversed the video until three large tanks on the floor came into view.

"Those look like the tanks we use to freeze cells at Vital Vittles. There could be thousands of cells in the tanks, ready to be grown later. They could have been prepared elsewhere, then brought here."

"I suppose that wouldn't be too difficult, given our proximity to Mexico. They could easily fit into a shipping container or the false bottom of a truck crossing the border near San Diego. They'd only have to smuggle tanks in once to have all they needed. Border Patrol agents are looking for drugs, not frozen cells."

We watched the rest of the video. Fran, of course, couldn't determine what they were preparing in the flasks or roller bottles by looking at them. When I told her the workers were required to wear protective gear around the flasks but not the roller bottles, she agreed that the flasks had to contain something highly toxic.

"They're certainly up to something in that lab," Fran said after we'd seen all the recordings. She helped me select still images from the video to load on my phone, so I could convince others I wasn't crazy. "Tomorrow, we'll try to start sorting that out, but now we need to get some sleep."

She distributed sheets and towels for CJ and me and headed off to bed with Tyler. The guest bed was only a twin, but we made do.

The next thing I remembered was Fran banging on our door, informing me it was time to get up. I was planning to go to work with her while CJ and Tyler went to the beach, where Tyler would give CJ a surfing lesson.

The drive to Fran's workplace took forty-five minutes due to traffic. We entered an industrial park, inland from her condominium, and drove to a modern two-story cement and glass building with a large sign reading "Vibrant Vittles."

Fran used her key card to enter her workplace and registered me at the front desk. I had to sign a nondisclosure agreement before going any further. Corporate spying was taken very seriously there. We walked down a busy corridor filled with people in white coats, business suits, and casual dress, some pushing carts of supplies, plants, and equipment. When we arrived at Fran's lab, she and I placed our purses in her locker. I held onto the specimens Bong had given me.

First, Fran introduced me to Dr. Mason, the director of plant genetic engineering. A balding, middle-aged man, I gave him a brief rundown of the goings on at Happy Sun Farm, which I had learned was owned by North Korea. He seemed skeptical until I showed him still pictures I had made from the drone video. I believe that convinced him I was legitimate. After I gave him the seeds Bong had collected for me, he agreed to test them.

Next, I met the directors of protein chemistry and microbiology together and repeated the information I'd given to Dr. Mason. I told them the sample from one of the flasks was likely highly dangerous and should be handled carefully. The other sample I had, from a roller bottle, might contain a non-toxic chemical or a benign microbe, but its purpose was unclear. Again, the images on my phone were instrumental in convincing them I wasn't delusional.

Each director was smart and asked many detailed questions, most of which I couldn't answer. I called Kwan several times, who in turn spoke to Bong to find out specific information, like, "What temperature were the roller bottles kept at?"—37°C, or body temperature; "Were any of the rooms kept at negative pressure?"—that would indicate an extreme biohazard such as smallpox, but Bong didn't know; "Had any workers become seriously ill, had rashes, other skin lesions, or other unusual symptoms?"—only an occasional cold; "Did any plants appear to be sickly or deformed?"—no.

Only the microbiology section at Vibrant Vittles had an isolation room suitable for handling deadly bacteria, viruses, or toxins, so the sample from the flask would be analyzed there. They would work on that first, as it appeared to be the most important of the two specimens, given its toxicity. The specimen from the roller bottle would be analyzed afterward.

It was 4:00 p.m. by the time we finished, and I was physically and emotionally worn out. Fran hadn't gotten any of her own work done, so she hurriedly did the least amount she could to get by, which took another ninety minutes.

I spent the time calling random stores in California and inquiring about their prices for Happy Sun produce compared to other brands. Most of the stores I contacted sold only Happy Sun produce when available. Customers were happy with the low prices, and there were no complaints. I called several stores in neighboring Nevada, Arizona, and Oregon. Same response. I branched out to other states, from the northern border to the Gulf of Mexico, and the Atlantic Ocean. I learned that Happy Sun was indeed squeezing the competition out nationwide. No illnesses or complaints had been registered.

It was 7:00 p.m. by the time we returned to Fran's place. CJ and Tyler were relaxing after a hard day surfing, drinking beer, and listening to country western music. We ate dinner at a local fish eatery and left for Melinda's house. I thanked Fran profusely for her help. As we left, she said, "I promise to let you know once I have information about those specimens."

On the way to Melinda's house, we stopped by Kwan's apartment to plan the next day's rescue of Nabi. Bong was there, and we conversed with him through Kwan, as we sat crowded around his kitchen table.

"Nabi will board truck headed for Albuquerque at 12:30 p.m.," Kwan said. "According to Google, most direct route to Albuquerque is go east on I-40 for eleven hours. If she can't get on 12:30 p.m. truck for any reason, she will try for next one going in same direction, which leave at 2:30."

"We need to intercept the vehicle before it gets on the freeway," I said. "How long does it take to drive from Happy Sun to I-40?"

"About forty minute."

"We'll have to divert the truck in that time frame."

We brought up the route from Happy Sun Farm to I-40 on Google maps. Studying the area using "layers" to show an aerial view of vegetation, we agreed on a spot where the road curved slightly, and trees grew fairly close to the road.

"We can park our vehicles there," CJ said, "so the Happy Sun truck driver won't see us when he approaches."

"Bong say there are always two drivers on produce trucks, so they can trade off driving," Kwan said. "It also makes them less likely to defect because workers don't trust each other. The cab on the trucks aren't locked. Most have a door on right side that is easy to open, and there is ladder permanently attached below the door so they can get into truck easily."

CJ turned to me and said, "I'll take you with me in my truck. Adam will take Kwan and Bong in his SUV. Adam and I will have flares ready to light and set up across the road as soon as we see the Happy Sun truck approach. The highway isn't traveled much, so with any luck, there won't be other vehicles around."

It was 11:30 p.m. by the time we had finalized the plan. Bong was beside himself with excitement when we left him at Kwan's apartment before returning to Melinda's. Nabi would be calling him in a half hour, at which time he'd explain what we had arranged.

CJ, Adam, and I would pick up orange vests and flares first thing in the morning. The orange vests would give us an official air, at least at first glance. We decided that adding a hard hat would be even more convincing. CJ would approach the driver's door, Adam the passenger door. If the drivers didn't speak English, Adam and CJ would use arm motions, and Google translate if necessary. Once the drivers were out of the truck, CJ would explain that they were agriculture inspectors, looking for illegally imported produce from Mexico, and they needed to quickly inspect the truck.

As Happy Sun was carrying legal produce, we expected the truckers to fully cooperate so they could be on their way quickly. They wouldn't want any trouble. Still, I gave a taser each to CJ and Adam to use if necessary, glad I'd taken them from my father's stash of weapons.

While CJ and Adam spoke to the men in front of the truck, Kwan, Bong and I would walk around the back and open the side door. Bong would greet Nabi and motion for her to keep quiet. She would put on an orange jacket we would carry, and the four of us would leave the truck and walk behind it back to our vehicles. Once Bong, Nabi, and Kwan were in Adam's SUV, I would shout that the truck passed inspection, and the Happy Sun truck would be on its way. Easy. That's what we all thought would happen, but things didn't go our way.

Chapter 44

WHEN WE REACHED MELINDA'S house, she was already in bed. I knew I wouldn't sleep well that night, and I wasn't concerned that we'd have to get up in less than eight hours. CJ and I were awake when the sun came up. If we got any sleep, it wasn't much. We had breakfast and left before Melinda was awake. After arriving in the nearest Home Depot parking lot, we waited for Adam to show up at 6:30. I was surprised at how many people—primarily men dressed in heavy-duty cargo pants, boots, and T-shirts—were there at that ungodly hour.

We purchased a dozen road flares and enough yellow vests and hard hats for all of us. As we walked by the area with protective goggles, we decided to buy a pair of them for everyone. We had time to stop for coffee before picking up Kwan and Bong at 10:00 a.m. CJ, Adam, and I left the coffee shop and drove directly to Kwan's apartment, Adam driving separately in his SUV. Once we were parked, I phoned Kwan. We waited outside our vehicles until he and Bong joined us a few minutes later. Bong was all smiles, and I suspected he hadn't slept much the night before, either. Kwan had prepared lunch for us, which was a nice surprise. It smelled delicious, even through the bag in which it was packed. I hadn't thought about eating later, but we had a long day ahead of us and would need sustenance at some point.

We drove to our destination, arriving at 11:00 a.m. CJ and Adam pulled their vehicles to the side of the road, as close as possible to the foliage. We had approximately two hours to prepare for the arrival of the Happy Sun truck. The trees by the side of the road were sparse, not large enough for Kwan, Bong, and me to hide behind. We decided to stay in the open. When the Happy Sun Farm truck approached, CJ,

Bong, and I would pretend to be surveying the area, taking pictures with our cell phones. Bong didn't have one, so CJ lent him his.

We put on the orange vests, goggles, and hard hats. After CJ got half of the flares ready to light up, I showed Adam how to use the taser I'd given him earlier. I didn't know much more than he did, but I had read the instructions in one of my father's survivalist reference books.

Several trucks and two cars whizzed by. One of the trucks had the familiar Happy Sun logo, but was too early to be carrying Nabi. At noon, we sat by the roadside and ate the barbecued chicken and pork Kwan had prepared. When finished, we all cleaned up with the wipes Kwan had packed. By 1:00 p.m., we were all on high alert, waiting for Nabi's truck.

Bong was the first to yell out at 1:08. I don't know what he yelled, but I imagine it was Korean for something like, "I see it!" or "There it is!" As a truck in the distance grew larger, the Happy Sun logo became clear. With no other vehicle in front of it, CJ set up the flares, and we all took our positions.

When the truck was close, Adam stood behind the flares, waving his arms above his head to alert the driver. With my stomach in knots, I turned to look busy photographing the trees and whatnot at the side of the road as I heard the squeak of the tires. The sound of the refrigeration in the truck cab was loud, and I could barely hear CJ yell that everyone had to get out so they could inspect their truck. The driver spoke broken English and agreed. I turned to see him and his passenger jump to the ground. Both men walked to the front of the truck, where CJ questioned them about what they were carrying.

Kwan, Bong, and I walked around the back of the vehicle towards the side. Bong looked like he was about to explode with excitement as he climbed the ladder and opened the side door to the cargo area without difficulty. Everything was going as planned.

Bong entered, but didn't immediately exit as I had expected. Instead, I heard him repeat Nabi's name multiple times. At first speaking quietly, he became louder and louder. Kwan climbed the ladder and told him to keep his voice down. Finally, after several minutes, Bong exited the truck. His shoulders were drooped, his back slumped.

I thought he might cry. He said something to Kwan in a low voice. "She's not there," Kwan told me, as if I hadn't figured that out.

The three of us returned to the side of the road, and I yelled to CJ, "We've completed our inspection."

CJ and Adam had a few more words with the truck driver and his passenger, who then boarded the vehicle and drove off.

We spent the next two hours trying to comfort Bong, as Kwan translated our sympathies and optimism that Nabi would be on the next truck. Having been through the exercise once without any problems, I was confident the second time would be even easier. My optimism soared when I saw the second Happy Sun truck approaching.

We all took our positions. Other than the truck, the highway was empty. CJ again spread the flares across the road. When the vehicle was close, Adam stood behind the line of burning sticks and waved his arms about his head. As before, the truck stopped.

While I pretended to take pictures with my cell phone, I heard CJ say to the driver, "We are government inspectors. Please, both of you need to step out of your vehicle and stand in front of your truck. I need you to answer some questions."

The driver answered, "Certainly, officer."

I realized I could hear the talking much better than I had with the first truck, although CJ, the truck, and I were in roughly the same positions. That's when I realized this Happy Sun truck was much quieter than the previous one—no refrigeration sound.

The driver got out, as did the passenger. However, the passenger refused to stand in front of the truck, remaining by his door, which was on the same side as the entry to the cargo area. Bong, Kwan, and I froze, not knowing what to do. Surely, if we opened the side door and let Nabi out, he would see us. CJ repeatedly told the man to step to the front of the truck, but he wouldn't budge. The two men from the Happy Sun truck spoke loudly back and forth in Korean.

Bong was trembling, his eyes open so wide I thought they might spring out of their sockets. Kwan whispered that they were agreeing not to cooperate with CJ, and that under no circumstances would they allow anyone to enter the truck.

After pausing a while, no longer having a clear plan to follow, I made the best decision I could at the time. "Let's enter the truck anyway," I said to Kwan. "I have no doubt CJ and Adam will fight with them if necessary. If we find Nabi, we'll have to make a run for it. I don't see another choice." Kwan turned to Bong to translate. I hoped he worded it better. I should have said, "When we find Nabi," rather than "If we find Nabi." When Kwan stopped talking, Bong shook his head ever so slightly in agreement.

My heart was pounding so loud, and my chest was so tight, I didn't know how long I could maintain my composure, but I pressed on. I led Kwan and Bong as casually as possible to the truck's side door. Bong was about to climb onto the ladder so he could enter, when a loud scream caught our attention. The Happy Sun truck's passenger was running towards us, his eyes glaring and his teeth bared. I froze when he raised his fist, expecting him to slug me. Without thinking, I closed my eyes, as if that would lessen the impact. The impact never came. By the time I opened my eyes, the man was on the ground, Adam on top. I surmised he had tackled my would-be attacker from behind, and I watched as Adam punched him in the head and pulled zip ties from his pocket.

He dropped the zip ties when the driver piled on, followed immediately by the appearance of CJ, who kicked the driver mercilessly, then rolled him off Adam's back. He continued to kick him, but the driver and passenger didn't give up easily. One of them had gotten to his feet and was reaching into his back pocket when Adam tasered him.

Realizing I had been wasting time while I watched the spectacle in front of me unfold, I sprung into action. I climbed the few steps to the side door of the cab and tried to open it. That's when I realized it was locked with a bolt on the outside. My heart sank.

Seeing my predicament, Adam, who by then was pulling the passenger's arms behind his back, yelled out, "Look under the seat in the pick-up. CJ still has the bolt cutter."

Thankfully, CJ hadn't removed it from his truck after we rescued Bong. I ran to his truck and returned with the bolt cutter. I probably looked lost when Bong grabbed it from me. Without ascending the stairs, he quickly snapped the metal rod securing the door.

As he laid the tool on the ground, I rushed up the stairs and swung the door open. Kwan and Bong followed closely behind.

Instead of a refrigerated space filled with produce, the interior was uncomfortably warm, occupied by stacks of oblong brown boxes bundled together, labeled with Korean characters. I looked around, but no one was in sight.

Despite the small space between the mountains of boxes, Bong pushed past me and Kwan and frantically shouted Nabi's name several times as he squeezed between the stacks. Seconds later, I heard a scream. Unclear if it was a scream of horror or happiness, I held my breath as I waited.

As Bong's heavy footsteps approached, I looked up to see him carrying a woman in his arms, the same woman I had seen with him in the shed on my parents' farm. She was stirring, and he had a broad smile on his face. He shouted something to Kwan, who disappeared. When he returned with a bottle of water, Bong had already carried Nabi off the truck and was gently whispering in her ear. Bong said loudly for all to hear: "Nabi."

Still standing in the truck, I watched through the door as he lowered her feet to the ground and, while continuing to support her, opened the water bottle and held it for her as she sipped, then drank more vigorously. I felt at peace as I witnessed the tenderness Bong demonstrated before CJ's yelling brought me back to the reality of the moment. I grabbed two of the boxes from the nearest pile, wondering what they held, and scooted to the ground.

Looking around, I saw that both the Happy Sun driver and passenger had been tasered and zip-tied. Despite having been bombarded with electrical current, both men were yelling and struggling to free themselves from the plastic strips holding their wrists together.

Instead of retrieving his shotgun, CJ grabbed a tangle of rope from his car and bound both men's feet. Then he and Adam loaded the Happy Sun drivers into the truck cargo area and shut the door.

We stood by our vehicles in the hot sun and drank water as we tried to relax.

I pulled Kwan aside and asked, “What’s inside these boxes?”

He glanced at the writing on the outside and said, “T-shirts.”

I figured there was a plan to distribute T-shirts with a propaganda message to the public after they had achieved their goal.

Nabi was now fully alert, standing on her own. She and Bong were speaking to each other softly, smiling and occasionally laughing. I couldn’t hear them speak and wouldn’t have understood them even if I did, but I was pretty sure I knew what the content of their conversation was.

After basking in the glory of our bold rescue of Nabi and multiple high fives, CJ called the local police and left an anonymous tip that a Happy Sun Farm cargo truck appeared to be abandoned on the highway to I-40. We all agreed to meet at Melinda’s house at 6:00 p.m. to plan our next steps.

Chapter 45

GENERAL BAI GLARED AT the soldier before him. "Do you understand?" he yelled.

"Yes, yes, general. I understand how important this is. I will do my very best."

"Don't forget what happened to the soldier you are replacing. You don't want to meet the same fate, do you?"

"No, sir. Of course not. But shouldn't General Jeong be making these plans? He is over there and has a better grasp of the situation."

General Bai's face turned red, and he clenched his fists as he bellowed. "Don't you know who he is? He is the favorite cousin of our Supreme Leader. He has his hands full with other issues. He can't be bothered chasing after some stupid woman who is getting in the way. She has caused a lot of trouble, and we must find her. It is up to you to make sure General Jeong has everything he needs. The best plans, the best equipment, the best people to guarantee success. No one can be allowed to get in his way."

"I have already contacted our sleeper cells there, and they are dedicated to finding the woman who is trying to interfere. They've come close, but she has eluded them so far. I am confident we will find her. It's only a question of time."

"I hope so, for your sake. Now go."

Chapter 46

WE WERE PRACTICALLY EUPHORIC when CJ and I left the scene of Nabi's rescue. It had been some time since I'd felt this optimistic. With Bong and Nabi, I thought we'd be able to quickly convince law enforcement that something nefarious was happening at Happy Sun. Before we would meet with the others again at Melinda's, CJ needed to stop by his pasta sauce company. Kwan wanted to bring the dirty plates and containers back to his restaurant, and Adam drove him along with Nabi and Bong.

I spent an hour familiarizing myself with the process of making large quantities of pasta sauce at Mama Baroni's while CJ spoke to the supervisor. It was hot and sunny when we arrived at Melinda's a little before 5:00 p.m., the agreed-upon meeting time.

Melinda didn't usually arrive home before 6:30 p.m., so we were surprised to see her sedan in the carport. CJ parked along the curb and waited for Adam to pull up behind us. When he arrived a few minutes later, CJ jumped out of the pickup, and I followed him to Adam's SUV. Adam rolled down his window and listened as CJ explained that he was concerned seeing Melinda's car parked at the house before she was expected home.

After a short discussion, Adam left Kwan, Bong, and Nabi in his vehicle, and joined CJ to look around the perimeter of Melinda's house and peek through the windows. We had left early that morning, before Melinda was up. Someone could have visited the house between the time we left and the time she usually drove off for work.

I returned to the truck and waited as Adam and CJ finished surveying the house. Minutes later, they returned. "Doesn't look good," CJ said. "I don't see any sign of Melinda, but the living room furniture is messed up, and there are broken dishes in the kitchen."

I felt horrible. Nauseated. Someone from Happy Sun must have learned we were staying there and came to find us. If we hadn't left early that morning, they would have found CJ and me, but Melinda would have been left alone. I closed my eyes as I reflected on the situation and hoped she was okay.

The front door was locked, so CJ used the key Melinda had given him to enter the house. He told me to wait outside while Adam followed closely behind. I waited a few moments, then entered. The house was eerily quiet, except for the sound of an irritating healthcare commercial emanating from the kitchen TV. Melinda often watched the news while eating breakfast. Her purse was on the kitchen counter.

Cold cereal was spread across the floor, admixed with pieces of a broken cereal bowl. I looked for blood but saw none. Partially relieved at the lack of blood, I broke into tears when I peered into the kitchen garbage can, which had been pulled out from under the sink. On top was an empty two-inch shiny silver cubicle box.

We stood in silence as we examined the surroundings, letting the scene sink in. I imagined the scenario that had happened there earlier. Melinda was probably questioned about our whereabouts, but she couldn't have told them because she didn't know. Perhaps they'd tried to beat the information out of her. From the looks of things, it appeared she'd put up quite a fight. She could have been given a deadly truffle as a peace offering or been forced to eat it. Either way, I was sure she was dead. Her body was nowhere to be found, possibly dissolving in a vat of sodium hydroxide by now. Melinda didn't have surveillance cameras, so we'd have to piece it together from the evidence at hand.

It was a mystery how they had found CJ and me. I looked outside. The street was empty, as usual. We hadn't spoken to any of Melinda's neighbors, but we could have been seen. CJ had been parking his truck on the curb in front of the house. Anyone driving by could have spotted it and reported our whereabouts back to Happy Sun. Thinking about it, it would be pretty easy for someone to find us if they had the resources.

Adam broke the silence. "Looks like some seriously bad shit happened here."

"Yup," CJ agreed, "there was a fight, but that box Berry found—it leaves no doubt Melinda was poisoned." He explained the significance of the box to Adam. "I don't think there's anything we can do now to save her. It's too late. Now we have to think about saving ourselves."

"And the world," I added.

"We need to get out of here before they come back," CJ said. "They already know we have Bong. Now they know we have Nabi."

"What about Kwan?" Adam asked. "Do you think he'll be safe if he goes back to his restaurant?"

"Good question," I answered. "I think he'd better stay with us. He's not going to like it, though."

"Where do you think we should go?" CJ asked, looking from me to Adam and back.

"We can't stay around here," I answered. "And I think we need to ditch your pick-up, CJ." I looked at Adam. "I don't know if they have a description of your SUV, too, but I think we better get hold of some other vehicles."

"I've got a buddy who owns a car rental company in Bakersfield," CJ said. "He can set us up with some new wheels. I'll call him right now."

"Great," I said. "As far as where we should go, I suggest we go to San Diego. It would be helpful to stay near Fran and her company."

CJ called the local police to anonymously report a break-in and kidnapping or murder at Melinda's house. CJ and I collected our things from the bedroom we were using, and explained to Kwan, who was still waiting in Adam's SUV with Bong and Nabi, that Melinda had probably been killed, and we all needed to go to San Diego, where we hoped to be safe. We left it to Kwan to explain what was happening to Bong and Nabi.

By 6:00 p.m., we were in two late-model SUVs CJ had borrowed from his friend. We had transferred everything from our vehicles to the new ones, and were en route to San Diego. CJ's truck and Adam's SUV were left parked in a secure area at the rental company.

I rode in a Honda CR-V with CJ, while Adam, Bong, Nabi, and Kwan, took a Nissan Pathfinder. I was right when I predicted Kwan wouldn't be happy about having to leave town, but he took the news in stride and instructed his daughter to close the restaurant until he returned. He didn't hide his excitement about being part of something big.

A half-hour into our trip, Fran called to report that her company had run a test similar to those conducted by companies looking for genetic modification, and all the seeds passed. No genetic modification was detected.

"Damn," I said upon hearing the news. "I was hoping you'd come up with a smoking gun, something we could use to show the company bribed someone to pass certification testing."

"I'd like to think none of the people doing the testing can be bribed," Fran said. "From what you told me, I doubted the Happy Sun people would try to bribe someone to pass the non-GMO test. After all, they're probably not altering genes to improve crops in the usual ways. I suspect that if they've done DNA editing, it involves other areas, ones that are not routinely tested for. It'll be another day before I get the results of the whole genome testing on the seeds."

"Turns out, we're headed to San Diego right now," I said, not wanting to alarm Fran by divulging the reason behind our sudden decision to visit her city. "Could I come by Vibrant Vittles tomorrow to see the latest data myself?"

"I don't see why not. Come around noon."

We reached San Diego around 10:00 p.m. that night. I was tired and hungry. We all stopped at a fast-food joint where I believe Bong and Nabi sampled their first hamburgers. At first hesitant, they dug in after a few bites, even eating all their fries. After finishing my fish sandwich, I was no longer hungry, but I was still tired. Most hotels already had their "No Vacancy" signs up so we decided to sleep in the parking lot of a Walmart. Two RVs were already parked there when we arrived, so I thought we would be allowed to stay. The store didn't close for another twenty minutes, so we all used the restrooms to attend to our needs. I escorted Nabi to the women's room and gestured towards the stalls. She figured out what to do with no further help from me.

Announcements that the store would be closing soon were coming frequently, but we had time to purchase foam camping mattresses before being kicked out. Despite the less-than-optimal conditions, I slept pretty well that night. We used the Walmart facilities again in the morning before dining at Denny's.

"I can't believe we've been so distracted with everything, we haven't opened the boxes I took from the truck," I said after sampling the coffee, which wasn't half bad. "I'd like to see what sort of message they have on the shirts, and if it's written any better than instructions for assembling things made in Asia."

We agreed to open the boxes which were in the back of our SUV right after breakfast. CJ did the honors as we all watched in silence. Rather than T-shirts, each box contained a metallic device protected by bubble wrap. It didn't take long for us to recognize them as drones.

They were powered by lithium-ion batteries. A gauge on the side indicated they were fully charged. They had two nozzles, one on each side, and empty pipe clamps near each wing where a canister could be secured, allowing the contents to be dispersed by the nozzle.

We were all silent for a few moments. I think everyone was thinking what I was—everything Bong had described earlier fit perfectly. Finally, I broke the silence. "These are the drones Bong told us about. They're planning to use them to disperse whatever is in those canisters. With enough of these, they could contaminate the air of the entire country." I turned to Kwan. "Ask Bong and Nabi if those clamps could hold the canisters."

Kwan handed a drone to the couple. Bong turned it over in his hands a few times. After a short conversation in Korean, Kwan said, "Yes, Bong says the canisters Happy Sun is producing would fit into the drone's clamps. They would snap right in." He paused a moment before continuing. "Like I told you before, North Korea is very, very dangerous. You must act fast."

As if I needed more pressure from him. I hoped my upcoming visit to Vital Vittles would open the door to a full investigation and an end to whatever the North Koreans were planning.

Not surprisingly, there was no information in the newsfeeds on my phone about an investigation into the break-in at Melinda's house. I picked up a copy of the LA Times for more complete news coverage. Lots of bad news—weather disasters in Florida and the Midwest, a school shooting in Montana claiming eleven lives, a mysterious illness causing diarrhea, vomiting, fever, and low white blood cell counts showing up sporadically across the country, and more violence erupting in Haiti. Nothing about a break-in at Melinda's house.

My attention was drawn back to the sporadic illnesses. So far, thirty-seven such cases had been reported in twenty-five states. Two of those affected, both children, had died. The course of the disease appeared similar in all cases, but the cause had yet to be determined. A toxin or virus was suspected, and there could be additional cases that hadn't been reported. The malady appeared to be contagious, as several family clusters had been identified, but no geographic area was impacted more than others. For a moment, I wondered if these illnesses could be related to the goings on at Happy Sun but quickly dismissed the idea. I was so focused on that company, it seemed to be distorting my every thought.

Chapter 47

WEARING KHAKI PANTS AND a matching shirt, Dr. Gang hung his head as he walked into General Bai's office. Instead of his usual white coat, he thought the semi-militaristic apparel might make him appear more dedicated and trustworthy. This meeting would be important. His life depended on the outcome.

General Bai sat behind a large desk, his military uniform with medals on full display. As Dr. Gang stood humbly before him, his legs quivering noticeably, the general did nothing to ease the scientist's discomfort. Although chairs were nearby, he didn't offer one to his guest. He waited a few moments before speaking, appearing to relish the unmistakable manifestations of fear Dr. Gang displayed. Finally, General Bai spoke. "Dr. Gang, what do you have to say for yourself?"

The scientist's body shook, his fear more intense. "I know I am unworthy, but I beg you. Without me, the program will fail. The Americans haven't figured anything out."

"Not yet, but I assure you, it's just a question of time. The illnesses have been noticed by their government, and their Centers for Disease Control are investigating. If they discover what's making those people sick, it will be a disaster."

"Just knowing what's making them sick won't be enough. They'll need to put all the pieces together before they can possibly stop us."

"Those scientists aren't stupid. How long do you think it will take until they realize what we're doing?"

"I don't know, but if we speed this up significantly, it won't matter. It will be too late for them."

"So that's your answer? Speed this up?" General Bai yelled as he pounded his desk, his face turning red. "You were instructed to take everything into account. Their diet, their fixation on organic and non-GMO food, their health care system, and their fixation on low prices. How could you have missed this?"

"I am stupid and irresponsible. I didn't think to investigate something that never occurred to me. Now I know the Americans are such idiots, they don't eat their dogs and cats. Instead, they call them pets and play with them like fools. I've been told they even hug them and kiss them. It disgusts me. I humbly ask forgiveness for my failure to realize the extent of the American's stupidity."

"I have a good mind to throw you to the dogs," the general shouted.

With sweat pouring down his face, Dr. Gang spoke, his voice quivering. "General, please understand. Everything I have been responsible for is ready right now. The produce has been widely distributed, and the Americans are buying all of it. We estimate that over eighty-five percent of the population is ready. Primed, as we say, like the prisoners in the orange jumpsuits. All the canisters we need have been made, and I am told many have been distributed. All we need to do now is speed up the distribution of the canisters and drones. It's in the hands of General Jeong. Please, General Bai, I humbly beseech you to order him to speed up his operation. You will be happy with the results, and our Supreme Leader will be very impressed."

"We just had a large shipment of drones intercepted."

"Were they loaded? I warned you against shipping them loaded."

"No, they weren't loaded, but the local police have confiscated them. And that American troublemaker I told you about has freed two of our workers. They were low-level and don't know much, but there's no telling what important information they'll reveal."

"Can't you eliminate them?"

The general pounded his desk as he shouted, "You think I'm an idiot?"

"Of course not, sir," Dr. Gang said, looking at the floor, seeming to hold back tears.

"They would be dead if we could find them."

Dr. Gang appeared to be mustering as much strength as he could before he raised his head. "If I may say, sir, it appears that there are now several reasons to speed this up. Not only the inadvertent illnesses of the American public, but the discovery of the drones and the escaped workers teaming up with the Americans. If we carry out the operation in a week, it will succeed."

"You think everything can be ready in a week?"

"I do."

"Will you bet your life on it?"

"Absolutely."

Chapter 48

CJ DROPPED ME OFF, and I checked in at the front desk of Vital Vittles at noon as Fran had instructed me. A minute later, my friend came to retrieve me, her face devoid of expression. "I think you'll be interested in what our molecular geneticists found."

I hurried to keep up with her as we marched down the familiar, busy corridor. We made a left turn, then another left into an office with an open door.

Dr. Mason was sitting behind his large desk, looking over computer printouts. He looked up as we entered. He had a serious expression on his face, different from the friendly smile he'd worn when I first met him.

"These seeds are interesting," he said. "All three types—the strawberries, arugula, and cucumbers—have been edited. They have the same modification, the insertion of a gene to produce a protein not native to them. So far, we haven't been able to identify that protein, and I'm concerned it might be something harmful to humans. I have someone comparing it to a database more complete than what we have here, and she should have some information soon."

I thanked Dr. Mason and told him I would have a hard time waiting. As I prepared to rise from my chair, loud footsteps approached. I turned as a young woman in a lab coat rushed in. She was sweating and breathing heavily, as if she had sprinted down the hallway. "I've got it, Jackson," she blurted out as she stood behind me. "I just got off the phone with Dr. Winters at UCLA. She has access to a huge database."

"Don't keep us waiting, Alice. You know Fran, and this is her friend, Berry, who obtained the samples."

Without acknowledging us, Alice continued. “The gene added to these seeds makes a human protein that’s never found in plants. The protein is called the transferrin receptor molecule.”

“What’s a receptor?” I asked.

“Receptors, in general, bind to specific molecules outside the cell,” Alice answered. “Each receptor acts like a doorway, letting the molecule it attaches to get inside the cell.”

“What exactly does the receptor made by the edited seeds do?” Fran asked.

“It normally attaches to a molecule called transferrin. Without this receptor, transferrin wouldn’t be able to enter cells. Before you ask, all I know about transferrin is that it carries iron through the blood. When it binds to its receptor, it goes into the cell and carries iron with it. While many animals have a transferrin receptor, it is slightly different in each species.”

“Why would anyone want to add a transferrin receptor to a plant?” I asked.

“I’m not done yet.” Alice paused to catch her breath before continuing. “The gene in the seeds has a number of changes, so the protein it makes is different from a normal human transferrin receptor. First of all, it makes only part of the receptor. Then, there are two major changes in the remaining part of the gene that alter the receptor it makes in significant ways.”

“It must have taken them years to do this,” Dr. Mason said. “Do you suppose this new gene was designed to interfere with human iron metabolism?”

“Probably not. I believe the North Koreans want to use the edited transferrin receptor in another way. One of the changes they made was to add a site that binds to a normal human protein called the CCK receptor. Most CCK receptors are on the surface of cells in the stomach, duodenum, pancreas, and gallbladder.”

“Interesting,” Dr. Mason said. “When the altered transferrin receptor is eaten with food, it will rub up against nearby cells before it is destroyed by acid and digestive enzymes. The edited receptor will enter the cells of the stomach and duodenum by binding to a CCK receptor. Then it will do something, but I don't know what."

"Probably something bad," I said.

Alice took a deep breath. "What I found out about the other edited site will throw some light on that." All eyes were on Alice as she continued. "At that site, a portion of human transferrin receptor DNA is replaced with a portion of DNA from the feline transferrin receptor gene."

"You mean this gene they've designed is part cat?" I asked, incredulous.

"It is," Alice said, "and the cat part likely holds the key to what they are planning. Interestingly, the feline transferrin receptor has a unique site not present on the human receptor. The feline site binds strongly to the virus that causes feline distemper. The normal human transferrin receptor does not bind the virus, and humans therefore cannot catch feline distemper."

"I'm getting lost here," I said.

"I'll make it simple," Alice said. "To summarize everything I found out, Happy Sun Farm inserted a gene into their seeds that makes a portion of the human transferrin receptor that's been edited to bind to the CCK receptor as well as the feline distemper virus. When we eat Happy Sun's produce, the edited human transferrin receptor containing the feline distemper virus binding site is incorporated into our cells, making all of us susceptible to feline distemper."

"Does anyone know what the symptoms of feline distemper are?" I asked.

Alice looked down at her paper and began reading. "Feline distemper is highly contagious, and can cause diarrhea, sometimes bloody, vomiting, fever, lethargy, loss of appetite, dehydration, low white blood cell count, seizures, and tremors." She looked up again, apparently pleased at being the one with all the answers.

Alice looked at Dr. Mason, who sat motionless, his brow furrowed. We all waited for him to weigh in on the information Alice had presented. Finally, he lifted his gaze, a somber look on his face, and began speaking. "Alice, you have presented compelling evidence that the genetic alteration introduced by the North Koreans will make us susceptible to the feline distemper virus, but I have a hard time believing that is the end goal of the North Korean government. While cats can die without the vaccine, the virus isn't nearly as deadly as many others."

"If the disease in humans is anything like it is in cats," Fran said, "it could be bad, but not catastrophic—no pun intended. Not nearly as dangerous as COVID-19. I agree that it wouldn't make sense for the North Koreans to dedicate so many resources to making us susceptible to the feline distemper virus. Most cats are vaccinated, so there isn't a lot of the virus around."

There was something familiar about the symptoms Alice had described. I tried to think of people I knew who had been sick recently, but nothing came to mind. Finally, I made the connection. "Did any of you hear about the recently discovered mysterious illness the CDC is working on? There have been cases of diarrhea, vomiting, fever, and low white blood cell counts reported, sometimes spread by close contact in families. Do you think this is related?" I looked around for confirmation. Maybe I was letting my imagination go wild and wondered if the others thought my idea was crazy.

"I suppose it's possible," Fran answered, scratching her head.

"Did those people have cats that could have spread it to them?" Dr. Mason asked.

"I don't remember reading anything about pets."

"It might be worthwhile to look into that," he said. "I have a friend who works at the Animal and Plant Health Inspection Service. She can find the best person at the CDC to investigate this. Even if it is shown that these people have caught cat distemper because they have the receptors introduced by food from this farm, I'm not sure we'd have the full answer about what's going on."

I left the meeting with Fran, satisfied we had made significant progress, yet uneasy about what we didn't know. Like Dr. Mason, I didn't think the North Korean goal was to infect as many Americans as possible with feline distemper. According to Bong, they were packaging something highly dangerous to be dispersed by drones. Did they think the feline distemper virus was extremely deadly? I didn't think so. The other samples from Happy Sun Farm were still being analyzed. Hopefully, they would fill in the blanks.

Chapter 49

"I DON'T KNOW WHAT to make of this, but I think it may be something important," Officer Riley said as she marched into her sergeant's office and presented him with a drone.

"What the hell is this?" the sergeant asked.

"We found a bunch of these—must have been hundreds—in a truck earlier today."

"Is that related to the call that came in earlier about a Happy Sun Farm truck?"

"Sure is. I went out there and found the truck, just like they said, and also, just like they said, there were two guys inside. Their arms were zip-tied behind their backs. What the caller didn't tell us was that both those guys were dead."

The sergeant looked up, seeming to be fully at attention for the first time. "Dead, huh? Shot, I suppose."

"I didn't find any bullet holes."

"Sometimes they can be hard to see. I assume you notified the coroner."

"Sure did. I stayed until they arrived to collect the bodies and any evidence left behind."

"Did you see anything?"

"Just two small silver boxes that looked like they'd been ripped open, lying next to them. And, of course, lots of these." She held up the drone again.

"You're saying a truck from our local farm was being used to ship a bunch of drones?"

"Exactly. We don't know if the company was shipping them, or if the truck was stolen and then filled with drones, but I did notice that both the dead men were Asian, like everyone at Happy Sun other than the pickers. They both had valid commercial driver's licenses and Happy Sun Farm identity badges, so I assume they were employees."

"We'll have to wait on the autopsy results. Hopefully, we'll have something tomorrow. Those silver boxes—do you think they had something to do with this?"

"I thought of that, given how close the boxes were to them. I wondered if they had a suicide pact. The boxes could have held cyanide pills."

"You have quite an imagination, don't you? How could they have committed suicide with both hands tied behind their backs?"

"They could have taken turns retrieving them from each other's pocket, even with their hands behind them. Then, one could tear the box open, and the other could bend over and eat the poison. The other one could drop the poison on the floor and lie down to eat it."

The sergeant rolled his eyes. "Sounds like something from a Hollywood movie. Meanwhile, while we wait for the autopsy results, why don't you visit Happy Sun? Find out if those men worked there or if they had stolen the truck and made forgeries of the ID badges. If you find out they worked there and didn't steal the truck, ask why they had all those drones. I don't see anything illegal about transporting those things, but I must admit to being curious. Just be sure you don't ruffle any feathers. That company has donated a lot of money to our local police fund."

When Officer Riley drove through the entrance to Happy Sun Farm, she was again stopped by the yellow arm blocking traffic at the sentry gate. Happy Sun, my ass, she thought as she looked at the Happy Sun Farm sign and the sculpture of the smiling sun behind it. She explained to the heavily accented Asian man who greeted her that two men had been found inside one of the company trucks. Both were deceased, and she wanted to find out if the truck had been stolen or if the men were employees of the farm and had been transporting drones.

The guard's expression didn't change, and Riley wasn't sure he understood her. He turned away and spoke into a shoulder walkie-talkie.

After overhearing a short conversation unintelligible to her, Riley was directed to pull into a parking space in front of the main building. Mr. Chen was walking out of the front doors as she exited her vehicle.

He smiled and greeted her. "Hello, Officer Riley. It's so nice to see you again. I would be happy to answer your questions about the employment status of these men for you. I know how difficult your job is, and I am always happy to help in any way I can."

Riley showed Mr. Chen pictures of the deceased men's licenses, with their names and photographs in sharp focus. He appeared to study the images, then shook his head. "These are not our employees. I have never seen them before."

"They listed this place as their home address on their licenses."

"I can assure you that they never lived or worked here."

"They obtained the licenses with this address over a year ago. Do you have an explanation for that?"

Mr. Chen chuckled. "Yes, they are stupid."

"What about the truck? Are you missing a truck?"

"Now that you mention it, I learned this morning that one of our trucks is missing. It was never returned yesterday as scheduled."

"Did you report it?"

"I thought it would come back today. It's not unusual for drivers to be delayed on the return trip. Between you and me, I think they often take a side trip for a little relaxation, if you know what I mean." Mr. Chen gave a wry smile.

"I'm concerned about your drivers. It looks like they were hijacked. Can you give them a call?"

Mr. Chen sighed. "I'll level with you. Some of our employees ditch or sell their trucks and disappear. They find a girlfriend and want to live elsewhere, but their visas only allow them to work here. I'm a sympathetic man. I don't want anyone to get in trouble, so I don't report them. If I lose a truck now and then, I write it off on our taxes."

"That's certainly very kind of you, Mr. Chen, but you really should report these incidents to us. Right now, I'm worried about your missing drivers and want to find them."

"They most likely sold the truck and could be anywhere by now. I don't want to cause problems for them."

"Do you mind if I take a look at your shipping records? I want to know when the truck we found left your facility, and the names of the drivers who took it. I have the license and VIN of the truck."

Mr. Chen stiffened as he maintained his friendly demeanor. "I don't think that would be helpful, and my people are too busy to look through the shipping paperwork."

"Don't you have a computer record of that information?"

"I've been asking my office workers to set up a program where we can track all our trucks, but unfortunately they haven't gotten around to it. I suppose I'm too lenient with them."

"If the drivers on the missing truck sold it to someone else, that would be a crime, and we'd need to be on the lookout for them. If the truck was hijacked, they may have been killed or be in danger right now. I'll need to know their identities."

"My apologies, but I don't know who the drivers were off the top of my head, and there's no time to look into that right now. In all probability, they're fine, living it up with their girlfriends. If they were smart, they got a lot of money for the truck."

"So I would need to get a warrant to see that information?"

"I'm afraid so, but I hope it doesn't come to that."

"One more thing. Do you know why hundreds of drones were on the truck?"

"Drones? I hardly know what a drone is, but I imagine whoever got their hands on the truck was transporting them for some reason."

"We didn't find any produce, but I suppose it could all have been dumped someplace."

"It's happened before," Mr. Chen said. "Those criminals probably thought nothing of wasting all that food."

"What about this?" Riley asked, holding up a clear plastic evidence bag. "I found two of these on the truck, next to the dead bodies. Is this something you were shipping?" Within the bag was one of the two ripped silver boxes found near the corpses.

Beads of sweat formed on Mr. Chen's forehead. "No, that's not anything we would transport."

Officer Riley thanked him and departed, escorted to her car by one of Mr. Chen's assistants, a young, muscular Asian man. She sat in the cruiser a moment before backing out under the watchful eye of the Happy Sun chaperone. All the while, she didn't stop thinking about her conversation with Mr. Chen. What employer, even the most benevolent, excuses the theft of their trucks? Something else was going on, but even if she got a warrant to look for information about the truck's cargo, the drivers, or their destination, there'd be plenty of time for Mr. Chen to make changes. As she headed towards the exit, the assistant returned to the building. Riley looked around and noticed that she was alone. She backed up her car and reparked in an open space.

The loading dock was a hundred meters away. Eight Happy Sun Farm trucks were lined up and were being loaded with goods. She got out of her vehicle and walked closer to the action. Six of the trucks were being filled with produce. Two of them were receiving a different sort of cargo. They were being loaded with stacks of boxes similar in size, shape, and color to the boxes in the truck with the two dead workers she'd seen earlier.

She spun on her heels and headed back to her car. Seconds later, she was speeding past the sentry gate, to the main road.

Chapter 50

I WAS THINKING ABOUT what I'd learned earlier in the day about the genetically modified seeds. If Happy Sun's intention was to ensure a large swath of the American public would eat their products, they were going about it the right way. Their wide distribution, effective advertising, and low prices were working their magic. All I had to do was figure out what the end goal was.

I was worried the Happy Sun goons were looking for me. Surely, they wouldn't stop looking when they discovered Melinda wasn't of any help. They knew we had rescued Nabi and had procured two of their drones. Their efforts to stop us were sure to intensify, if anything.

As we exited the parking lot of Vibrant Vittles in Fran's car, I looked around and monitored the vehicles behind us. Whenever I thought we were being followed, the car in question turned off or failed to turn when we did. I didn't know how many people the North Koreans had at their disposal to look for us, or how wide a net they could cast, but I knew I couldn't let my guard down.

We met up with Adam, CJ, Tyler, Nabi, Bong, and Kwan at the beach near Fran's condo. Neither Kwan, Nabi, nor Bong knew how to swim, so they had spent the day sitting on the sand, fully dressed, watching the other three surf, or at least attempt to surf.

"I don't think that was a good idea," I said. "Three Asians in long pants sitting on a sandy beach look nothing if not conspicuous.".

"We weren't there the whole day," Kwan said. "I took Nabi and Bong to lunch at a Korean restaurant I'd seen nearby. The owner was Korean, of course, and very friendly. He spoke to us, especially Bong and Nabi, a long time. I think they were happy to talk to a Korean other than me, especially since he spoke with a North Korean dialect."

"Another defector?" I asked.

"Yes. Years ago, he escaped from the prison where he lived with his mother and sister. They had life sentences because his father had been accused of being a spy. Not many escape North Korean prisons so we were impressed."

"What about his mother and sister?"

"He thinks they're dead, but tries not to think about them. He didn't let me pay for the lunch. The food was very good, and we want to go back there."

I learned that CJ, Adam, and Tyler had spent the day in the water, only stopping to grab lunch at a nearby Taco Bell. While CJ was starting to get the hang of surfing, Adam had a long way to go. Nevertheless, they all enjoyed the day in the ocean.

We returned to Fran's condo, where CJ, Adam, and Tyler changed, and the rest of us freshened up. We walked to a local burger joint and ordered. I was nervous sitting there and kept checking for anyone suspicious in the vicinity. When a man who'd clearly had too many beers stumbled and bumped up against Bong's chair, I froze. I didn't breathe until he apologized and was on his way. I realized at that moment I was mentally unprepared to do anything meaningful should we face real danger.

After dinner, Tyler showed us the house of a friend who was away for a month and suggested we stay there. He retrieved the key from under a fake rock, and we entered. Three bedrooms, two baths, and near the beach—we were elated. Most elated were Bong and Nabi. This would be the first time they could spend a whole night together in the privacy of their own room. They retired for the evening shortly after we arrived.

Before going to bed, I jammed a chair under the front door knob to prevent anyone from entering. I tossed and turned that night, worried about the Happy Sun people who were most likely looking for us. I shared my concern with CJ, who confessed he had been nervous about the same thing. Since we'd left Melinda's house, he had been looking out for danger, but didn't mention anything, hoping to spare me from anxiety.

The first thing I did after getting up the following morning was to check if the chair was still in place by the front door. It was. Then I turned my attention to breakfast. We'd need to go shopping later that day. There was no milk in the house, so CJ and I had a breakfast of dry cereal and stale bread toast with Kwan and Adam. They had shared a bedroom the night before, thankful they each had their own twin bed. No sign of the happy couple.

"They probably want to sleep in this morning," Kwan said. "Our room next to theirs, and I hear a lot of noise from them last night." He chuckled. "Remind me of my honeymoon." He turned to Adam. "You didn't hear anything. You snore most of the evening."

"Yeah, I missed all the excitement. I took an Ambien pill I found in the medicine cabinet because I knew I wouldn't be able to sleep without it. I was knocked out pretty good."

Fran called me at 9:30 that morning and told me to meet her at Vibrant Vittles in an hour. One of the liquid samples had been analyzed, and she wanted me present when she learned the results.

Bong and Nabi were still in their room as we got ready to leave. Kwan was watching TV and barely acknowledged us when we left the house to drive to Vital Vittles. Our car was parked down the street. It would have been nice to have an attached garage, but I was in no position to complain.

Shutting the door, CJ said, "I'll bring the guns inside tonight. I think we'll sleep better." I agreed.

As we turned from the house walkway to the sidewalk, heavy footsteps approached from behind. I looked back and saw two men in gray suits running towards us. One was Asian, the other Caucasian.

My first instinct was to freeze. I didn't want to repeat my response of inactivity when real danger was lurking, so I started to rummage through my purse for the taser I still had. Damn, I thought as panic set in, where is that thing? I need to get rid of all this junk I carry around.

"Are you Strawberry Fields?" one of the men yelled out.

As I was trying to decide how to answer that question, CJ spun around and shouted, "Who wants to know?"

With my hand still in my purse, searching for the elusive taser, I turned around. The men were standing a foot away when the Asian man spoke up. "FBI." Both men held up their identification. Their badges looked legit, displaying their names, faces, and the FBI seal. The pictures of Special Agents Hatanaka and Jankowski matched the faces staring at me. Despite that, I was skeptical.

"How do I know these badges aren't fake?" I asked, stalling for time as I tried to think of a way to escape should that be necessary.

"Ma'am, I'm going to have to ask you to remove your hand from your purse," Hatanaka said.

I still hadn't located that damn taser, so I complied. I wouldn't have time to find it, pull it out, aim it, and discharge it before one of them stopped me. Anyway, I only had one taser, and there were two of them.

"I'll ask you once again. Are you Strawberry Fields?"

I looked towards CJ for an indication of what he thought I should do. He looked at me and shrugged.

"Okay. Yes, I'm Strawberry Fields."

"We're here to investigate the suspicious activity you reported recently."

I relaxed. "Damn," I said. "I thought your people just ignored me. Never heard a thing."

"They leave it up to local agencies to investigate if they believe it's warranted. An Officer Riley in Kern County was concerned about Happy Sun Farm and called the FBI field office in her area to alert them to her suspicions. They had a record of you calling about Happy Sun earlier, and thought there was enough there to warrant an investigation. They asked the local precinct to locate you but didn't think it would be safe to call you because they figured your phone was probably being tapped."

"They can do that?"

Jankowski smiled. "It's illegal, but we know criminals sometimes break the law."

"Point well taken," I said, feeling foolish.

Ignoring the interruption, Hatanaka continued. "When the local officers couldn't find you, they notified other precincts in the state to look for you. Police in Bakersfield identified you on a street camera video, getting into a truck owned by Curtis Bledsoe. Are you Curtis Bledsoe?" he asked, turning to CJ.

"I am, but everyone calls me CJ."

"They've been searching for both of you and learned you had swapped vehicles. The police have been on the lookout for the Honda CR-V and Nissan Pathfinder you rented. They were located parked on this street last night by local police, who notified us. We're from the FBI's local field office."

"I can't tell you how relieved I am to see you," I said as I became aware of my body relaxing.

"Can we go inside and talk?" Jankowski asked.

"I was just on my way to learn the results of the analysis of a sample we got from a secret lab run by Happy Sun Farm. It could be very important."

The two agents looked at each other. "I think we should talk first. In fact, if you have obtained samples from a lab run by Happy Sun Farm, I suggest you hold off on doing any more analysis for now. It's possible you'll be putting people in danger."

I was glad my earlier report was being taken seriously, yet frightened by his words. He handed both me and CJ new phones and instructed us to use them exclusively. He forwarded incoming calls and messages from our old phones to the new ones, assuring us they had been loaded with the most sophisticated anti-spyware available. I used my new souped-up phone to call Fran, relieved she answered the unfamiliar number. I told her I'd been delayed and she should inform her colleagues to hold off on any further analysis.

Kwan was bent over, watching TV when we entered, laughing at something he had just seen. I introduced him to the agents and asked if Bong and Nabi were up yet.

Kwan smiled. "They like newlyweds. I not hear a thing from their room."

"I hate to do this," I said, "but I think I should get them out here." I turned to the agents. "Bong and Nabi are two North Koreans we rescued from Happy Sun Farms. They were low-level workers but want to help and will answer any questions you have if they can. Unfortunately, there's a lot they don't know. Kwan can translate."

"I'm impressed," Hatanaka said. "We didn't know you had some Happy Sun Farm people with you. It would be extremely helpful if we could speak to them."

I walked down the short hallway and tapped lightly on the door. No response. I knocked louder. Still no response. The last thing I wanted to do was open the door and find them doing what couples do in private.

I called for Kwan to help. He banged on the door, then yelled several phrases in Korean. Still no response from the other side of the door. He turned the doorknob, but it was locked.

"Do you think they might have left?" I asked Kwan. "There's a window in their room. They could have climbed out."

"That make no sense. They speak no English, have no money, and trust us completely. Why would they leave?"

Kwan and I returned to the living room where the agents were seated and explained that we needed to open the locked bedroom door.

"Do you still have that kit?" Hatanaka asked his partner.

"I do, but I don't think I'll need it." He retrieved a credit card from his wallet and walked towards the door. We all followed and watched as he jiggled the card between the door latch and strike plate. It took less than a minute for him to free the lock.

He knocked on the door as he slowly opened it. None of us were prepared for what we saw.

Chapter 51

NABI AND BONG WERE naked, sprawled out on the floor, motionless. The agents quickly checked for pulses and found none. Rigor mortis had not yet set in. Bong's body partially covered Nabi's, as if he was trying to protect her until the end. Jankowski rolled Bong off of Nabi, onto his back. There was no blood, no evidence of gunshot wounds, only a small amount of vomit on the bed and the floor.

I stood in horror, unable to move, before the tears came. How could this happen? We were all rooting for this young couple who seemed so much in love, and so enthusiastic about starting their lives in America, where they would be free to pursue their dreams, say and think whatever they wanted.

As the initial shock wore off and my tears dried, I realized the FBI agents had wasted no time checking the window which they found to be locked from the inside, then searching the room. The couple had little more than a few clothes which were scattered around. As I scrutinized the room with my eyes, I detected a glint of light off of something on the bed. I approached and found two silver metallic cubicle boxes, each two inches on a side. I held one up and announced, "I think we have our answer."

"What do you mean?" Kwan asked. "Those are just truffle boxes. We each got one at the restaurant where we had lunch yesterday. The owner gave them to us for free."

"Did you get one?" I asked.

"Yes," Kwan answered, "but I didn't eat it. My daughter love sweets, so I save it for her."

I explained where I'd seen similar boxes before, and my certainty that they contained a deadly poison. Kwan looked sick as he sank to the floor. Not only had Bong and Nabi died tragically, but he realized he had escaped the same fate because of his daughter. Furthermore, had he not seen the result of eating the candy, his daughter would have died.

"You couldn't possibly have known," I said to Kwan. "I never mentioned anything about the boxes to you because it didn't occur to me that you needed to be told. I was wrong. I'm so sorry."

"We need to find out everything you know, but first, we have to get you out of here," Hatanaka said. "Give us a moment while we locate a safe house for you. It won't take long for them to find you here. After all, we did it without too much trouble. Meanwhile, Kwan, give us your candy. We'll have it analyzed."

I looked forward to learning what was in the candy Happy Farms distributed to select people. Unfortunately, too many people had already fallen victim to it.

Kwan retrieved his toxic gift and handed it to Jankowski as his partner spoke on the phone. Finally, Hatanaka informed us he had a safehouse for us to relocate to. He instructed us to leave our cars where they were, parked on the street. A van would come to transport CJ, Kwan, Adam, and me to the new location. They would stay with us until it arrived.

While we waited, Hatanaka instructed me to phone Fran and tell her someone from their office would come by Vital Vittles to pick up the specimens I'd given her and transport them to a government biosafety level 4 laboratory, capable of handling the pathogens most deadly to humans.

When I called her, she was in tears and could hardly speak.

"What's going on?" I asked.

"It's awful, " she said. "The three scientists who began working on the roller bottle specimen yesterday became ill hours after they started, and—." Fran sobbed loudly before continuing. "Two of them died early this morning, and the third is in critical condition. She's not expected to live."

"Damn," I said. "This is awful! The specimen must contain a deadly pathogen or toxin, but the Happy Sun people were exposed to it without getting sick. This doesn't make any sense."

"Sense or not, that is what happened. This morning, electron microscopy showed that the roller bottle specimen is loaded with viral particles."

"Holy cow," I said. The news was shocking. "Any idea what the virus is?"

"No one here knows. All I know is the viruses average 36 nm in diameter."

I thought a moment before asking, "What about the sample from the shaker flask?"

"It's a cell-free extract containing a mixture of RNA and other chemicals which was being used to produce a protein. It's a common way to produce large amounts of a desired protein."

"What exactly were they making?"

"They isolated it, but were waiting for the protein analyzer to be repaired so they could identify it. Now, nobody wants to touch anything from those specimens."

"Of course," I said. "No one should handle them. I'm in contact with the FBI now, and they will send someone by to pick up everything you have from Happy Sun. They'll take it to a government facility where it can be handled safely."

"I wish them luck," Fran said. "We need to find out what's in those specimens."

The conversation ended with Fran eager to tell her colleagues about the pending specimen collection.

After I filled in the FBI agents about the latest developments, they spoke among themselves privately and began making and receiving phone calls. The California Department of Public Health ordered a quarantine of all personnel at Vibrant Vittles. No one would be allowed to enter or exit the building until further notice. Someone from the county health department would set up procedures for delivering food, medicine, and other provisions. I knew the people at Vibrant Vittles wouldn't be happy.

The van to transport us arrived, and we piled in. Jankowski stayed behind, but Hatanaka accompanied us. On the way to the safe house, I received a text on my new phone from my mother telling me about the beautiful birds she had seen that morning. Several attached pictures showed palm trees with the ocean in the background. She included a picture of Harrison, the first one I'd seen. A nice-looking, middle-aged man wearing a smile and a Hawaiian shirt, I knew one day I would have to accept him, but not just yet.

Perry phoned, but I wasn't about to talk to him in the van where everyone could hear, so I let his call go to voicemail.

After an hour-long drive, we arrived at a defunct farm east of San Diego. The house was old but solidly constructed, and fairly large. I figured it was built at the turn of the century—not 2000, but 1900—by a family with lots of children. Although it had been renovated, the last update was probably fifty years earlier. The furniture was old and worn, but we were happy to be in a safe place, with plenty of room to be comfortable. CJ and I took the master bedroom. Adam and Kwan each took a smaller room, leaving another bedroom unoccupied. We were guarded by two local police officers who received instructions from Hatanaka. With ample open space around the house, it would be easy for them to spot anyone approaching.

Shortly after we were settled, our rental cars arrived, driven by agents who parked them close to the house. CJ checked and confirmed that our firearms were still under the tarp where he had left them.

Although we were told to relax, that wasn't possible under the circumstances, at least not for me.

Chapter 52

AN HOUR AFTER WE arrived, Dr. Esther Parks, a physician from the local Public Health Department, visited. Hatanaka explained that he had requested her help after learning about the deaths at Vibrant Vittles. He asked CJ and I to start at the beginning and describe everything we knew about the Happy Sun Farm operation with the exception of what we'd learned about the specimens Bong had obtained for us.

He and Dr. Parks listened attentively, both taking notes, as I described the aggressive takeover of farmland near my parent's home, my father's suspicious death, the strange farming practices of Happy Sun Farm, the body in the vat, and the attempts on my life.

CJ summarized our discovery that the Happy Sun employees were from North Korea rather than China as they claimed, our rescue of Diego, and what we saw when we surveilled the Tulare compounds. Listening to him re-hash how we freed Bong and Nabi, found the large drone shipment, and learned of Melinda's fate made me realize how much we'd been through. Thankfully, CJ didn't talk of Bong and Nabi's murder. The horror was still raw in my mind. Hatanaka knew of it, and Dr. Parks didn't need to know.

When CJ was finished, Hatanaka turned to Dr. Parks and said, "Now you're caught up on what we know about the extent of the Happy Sun Farm operation, and the extreme measures they've taken to protect it. What we need to figure out is what exactly they are planning, and how we can stop it."

"I'm not sure how I fit in," Dr. Parks said. "You mentioned an investigation into deaths at Vibrant Vittles. You think they are related to Happy Sun and present a public health risk?"

Hatanaka turned to me and said, " Now it's time to explain to Dr. Parks everything you know about what Happy Sun Farms is producing."

I took a deep breath as I tried to organize my thoughts. "Bong brought us three types of specimens from Happy Sun, which I turned over to Vibrant Vittles for analysis. The first to be analyzed were the seeds Happy Sun was producing. What we know now is that the seeds were genetically modified so that plants grown from them would synthesize an altered human transferrin receptor that binds to both human cells and the feline distemper virus. The workers at Happy Sun were strictly forbidden from eating any of the genetically modified produce."

"Curious," Dr. Parks said. "For some reason, they considered the altered receptor to be extremely dangerous. At worst, exposure to it could make people susceptible to the feline distemper virus."

I continued. "The second specimen came from one of their shaker flasks. According to Bong, the Happy Sun lab workers needed biohazard gear when coming in contact with the contents of the flasks. Material from them was sprayed on produce before it was sold. After it was sprayed, the workers weren't allowed to touch it. Based on that, we assumed the flasks contained something highly toxic, although, to my knowledge, people haven't gotten sick from any Happy Sun products."

"That's true," Dr. Parks said. "I would know if that happened."

"Not wanting to take any chances, Vibrant Vittles scientists took strict precautions when analyzing it. They recently determined that inside the shaker flasks, they were producing a protein that hasn't been characterized yet."

"Perhaps it's a toxin," Dr. Parks said, "one that's not very potent. It shouldn't take long to sequence it and figure out exactly what it is."

"The most confusing part of all this is the roller bottle specimen. Personnel at Happy Sun took no special precautions with the roller bottle contents, so we all assumed it wasn't dangerous. Everyone at Vibrant Vittles who handled that specimen has died or probably will die. By electron microscopy, it appears to be loaded with a virus—a virus deadly to the lab personnel at Vibrant Vittles, but not to the Happy Sun workers. None of them got sick."

"Perhaps the Koreans were vaccinated."

"Bong said they weren't."

"Any idea what type of virus it is?"

"No, but I was told the average diameter is 36 nm."

"Let me check something out," Dr. Parks said as she tapped into her phone. Seconds later, she looked up. "The feline distemper virus is only 18 to 25 nm, so the deadly virus from Happy Sun Farm is definitely not the feline distemper virus. This certainly is baffling."

"I agree," Hatanaka said, "the information we have is very confusing. The roller bottle specimen appears to contain a highly dangerous virus. I suspect it's a designer virus that has yet to be characterized, yet the Happy Sun employees were exposed to it without ill effect."

"I don't know how that could be the case if they weren't vaccinated," Dr. Parks said.

"We'll have to look for another reason why the Happy Sun personnel weren't affected by the roller bottle virus. We'll also have to figure out why they weren't allowed to eat their genetically modified produce and took strict safety measures when handling the shaker flask materials. The virus from the roller bottle, the protein made in the flask, and the protein made by the seeds must be related. So far, the only deaths we know of are the people from Vibrant Vittles exposed to the roller bottle specimen."

Hatanaka's narrative was interrupted when Dr. Parks received a call. We all watched as she spoke quietly, a concerned look on her face. When the call ended, she turned to us. "Unfortunately, another person, someone exposed to a lab worker who just died, has taken ill with the same symptoms, and will likely die also. He wasn't directly exposed to the specimen from Happy Sun Farm but caught it from someone who was. Now we know the virus is contagious. But like you," she said, looking at me, "I don't understand why no one in the Happy Sun lab who was exposed to it died. Any ideas?"

"This has bioterrorism written all over it," Hatanaka said.

Chapter 53

"THE INFORMATION FROM BONG indicated the roller bottle material isn't harmful, while the flask material is, "Hatanaka said. "I suspect he may have been a plant, and he gave you false information on purpose."

"I can't believe he intentionally misrepresented anything to us. If he did, why was he murdered? He didn't come looking for us. We found him and offered him a chance to defect because we knew he wanted to escape North Korea. He said he double bagged the specimen from the flask as soon as he collected it, while he was wearing protective clothing. He couldn't have been confused. I think we're missing something."

"I concur," Dr. Parks said. "I think a key to this may be figuring out why they want Americans to ingest a modified portion of the transferrin receptor."

"I've been racking my brain about that," I said. "The scientist at Vibrant Vittles said the receptor isn't harmful."

"But what we're dealing with here isn't a normal transferrin receptor," Dr. Parks said. "You said two sites have been modified. One was changed to be the same as the site on the feline transferrin receptor that binds the feline distemper virus."

"That's right," I said. "There's a vaccine for feline distemper, so most cats don't get sick from it, but even if they do, they usually survive."

Dr. Parks was quiet as she turned her attention to her cell phone. After a few minutes of reading and sending messages, she looked up. "This is all starting to make sense," she said.

"It is?" I asked in disbelief.

"We know that humans absolutely cannot catch feline distemper from cats because they do not have the proper receptor. Without the receptor, the virus cannot get into human cells. But that no longer seems to be the case." All eyes were on her as she explained. "You may have heard about the scattered cases around the country of people getting ill with various symptoms, including nausea, diarrhea, and vomiting."

"Yes," I said. "I read about that in the paper. I believe the CDC is studying it."

"They are, and they have some interesting findings. These cases started popping up about a year ago. Two months ago, they came to the attention of the CDC, and they have tested a number of the people affected. The way it spreads by close contact has the appearance of an infectious agent, and they have sent alerts to local public health agencies to be on the lookout for additional cases."

"That doesn't sound like it has anything to do with the virus from the roller bottles," I said.

"So it would seem," Dr. Parks said. "People at Vibrant Vittles died, while the people being studied by the CDC aren't terribly sick. At first, CDC scientists thought this relatively mild illness was caused by a new virus—one we haven't seen before. The public hasn't been notified yet, but the CDC has recently identified it. Surprisingly, it's an old virus—the same virus that causes feline distemper. Until now, everyone at the CDC thought it was impossible for humans to catch feline distemper. They didn't believe it until they reconfirmed their findings at least a dozen times."

I began to put the pieces together in my mind. Not all of them, but some of them. I eagerly awaited what Dr. Parks would reveal next.

"All the patients with this new illness had pet cats infected with feline distemper," the doctor said. "The CDC studied the virus isolated from several of these patients as well as their cats. They've been looking for a mutation that would enable it to enter human cells by attaching to the human transferrin receptor, but so far, they haven't found it. There were no significant changes in the virus isolated from these patients or their cats. It's the same distemper virus they are familiar with."

"Maybe the CDC should be looking at this from a different angle," I suggested.

"I concur. They should study the transferrin receptor in the humans who have caught the disease and determine if it is abnormal, and binds the feline distemper virus. I suspect that it does."

"I don't understand," Hatanaka said. "You think the North Koreans want to give this modified transferrin receptor to all Americans so they can infect them with feline distemper? Can't we simply vaccinate people with the cat vaccine?"

"Good thinking," Dr. Parks said. "The vaccine would probably work in humans, but of course, it would need to be tested. Can you imagine trying to vaccinate people with a cat vaccine that hasn't been tested for safety in humans? I think the public reaction to the COVID-19 vaccine, which had gone through many months of testing, tells us a lot of people would refuse it."

"Maybe they're counting on the skepticism of the American public when it comes to vaccines," Hatanaka said, "but even without a vaccine, it's hard to believe the North Koreans are going to all this trouble for something that will hardly bring down the government. I'm more concerned with the deaths at Vibrant Vittles."

"I understand," Dr. Parks said, "but the people who were infected with the feline distemper virus provide an important clue. I believe the novel transferrin receptors are directly related to the illness of the workers at Vibrant Vittles. Blood and swabs from those who died will be studied at the CDC. I believe the people at Vital Vittles were infected by a lab-made deadly virus present in the roller bottle sample, and that virus binds to the transferrin receptor created at Happy Sun. I suspect that the protein sprayed on Happy Sun produce is, in fact, the same altered transferrin receptor produced by the genetically modified plants."

"Are you saying only people with the altered receptor in their cells can get infected with this new virus?" I asked.

"That's what I'm thinking," Dr. Parks answered. "It seems to me that North Korea is wisely trying to avoid a likely reason there haven't been significant bioterrorism attacks yet. They want to limit the spread. An uncontrolled virus attack, such as with smallpox, would not only be devastating for the targeted country, but would likely travel around the globe and include the instigating country. Just look at how widespread the COVID-19 epidemic was, despite efforts to control it. Fortunately, no world leaders have been crazy enough to intentionally unleash such an attack on the world. I doubt it's for humanitarian reasons. It's because they could be directly affected themselves. Once the genie is out of the bottle, it can't be contained."

"I hate to be complimentary," Hatanaka said, "but this seems like an incredibly brilliant plan."

"I can't disagree," Dr. Parks said. "Only people who have ingested the modified receptor, whether in genetically modified produce, or food that was sprayed or mixed with it, will have it on their cells. According to Bong, Happy Sun Farms made sure not to ship the contaminated food to other countries or expose their workers to it. That receptor has been distributed to Americans only."

"You think the lab-made virus is related to the feline distemper virus?" I asked.

Dr. Parks nodded in the affirmative. "Viruses are held together by an outer coat, or capsid, made mostly of protein. They enter cells when a site on the capsid binds to a specific receptor on the cell surface. I imagine the Happy Sun virus has a capsid the same as or similar to feline distemper virus. That virus will infect any human cells with the modified receptor they have created to bind the feline distemper virus. Happy Sun workers were prevented from being exposed to the receptor, so they couldn't be infected with the novel virus. Therefore, they didn't need to be careful when handling it."

It all made sense now. I hated to agree with the others—the North Koreans had devised an amazingly clever plan to attack the United States. I thought about my own vulnerability, having eaten Happy Sun Farm yogurt and produce laced with the potentially deadly receptor.

Dr. Parks answered several text messages and resumed her explanation. "The cornerstone of their plan is the genetic material within the lab-made virus. Remember, a virus is basically a protein capsid that encases genetic material, which is the source of the damaging effects of the virus. I speculate the happy Sun virus, while binding to the feline distemper receptor, doesn't contain the normal feline distemper viral DNA. Rather, it harbors something deadly, possibly the genetic material of a virus we already know about. All of this will need to be verified, of course." Dr. Parks looked at me. "If you hadn't persevered and started the ball rolling, and those people hadn't come up with feline distemper, we never would have figured it out until it was too late." Then she paused. "If it isn't too late already."

Chapter 54

WE ALL SAT QUIETLY and reflected on Dr. Parks' words. Finally, CJ broke the silence. "What have you learned from the truck with the drones?" he asked Hatanaka. "Did the drivers help?"

"They were dead when found. We're pretty sure they committed suicide. I received a report from the coroner shortly before we left the beach house. The autopsy didn't show anything specific—organ congestion, fluid in the lungs, cerebral edema, and pupil constriction. They did find torn, empty silver boxes near the bodies. I suspect they're identical to the ones Kwan, Bong, and Nabi were given, and the ones you've both come in contact with earlier. The coroner will run the usual toxicology, but I doubt it will show anything. We're sending samples to the FBI lab for a more specialized analysis."

I was struck by something he mentioned. "You said their pupils were constricted. When I saw my dad's body in the funeral home, I noticed how tiny his pupils were. I thought that was normal for someone who died of a heart attack."

"It's not," Dr. Parks said. "I'm not a medical examiner, but I do know there are a host of drugs that can cause pupil constriction, including opioids, nerve agents, and some insecticides."

"I would put my money on a nerve agent. North Korea seems to favor them," Hatanaka said.

I'd been certain my father had been poisoned, but the thought of a specific poison, a nerve agent, made it seem more immediate and horrific. I dabbed my eyes with a tissue, trying to hide the tears beginning to well.

CJ put his arm around me. "Sorry, Berry," he whispered. "Do you want to be alone?"

"No, this is important. I want to be here."

"Of course we can't be sure what poison was used until the testing is complete," Hatanaka said. I think he was trying to make me feel better, but he didn't. After a few awkward moments, he continued with his narrative. "As you know, the truck was full of boxes containing drones capable of holding canisters and delivering their contents. Although Happy Sun claimed the truck was hijacked and subsequently filled with drones, a local officer recently saw boxes identical to those containing the drones being loaded onto a Happy Sun Farm truck at their loading dock."

"Thank goodness," I said. "I'd hate for Happy Sun and Mr. Chen to evade the law."

"That's not going to happen," Hatanaka said, "but our first priority has to be stopping the attack we think is being planned. We don't know when it's scheduled to take place, but we can't take any chances by delaying things. It's likely the canisters you mentioned contain the same virus that infected the workers at Vibrant Vittles."

I was struck with horror. "They could kill millions!" I said. "How are you going to stop this?"

"Our best people in the FBI and Homeland Security are already working on this. There is already a high index of suspicion that the drones discovered in the truck are being distributed widely and are part of a plan to do something horrible. We assume they are programmed to respond to orders from a central command post which will transmit instructions via satellite. Many drones and canisters have probably already been delivered. Finding all of them could take weeks or months. We don't have that much time. Instead, we need to cut off the head of the snake which is the source of signals for the drones."

"Hell, tell me where it is, and I'll take care of it," CJ said. "I'm not afraid to take action for something like this without a warrant."

"It's not that simple. We don't know where their command center is, and we don't expect the people at Happy Sun to help. Remember, the two truck drivers killed themselves rather than face questioning by police, and we suspect others are equally dedicated to the cause."

"How about flying drones over all the land they own? You could find their command center from the air."

"That's been tried. Overhead satellites have also provided high-quality pictures, but we haven't found anything. We anticipate they will use satellite transmissions to pull off their operation but haven't been able to locate any of their communication equipment.

"Can't the military jam their satellite?" CJ asked.

"No. North Korea has its own satellites, or might be using one from China. We don't know what frequency they're using. We have electronics experts studying the area around the farm for signals but haven't located any. It's possible they won't transmit anything until they start the operation, and they may use a sophisticated technique called frequency hopping, where they avoid jamming by changing the transmission frequency."

"Is that it?" CJ asked. "You're just going to wait until they start to launch the drones and hope to jam the satellite then? That could fail."

"We have a group of lawyers working on obtaining a search warrant for the main Happy Sun farm right now. It can be challenging to get a warrant allowing us to search a facility so large, and we expect Happy Sun to lawyer up, so they're trying to make it bulletproof. But even a warrant won't help if the command center is well-hidden, underground, or at a different location altogether. They need to search their other sites so we have people working on getting warrants for them, as well. All we can do now is wait. Wait for warrants and wait for results from the CDC and the FBI toxicology lab. The FBI lab is analyzing the truffle from Kwan, and specimens collected from people we suspect were killed by the same poison."

I turned to Dr. Parks. "Any word on the people quarantined at Vibrant Vittles? I want to find out how my friend there is doing."

"I haven't had an update on them," Dr. Parks said. "I suggest you call her. Phone contact hasn't been cut off." She turned to Hatanaka. "I don't think there's anything more I can do here, so I'll get back to my office. Don't hesitate to contact me if you think of something important." Moments later, she was gone.

I called Fran and was relieved when she answered, sounding like her usual self. I learned that while she hadn't slept well on one of the thin mattresses that had been dropped off in bulk, she felt fine and had no fever as of the last time she was checked, a half hour earlier.

Another call came in shortly after I disconnected. I was afraid it was Fran calling back to tell me she had been retested and now had a fever. I answered without looking at caller ID and was surprised to hear the voice of another female. It took me a moment to place her. "Martina," I said. "I hope everything is okay."

"For the moment, yes. We're fine, but I think people from Happy Sun are looking for my dad. He found work on a small farm here in Salinas and I'm working part time at a nearby daycare. We're living in a trailer we found for rent in a trailer park. Dad hurt his back and can't work today, or rather, I forbade him from working. He's so damn stubborn, he didn't want to take the day off. We went to the grocery store this morning, but when we returned to the trailer park, the woman in the front office there told us two men were looking for him earlier. Both Asian. Spoke very bad English. We don't know of any Asian men who might be looking for him other than people from Happy Sun, so we drove away. We're in a coffee shop near Coalinga right now. We hope you're okay, and wonder if you know any more about what's going on at the farm."

I sighed. "I'm glad you called. A lot has happened, and I'm hiding out myself right now." I excused myself for a moment and had a short discussion with the FBI agent while Martina was on hold, then resumed my conversation with her shortly. "Me, CJ, Adam, and a man named Kwan, who has helped us out, are staying in a safe house where the FBI is guarding us. They'll send someone to pick you and your dad up and bring you here where you'll be safe."

The relief in Martina's voice was unmistakable as she thanked me and told me where she and her dad would wait. Fortunately, most of their possessions were in her car's trunk.

There was nothing to do but wait for things to unfold, but relaxing while I waited wasn't possible. I told the others that Martina and Jose would be joining us later. Adam tried to act disinterested, but his sudden pacing around the room told me he looked forward to seeing Martina again.

Hatanaka went outside where he spoke to the officers guarding us, then began to walk around the property.

CJ found a Monopoly game in one of the cupboards, and he, Adam, Kwan, and I sat down to play. Kwan said he was unfamiliar with the game but caught on quickly. I had a hard time concentrating, and soon Kwan was the proud owner of Boardwalk and Park Place, as well as all the yellow and red properties. Hotels were on all. I was the first one out after landing on Boardwalk and defaulting on the rent.

I roamed around outside and overheard Hatanaka yelling into his phone, frustrated that a judge had refused to issue a warrant to search the entirety of the Happy Sun Farm. Apparently, they would need to designate specific places to search. I understood every iota of his frustration. I checked my watch. It would be another four hours before I expected Diego and Martina to arrive.

After Kwan triumphed over the remaining Monopoly players, Adam excused himself and went down the hall. At first puzzled by the sound of water running in the shower, I realized Adam was prepping for Martina's arrival. He wanted to dazzle her with his outstanding hygiene.

Fran phoned. "I'm so dang bored," she complained.

I was glad that was the main reason she was calling. "Any news about your colleagues?" I asked.

"Everyone affected so far has died. The precautions they took at the hospital where they were treated has fortunately prevented the virus from spreading. If no other cases break out, they'll stop the quarantine a month from when it began."

"Who decided that?"

"The CDC. I just hope I don't lose my mind all cooped up in here."

"How is everyone else coping?" I asked.

"Not well. Most of these people are introverted scientists, but they've started bickering like preschoolers. Instead of arguing about who gets to be first in line, they're quarreling about things like whether it will be possible to sustain life on Mars, and should self-driving cars be allowed on public streets."

"I imagine some of the discussions are pretty interesting."

"They were at first, but now two political camps have emerged. Approximately twenty percent are on one side, and eighty percent on the other. Neutrality isn't an option. Each side has taken over a different area of the building. So far there hasn't been any bloodshed, but when supplies are dropped off several times a day it's uncomfortable for all of us."

Our conversation was cut short when Fran received notification of an incoming call from her mom. We had pretty much run out of things to say by that time, so I was thankful for that. I was back to waiting for more answers to my many questions, which was hard.

Adam emerged from his bedroom, clean-shaven, hair washed, and wearing what I assumed was his cleanest shirt. CJ and I ribbed him a bit but backed off when he became upset.

I was about to check out what was in the refrigerator when my phone rang. I didn't recognize the number but took the call anyway. I didn't want to miss something important. I was glad I answered. It was Dr. Parks.

"They've finished analyzing the sample from the shaker flasks," she said. "They determined the North Koreans were synthesizing their modified transferrin receptor in those flasks. I imagine they sprayed it on all the produce that wasn't genetically engineered, so the receptor was in everything they sold."

"I suppose it isn't stable if it's heated," I said.

"That's right. Preliminary studies show it is destroyed around a hundred eighty degrees."

"That explains why they only sold dairy, fruits, and vegetables that aren't typically heated."

"That's what I'm thinking. Any food that isn't heated can deliver their edited receptor. It doesn't matter if it is made by genetically engineered produce, sprayed on other food, or mixed into dairy—the results are the same. By now, most of the population has eaten Happy

Sun Farm products, and the edited receptor has been incorporated into their cells."

"People need to be warned not to eat any Happy Sun products."

"I agree. Scientists at the CDC are speaking to Homeland Security about issuing nationwide public service announcements."

"This can't wait!"

"I'm not sure our attention should be focused on stopping people from eating their products. The receptor itself doesn't seem to be harming anyone and will probably remain in people who are exposed for quite some time. It will only be important when their virus is released. Stopping that has to be the focus right now."

I couldn't argue with that logic. After our conversation, I thought of all the people going about their day, oblivious to the looming threat. I was terrified by the thought of a deadly virus being released nationwide, killing millions, but there was nothing I could do.

Chapter 55

I TURNED ON THE TV for some news. Nothing about Happy Sun Farm, or a warning not to eat their products. Only a short piece on a contamination incident at Vital Vittles, followed by a description of a brazen bank robbery. I was starting to doze off when the door burst open.

Diego and Martina entered full of excitement, carrying two large pizzas. We introduced them to Kwan, and questions began to fly back and forth as the pizza disappeared. Adam dominated the description of our encounter with the Happy Sun truck and rescue of Nabi. I couldn't help but feel sad, thinking about what had happened to her and Bong later. During his delivery, Adam repeatedly looked towards Martina, who appeared to be impressed. Maybe something good would come out of all of this for Adam. And Martina.

Hours later, the conversation started to die down. Hatanaka left us in the care of the police officers guarding the farm. Martina and Diego shared the fourth bedroom which had two twin beds. Adam went to bed, followed shortly by CJ and me, leaving Kwan, who was watching TV. The following morning, I found Martina and Adam having coffee together at the kitchen table. Diego was sweeping the kitchen floor.

As CJ and I dined on toast for breakfast, I received a call from Hatanaka. "We have the toxicology results," he said. "You were one hundred percent correct in suspecting the truffle was poisoned. I just received word that it contains VX."

I wasn't sure what VX was, but it sounded familiar. I was about to ask for more information, when the agent refreshed my memory. "That's a potent nerve agent favored by the North Koreans. It was used in the famous assassination of Kim Jong Un's half-brother at the

Kuala Lumpur Airport. The poison was smeared on his face by two women, who were told they were helping to pull off a harmless prank. The half-brother died fifteen minutes after he was exposed."

"I remember that. Everyone was sure Kim Jong Un ordered the assassination, but of course, he'll never face any consequences. Seems very similar to using the two girls to poison my dad, although the poison was eaten, not smeared on his skin."

"VX is most predictable when delivered by aerosol or skin contact, but ingestion is also deadly. There was quite a bit in the candy."

The results weren't surprising, but I was quiet as I thought again about my father's last minutes, most likely suffering greatly from the poison. "I don't feel better knowing the details about how my dad died," I said, "but thank you for getting the testing done so quickly."

"Normally, it would have taken our lab much longer to identify VX, but knowing the source of the poison was North Korea, they started testing for it immediately. Be sure to warn everyone in your group about the findings. Even touching the candy could be lethal if any VX is on the surface. It's quite potent, even in small amounts."

I told the others what I had just learned. If we didn't know it before, we knew it then. We were dealing with an enemy of the worst sort.

After the call, Adam was outside speaking with one of the guards, and Diego was carrying a bag of trash to the garbage receptacles at the end of the long driveway. Martina used that time to show me something amongst the few possessions her father had on him when Adam freed him from my dad's underground shelter. She had found the small spiral notebook in his shirt pocket and was so moved she wanted to share it but didn't want him to know she had seen it. The note was a farewell letter to her, telling her how much joy she had given him, how smart and beautiful she was, and expressing his faith that she would be a success in life. She shouldn't be sad he didn't survive, as he was again with his beloved Camilla. Martina began to cry, so I took the notebook and tried to comfort her with a hug and soothing words. I pointed out that her father had indeed survived and was very much alive.

As Martina's eyes started to dry, I absent-mindedly paged through the notebook. Going backward, I realized it had been left in the bunker by my dad, who had scribbled notes and sketches before his death. Some of what he'd written appeared to be the rantings of a madman, full of conspiracy theories about the owners of Happy Sun. My eyes fixed on a diagram he had drawn. Crude, yet still clear, it appeared to be a drawing of a sun, similar to the Happy Sun logo, but viewed from an angle rather than straight on. With the roughly triangular rays dancing around the perimeter, the smiling face of the sun formed a cup instead of a flat disc. The perspective allowed the viewer to appreciate that the sun had raised edges, while the center was concave. Thin lines emanating from near the disc perimeter met in the middle. The sun was attached to an A-frame. Where had I seen that before?

I studied the picture more closely. A line ran down one of the support legs, into the ground. I focused on the small, illegible writing near the center of the concavity. I squinted, then moved the paper back and forth. I made out the first part of the word. "Trans." More squinting allowed me to read the complete word. "Transmitter." Could that line on the support leg represent a pipe containing a bundle of wires?

I stopped breathing as I realized where I'd seen that sun before. A welcoming sun, exuding warmth and happiness. I hadn't paid much attention to it when I'd gone through the pictures on my father's computer. Looking at it straight on, the curvature wasn't evident, and I didn't notice any wires. Certainly, many people had passed by that display and received the warm and fuzzy feeling it was intended to evoke.

It made sense. The transmitter to send signals to the drones via satellite was hiding in plain site on the grounds of the command center of bioterrorism. Before I had a chance to call Hatanaka, my cell phone rang. I couldn't ignore another call from Dr. Parks.

"Any news?" I asked.

"Yes," she said. She sounded out of breath with excitement. "Scientists at the CDC just released the results of their testing to me and others that need to know. The roller bottle specimen contains a novel virus that has a capsid made of the same components as the capsid of the feline distemper virus."

"That confirms that their new virus can infect any humans who have incorporated the modified transferrin receptor they add to their food."

"Right. As I suspected, the feline distemper virus DNA is not inside the capsid. In its place is the genetic component of the Marburg virus."

"I've never heard of that. How bad is it?"

"Marburg is one of the deadliest viruses in existence. It's related to the Ebola virus, which you must be familiar with."

"Of course."

"Both Marburg and Ebola cause hemorrhagic fever. Symptoms include fever, aches, nausea, vomiting and weakness. Blood clotting is abnormal, and small blood vessels are damaged. Bleeding from under the skin, the mouth, eyes, and internal organs becomes uncontrollable. Organ failure, coma, and death follow. This is precisely what was seen in the patients from Vital Vittles. The only difference is the speed of progression. Normally, symptoms don't start to appear until several days after exposure. The CDC scientists noted several changes in the virus, and believe they were introduced to make it act more quickly and be more deadly than the natural form."

"You think the virus was changed intentionally?" I asked.

"There's little doubt. The North Koreans took a deadly virus and made it deadlier. They have designed a virus with an outer capsid constructed of the same molecules as the feline distemper virus, but with the internal genetic material of Marburg. Since the Marburg virus has more genetic material than the feline distemper virus, it is larger in size."

"Let me get this straight. The North Koreans have made a variant of the Marburg virus that is more virulent than the already terrible original virus, and has a capsid similar to that of the feline distemper virus. They contaminated their produce and dairy with a receptor for the feline distemper virus. That receptor has been incorporated into our cells and will invite the weaponized super Marburg virus as well as regular old feline distemper inside."

"That's right. By strictly limiting the distribution of the receptor to people in the United States, there is no danger of a worldwide pandemic when they spread their virus over our country. North Korea will be safe."

"Their workers here will also be safe," I added, "as they weren't exposed to the receptor. I imagine whatever members of sleeper cells they have here were also warned not to ingest any Happy Sun Farm products."

"Although we can't yet prove everything, it's the only scenario that makes sense. We need to act right away, before the drones take off and the virus is emitted. Otherwise, many millions would die."

"What is being done to stop this?" I asked.

"Good question. I only know what the danger is. I don't know what the government is going to do about it."

"How much time do we have?"

"I don't know. Hatanaka told me all their resources and Homeland Security are on it. They have found a few stockpiles of drones and canisters in the Midwest and East Coast, but don't have the means to find all of them. That could take years unless we can find a person or document that leads us to them. A helicopter flying over Manhattan spotted someone arranging drones on top of a building. When police arrived to investigate, they found a hundred drones unboxed and ready to go. Most of them had been loaded with canisters. A pile of canisters was nearby. They assumed the person seen getting the drones ready fled when he heard people approaching."

I couldn't imagine worse news. My stomach was in a knot. "They need to prevent the North Koreans from deploying all those drones!" I was yelling, frustrated with the messenger who, like me, was powerless to find and stop the drones.

"Unfortunately, no one has been able to locate their command center. We don't know how much time we have before they strike, but I imagine they are getting ready to do it in days. A few weeks at the most. Meanwhile, Homeland Security is preparing a public statement warning of the danger, telling people to avoid eating anything from Happy Sun Farm, and to wear N95 masks."

"Good idea," I said, "but given the public reaction to masking during COVID-19, I think there will be a great deal of resistance. There probably aren't enough masks to go around at this point, anyway."

"You have a better idea?"

I didn't. The mystery behind Happy Sun Farm was finally solved, but I felt more uneasy than ever after our call ended. We still had to prevent the plan from being implemented. The North Koreans had designed a brilliant, diabolical plot to wipe out most of the US population. I imagined large cities, government buildings, and military installations would be highly targeted. Taking over our whole country would be easy after that. Worries about inflation, taxes, the national debt, or illegal immigration would be a thing of the past. Those of us who survived would be subjugated by a dictator with no interest in our values. We could be enslaved or imprisoned. A dystopian future might be close.

Dr. Parks' phone call had drawn my attention to the findings at the CDC, but my mind soon drifted back to the sketch in the notebook from my father's bunker. I phoned Hatanaka and described the drawing. He asked for a picture, and I wasted no time in capturing an image on my cell phone and sending it to him.

I turned on the TV and saw the first of many public service announcements prepared by the Department of Homeland Security. I was glad they had acted quickly. The public was warned to refrain from eating any Happy Sun Farm products and implored to mask up. Watching from the isolation of the safe house, I had no way of knowing how the public was responding, if they were accusing the government of conspiring to force people to wear masks, if they were frightened, or if they were following the advice. I figured it was a mixture of all three.

Chapter 56

THE CALL CAME AT 9:00 am. The sergeant looked around the main work area and saw that Riley was the only one wearing an N95 mask. She was at her desk filling out paperwork when he gave her the assignment.

"Special Agents Hatanaka and Jankowski need an officer to accompany them to Happy Sun Farm, and they requested you of all people. They said N95 masks are mandatory, but it doesn't look like that will be a problem for you. You probably heard that something is brewing there, but I doubt you'll find anything. Seems folks have been trying to get rid of them 'cause they've been buying up so much land, but I've never found anything illegal. Don't look too close, though. We're counting on their donation for the end-of-the-year party. We'll have it someplace real nice."

"I'll do my best," Riley said, keeping her thoughts to herself. Minutes later she was in her cruiser, headed to Happy Sun. When she was fifty yards from the main entrance, she was surprised to see twenty men and women wearing jackets labeled "FBI" gathered near squad cars. All were wearing N95 masks around their noses and mouths. None were only partially in place, below their nose, or loose. Each and every mask looked like it was charged with protecting the wearer from something dangerous.

She spoke to one of the agents, who directed her to two men in FBI gear deep in conversation with each other several yards away. One was Asian, the other Caucasian.

"I'm Officer Riley from the local precinct," she said as she approached.

The two men looked her way. The Asian man said, "Thank you for coming. I'm Special Agent Hatanaka, and this is Special Agent Jankowski. It's a pleasure to meet you. We were very interested in the information you have already supplied, and are glad you could join us. How much of Happy Sun Farm have you seen?"

"I've been there twice but haven't been able to see the entire farm. Only parts."

"That should come in handy, as none of us have been here before," Hatanaka said. "We are particularly interested in a large sun sculpture that looks like their logo. It's near a large sign that reads 'Happy Sun Farm.' We believe the sculpture is hiding equipment for satellite communication."

"I can assist you with that. As I recall, there's a large metal sun to the right as you enter via the main driveway."

"That's very helpful. We have a warrant to search the entire premises, which will take about two hours. Before we start, we plan to clear everyone from the area. We are prepared to meet with some resistance, so we have plenty of tasers and handcuffs. We don't expect to need our firearms, but we'll do whatever is necessary."

"Where do expect the workers to go?" Riley asked.

"We have buses to hold those we arrest waiting along this road on the other side of the entrance. We also have stations set up where employees we don't arrest can stay while we search. I will introduce you to our two communication electronics experts. Please take them to the sun sculpture as soon as possible. Then you will be directed to join our search of the rest of the premises."

"Understood," Riley said. She felt more awake than she had in quite some time as the adrenaline surged in her blood and her pulse quickened. She was looking forward to this.

Hatanaka introduced her to their communications experts, two special agents—one a tall, thin woman, the other a short, husky man—both of whom would be inspecting the sun sculpture. They carried with them large shoulder bags containing tools and electronics gear.

Minutes later, Hatanaka stepped to the front of the group and called for everyone's attention. A hush came over the waiting agents as he explained they would be going in momentarily, and it was time for everyone to suit up. "As you know," he said, "the area may be contaminated with an extremely deadly virus. Be careful."

All the agents headed to the rear of a van with the doors open, exposing several stacks of disposable white hazmat suits, gloves, and shoe coverings to protect the wearer completely, head to toe. Riley joined in and donned a suit. They were one-size-fits-all, with some clearly too large for the person inside, their arms and legs bunched up to varying degrees. The tallest person there, a heavyset Black man, barely fit in his suit. He was entirely covered but had no arm or leg length to spare. Tasers, handcuffs, and other supplies were carried over their shoulders in black purse-like fabric bags.

Hatanaka looked over all the officers individually, making occasional small adjustments to ensure that all were completely covered. When he came to Riley, he handed her a shoulder bag similar to the others. When finished with his inspection, he stood in front of the group and started walking, search warrant in hand. The others followed behind in silence.

As they approached the security guard's house in front, Riley was surprised no one stepped out to stop them. When she was close enough to see within the small sentry kiosk, it was empty. The group marched forward, circumventing the yellow traffic-stopping arm.

Straight ahead, she recognized the sun sculpture and pointed it out to the electronics duo. They rushed ahead and got to work moving equipment around the base. Riley was interested in learning exactly what they were doing but stayed with the others as they walked further into the compound. Nearing the building where she'd met with Mr. Chen previously, she expected they would be confronted by guards, but none came. Looking to her left, the loading dock, previously a jumble of activity, was deserted. Parked trucks had no drivers. A single forklift was still on the dock, but no workers were in sight.

The agents pressed on, and a group of four, including Hatanaka and Jankowski, entered Chen's building. The rest stopped to listen for signs of conflict, but none came. A minute later, Hatanaka emerged and yelled, "No one is here. We'll search this entire structure, but the rest of you should continue to the remaining areas. Remember to swipe lots of surfaces so the CDC can check for the virus."

Riley felt lost as the officers dispersed in groups of two until a middle-aged female agent approached and told her she would be her partner. Special Agent Hernandez told Riley that earlier, each agent had been given a map in which the entire property had been divided into zones. They were assigned to zone 5. As they approached their area, they passed a group of farm laborers huddled in a field. A pair of agents were speaking to them in Spanish.

Zone five included the dairy with approximately three hundred black and white cows penned and mooing. Some of them were lined up adjacent to the five robotic milking machines that were still operating, a cow in each station being milked as we walked in. When one finished, she would leave, and another would take her place. Riley had never seen an automated milking system in operation and was amazed at the orderliness of it all, the cows waiting patiently for their turn with no pushing or fighting. She wondered what it would look like if bulls needed to be milked.

Hernandez removed kits for swiping surfaces from her bag, and the two began taking samples. They found a large room nearby housing twenty computers with large monitors lined up on four long tables.

"The milking robots are computer-operated," Hernandez said, "but only one computer would be needed. Perhaps two would make sense to ensure redundancy. I have a feeling all the others are here to operate the drones."

Hernandez walked down the rows of computers. The screens were dark but came alive when she shook each mouse. "The computer closest to the door is displaying the milking software," she said, "but these others are obviously used for a different purpose. They all show maps of various areas of the US, with scattered red dots. These may be sites where the drones are stored, ready to launch."

As the officers continued looking around, they noticed that the chairs were haphazardly pushed back, cups of half-empty room temperature coffee and tea near some monitors.

"Look at this email," Riley said, leaning over to get a better look. "It's been opened. I can't read it because it's written in Korean, but the time stamp indicates it was sent at four a.m. this morning."

"Looks like the room was deserted, probably suddenly, sometime after four in the morning."

As they started to home in on the maps being displayed, the images suddenly disappeared, and a message in Korean appeared on all the screens simultaneously.

"Looks like our electronics team just disconnected everything from the satellite feed," Hernandez said.

The officers continued to search the buildings and nearby fields in Zone Five. Other than the room of computers, they found nothing of note. No people, no papers. Two hours later, Hatanaka drove by on a cart and directed them to the loading dock.

Once all the agents were assembled, Hatanaka summarized the findings thus far. They had been unable to find Mr. Chen or any of his team. All the North Koreans had evacuated the facility at 5:00 a.m. that morning, according to the farm workers. All other workers had been roused and told to wait in the lot where they had been found. No explanation had been given, and the destination of the North Koreans was undisclosed. Law enforcement officers throughout the state had been notified to be on the lookout for them. FBI agents dispatched to the two facilities in the Tulare area likewise had found them to be deserted.

A stockpile of cans for spraying fruit would be analyzed, as would the small canisters they'd found on a truck. More drones had been discovered in a stack of mattresses shipped from China. Hatanaka assumed North Korea sent the drones and other items as needed, embedded within mattresses that were routed through China, most likely with China's knowledge and approval.

A supply of silver boxes identical to those previously found at poisoning sites was in a closet near Mr. Chen's office. Also within the closet were bags of a white powder. A field test for fentanyl had been positive, but the results needed to be confirmed by a more rigorous analysis.

Eighteen drums which appeared to be full had been located in a newly constructed shed between the fields of romaine lettuce and arugula. Agents had opened two of them and identified human remains in a caustic liquid. The others would be opened later. That task, and the task of identifying the remains, would be left to others.

With Mr. Chen gone, no North Koreans to be found on the premises, and the satellite connection cut off, their work at Happy Sun Farm was done. The field hands were taken to a hotel in Bakersfield, where they would be individually questioned by bilingual officers and housed until the local government made a decision regarding their disposition. It wasn't expected they would provide additional helpful information.

Hatanaka finished by announcing, "The threat of biowarfare has been neutralized."

After leaving the farm and removing their protective gear, Riley and the FBI agents met for drinks at a local pub. The air was celebratory. Looking around, Riley liked what she saw. After receiving encouragement from Hernandez and other agents, she set her sights on doing whatever it would take to join the FBI.

No sign of Mr. Chen and his associates was found despite alerts at airports, border crossings, and police stations throughout the country.

Chapter 57

SPECIAL AGENT HATANAKA PHONED me at 11:30 a.m. I'd been expecting his call and answered right away.

"Our agents did a thorough search of Happy Sun Farm, but it was already deserted. No sign of Mr. Chen and his entourage, but their communication system has been shut down and the threat has been eliminated."

"That's great news and terrible news," I said. "Millions of lives no doubt were saved, but Mr. Chen is still out there someplace."

"We have alerted authorities to be on the lookout for the North Koreans. Airports and the borders with Canada and Mexico are being watched closely, so I'm hopeful they will be caught soon. Meanwhile, all Happy Sun Farm products are being removed from stores, and we no longer need to live in fear. Our Office of Public Affairs is preparing to address the public about all of this soon."

I turned on the TV which was broadcasting a message:

"Scientists at the CDC say that the dangerous receptors that had been introduced into our diet by Happy Sun Farm will likely disappear with time, as cells constantly break down proteins and synthesize new ones. They will conduct studies on volunteers to test the amount of the receptor remaining in tissue over time. They highly recommend the public vaccinate their cats against feline distemper if they haven't already done so, as people are at risk for catching that disease from their pets."

I called Fran. "No other cases of Marburg virus here," she said, "but the dang CDC is holding firm, insisting we stay in quarantine at least a full thirty days. After that, they're going to test all of us, and if we're virus-free, we can leave."

"I just hope nobody there kills any of their colleagues in the next month," I said.

"Some are saying they will never return to the building after they're released, but so far, no significant violence."

"I feel a twinge of guilt being responsible for so many people being confined," I said, "but I'd do the same thing again if I found myself in a similar situation. It's not every day you can save millions of your fellow Americans from contracting a deadly virus." I paused a moment before continuing. "I'll send two large flat-screen TVs to Vital Vittles. Someone there should be able to connect them to the internet, and access their Netflix account. That should help to pass the time."

"I have to admit, there are a lot of shows I'd like to see, but have been too busy to watch."

After our conversation ended, I found Kwan contacting the most prominent Korean Buddhist temple in Los Angeles Koreatown and arranging for the proper burial of Bong and Nabi. I don't believe in an afterlife, but if there were a chance I was wrong, I was glad they would be in a place where they could hang out peacefully for eternity. We would bring Kwan with us when we attended the burial.

After hugs and a promise to visit Best Korean BBQ soon, Kwan took the Honda CR-V to drive home. He planned to go back to the Bakersfield car rental agency with his daughter in a few days to return it.

At Diego's urging, I phoned Hatanaka to learn the whereabouts of the farm workers who had been found at Happy Sun. CJ, Adam, Diego, Martina, and I drove to Bakersfield in the Pathfinder. There was much conversation during the trip, and I overheard Adam describe his confirmation at a Catholic church when he was a teen. I figured he mentioned that to get on Diego's good side.

In Bakersfield, CJ returned the Pathfinder to the rental agency where Adam and CJ's vehicles were still parked. I could almost feel the sexual tension between Martina and Adam. After some awkward back-and-forth, Adam left with Diego and Martina in his SUV. I suspected he wanted to take Martina to his apartment after dropping her father off at the hotel near Bakersfield to visit his friends.

Diego had warmed up to Adam after learning he was Catholic, and I envisioned a Catholic wedding in the near future. I hoped CJ and I would be part of the wedding party.

CJ visited briefly with his friend at the rental agency, and transferred our belongings, including our guns, to his truck before leaving. We drove to the site of my parents' old home. I expected to find scorched earth where it had once stood, but was surprised to find the structure still standing. From the street, I could see it was badly damaged, with smashed windows, bullet holes, and a missing front door. Guards in hazmat suits were stationed every fifty yards around the entire Happy Sun Farm property. CJ and I approached the one stationed closest to the house.

"That's my old house," I said. "Can we go in there?"

"Sorry," she replied. "No one is allowed on the property until the tests for viral contamination are complete. Probably tomorrow or the next day."

"What if I wore a hazmat suit? I won't take long. I just want to see how much damage was done."

"Let me check," she said. She bent her neck to the side and spoke softly into her shoulder radio. Moments later, I detected a smile through her plastic face covering. "Someone will be by with a hazmat suit, but only one of you can go in, and you can't bring anything out."

"Thank you," I said. I turned to CJ. "You don't mind if I go in alone, do you?"

"Of course not. I'll wait in the truck."

I knew he'd be happy to listen to his country music without his choice of recordings being judged by me.

After a short wait, a black car drove up, and the driver handed me a shrink-wrapped hazmat suit. The guard helped me open the package and suit up. Not wanting to litter, I stuffed the wrapping into my bootie, which was much too big for me.

I turned towards the house which, although ravaged by recent events, still held many memories. As I entered, I thought I heard a noise coming from my parents' bedroom. Probably an animal that got in. There was easy access with the front door gone, and windows smashed. I stood still for a moment in the living room to look around. The furniture was still in place, and I pictured my mother, father, and I watching TV in there in better times. Boxes were still piled up, as I hadn't had a chance to start moving things out before Danielle tried to kill me. Thinking about Danielle made me sad, but only for a moment.

I turned and gasped. A man was standing five feet from me. He was young, Asian, and held a large kitchen knife in his right hand.

Chapter 58

WE STARED AT EACH other several long, uncomfortable seconds as I tried to make sense of the situation.

He wasn't trying to kill me, although he held a lethal weapon. Perhaps he was as scared as I was. If I screamed, the guard would likely hear me and rush in, but that might cause him to panic.

I took several deep breaths to calm myself. "Do you speak English?" I asked, my throat so tight my voice croaked.

"Little."

"What do you want?" I asked. My words were met with a blank stare. My gut feeling was that this man was hiding from General Jeong and his henchmen. Like Bong, he wanted to defect.

What I should have done was alert the guard outside. What I did was work my phone out of my pants pocket, down the inside of my hazmat suit pants leg, and into the crumpled but clean shrink wrap in my bootie. My phone was now protected in a see-through bag. I held my breath as I tapped the phone, not sure if it would respond through my glove and the shrink wrap. I exhaled when it did. I wasted no time in calling Kwong.

He answered on the third ring. I started talking before he had a chance to finish saying "hello."

"I need your help," I said. "I'm with a North Korean who was left behind at Happy Sun."

"How—"

"I'll explain later, but right now I need you to translate. I'll put you on speaker. Ask him what he's doing here and what he wants."

As Kwan spoke, the man came closer to the phone and began to speak. After some back and forth, Kwan said, "He wants to be an

American. Says everyone else left in four Happy Sun Farm trucks headed to the coast. They will board submarines and return to North Korea. He knew Nabi, and wants to know how she is. I couldn't tell him."

His last words were like a knife through my heart, but there was no time to reflect on something that couldn't be undone. "Bad news can wait. Now I need to know how the trucks escaped our police, and where exactly they will catch the submarines."

After more discussion in Korean, Kwan told me, "They changed the writing on the trucks to read 'Amy's Bakery.' He doesn't know if the submarines have arrived yet, as they are coming from North Korea. The people will be camping until they arrive. He heard they would be waiting near a castle, but will have to sleep outside on the ground."

Leaving on submarines meant they had to be near the ocean. There was only one castle near the coast that I knew about. Hearst Castle, the previous over-the-top luxurious estate of William Randolph Hearst, currently a popular tourist attraction.

"Tell him he is safe now. I will tell the officer outside he wants to defect, but they will likely quarantine him until they can test him for the virus."

The man smiled after Kwan spoke to him, then sat on the couch. We nodded to each other, and I left.

I told the guard outside about the North Korean who wanted to defect, and she said she'd take care of it. After she helped me remove my hazmat suit, I got into CJ's truck and told him what I had learned.

"Well, what are we waiting for?" he asked. "It'll take over three hours to get there."

"You sure you want to find them?"

"Of course."

"I was hoping you'd say that. By the time the FBI interviews that guy and organizes a search, the North Koreans will be gone. I want that bastard General Jeong to pay for what he's done."

A moment later, we were on our way to San Simeon, the small coastal town near Hearst's Castle. We had no clear plan, but couldn't afford to wait until we had one.

It was after 6:00 p.m. when we reached a vista point overlooking the ocean near San Simeon. Despite the beautiful view, we concentrated only on looking for a group of trucks. None were in sight. We drove north on the Cabrillo Highway portion of the Pacific Coast Highway, which hugged the coast. The fog was rolling in and there was little traffic. We pulled off the road and headed towards a group of cars parked near the beach.

I jumped out of the truck and I addressed the couples gathered there who were sitting in beach chairs, drinking wine and beer. "Have any of you seen four delivery trucks from Amy's Bakery around here? They're mine, and one of the drivers phoned me and said they were lost in this area."

They all shook their heads "No," and I was about to leave when one more car drove up and another couple got out. I asked them the same question.

The young man said, "Sorry, no," but his companion said, "Wait a minute. I saw a group of four cargo trucks parked close to the water about a mile back." She pointed north, and continued, "I thought it was weird. Don't know if they were from Amy's Bakery, but I figured they might be lost."

"Thanks," I said as I rushed back to the car. We were on the road, going north, in no time.

As CJ drove, we both scanned the beach below and to our left, looking for four box trucks. It was becoming hard to see, with the sun getting low, and the fog rolling in, but we both shouted at the same time. "There they are."

No other cars were in sight. CJ crossed over the opposite lane, and rolled over the edge of the highway, onto the rocky dirt next to the road. He stopped the truck and we got out. The trucks were a distance away, but I could make out the lettering spelling "Amy's Bakery" on two of them. Dozens of people were walking and lying in the surrounding sand.

CJ grabbed the shotgun from behind his seat where he had left it, and tossed me my gun and holster.

"Let's walk down there and see what's going on," I said. My heart was pumping as I secured the holster around my waist.

"Right. And stay low."

It was difficult walking down the steep slope covered with brambles. We approached cautiously for what seemed like an eternity. The trucks were farther away than they looked from above. When we were close enough to hear voices, we stopped.

Everything—the sky, the water, the ground—looked gray in the dim light and mist. Straining my eyes, I saw people wading into the water a ways, then seeming to disappear.

"They're getting into the submarine," CJ whispered.

I peered more intently into the gray haze, and made out an oblong shape in the water. In the middle was a black circular structure that people were descending into.

"Damn," I said. "It's so close to the shore. Wouldn't our military have detected it?"

"Must be like one of those narco-submarines," CJ answered.

"I've never heard of that."

"They're small semi-submersible vessels that are very hard to detect. Due to their size, they can get pretty close to the shore. Was probably carried by a larger ship anchored a ways out. I've heard about them because they're used by South American cartels to smuggle drugs into the US. They get people to custom build them."

I didn't have time to think about this amazing revelation. "I can't see Jeong. We have to get closer. If we can capture him, he can get the rest to surrender."

We inched forward and I drew my gun. In the twilight, I was finally able to make out my nemesis. He was directing the others to board the submarine in single file. All but about a dozen people were already on board.

Out of the darkness, a man exited one of the trucks and approached General Jeong. He whispered in his ear, and the general suddenly looked in our direction. The other man shone a bright light on us and a shiver went down my spine.

"Miss Fields, what a pleasant surprise," Jeong said. In the dim light I made out a devilish smile. "Perhaps you and your friend would like to join us on our voyage to our homeland."

"Not a chance," CJ said as he began to raise his shotgun.

Mr. Chen retrieved a small black canister from his pocket and held it up, his finger ready to press the nozzle. "I would think twice before trying to stop me," he said. "This canister contains enough virus to kill both of you and a thousand others. You can see that several other of my people have similar canisters."

I followed his gaze and saw three men and a woman nearby, holding black canisters, ready to release their contents.

"Put down your weapons. We'll leave, and both of you will live. I have no reason to kill you now unless you try to interfere."

"You killed my father," I yelled.

"It was nothing personal."

"It was personal to me," I said as tears welled in my eyes.

"I am not a patient man. It makes no difference to me if you live or die. The choice is yours."

"It looks like they win," I whispered to CJ. "I don't see a way out of this. Even with the best treatment possible, a huge dose of the virus would kill us."

CJ and I put down our weapons.

"May you rot in hell," I yelled.

"Hell is just make believe," Jeong replied. Then he turned to two of his men. "Tie them up."

They retrieved rope from one of the trucks and tied our wrists behind our backs. Ten minutes later, they were gone, swallowed by the ocean.

It was two full hours before CJ and I had freed ourselves and ascended the cliff where we could access cell phone service.

I phoned Hatanaka immediately and told him exactly where we were and what had transpired.

"I'm on it," he said, before disconnecting. I trusted him to follow through and hunt down General Jeong and the others. Unfortunately, they had at least a two-hour head start.

CJ and I found a hotel in the town of San Simeon. Three hours later, Hatanaka called.

His first words were, "There were three submarines, and we located all of them."

"Thank goodness," I responded as a sense of relief enveloped me.

"We found them, but unfortunately, two were already in international waters, headed to a large ship. Fearing a confrontation could escalate into a major international incident, they weren't stopped. One submarine, however, probably experienced engine trouble or a strong current and lagged significantly behind. It was intercepted in our territorial waters. Twenty men and women were on board, none of whom speak English."

"Did they get General Jeong?"

"Unfortunately, no. He got away. But the others will be processed and fully prosecuted if appropriate. We are bringing several Korean translators to meet with them."

I was massively disappointed, but had to let my feelings go. There would be no getting the general, no final reckoning. He would be safe in North Korea unless the Supreme Leader decided otherwise. I didn't sleep that night, but knew that in time I would be able to move on.

Chapter 59

CJ AND I RETURNED to his house the following day. I should have been more relaxed than I had been for a long time, but I felt wound up, ready to explode. CJ left me alone to take a bath and try to relieve my anxiety while he went to his factory to take care of issues needing his attention, then to baseball practice at his school. I don't know how he managed to carry on like nothing had happened, but, then, he hadn't just lost his father to poisoning, his mother to a new lover, and his family home, which was to be the cornerstone of life after college.

After a warm bath and a short attempt at napping, I was ready to face the world. I made a list of things I needed to do. CJ called to tell me baseball practice was over, he'd be home after picking up something for dinner, but he had to attend an event later and wanted me to accompany him. The call ended before he told me what the event was about.

Over sandwiches from Subway, CJ explained that his backers were holding an important get-together that evening. Support for his candidacy was stronger than ever, given his previous opposition to Happy Sun Farm. Word had spread quickly about the dangerous operation the North Korean company was close to carrying out. CJ's main challenger had received generous donations from them and been a vocal supporter of theirs. Her campaign was now in shambles.

Our meal was interrupted by a call from Dr. Parks. "Good news," she said. "The CDC has completed the testing of all the samples the FBI had taken on their search of Happy Sun Farm, and no virus was found."

"Including my parents' old house?"

"Including your parents' old house."

It was nice to have some welcome news. Although I no longer owned it, I expected to be able to collect whatever items I wanted to save.

The meeting at the local high school was well attended. We arrived several minutes late and were welcomed by loud applause. The air was electric as we took the seats on the stage reserved for us. I was surprised to be included. For the first time, I realized just how devoted CJ's supporters were. I understood the intoxicating effect of having a crowd of enthusiastic backers, even for a local election.

CJ delivered a short speech in which he credited me with doing most of the planning behind our unraveling of the Happy Sun plot. Someone in the audience suggested I run for a position in the county government. This suggestion received lots of applause. Several people spoke of CJ and me being a formidable power couple, as we moved up in state government. National prominence was sure to follow. I was flattered and supported CJ's candidacy but had no desire to enter politics on any level myself.

The State Controller's office was charged with the task of selling the land Happy Sun Farm had abandoned, and several local citizens planned to petition the office to sell all of it to me at a discount if I wanted it. For the first time since my first encounter with General Jeong, I dared to think my lifetime dream of running the farm might be realized.

Before the meeting, I had envisioned collapsing in bed afterward, but I left feeling invigorated. On the way back to CJ's house I called my mom to tell her I was optimistic about getting the farm back, in which case I'd move back to the area after graduation. She was in Vancouver, planning to go whale watching the following morning, and asked if I knew anything about the North Korean plot she'd heard about on the news, as it was centered around Kern County. I told her that, being a local concern, I knew a thing or two about it and would fill her in on the details when I saw her again.

She sent more pictures of her and Harrison at a restaurant, under the sign at the Granville Island Public Market entry, and enjoying the VanDusen Botanical Garden. Harrison was starting to grow on me.

He had a nice smile. I didn't know if Mom's fling with him would last, but she seemed happier than she'd been in years, and I was glad about that. Regarding the farm, she assured me I could have it as far as she was concerned.

CJ and I spent hours making plans. I'd call my advisor at Purdue in the morning and arrange to take the next quarter off. If no signs of Marburg virus were found on the samples taken at Happy Sun Farm, I would renovate my old house and assess the surrounding land.

I didn't have much money but would come up with a tight business plan and leverage what funds I had to buy all the available property. CJ had confidence I could pull that off on my own, but wanted me to know that he was in my corner and would kick in financial support in the unlikely event I needed it.

Once my ownership of the land was secure, I looked forward to offering Diego a supervisory position. I trusted him to hire the other workers we would need. I hadn't envisioned becoming a dairy farmer, but the cows were already there, and milking machines took care of the most strenuous labor, so my answer to the question, "Got milk?" was "Yes."

I looked forward to destroying the genetically engineered crops and replacing them with the produce that had been growing well there for years. Most fulfilling would be re-planting the strawberry fields my father had established, using the same breed he had used. That would be a place where, if there is an afterlife, his tortured soul could rest, free of whatever demons had plagued him during his lifetime.

With tomatoes again flourishing in the area, CJ's pasta sauce factory would never face a shortage of their product's main ingredient. He would campaign hard for the State Assembly seat, and I would be by his side as an assistant to his campaign manager. We'd hash out the details of his campaign strategy and platform together.

We didn't talk about marriage or anything permanent, but things were moving in that direction. For the time being, we were partners in every sense of the word.

"One more thing," CJ said when our plans had jelled. "Call that guy I know you've got waiting for you back in Indiana, and tell him you're not going back to be with him. I know you'd prefer to text him, but calling would be the right thing to do."

I promised I would.

Chapter 60

ESCORTED BY GUARDS, DR. Gang shuffled into the office of the Supreme Leader, his head hung low. With legs like jelly, he would have collapsed if not supported by the uniformed men accompanying him. He wore the blue pajamas of the inmates in the prison where he'd been housed after the catastrophic failure of his plan. His legs wobbled noticeably as he stood in front of the large desk. He hoped for a firing squad. All other punishments would be far worse.

Afraid to meet the eye of the one who would be meting out his sentence, it took all his effort not to crumble completely. He still had his pride left. His analysis of proteins, plant genetics, and viruses, combined with his ability to synthesize edited versions, was an accomplishment to be admired by generations to come. The facilities he designed where the modified products he engineered could be mass-produced had operated flawlessly. He was a genius, and he knew it.

Once an exalted scientist, hailed as brilliant, the recipient of the Korea Hero of Labor Medal, he had fallen from grace due to the failure of his program. If only he had known about the Americans' ridiculous proclivity to adopt pets as if they were children. He knew they were corrupt and decadent, but had never imagined such an unnatural alliance between man and an excellent source of protein—cats and dogs. That alliance had tipped the Americans off to the presence of the mutated receptor, and, ultimately, led to the failure of the entire plan. Perhaps he should have focused on a virus that only infected elephants, bears, or kangaroos. Platypuses might have been even better. Only in one American zoo. Too late for that now, unfortunately.

General Bai, once his greatest supporter, had deemed him an enemy of the people once the scheme failed. General Jeong and most of his colleagues had returned to North Korea. Those who had been arrested at sea were unskilled laborers. They knew very little and could easily be replaced, but a great deal of time, money, and hope had been wasted on the operation.

It had been five weeks since General Bai had ordered him to prison to await his final sentencing. Death for sure, but in Dr. Gang's mind, the means loomed large. All he could hope for at this point was a quick and relatively painless exit from his predicament.

When he was summoned that morning, he had anticipated his final appearance before the general. Once he learned he'd be brought before the Supreme Leader, he was filled with an intense, indescribable feeling of horror.

The Supreme Leader began to speak. "You are probably wondering why I have brought you before me."

Dr. Gang was surprised by the words. Of course he wasn't wondering. Was this an attempt at humor?

"You had been told your final sentencing would be carried out by General Bai."

It took all of Dr. Gang's strength to nod in agreement.

"I want you to know General Bai will no longer be involved in your activities."

Strange wording, Dr. Gang thought. Why use the word "activities" instead of "sentencing"? The general would have relished sentencing him.

The Supreme Leader cracked a smile. "Right now, General Bai is in a helicopter, flying over a remote area of the Taedong River. I was in a good mood this morning, so I gave him a choice of being dropped to his death from a helicopter or torn apart by my dogs. He chose the helicopter and will be dropped in . . ." he looked at the clock on the wall, "approximately two minutes."

Dr. Gang looked up and glanced around the room. His mind raced as he tried to make sense of what he'd just heard.

The Supreme Leader continued. "I have studied Operation America Takeover in depth. Your scientific expertise is most impressive, and your plan amazingly original for a scientist. You have an extraordinary, brilliant mind."

Dr. Gang didn't know where this conversation was going, but he was at full attention as he wondered what this meant for himself. Rather than death, perhaps he would be sentenced to a labor camp. Maybe even released after a long sentence, if he survived.

"General Bai is an idiot. Or was an idiot." The supreme leader chuckled. "He blamed you, a brilliant scientist, for his own failings. He's the one who should have known all about the American's peculiar customs. You are a scientist, not responsible for knowing their language, their dress, their holidays, their favorite TV shows, or their affinity for animals. General Bai failed and blamed you. He would have destroyed our most exceptional scientist to save face. Such deceit will not be tolerated."

Dr. Gang didn't want to think the unthinkable. Still, he couldn't help but wonder if he would be freed.

"You will be released from prison this afternoon. Take a few days to relax. Then come back and be prepared to start work on Operation North America Takeover."

Dr. Gang looked up. "I would be most honored to participate in such a noble cause. May I ask what is planned?"

"We were unable to take over the United States with your virus, but I am confident that you can devise a scheme to attack Canada and Mexico in a similar manner. Once we have control of those countries, we will move our missiles in. We have had difficulty directing them from long distances, like across the Pacific Ocean, but launching from Canada and Mexico will be easy."

A smile spread over Dr. Gang's face. "Excellent idea. I look forward to begin working on Operation North America Takeover."

Acknowledgements

Thanks to everyone who helped me write this book. In particular, I want to thank my brother, Seth Greenberg, for his valuable suggestions, and my Amazing Husband, Glen Petersen, for his recommendations and daily support.

About the author

Deven Greene lives in Northern California. She enjoys writing fiction, most of which involves science or medicine. Deven has degrees in biochemistry (PhD) and medicine (MD), and practiced pathology for over twenty years. She has published *The Erica Rosen MD Trilogy*, *Ties That Kill*, *The Organ Broker*, and several short stories.

Also by Deven Greene

The Erica Rosen Trilogy
Unnatural
Unwitting
Unforeseen

Ties That Kill
The Organ Broker